SHADOWS OF THE VALLEY

SHADOWS OF THE VALLEY

A McCade Family Novel
Book Two

BRITT HOWARD

To Joe—the love of my life and my daily source of inspiration. I love you.

And to Finnegan—my best little buddy forever. Never forgotten.

"Yea, though I walk through the valley of the shadow of death,
I will fear no evil;
For you are with me"
(Psalm 23:4).

Chapter One

Kasey
Late June

I need your help . . .

The lone line of dark text stands out in sharp contrast to the glowing white screen.

Instantly, my stomach drops. I stare at the cell phone with more distrust than one of the venomous desert vipers we occasionally encountered slithering through our barracks on deployment. Tossing the phone on the kitchen table, I try to walk away, but each word of the dreaded message floats through my brain. I want to ignore it and go back to bed, but my gaze is drawn to the phone again, and I watch three bubbles dancing across the screen. The sender isn't waiting for my reply. She's already typing another message, and it appears a few seconds later, landing just below her first.

AMY: I'm in trouble. I need your help.

A sigh originates deep within my chest. The rumble of the ocean waves beyond the door mimics the angsty churning pounding inside my head.

The timing feels cruel. Why this message now, when I'm feeling more settled than I've felt in years?

I don't want to deal with everything her message represents. And yet, I know I will.

Because just like before, I'll always come running when Amy calls. And just like before, the prospect of coming to Amy's rescue triggers both my sense of duty and my fears.

Attempting to calm my breathing, I debate whether to reply tonight. I'm not taking her messages lightly, but I need time to reflect. Do I want to get involved in this? We haven't spoken in months . . . or has it been nearly a couple of years? The timeline is hazy—pain and surgery and months of physical therapy dulling my memory—but some time ago, the email updates she used to send simply stopped, probably because I rarely replied.

Tonight's messages are nothing like the lighthearted family updates I'm used to receiving from her. The words are urgent and random, triggering my sense of alarm. Because Amy is the bubbly sister, the carefree, happy-go-lucky, everything-always-works-out-for-her sister. Though she had plenty of little crises over the years, and once she turned eighteen, her habit was to call her big sister, Kasey, and beg me to spin some story if our father came asking questions about her petty rebellions, Amy has otherwise lived a charmed life.

My younger and only sister.

My lips twist into a mirthless smile at the thought of the two of us being related. We couldn't be less alike. A sister is supposed to be your best friend, a trusted confidante.

Instead, Amy is me . . . or the person I should have become if life had handed me a fair deck. She inherited the life I could have had if Dad hadn't chosen her mother—and all her generous inheritance and Wall Street connections—over mine. He gave his second daughter a safe, peaceful, privileged, and happy upbringing. She's always had everything she ever wanted. And yet, I can't find it in myself to resent her, even though there are times when I wonder if I'm destined to endure a double portion of misery. Amy got the husband, the house, the cute kids, and the inheritance. And then there's me: a broken veteran, alone, just as I've been since the beginning.

Now, she's texting me at midnight on a random Tuesday in late June, begging for help. My phone buzzes a third time.

AMY: Please, sis. I think I'm in real trouble this time.

For all she knows, I might be on deployment. She doesn't even know if I've received her texts. She could be reaching out into the void. I haven't initiated contact in years, but I've also never changed my phone number. I couldn't . . . just in case. She knows I'll reply. It's just a matter of time until I text her back and officially get involved in whatever mess she's gotten herself into. It doesn't matter how often I've distanced myself. I can't turn my back on my sister. We are inextricably bound by blood.

After all, she had no control over what our father did some thirty-odd years ago.

I lift the cell phone off the table, walking toward the open slider to let the chilly night breeze cool my overheated skin. I'm at home, my new home, the only permanent home I've ever allowed myself to have. The cottage is mine. The Oregon coast stretches only a few hundred yards from my door. I still can't believe I was fortunate enough to snag this piece of property months ago. It took me years to save and a VA loan, and the cottage was little more than a shack when I bought it. But renovations have made it feel more like a home than any other place I've lived in.

Tranquility Bay Beach.

I tend to avoid the village shops, and I've barely done more than explore the trails and surrounding beaches in the time I've lived here. But I appreciate the sentiment of the name.

Though the irony of living in a seaside village named Tranquility Bay, yet rarely getting a full night's sleep as the loop of endless memories and nightmares keeps me awake, isn't lost on me.

There's just so much to regret.

Only ten minutes ago, I gave up tossing and turning in my bed and threw the sheet aside. Walking the short distance to the kitchen, I set about making a cup of tea, thinking the hot drink and watching a few *I Love Lucy* reruns would lull me back to sleep. It doesn't matter if I'm up late. I've nowhere to be in the morning since my disability benefits suffice to cover my meager needs for now.

It was while I waited for the chamomile tea to brew that the blinking light on my phone alerted me to the waiting text. I should have checked it in the morning because I'm surely not returning to bed now.

On the other end of the screen, she's waiting for my reply. Frozen, my fingers hover over the phone. There's no turning back once I respond. I'm either all in, or I need to tell my younger sister to leave me alone once and for all. But I'd never do that to her.

We may only be related due to our shared paternal heritage, but I knew I loved her since the day I learned of her existence. I'd always wanted a sister. And now she's asking for my help. My fingers fly across the screen.

ME: I can leave in the morning and arrive in about four days. I'll check

Holding onto the phone, I turn back to the tiny kitchen, needing the comforting influence of hot tea. I must move too fast because it triggers a sharp, stabbing pain that runs down my thigh. I stumble on the wood floor, one leg moving forward but the other temporarily refusing to cooperate, as it sometimes does. My agonized gasp breaks the silence as my loose sleeping shorts ride up, exposing the scar running along the top of my thigh. Its wrinkled, purplish length is a grim daily reminder that merely an inch to the right, and I probably would have bled out that day in the desert.

Using my knuckles, I knead the throbbing length of the scarred-over wound. When I left my job as a waitress and signed up to become a combat medic in the army, I knew I'd have to grow accustomed to dealing with emergency crises and battlefield wounds. I figured if I couldn't rescue myself from the disappointment of my own life, I could at least be of use and save someone else.

No amount of training prepared me to endure the day the battlefield shattered my carefully controlled world. When I first woke up in the hospital bed, half my body was wrapped in bandages, and I was given the news that I would sport a pin in my thigh for the rest of my life and be fortunate to walk again. There were days when the pain was so intense, I wondered if I should have simply let the desert claim me as it had my friends.

The months of physical therapy were brutal, drawing on the final reserves of my grit. I pushed through the punishing pain, considering it the least I deserved for the ones who didn't make it home. But now, there are days and even some weeks I can ignore the ache completely if I'm careful. The world has moved forward, the families were long ago notified, and the bodies brought home and buried at funerals I didn't get to attend.

To an outsider, the only lingering sign of my honorable discharge from the army months ago is my disability benefits classification and the slight limp that gets aggravated frequently. They can't see the other scars scattered in random patterns across my body that remind me of that day, and I don't want them to. The worst scars are on the inside anyway, where no one can see, where they've always lived. Though, to be honest, no one is left in my life who would care to see them anyway.

My leg flares up when I'm stressed, and panicked, midnight texts from my sister are definitely cause for stress. With a grimace, I take a deep breath, and a minute later, the throbbing sensation in my leg begins to recede. With a tentative step, I test my weight on my stronger leg and try not to let the weaker limb drag as I move into the kitchen. Usually, I fight the limp, refusing to let my weakness show in public. But when it's late at night and I'm alone, I let my guard down just a little.

The sliding door that leads to the back deck is open; the scent of briny water and the sound of a rolling tide drift into the cottage. I'm not afraid of the darkness. My favorite handgun sits within reach on the countertop. It's loaded, as it always is. Between Finn and me, no one would make it through the door unchallenged.

Absently, I reheat the cooling tea, wondering if brewing a pot of coffee would make more sense at this point. I'll need the soothing softness of the chamomile on my nerves, though. Already, they are thrumming with discomfort at the thought of returning to the East Coast. When the army discharged me, moving back to my home state had never been an option. Oregon was as far away as I could get stateside.

As I sip the floral brew, my brain kicks into work mode, the rigidity of making lists and planning logistics a comfort. I run through a checklist of what I'll need to pack for the drive that will commence just after sunrise: food, water, cash, a sleeping bag, blankets, several changes of clothes, car tools, the emergency backpack I keep in the closet, my medical kit, and my firearms. More than my trusty SIG Sauer will be making the long drive from the West Coast to the East Coast with me. Taking a flight is out of the question. Driving allows me to bring essential supplies that would be frowned upon on a commercial flight. Besides, I trust airplanes about as much as I trust people.

Instead, I'll load up my forest-green Jeep with everything I need to feel safe and secure.

Amy's final message comes through two minutes later, and the sense of dread in my chest deepens as I stare at the screen.

AMY: *We're safe enough for now. But hurry, Kasey. We need you.*

Chapter Two

Dean
Mid-August

"Was it just me, or were those wolves out in full force last night?" Vincent's deep, unhurried voice carries down from the hill across the clearing. I can just make out his figure in the gray predawn light.

I'm repacking the solar panels that power the temporary electric paddocks we use to safely confine our cattle herd at night. The cows and their calves are already stirring in the open space between me and my brother. They are ready to move on for the day, despite the early hour.

I would have preferred to stay in the warmth of my sleeping bag this morning. Forcing myself out of its depths into the chilly damp before sunrise is a struggle that never gets easier. The best option is to throw back the flap and rise in one swift motion. Getting dressed and starting a fire is the quickest way to warm up my muscles and mind. Now, as I finish the task of repacking the panels, I reassure myself that a cup of freshly brewed coffee will banish the last of the fog from my brain. Since I started the fire already, Knox should be finishing up breakfast right about now at camp.

Vincent strides down the hillside that we'll climb today as we allow the herd to graze. My brother's steps are long and sure across the dewy carpet of wild grass. We made camp last night not far from the base of the hill. This morning, he walked up the slope to get a better view of our route for the day.

"It wasn't just you," I reply when he gets closer. "I reached for my rifle a couple of times when it sounded like they were getting too close. They were probably miles away, though. Those howls carry."

"I walked out a couple of times to check on the herd," Vincent admits, falling into step next to me as we turn toward camp. "We might need to start a nightly watch rotation again if they don't move on."

I grunt in agreement. "Probably should anyway for the time being. We haven't lost any cattle to the wolves in what, two years? I'm not interested in starting again now."

As much as I respect the wolves' territory, their presence in Montana has resulted in quite a few ranchers losing cattle—mostly vulnerable calves—whenever they were left to graze alone. Every ranch has a different tactic for dealing with the predators. When it became obvious that the wolves were going to be a pressing problem for our operation, my tactic was to change direction entirely. A few years ago, we launched a conservation program that includes a full-time team of range riders who live with the herd during the summer months as we graze it across the Montana mountains. The extra wages cut deeply into our already slim profit margins, but so far, we haven't lost any of the herd to wolf attacks.

"Changing up our grazing strategy was a game changer," Vincent acknowledges. "We may need to add a couple of guys to the team if we're going to go back to night shifts."

I consider his advice as we cross the distance to camp. Being the oldest of our group of five siblings, I assumed leadership over the McCade family's cattle operation when Dad passed away in a horseback riding accident four summers ago. Though I spearheaded most of the decision-making and shifted our ranching philosophy to a regenerative, hands-on approach, I make it a point to value the input of my entire team. Each cowboy who rides with us has years of experience wrangling cattle or living the ranch hand life. They are all excellent shots and even better horsemen, traits needed out here in the land of snakes, predatory animals, and unpredictable elements. Still, I can't help feeling frequent bouts of frustration as I try to be a strong leader for the team, manage the herd, compete with cultural shifts against ranching, and somehow, someway, scrape together enough money to pay my men and put a little away for whenever disaster strikes the ranch in the future. Almost daily, I fear I'm not the leader Dad would have expected me to be.

A voice shouts at us, breaking into my troubled thoughts.

"Dean! Vince!" Knox throws up his hands as we approach, the two other men on our team hunkering over their camp mugs a few feet away. "You two have held up breakfast for ten minutes already. Hurry up. We're starved." The grin that flashes across my youngest brother's face opposes the chiding tone in his voice.

"You only finished cooking faster today because I started the fire for you," I reply. "You're welcome."

His head falls back as he laughs, the hearty sound ringing across the hills as we take seats around the fire and our small group settles in for breakfast.

The McCade brothers have three things in common: our father's height, our mother's cocoa brown hair and eyes in varying shades of blue, and laughs that can echo for miles. In addition to these qualities, we all possess a deep sense of protectiveness toward children and the women in our lives. Our commitments are to God, family, community, and work—in that order.

However, we don't share many other qualities. Vincent is only a couple of years my junior, hitting thirty-two in a few months. He's spare with his words, though notably kind and possessing a steely inner strength that makes me reluctant to provoke his ire. On the few occasions Vincent's had to step into the figurative ring, the fights haven't been pretty for the other guy. And then there's Knox, our youngest brother—lovable, slightly goofy, and basically a golden retriever. He keeps us rolling with his antics and jokes, but he is also a crack shot and a workhorse when he wants to be. Which isn't often enough in my opinion.

Knox dishes out breakfast, joking all the while, and inwardly, I cringe as the uncharitable thought enters my brain. It's hard to admit it, but my biggest struggle seems to be giving grace to others as well as myself. I find myself wanting to control the outcomes to the detriment of my patience.

Since I was thrust into the role of family leader without warning, taking over the ranch could have been a huge failure. To my shock, the last couple of years have been decent, and our books are in the black. We even have enough money set aside to start diversifying our business ventures should we want to, and we've been discussing the possibility of branching into another business. But I'm not naïve enough to think our good fortune couldn't turn on a dime.

And that worries me.

Coming fully awake as the caffeine hits their systems, Jerome and Abraham join Knox's wisecracks from their seats on the logs we dragged together last night to form a mock firepit. Steam rises from the enamel mugs and plates of food balanced on their laps. I hold out my mug for Knox to fill with the nearly black brew. We like our coffee black, strong, and piping hot around here. Breakfast is our usual daily fare of grits and reconstituted scrambled eggs. It's bland and boring but certainly beats eating an MRE for every meal on the range.

Breakfast triggers memories of Mom's home cooking. Currently, she's back at the ranch, but she's left the state a couple of times this year to go on vacation. She even embarked on a cruise this spring with friends, quite an adventure for a McCade. If someone asked Mom what she anticipated life looking like four years ago, before we lost Dad, she would probably say she expected to be surrounded by daughters-in-law and grandchildren, enjoying a semi-retirement with her husband. Instead, she's a widow with five grown (and all still unmarried) children. It's no wonder she's been taking herself on solo vacations just to see more than the mountains of Cascade Valley, Montana, day after day.

Scraping the last bits of egg and grits off my plate, I hand it back to Knox. He's on dish and meal duty this week. While he cleans up the firepit, the rest of us quickly clear the rest of the camp and saddle the horses.

It's still dark, and I can barely see the outline of the ebony horse waiting at the perimeter of the electric fence where we penned them last night. Midnight bobs his head as I approach. I rub the white stripe between his eyes affectionately.

"Ready for another day, buddy?"

It's my habit to talk to him as I saddle up for our twelve-hour days. Usually, it's random nonsense. More often of late, I slip into a quiet conversation with God as the morning sun ascends.

Contrary to what I tell myself about being content with a simple, work-focused life as a regenerative rancher, lately, I've had the sense that something is missing. An urgency nags at the back of my brain.

The feeling may be prompted by my recent breakup with Shelby Gentry. I was unofficially courting the "Cascade Valley Widow" during the spring and into the early summer. Her husband's tragic death in the line of duty overseas rocked our entire community when the news came. While he was raised in Cascade Valley, Shelby was transplanted by marriage. That didn't stop the community from rallying around her when the news of Paul's loss hit.

Paul Gentry isn't the only member of the valley we've lost over the past few years. We still aren't over the death of Danny Gardener, who grew up here. Almost a decade ago, he joined the army and became a specialist and squad leader. He was a few years older than I, but Caleb Kane, Vincent, and I formed a brotherly friendship with him early on in our youth.

There aren't any Gardeners left in Cascade Valley now. They've all passed or moved away. When he was a teen, Danny and his grandpa built a hunting cabin deep in the mountains above our ranch. We used to throw a few days' worth of food and water into our backpacks and hike up to it to go rabbit hunting. The small structure has probably been worn down by the elements at this point, but Danny's legacy and sacrifice remain embedded in our hometown.

My thoughts swing back to Shelby and the price she paid for loving a soldier. Initially, I had hope for us. There aren't many women with dating potential in the valley, most of the single women being too young for me or already paired off.

My thirty-third birthday is looming. I thought marriage might be a possibility. But a month ago, when I went to town to pick up fresh supplies, I took Shelby on our usual coffee date at Sherry's. Halfway through, she'd reached across the table and pressed her hand over the back of mine. Her indigo eyes locked on me.

"Dean . . ." She bit her lower lip. "I have something to tell you. I'm so sorry I've wasted your time."

"What do you mean?" I replied.

She paused briefly. "I'm selling my house and moving back home. I miss my mom. I miss my sisters. And it's just time. It's been long enough, and I'm ready to be with my family again."

It took me a minute to process her announcement. "But your home is here. You live *here*. Don't you like Cascade Valley?"

"Of course. I love it." Her soft brown hair brushed her shoulders. "I've made so many friends. I'll miss you all. But this was my home with Paul. I came here as a bride nearly eight years ago. And I've tried to make it work without him. But I can't see myself making a home here forever. The memories are just too painful, and I'm ready to move on."

I couldn't blame her, but my reply was unintentionally husky. "I understand. But my family's business is rooted in this valley, Shelby. My life is here."

"I know," she'd murmured. "And it'd be so easy to imagine a future with you, Dean. You're a good man. But I need to go home."

"Are you going to finish saddling up, or are we just hanging out under these trees all day?" Knox's good-natured words break into the memory, bringing me sharply to the present.

Quickly, I tighten the straps on the horse's saddle. Shockingly, my heart hadn't urged me to ask Shelby to stay. And after a month of reflection, the closing of our chapter doesn't feel like a mistake.

I turn to Knox and give him a playful shove. "I just thought I could take extra time because we'd be here forever while you cleaned up breakfast."

He snorts, turning away to saddle his own ride, while I walk toward Vincent, letting Midnight trail behind me.

"I'm thinking I should ride ahead this morning to make sure we aren't bringing the herd right up onto wolf territory tonight. What do you think?" I say when I get within earshot.

Vincent fastens a buckle on his saddle and glances at me. "Are you thinking we should reroute the herd and go farther west instead of east?"

I shrug. "Possibly. I want to check out Fisherman's Gulch before we get there anyway. We haven't grazed on that pasture for a couple of years, and I'd like to see how that reforestation project we started has progressed. It should be well-established by now."

The mountains above Cascade Valley have seen their share of fire and destruction over the last twenty years. A forest fire can change the weather pattern of a region, making the land ever-increasingly arid and useless. Less rain means less water in the rivers and lakes. Trees and native grasses struggle to grow and hold onto the earth. When a storm inevitably hits the mountains, mudslides and flash floods are a significant threat.

We approach our ranching philosophy as stewards of the land. As the herd moves across the mountain, the cattle's hooves till the ground. Their droppings provide fresh fertilizer for the struggling soil, replenishing it and allowing grass and wild plants to grow. We are intentional in scheduling where we allow them to graze, steering them away from sensitive areas and toward the spots where they could exert the most benefit over the land. It's a pattern that mimics the grazing habits of native bison, and so far, we've been successful in our mission.

On a few occasions, we've worked hand in hand with the forestry service to plant new trees and restore the banks of several key stream beds that were washed away by a flash flood five years ago. Fisherman's Gulch was one such project. Our plan was to graze the herd on the perimeter of the stream, but if there's a chance we could damage the sensitive waterway, I'd rather avoid the area entirely.

Vincent nods in agreement. "The boys and I can handle the herd for the day if you want to ride ahead and check it out. If a wolf pack has established itself in that direction, I'd rather not stay awake all night waiting for them to break into our camp."

I check that my rifle is in its case and secured to the saddle. I touch the pistol on my hip and the walkie-talkie on the other side before swinging up on top of Midnight. "Alrighty then, I should be back by tonight. I'll use the walkie on the way back if we need to adjust the route."

The rest of the team is already on their horses, prompting the cattle forward. I ride past and wave.

"You headed to the valley, boss?" Abraham calls.

I shake my head. "Just riding ahead toward Fisherman's Gulch to scout out our grazing route. I'll try to be back soon."

"Take your time," Abraham replies, adding hopefully, "Maybe you can catch us a few fish to fry up for dinner. I could use a break from Knox's reconstituted chili and dry cornbread."

Knox shakes his fist at the cowboy's good-natured dig. With a laugh, I nudge Midnight's flank and leave the meandering herd behind.

The mountains that border this part of Montana are one interconnected mass of rolling hills, ridges, valleys, and gorges. We're deep in the backcountry out here. Cell service is spotty at best, so the walkie-talkie comes in handy if it's within range. Otherwise, I'm on my own for the day. I crest the first hill and begin my descent into the small valley that stretches between me and the slope of the forest rising in the distance. The herd will pass this way, too, albeit more slowly.

I set Midnight to a brisk pace. Within an hour, the pines ahead of me take on a clearer shape, and the earthy, spicy scent of the forest hits me again as I leave the open rangeland. I opt for taking the same path the herd will travel, rather than a more direct route, my eyes open for any signs of wolf presence along the way.

A couple of miles ahead, Fisherman's Gulch is one of the best-kept secrets of the mountains, providing savory Kokanee salmon during the spawning season and rainbow trout at other times to those fortunate enough to know about the out-of-the-way spot. There's also a lush meadow stretching just before the stream that will allow us to graze and water the herd for a couple of days. We'll have to share the fishing spot with the elk and deer that frequent the watering hole, but the thought of crispy, smoky trout for dinner makes me spur Midnight forward into the cover of the trees.

We wind around exposed roots, taking the wider trail worn into the ground. It'll be a tight fit to guide the herd through the trees, but the rich meadow once the journey is over will be worth it. Bird calls and the chatter of red squirrels warn the forest of our arrival. This side of the mountain is remote. It is the perfect place for a pack of wolves to establish their territory. So far, I haven't seen evidence of a den, but that doesn't mean it isn't located closer to the water.

The steady *clomp* of Midnight's steps echoes above the morning bird calls and the sound of wind passing through the tree boughs. I spend twenty minutes crossing back and forth, leaving the trail often, but finding nothing that would indicate a wolf den. Finally, I steer my horse toward the ridge that leads up and over toward the fishing hole. We emerge at the top a few minutes later, and Midnight's stride pauses with my gentle tug on his reins. The meadow stretches out far and wide, ending abruptly at the wall of pines ahead. Running through the middle, the stream glistens in the soft light of morning. It hasn't even been two hours of riding. Since I left before the sun rose, it has now just crested the top of the trees. The heaviness of midsummer warmth is rising steadily. Our slow-moving herd will take much longer to arrive, so I can take my time searching the clearing.

It's a peaceful view, nothing but forest, water, earth, and sky. God's country. I consider crossing the wide stream and checking out the forest on the other side. The banks are narrow enough at this time of year, the heat having depleted some of the watershed from the glacial runoff that floods the waterways in spring. It'll be easy to cross and scout for any indication of gray wolf territory.

Midnight shifts restlessly under me. Leaning forward, I pat his withers, my eyes scanning the clearing again as I ready myself to continue the search. But then, out of the corner of my eye, I catch sight of her.

A woman stands in the middle of the stream, the swiftly flowing water rising past her waist. She is dressed in brown waders that look to be three sizes too big for her, but she is holding her own against the chilly flow of the water. She's half-hidden behind the overgrown bank, its shadows obscuring her. My eyes only caught sight of her now because she took a step backward, her arm coming up and over her head as she cast a line into the river.

She's fishing, a not-unusual sight in Montana. What is unusual is seeing a woman deep in the woods fishing alone this early in the morning. I lean forward again, scanning the clearing a third time for any sign of her companion, reasoning that she is probably camping up here with someone who is currently out of sight.

But I see no sign of a second figure near the fishing hole. There are no tents or a fire in sight, and the woman hasn't spotted me yet since her back is still turned away from me. From the hunch of her shoulders, it's obvious she is focused on staying upright as she works the fishing line.

A minute ticks by as I debate backing away and leaving her alone. Depending on how fast the herd moves, it may end up taking us a couple of days to move fully out this way. By that time, she'll be long gone, and I won't have needed to disturb her.

But my conscience pricks at me. Wolf packs hunt in large territories, covering up to a thousand or more square miles. They could have easily traveled this far in a night. If there is wolf presence in the area, she needs to know. My concern has nothing to do with the fact that she appears to be a woman who has ventured out alone in the woods, and I'm worried for her safety; any lone hiker or camper needs to be aware of the risk of nearby wildlife.

Without giving it further thought, I spur Midnight down the ridge. Moving at a mild gallop, we close the distance swiftly. As I approach, her shoulder-length, golden blonde hair falls over her shoulders in pretty waves, capturing the soft rays of early morning peeking over the trees. She's still unaware of my presence, her back to me, and the sound of the swiftly rushing water covering Midnight's approach. Not wanting to startle her, I call out fifty feet away.

"Hey there! Hello," I shout, ensuring my voice carries over the gurgles of the water.

The woman's reaction is swift, decisive, and without hesitation. Swinging her head to look back over her shoulder, her eyes sweep over me. Within the same movement, she is already striding toward the far bank, fighting the push of the current but making fast progress. Tossing the fishing pole toward the muddy bank, her arms come down to help propel her through the waist-deep water.

Before I can call out again, she's already scurried up the embankment as Midnight trots forward, eager for the promise of a drink. Caught off guard, I let him amble unchecked, watching the woman's movements. Quick as a flash, she runs to something tossed on the far shore, her posture low and tight. She reaches down and slides out something slim and black from its carrying case.

I watch as she lifts a rifle to her shoulder and points it straight at my head.

Chapter Three

Kasey
Late June

Before the break of dawn, the coastal air is sharp and chilly. The strong northwestern wind whipping off the coastline is still too icy for my blood, even after months of living on the Oregon coast. I prefer the warmth of the sun, but when I left the army, I found myself drawn to the notoriously misty Pacific Northwest. It fits my gloomy mood.

Burying my chin in the collar of my fleece-lined parka, I carry the final load to the Jeep. Finn paces at my side, the German Shepherd sensing my tension. Last night, he'd stayed out of my way as I'd moved about the cottage, his dark eyes and somber face watching me from his cushion as I paced in front of the television, not hearing the laugh track that played on the screen. Forgotten again, my tea grew cold as I wore a trail in the rug.

The deep blues and grays of the night soften as the sun rises to greet the day. I double-check my cottage—back door locked and bolted, alarm set, windows latched. Locking the front door, I walk the seashell path to the street one final time. My Jeep idles in front of the cottage. I pause just beyond the white picket fence to stare back at the mustard yellow front door of my beach cottage, the color a reminder of the sun that rarely peeks through the clouds. The soft gray siding, gabled roof, and cheerful door stare back at me with a strange and mystical gaze as the morning fog lingers, caressing the edges of the small house.

A perfectly normal house on a perfectly normal beach on a perfectly normal day. It's a feeling I crave after a lifetime punctuated by what I'd label "not normal" experiences. Now, it stands as a tiny slice of sweetness to give me a respite from the bitterness of what my life has become.

And just as I've walked away from everything that felt like home before, once again, I'm leaving it all behind with an all-too-familiar eerie feeling that I won't be back for a very long time. In an act of premonition, I set up automatic mortgage payments last night. When the federal government deposits money into my account every month, an outgoing payment will keep my mortgage current. I did the same for all the utilities and put my mail on hold. I keep my monthly expenses low, and beyond that, no one in my life will worry if I don't reappear for a while. But I want the reassurance that my home will be waiting for me when I get back.

"Ready, boy?" I glance at the handsome dog waiting anxiously at my side. Finn always grows jittery when he sees me packing up the Jeep. He seems to remember the times over the past few years when I packed my army-issued bag, knelt in front of him at the boarding facility, and promised I'd be back soon. I never knew if I was telling him a lie, and once, I almost did. As my official ESA companion, he's been my constant shadow since I returned to the States for good.

I kneel on the dirt now and put my hands on either side of his broad, furry face. His dark eyes meet mine solemnly. My fingers bury themselves in his ruff.

"I'm going to need you to watch my six when we get there." My forehead falls forward to rest against the slope between his eyes. "I don't know what we're walking into, but if it looks bad, I'll get us out of there. Okay?"

Am I comforting the dog or reassuring myself? Probably the latter. Finn holds still while I gather my courage, his hot breath brushing against my face. After a minute, I rise, ready to face what's next, if only to comfort my dog.

"Let's go for a ride!" The forced excitement in my voice doesn't match what I feel.

But I'm satisfied when he brightens, his fluffy tail wagging.

"Up," I instruct him, and he leaps into the passenger seat. He stares through the front window, the soft loll of his tongue giving away his secret enthusiasm for car rides. I already set up a comfortable resting spot for him across the back seat, but for now, I need to be able to reach over to stroke his coarse fur whenever I feel the anxiety creeping up in my throat again.

As we leave the quiet seaside street and take the road that will eventually lead us east, I can't shake the feeling that this is the last time I'll see the happy yellow door of my cottage welcoming me home.

. . .

The drive takes almost four days, just as I predicted. Already, I wish it could be longer. The address Amy gave me when I checked in yesterday afternoon is leading me to a ritzy Greenwich address.

The last I knew, she was living in a glamorous Soho apartment. Now, it seems she has made the transition to suburban housewife.

I wonder how the role will fit the Amy I once knew. My sister used to live for cocktail parties, shopping excursions, travel, jewelry, and Pilates classes. Not that I experienced even an inkling of that lifestyle with her, but she told me—effusively—on the few occasions I accepted her invitation for a lunch date over the years. That was before I signed up for the army and went away.

Though she's kept me fairly updated on her life via email, it's been years since I last saw my sister in person. As Finn and I travel the highways with too many cars and blaring horns, I realize I don't really know her at all. Certainly not well enough to feel surprised that she would take her young family and move them out to the suburbs, escaping the smoke and chaos of city life. Most likely, she's transitioned smoothly into the role of gracious heiress, wife, and mother, just like her mother before her.

I've never met Amy's husband. I've never met my nephew and niece either: Dmitry Junior and Jane, or DJ and Janie as their mother calls them. Five years old and just about fifteen months, respectively. I remember their ages because Amy sent emails after each of their births with candid photographs of her in the hospital room, holding her newborns, and in the nursery. She probably wanted me to respond with more than a curt congratulations. But I've avoided encouraging her to make me a part of her life. I don't want the rejection that I know will eventually come when she realizes I can't be who she needs me to be.

Though at first, I stayed away because I was hurt and angry after Dad passed and Amy's mom kicked me out of the memorial service. I didn't care about the inheritance; I knew there was nothing for me. I just wanted to say goodbye to the father I never really knew.

Then I enlisted, and I stayed away because I was overseas on a tour of duty. And I'd kept going back, rushing to return to wherever I was deployed after short furloughs, and there was never time—or I didn't make time—to visit my sister in New York City for nearly the past decade.

It's all just as well because some of us are simply destined to be alone.

But then I nearly died on what was supposed to be a routine mission. Months of recovery led to months of physical therapy to learn how to use my leg again. I've never told Amy anything about what happened. And yet, despite how strictly I've avoided her, Amy knew how quickly I'd come running if I could. Because, after all, that's what older sisters are supposed to do, and it's what I promised her years ago.

Now, I wonder if whatever awaits me is going to make me regret that promise.

When I make the turn onto Amy's swanky suburban street, my stomach tightens. Houses that would be better qualified as mansions on luxurious estates flash by on both sides of the street. Immediately, I feel out of place. Given my humble city roots, I would never fit in here.

Glancing down, I side-eye my green utility pants, basic black t-shirt, and biker boots. I hadn't even thought to pack the frillier, softer clothes that are probably standard in Amy's social circles.

My voice rises over the mumble of the radio speakers. "We get in. We find out what's going on. And then we get out if things start getting dicey. Deal?"

Finn's eyes meet mine as I reach across the console to stroke his cheek.

My sister's last text instructed me to park down the street and walk up the side lane where delivery drivers drop off packages. I comply, leaving the Jeep parked several estates down, tucked behind a copse of decorative trees. It isn't hot, so I opt to leave Finn inside for now with the windows rolled down, unsure if he'll be welcome in the house. I texted her of my arrival as instructed.

ME: I'm here.

Maintaining a casual pace, I walk along the street toward the address Amy gave me. Earlier, I rolled my blonde, shoulder-length hair into a baseball cap, the collar of my tan canvas jacket tucked up around my ears. Though I'm trying to blend in, I wonder if I look as suspicious as I feel as I duck toward the side entrance of my sister's mansion.

The estate is surrounded by a high rock wall. The property sits on a corner, and to the rear, a secluded walkway with a towering hedge on either side leads me to a gate. Not a single stray leaf litters the ground. The bubble of a fountain catches my ear as I rap on the wooden gate. The latch gives way under my gentle push, and I peek my head around the corner.

"Amy," I call softly down the ivy-strewn corridor, unsure of whether to proceed or go back to the front gate to come in via the intercom like a normal person. Secrecy makes me nervous.

"Come in, Kasey. I'm here."

I jump when her voice speaks softly behind the gate. It swings inward to reveal a wisp of a woman in the shadows under the trees. In disbelief, I stare at my sister, shocked at the change in her features. The last couple of years haven't been kind.

Her once joyful, pretty face is hollow and gray. Expensive cream linen pants and a green silk top hang off her emaciated frame. Gone is the pert, toned Pilates body she used to have. Gaunt is a better word for her now. Her tiny shoulders shake as her bony fingers reach to pull me past the gate's threshold. Before I can react, I'm enveloped in a frail pair of arms as Amy begins to sob against my shoulder.

I only hesitate for a moment before my arms come up and wrap tightly around her. My pulse quickens as I try to find the words to ask how and why.

"Thank you for coming. I've been so scared." She is the first to break the silence, her soft tears sounding like a wounded animal.

I pull her closer, guilt washing over me in waves. I should have been here. I should have known when her emails stopped that something wasn't right. But I've been too focused on my own survival and recovery after . . .

"Are you sick?" I demand, anxiety making my voice come out harsher than I intend. I clear my throat and force myself to soften, continuing in a gentler tone. "What's wrong, Amy? Tell me everything. Is it bad?"

Finally, her arms release me as she steps back. Her tears have soaked through my jacket. I'm just around average height, but she is a couple of inches shorter, so I have to lean down to see her face. My breath catches as her pale, watery eyes look up at me for the first time. The hollows under them are deep and purple.

The silence stretches on, and I think of how much she resembles her mother. They share the same strawberry blonde hair, the same sharp, Waspish features, the same pale ice-blue eyes, and fair skin. I took after our father, inheriting a muscular and athletic frame, thick golden blonde hair, aquamarine eyes, and easily tanned skin. Never in a million years could I have mimicked the delicate figures of my half-sister and her mother. Another thing separating me from their world of glitz and glamor.

"It is bad." Amy finally gathers herself enough to speak, dabbing at the clumpy mascara running below her eyes. "But it's not that. I'm not sick. Or, I mean, I'm not sick like that."

I shake my head, trying to understand. "So it's bad, but you're not sick? Can we go inside where you can warm up? Maybe make some tea?"

She shivers in the shadows of the mature trees that arch over the alcove. We are just beyond the gate on a mossy, cobblestone path. A short distance ahead, a door leads into the house.

"Yes, come inside." Amy steps past me to lead the way. "There's no one here, and we won't be interrupted."

I see that she is trying to recover her composure, but her hand trembles as she turns the doorknob to enter. Following a dark hallway, we emerge in the rear of a grand kitchen. Marble seems to touch every surface. Amy busies herself with setting a kettle of water to boil on the massive gas range, and I find a seat on a leather barstool at the island.

We don't speak. The silence stretches on as I realize what's wrong.

The house is too quiet.

"Are the kids here?" I look around, expecting to see two tiny bodies flinging themselves from one of the dark corridors that fan away from the kitchen. "Or your husband?"

Amy turns away from the stove, shifting from one foot to the other, her fingers scratching at the skin of her arm absentmindedly. I notice several scabbed-over scratch marks already on the skin.

"The kids aren't here. I hired a babysitter to take them to the park for a few hours so we could be alone when you arrived." She lifts her head. "And Dmitry isn't here either. He hasn't been here for a long time."

My eyebrows rise. I feel my lower jaw drop open a little at the unexpected news. "Oh," I manage, "are you two . . .?"

Amy plants her hands on the marble countertop. Her face

contorts. "I don't know . . ." Then her eyes harden, turning into two orbs of ice. "Something's happened, and I need to make a change . . . but he doesn't know yet."

As the tension builds, the kettle whistles, the high-pitched squeal piercing the lofty space. Amy turns away, pouring the hot water into a teapot and reaching into a glass-fronted cabinet for two bone china teacups and saucers. She walks to the refrigerator and pulls out a small pitcher of cream and a bowl of quartered lemons. Setting them all on a silver tray with a crystal sugar bowl, she carries it toward me. The cups rattle in her fragile grip.

"I have a sitting room that overlooks the gardens. Shall we talk there?"

Silently, I stand and follow her through the house. I try to sneak a few peeks into the front rooms, but my sister leads us through a series of dimly lit, interconnected back passageways, our footsteps reverberating off the floors. The room we end up in is bright and lovely, painted a soft forest green and filled with rays of sunlight that filter through gauzy sheers that cover the floor-to-ceiling windows. I sink into the corner of a cream-colored sofa that is surprisingly comfortable, taking care that my boots don't dirty the rug.

"Lemon or cream?"

"Amy?"

"Do you take sugar?" She avoids eye contact, carefully pouring the fragrant chamomile tea from the pot. I note the tremor in her hand.

"Just plain, please." I accept the delicate teacup and set it on the table in front of me. "What's this about? What is going on? Why am I here?"

She sinks into a wingback chair, a teacup clattering in her hands. "Kasey, do you remember about thirteen years ago when you said I could come live with you? I had barely turned eighteen. You hadn't gone into the service yet. I think you were working at that diner uptown. You were talking about going to nursing school. And I was having trouble with Mom and Dad, and you said I could live with you for a few weeks if I needed space."

"I remember," I reply softly. A spot on my sofa and leftovers brought home from the diner were all I had been able to offer her.

Amy's shoulders slump forward as if she is too exhausted to hold herself up anymore. "I wish I'd just done it. I wish I hadn't talked myself out of it and convinced myself that vacations and shopping trips were worth staying for. Maybe then I wouldn't have made such a mess of things."

"We all have regrets, Amy." I try to soothe her. "But everything can be fixed."

She shakes her head. "I'm not sure this can be fixed. I've done this to myself, and I'm suffering the consequences of it." She leans toward me, reaching out with alien-like fingers. "I just can't bear the thought of my children being the ones hurt by my mistakes." She grabs my hand, and I squeeze it gently. "Promise me, Kasey," she continues with intense focus, her eyes too bright, their pupils too wide, "promise me that no matter what happens, you'll protect them. You're the only one I've ever truly trusted."

"Just breathe," I reply. "It's going to be okay."

A sad grimace comes across her thinned lips. "You're the strongest woman I've ever known. Nothing ever seemed to faze you, even when life threw struggle after struggle at you. You just pressed on. And now look at you. You've fought for our country; you've done something important with your life." I shake my head, but she squeezes my fingers. "Honestly, though, I'm not sure even you can fix this mess."

"Why am I here then?" I press.

Amy settles back into the chair, dropping my hand. She crosses her legs and places her hands in her lap. Her expression hardens. "It's simple. I need you to take the kids and go away. Run where no one will find you. Where you'll all be hidden until it's safe."

I frown. "And where will you be? What about Dmitry?"

"I don't want that man near my kids ever again." Her voice is harsh and guttural, surprising me with the sudden show of energy.

I stare at her in alarm, never having seen my sister this angry yet also so vulnerable and afraid. "Can we back up? What's going on? Are you and Dmitry getting divorced? You know he's entitled to custody of the kids too? Asking me to take them away is . . . crazy and probably illegal."

"I know it's crazy, but in this case, it's most likely not illegal," she replies. A chilly calm settles over her frail frame, but her words come out fast and slightly slurred. "Kasey, Dmitry has been in prison for the last three months. Last year, he got into a fight with a man at one of his nightclubs. He hurt him . . . badly. The man has been in a coma ever since. They have no idea if he'll recover, and it's likely he won't. They gave my husband five years."

I try—and fail—to hide the shock in my expression. Years ago, I dug into Dmitry Volkov's past when Amy first announced their engagement. The man was all glitz and glam, charming even the most vicious tabloids. And I didn't trust him for a single second. Anyone that level of slick had to be shady, and when I dug into his past and discovered faint whispers of drug dealing, mafia connections, and organized crime surrounding him, I feared his connection to my sister. Most of his family didn't even live in the States. But he'd purchased a series of nightclubs throughout the East Coast and had his hands in at least half a dozen other businesses up and down the coastline. He wasn't anywhere close to as wealthy as Amy after her inheritance, but he wasn't hurting financially.

And Dmitry's underhanded dealings were only ever rumors, investigations that never went anywhere, charges dropped. I told myself it wasn't my place to stop my sister's marriage. Dad always did love a good social and financial connection. I didn't attend the wedding eight years ago. By that time, I was over my adolescent desire to be part of the Carter family tree.

Amy continues, "That incident wasn't the only one, but the others were swept under the rug. He would . . . get angry at home too. I wish I'd done something to stop it years ago or put my foot down and made him get help. He always said he was stressed, he didn't mean it, or that I had provoked him. Maybe I could have stopped him from hurting that man if I'd just done something."

When she pauses to take a deep breath, I struggle to control my rising anger. "Amy, are you saying . . .? Did he hurt you?"

Unconsciously, her hand rises to the base of her throat, and the look in her eyes tells me everything I need to know. "It wasn't just the fits of rage. Over the years, I caught him doing . . . Let's just say I knew about the drugs. But he always seemed to have it under control. Now, I don't know. After the wedding, with the drinking and the strange men he always had around here and the clubs, I didn't know what to think anymore. During the trial, things came out that I only had suspicions of . . . illegal things, shady connections, illicit dealings. I only had suspicions, but I didn't dare testify as his wife. So they could only give him five years for the assault." She steadies herself. "And now I'm scared. That's it in a nutshell."

"You can hire protection." I lean forward, hoping to dissuade my half-sister from making a disastrous decision. "You have money. He can't touch your inheritance, can he? But you can't just disappear with the kids and not expect there to be legal retaliation from your husband."

"My inheritance is safe. My attorneys have made sure of that. And I won't be the one disappearing with them. You will."

When I open my mouth to protest, Amy holds up her hand, and I notice several small prescription medicine bottles clasped in her palm for the first time. They are half-full.

"I'm afraid there's more." She exhales sharply, the shame caving her shoulders in. "I'm also an opioid addict. I've tried and tried to quit, but I keep failing. I have to go into rehab, because if I don't, I'm afraid all hope is lost."

My breath catches in my throat. I stare at her, the edginess, the tremors, the waif-like emaciation, and the purple shadows under her eyes suddenly making sense. "For how long?"

"Full-blown? It's been about a year. It started after I had a minor car accident. There was lingering whiplash and some other issues, and my good old family doctor didn't hesitate to prescribe pain medication to treat my discomfort . . . at my husband's insistence, mind you. He wanted me to get back to normal because Janie was starting to teethe and keeping us up at night. I was already struggling with the antidepressants my psychiatrist prescribed me five years ago. I thought I could handle both medications, but when my prescription ran out and the pain and depression just got worse . . ."

"Maybe you just need to talk to your doctor again? Come up with a treatment plan," I suggest, holding onto the last vestiges of hope for an easy solution.

The shame in her voice is mixed with anger as she continues, "My doctor is the reason I'm in this mess." She pauses. "That's not true. I couldn't stop. I liked the way the pills made me feel, the way they softened the hard edges of my life. I didn't care about the things happening around me when I had them. Turns out, it's not hard to find a dealer around here. Most of the moms are on something anyway . . ."

"I'm so sorry." When her words trail off, I clear my throat to hide the sudden lump in it.

"It's my own fault. I ignored the red flags because it felt good at the time. The same way I handled my marriage, I suppose." Harshly, her laugh rings out. "I've got plenty of mental clarity for a drug addict. Time and time again, I've wondered if he encouraged me to use them on purpose. I can't blame him for my choices, but maybe a dulled, apathetic wife seemed easier to manage. I was asking a lot of questions before the accident happened."

"You could just file for divorce. Spousal abuse isn't to be taken lightly, Amy. When's the last time you . . .?" Rather than say the ugly words aloud, I nod toward the bottles clutched in her palm.

She doesn't hesitate to meet my gaze, but her eyes are full of pain. "A few hours before you arrived. I tried not to, but I . . ." She swallows. "There isn't a judge in the county who will give custody to a woman addicted to painkillers. And Dmitry will use it against me. I know he knows. And when he gets out of prison . . ." She shivers.

"But he'll be in prison for years." A tingling sensation creeps up my limbs.

She shakes her head. "That's why I text you. I just found out that he's being considered for early parole. There's a very real possibility he might be out by the end of the year. Can you believe it?" The whites of her eyes show as she casts them about the room wildly. "Puts a man into a coma and doesn't even serve a year. It was a bad case. People talked; the tabloids went crazy. Even though I suspect the judge was on his payroll, there were expectations. It couldn't be swept under the rug. But he gave him a remarkably light sentence, the barest minimum. It wasn't even a maximum-security prison. And if I'm still in rehab when he gets out . . . That's why I need you. You're my rock, and—"

"What's your plan?" I interrupt her. "Rehab is good, but what are your long-term plans? How are you going to stay sober when I'm gone?"

She leans forward eagerly, her pupils large black dots. One of her legs bounces. "I must completely annihilate this ugly thing inside me. There's a state-of-the-art, private treatment facility I want to go to, but it's an immersive program out of state with no contact with the outside world for at least a couple of months. You are required to stay ninety days, at a minimum. No exceptions."

"Why don't you just go to rehab here in Connecticut?"

"Because I think Dmitry is watching me, and I can't let him find out I'm trying to get help so I can leave him." Amy's face pales. "Before the trial started, his cousin showed up with a team of security guards. He claimed they were to make sure the media didn't try to disrupt our lives. Yet, even now, they follow me and the kids everywhere when we go out. Plus, there are the cameras."

I glance around in alarm, visually sweeping the room for surveillance equipment, my hand going to my hip under my jacket. "Are these guards here now?" I demand.

She shrugs. "When the media attention died down, they stationed one guy in front of the gate. Pretty much every night, they'll come into the house to do random security sweeps. They usually show up before we go to bed."

"And the cameras?"

"When Dmitry wanted to install them inside the house, I

refused. I told him there are too many ways for someone to hack into the feed, and I didn't want the kids exposed to some creep. But they are all around the perimeter of the house. I messed with the one at the service gate, though, so they couldn't see you arrive, and there's a blind spot on that side. It just looks like a leaf blew in front of the lens."

"This isn't good." Tension builds in my stomach, and I feel foolish stating the obvious. "If you feel unsafe, you need to involve the police."

"But there's no one I trust besides you and my lawyer. Do you remember Bill, Daddy's estate attorney?"

I shake my head. I never met the man, but that's not important.

As if she can't sit still any longer, she stands and paces the floor in front of the windows. I note the slight jerkiness of her movements. "I've worked everything out with him. He doesn't know the details, but all the bills are paid in advance, and he privately booked a long-term rental in California for us. He thinks we're going there to get away from the negative press, but we'll never actually stay there." Her shoulders slump inward. "I'm so tired of it all, Kasey. I just want to be free."

Her multi-layered words hang heavily between us.

I rise to join her on the fluffy rug, staying away from the windows so I can't be spotted by the exterior cameras. I can't imagine her fighting anyone, let alone a violent husband connected to illegal dealings. I've been a fighter my entire life, and even I want to run at the thought of entering this battle. My sister's lips are set in a stiff line, her eyes haunted with the secrets that terrify her.

My tone is firm but soft. "I can't disappear with your kids, Amy. What about your mom, your friends, the kids' friends,

Dmitry's family? Someone like you can't just up and disappear. People will notice."

She shivers, wrapping her arms around herself and shaking her head. "Dmitry's family and I never got along. They don't live in the States anyway, and they never wanted anything to do with me and my children. I expect his cousin and the security guards to alert him quickly, but as I said, they'll think we're in California. As for Mom . . ." Her voice goes husky, a deep sadness creeping into it. "She's been in a private home upstate for the past couple of years. She's getting the best care possible, but her mind just isn't what it once was. All her expenses have been paid in advance, and she probably won't notice if we don't come by for a few months."

"What about your friends? You can't just pull the kids out of school."

At this, Amy smiles sadly. "When Dmitry's trial started, most of my friends—or the people I thought were my friends— distanced themselves from me. Suddenly, I was the social pariah Mom always taught me to fear. That's when the pills started getting me through the long, excruciating days, and I haven't really been able to . . ." Her voice thickens. "We've kept to ourselves for quite a while." She gestures toward the framed photograph of two small children on the table. "I didn't want DJ hearing gossip about his dad, so I've been homeschooling him this past year. And Janie is too young for more than preschool. So you see, there isn't anyone to miss us, and the official story will be that we're vacationing in California until at least the end of the year."

Wearily, I close my eyes and rub them. "It sounds like I've missed out on a lot of things."

Amy's eyes fill with tears. "I wish you'd been here, Kasey. I've needed you." She pauses, her face filling with dread. "I didn't even ask how long you're in the States. Is there any way you can get a furlough?"

There's no malice in her tearful words, but they hit me like a punch in my gut. Since I was born, I wasn't needed, nor was I wanted. Then I joined the army, and suddenly, I was both needed and useful to many. I was trained to save lives. I patched up wounds. I got people home to their families while my own forgot me. How could I know my sister would need me? Even as I wish I could push away the crushing weight of guilt, I know my rating as a sister is currently hovering at less than zero. At the very least, I could have checked in from time to time.

"Where would we even go?" I hear myself muse aloud. "If Dmitry is connected to the people you say he is, it won't be hard for him to find us."

Amy's lips tighten. "You were in the army. Didn't they teach you those things? How to disappear and survive." She peers up at me. "It has to be you."

"I don't know . . ." I sigh.

"And you can't tell me anything about where you are going, just in case." She points to the second story above us. "I've purchased two burner phones. I used cash, and I don't think any of Dmitry's security team saw me buy them, but I can't be sure. I'm going to give one to you. Keep it charged and turned on. I'll tell you when I arrive and keep you updated on my progress when I can. We aren't supposed to have cell phones or outside contact while we're there, but I'll find a way to sneak it in, and I'll try to reach out regularly. And when I'm finally free of this, I'll call that phone and join you wherever you are. Then I'll figure out how to deal with this mess I've made of my life."

She looks at me, and I recognize hope finally dawning in her eyes. "Did I do it right? Is that what you're supposed to do?"

I chew on my lower lip, my heart beating faster as I feel the pressure of what she is asking me to do. "This is crazy, Amy. I wasn't expecting this when I drove out here to see you, so I need to think. Pardon my bluntness, but I'm not prepared to get mixed up in your marriage troubles."

When she takes a step back, I realize I hurt her. Tears spring to her eyes.

"You're absolutely right," she murmurs. "You don't owe me anything, especially not after the way Daddy and Mom . . ."

My heart constricts.

There's a sudden commotion at the front of the house, the sound of the doorbell, and gentle rapping on the door. Instantly, Amy's face softens, and she casts her eyes back to me. "I can't ask you to do this for me, Kasey. But please . . . do it for them?"

Before I can reply, she turns on her heel and walks down the shadowy hallway to welcome my niece and nephew home.

Chapter Four

Dean
Mid-August

"Whoa, whoa, whoa."

Dropping the reins, I lift my hands to show the woman I'm not a threat, but the rifle remains aimed at my head. Her stance is steady; her feet are planted into the earth. The butt of the rifle is pulled securely into the crook of her shoulder. I have no way of knowing how good of a shot she is, and I don't intend to put her to the test.

Across the stream, our eyes connect. The water gurgles between us. The channel narrows in this spot. It would be easy to ride Midnight across to the other side, but I don't dare until I know her intentions.

"Who are you? What are you doing here?" Her voice is strong but also softer than I would expect from such an aggressive stance. I don't hear any fear in her tone. The words carry across the water, falling on my ears in a short, staccato burst.

"I didn't mean to startle you, ma'am," I shout. "My name is Dean McCade. I own a ranch in the valley."

Her gaze is locked on me, but she makes no reply.

"Would you mind lowering the gun?" I venture, keeping my expression nonchalant and relaxed. I keep Midnight still. Getting shot isn't on my to-do list today. From the way she has me sighted down the barrel, she doesn't look like she'll hesitate to put me down if I make the wrong move.

The seconds tick by as she waits. It takes a full minute before she finally lowers the rifle from her shoulder. Yet, her tight, two-handed hold on it isn't lost on me.

"Thank you," I call.

"What are you doing here?" she shouts again.

"I'm just scouting for a spot to graze and rest my herd tonight. My cattle are headed this way. I really didn't mean to startle you." I gesture to the water between us. "May I cross?"

She gives me a curt nod, which I take to be permission. But she lifts the rifle again in a warning gesture, and I'm careful not to move too quickly as I urge Midnight forward. He enters the water, moving easily across the stream. With a bound, he leaps up the embankment as the woman takes a few measured steps backward, the gun's presence never wavering.

While I'm confident I'm an equal, if not better, shot than this woman, a chill runs through me as I ride closer. Her expression is unflinching. She means the threat. Of that I'm certain.

"I'm dismounting," I call to her. Swinging out of the saddle, I keep her in my peripheral vision. The rifle rises higher as I turn and take a few steps toward her.

When the distance between us closes to ten yards, I take a moment to get a good look at her. The woman is just around average height and what I'd call petite, yet with a shapely and muscular figure. Her arms are toned and defined, her jawline sharp, and her cheekbones high and carved into her face. Her hair grazes her shoulders, the golden strands catching the rays of the early morning sun. Even from a distance, the woman is undeniably pretty. It's with some effort that I manage to pull my eyes away from her face long enough to scan the surrounding meadow for other threats.

She still hasn't spoken, her eyes never wavering in their intense study of my face. A large hunting knife is strapped to her waist, and I wonder if she has other weapons hidden on her person.

"Are you out here alone?" I venture to break the silence, turning my gaze back to her.

"I don't see that being any of your business," she snaps.

It seems that permitting my approach hasn't done anything to soften her mood.

I sigh. "Ma'am, I'm not here to bother you. But there's been a pack of wolves out hunting about ten miles south of here the past couple of nights."

"I haven't heard any wolves," she retorts.

"This area might not be part of their territory, but I'm not in the mood to lose any cattle tonight. I came out scouting to see if I could locate their den."

"I thought you said you came to find a grazing spot for your herd?" Her expression reflects fresh suspicion.

"That too." I lift my hands, Midnight's reins clutched between my fingers. "Look, I only rode down here to let you know that a wolf pack could be using these woods as a hunting ground. You should be careful out here, especially if you're alone." I level my gaze at her, letting my expression harden. "They are dangerous, and they can gang up on you pretty quickly, especially if you have something they want, like fresh fish."

She tosses her head and shakes the rifle. Her hair brushes her collarbone. The waders drip, quickly drying in the warmth of the August sun. "Thanks, but I think I can handle myself."

Somehow, I'm in little doubt that even as petite as she is, she could do some damage. The woman seems made of steel.

"Do you have extra ammo?" I ask. I risk a step forward. Midnight ambles behind me, his head dropping to munch on the grass whenever we pause. "I have some extra rounds you can have."

She lets me approach. I pause ten feet from her and turn to my saddlebags. Moving slowly, I reach into the leather pouch and pull out a box of .22 rounds.

"Here." I turn back and step toward her. Almost imperceptibly, she flinches as I approach, but she holds her ground when I extend the box. She reaches out and plucks it from my fingers.

"Thanks." The word is uttered begrudgingly.

"You're welcome."

Up close, I take the opportunity to study her features again. She is even prettier than I thought. My best guess is that she's in her mid-thirties. Her smooth, unadorned face glows with a golden summer tan. Her lips are pretty and notably full, colored a particularly appealing shade of pale peach. I imagine them frowning more than they smile. Her lashes are thick. But as her gaze lifts to mine, my breath catches. Her irises are a shade of aquamarine that I've never seen. Like the sea on a sunny day. Unforgettable eyes.

She could freeze a man in his tracks with those eyes alone.

Silence stretches awkwardly between us. With her eyes pinned on my face, I get the feeling that she is studying me as much as I am her.

"Well, if you don't mind, I'd like to get back to fishing now." Finally, she speaks, and I know I've been dismissed.

With a nod, I turn and lead Midnight away. Unable to stop the uncanny feeling pressing at my back, I pause and look over my shoulder. A sudden sense of protectiveness grips me. I'm worried that she doesn't understand the gravity of my warning.

"Just promise me that you'll be careful out here," I say after a hesitant pause. "If you're camping alone, keep a fire burning all night. Do you know how to build a fire?" Why does part of me hope she'll say no just so I can linger to demonstrate the skill to her?

The faintest flicker of amusement passes over her face. "Thanks," she replies, "but yes, I know how to build a fire. Actually, I know how to do lots of things. So don't you worry about me."

We seem to have progressed from open hostility to sarcasm. A good sign, in my opinion. Maybe she'll let me ride out of here without shooting me in the back. Matching her sarcastic tone, I allow my native Montana drawl to slip out. "I've no doubt in my mind that you can do many things, ma'am."

A flicker of one arched eyebrow. "Okay, then . . ."

That's my cue. "Well, I'll leave you to it. If you run into trouble, our team will progress this way over the next day or so . . ."

"Thanks. I'll be sure to trek out of here to find you if I have any problems." More sarcasm. "Thanks for sparing the ammo." She lifts the box as I step into the stirrup.

Dipping the brim of my hat, I settle into the saddle, tap Midnight's flank, and direct him toward the water. We cross the stream and emerge on the other side before I allow myself a glance back. The woman is standing in the same spot I left her. Her stance hasn't wavered, and she is still holding the rifle securely between her hands.

"Is it just me, or does that woman seem a little paranoid to you, buddy?" I mumble to Midnight as we trot across the meadow. His head shakes, his mane fluttering with the movement. "Yeah, I knew it wasn't just me."

I don't look back again. Instead, I spur my horse into a canter as we approach the ridge. He climbs the slope easily. The timberline beckons ahead. I'll disappear under the shadowy boughs within a few seconds. Slipping into the forest, I ride forward a dozen paces. Only when the ridge is well behind us do I prompt Midnight to stop. Dismounting quickly, I loop the reins around a log on the forest floor. Reaching into the saddlebag, I grab a small pair of binoculars I always carry with me.

"Be right back," I tell him, turning to retrace my steps, my strides long and quiet. I slow and duck down as I approach an opening in the trees. I have no intention of letting the woman spot me this time. Staying low, I creep forward. With caution, I peek around the trunk of a particularly large pine.

It takes me a few seconds to find her in the binoculars. The woman must have sprung into action as soon as I rode away. Already, she's collected her fishing supplies, and I watch as she cuts across the meadow. She heads for the deep forest just beyond the clearing. On her back, I see a rucksack, the rifle, a fishing pole, and a basket that I assume was intended to store any fish she caught.

Her pace through the tall grass is quick and steady, but to my surprise, I observe a noticeable limp in her stride, which escaped my notice the first time. One of her legs seems to lag a second or so behind the other. Still, she's moving at a quick trot as I track her across the meadow. She approaches an opening in the trees, and I watch as she reaches the shadowy boundary of a trail.

"Well, you sure hightailed it out of there right quick, little lady," I drawl sarcastically. "What? Fishing without a license, are we? Depleting our natural resources without paying your dues? *Tsk, tsk, tsk.*"

She couldn't possibly hear me, but I'm kidding anyway. It's Fish and Wildlife's job to police the mountains, and I'm not concerned with her having the proper paperwork to catch a few fish from the stream. But I have to acknowledge the possibility that she viewed *my* approach as a threat and thought the safest course was simply to disappear. A disquieting feeling hits me at the thought of making her uncomfortable.

Pausing, she looks back over her shoulder and surveys the zigzag trail she's just broken through the grass. Her body moves in a slow half-circle, following as her head turns from one side to the other. She seems to pay particular attention to the very spot from which I am now observing her, but I reason it's unlikely she can spot me from such a distance.

Finally, the woman seems satisfied. Hoisting the rifle higher on her shoulder, she turns around, takes a step forward, and disappears into the forest.

Chapter Five

Kasey
Late June

"I didn't know how bad all of this could get until I woke up and realized I was right in the middle of a nightmare. You hear stories about people ruining their lives over their addiction, but I didn't know how completely it could take over your mind until I couldn't think of anything else. I told myself I had it under control, but when I woke up from a blackout a couple of times—"

Amy's voice cracks, and my heart cracks with it. I recognize how hard she is trying to hold herself together and how scared she is. Her hands shake as she prepares dinner in the kitchen. I wonder if the last pill she took has faded by now.

I didn't hesitate to take the prescription bottles and dump their contents straight into the toilet when she was occupied with the children. The paleness of her face when she realized what I'd done sent a chill racing through my heart. But she'd accepted the loss silently, and now I wonder if she simply has more stashed elsewhere in the house.

"Here. Let me cut that." I use my hip to nudge her aside, taking the knife from her cold fingers. I slice the vegetables she pulled from the refrigerator. The moment feels surreal, casually preparing a salad for a family dinner while my sister recounts her spiral into addiction. With every word, my anger seethes a little hotter inside my chest. I'm not angry with her, and yet, I am. And with her husband and with every person who played a part in leading her down this road.

Finn, whom I snuck into the house an hour ago, observes my every move from his station in the corner.

My sister leans against the counter, her thin shoulders slumping forward, her eyes too bright, too wide. "At first, I was handling them fine," she explains in a low tone. "I'd been depressed before the accident, but everything got worse afterward because I was in so much pain. Janie was a fussy little thing. I was clumsy and forgetful because of the medication, and I was crying all the time, and Dmitry . . . well, he was never as charming after the wedding as when he was courting me." Her head drops, her flat, dull hair falling over her face. "But after a while, I think he recognized that the pills made life easier for us both. I was so fuzzy and lightheaded; I didn't even have the words to protest when he was mean to me. Sometimes, I didn't even care. And then, when my prescription ran out, he encouraged me to ask for more, so I did."

The knife slams down on the counter next to the cutting board with a sharp *thwack*. Instantly, Amy's head pops up, her eyes widening with alarm, and a flash of regret surges through me at my lack of self-control. This moment isn't about my righteous indignation at the injustices I'm just discovering. It's about protecting my very scared, very lost little sister.

DJ and Janie scamper through the kitchen, screaming and laughing simultaneously. From the corner, Finn snorts loudly. He isn't used to this much commotion. Janie stumbles against the back of my leg, and I look down at her in alarm. She appears to be okay, now chasing her brother on all fours through the house as if they don't have a care in the world. Which I suppose they don't. Amy seems to have done a good job of hiding her struggles from them. Despite the fiery urges roiling through her veins, her calm demeanor is notable, and I wonder if that's what motherhood does to a person.

As an only child, I didn't grow up around babies or children in general, and I wasn't around Amy until she became an adult. The thought of being alone with a tiny human for any length of time sends jolts of panic through me, but that doesn't mean my protective instincts weren't immediately activated as soon as I found out what my sister is facing.

"They don't deserve a life filled with their father's violence and lies . . . or my failures as a mother. They deserve the world." As if reading my thoughts, Amy murmurs next to me. She drags herself upright and walks to the butler's pantry, emerging a minute later with a sleeve of pasta. She sets a pot of water to boil before looking at me with the most mournful expression I've ever seen.

My heart cracks fully in two. "Amy . . . I just can't. Surely, there's something else you can do besides leaving the kids?"

I recognize the desperation on her face. "I'm fighting a battle I can't win, Kasey. I can feel even the will to fight slipping away, and I have to do this while I still have the presence of mind to care. There's only a short window of time for me to get free of this without Dmitry stopping me."

My heart shatters. "But I'm not their mother. I don't know

anything about raising children."

"You don't have to raise them. Just keep them safe until I'm myself again. It'll only be a couple of months. Kasey, you have to. There isn't anyone else."

"A couple of months . . . That's too long. You need to appoint a proper guardian." I shake my head, knowing it has to be anyone but me. "Taking your kids away—even with your permission—is walking too morally gray of a line for me. Maybe you can hire a family law attorney and sue for custody on the grounds that a convicted felon is a danger to you and your children. That'll at least buy you some time."

She simply stares at me with a hopeless expression and shakes her head. For the next few hours, I listen as Amy insists her plan is the only way to ensure the children are fully protected while she goes through rehab. She seems to have made up her mind: It's rehab and unofficially turning temporary protective custody of the children over to me, or she is convinced she'll lose them and possibly worse when Dmitry is released on parole. I let her talk, but inwardly, I'm determined to find a way out of this that doesn't involve me running away to hide with two children I hardly know.

Besides, where would I even go? It isn't as if I can leave the country with them. Taking them back to my house in Oregon is out of the question. Once my brother-in-law realizes his wife and children have left Greenwich, he'll send his people to hunt us down. He'll quickly discover they aren't vacationing in California and then turn his attention to the other connections in her life.

Discreetly, I've been conducting a search engine deep dive as Amy moves about her family's evening routine. My research has given me enough new information about Dmitry Volkov to get the same sinking feeling in my gut I had the last time I checked him out . . . before he married my sister. Just from the media coverage during the trial, my suspicions have tripled.

It's clear he's not a good guy, and she's in danger the longer she stays where he can control her every move.

But it's out of the question. I can't do what my sister is asking.

I'll find another way to keep her safe. Yet, despite my determination to avoid doing what I know I can't do, my mind reminds me with alarming frequency that there is one place in the world with which I have no association. And it's two thousand miles away from here in the middle of nowhere.

I picture the photograph of the tiny, primitive cabin Danny showed me during our grueling months in the desert. He was so proud of the hunting cabin he and his grandfather built together to be their retreat in the deep woods. The log structure was cut and built by hand from the very forests of Montana. Danny clung to its memory during the hardest of days of military service, a comfort and token to carry him home.

"It's the safest place in the world, Kasey," he once told me. *"If you're ever in trouble, run to the old forest. There's healing in those woods."*

I would run to my old teammate, except for the fact that Danny is gone now, lost to a ruthless war that claimed more than it ever gave.

And Cascade Valley, Montana, is far, far away.

But I won't do that.

As I observe my nephew and niece chattering and laughing over their dinner, their faces aglow with the ease and joy of childhood, an uneasy feeling creeps into the pit of my stomach. Even though I won't do as Amy has asked, I reassure myself that, whatever comes, I'll make sure this little family is safe before I return home.

. . .

I'm given a large and comfortable guest room in the basement for the night. As Finn and I settle in, Amy comes down to inform me that she managed to persuade the security team to forego their nightly interior security check by claiming the kids are extra tired and fussy, and she doesn't want to disturb them.

"Dmitry's cousin knows I hate those men tramping around the house with their dirty boots, so he let it slide."

She sinks onto the bed. Her shoulders cave in, and my heart constricts again at the sight of the aged and unfamiliar woman in front of me. She's barely entered her thirties, far too young for this heartbreak.

Amy rises, a cautionary hand lifting. "Stay away from the windows if you venture upstairs tonight."

When she leaves for the night, I stare at the dark ceiling, the silence roaring in my ears. It takes hours for sleep to find me, and when it does, I toss and turn, my brain tormented with fitful and uneasy nightmares. At one point, I sit straight up in the darkness and stare at the door, convinced someone is standing just outside of it. Finn's low, throaty growl from the floor next to the bed makes me reach cautiously for the pistol I stashed in the nightstand drawer.

And then I wait.

But though I listen, barely breathing for what feels like hours, the eerie silence never breaks. Eventually, I lean back against the headboard, slipping the weapon under the pillow next to me. The darkness presses against my heavy eyelids.

And then I'm awake and staring straight into the bright hazel eyes of a five-year-old boy who is trying to hold back the big tears threatening to spill over onto his chubby, rounded cheeks. When he speaks, his voice trembles.

"Kasey, where is Mama?"

Chapter Six

Dean
Late August

Coming home to the McCade family ranch is always bittersweet.

Only a few years ago, it was Dad, Vincent, and I riding into the barnyard after a long day in the pastures. We'd be sore and spent, but nothing beat the sight of our faded butter-yellow farmhouse, lights glowing in the windows, two heads popping up every few seconds to check the yard. As twilight fell, the chirping of the cicadas would cease as we passed through the tall grass, always resuming a moment later.

Once we went inside, it used to be all smiles and laughter and talking excitedly over each other. Knox and Samantha were still in high school at that point. We'd sit around the table in the kitchen, stuffing ourselves with Mom's dinners like ravenous wild animals.

But Dad isn't here anymore, and I wonder if the sharp sting that stabs my chest every time I approach the house will ever fade.

Being a McCade was always easy when I had Dad to turn to for wisdom and guidance. Now, I think I have more days than not when the weight of leading and protecting the legacy he began feels too heavy. I just wish I knew if my mission to protect what we've built is doing any good.

Especially on nights like tonight, when Samantha has finally returned home.

Knox, Vincent, and I started our journey down the mountain before the break of dawn. Our youngest sister's unexpected return from New York City this week coincided with the arrival of our relief team, and they brought a message from Mom asking us to head home right away. After the four of us siblings had an unfortunate argument about her plans for the future earlier this summer, Samantha left to stay with our sister, Demi, in New York City for several weeks. Things were said, feelings were hurt, and we've been beating ourselves up for pressuring her to forego her dreams ever since.

I've had an uneasy feeling for a couple of weeks now. After riding for hours to the valley, something still nags at my subconscious, but I can't put my finger on what it is. My brain keeps casting about for a cause, even while I focus on making amends with my youngest sister before she moves to Europe to start a new life in ministry.

As we ride into the barnyard, Samantha waits for us on the back porch steps, her mahogany hair loose and falling over her crossed arms. Her face is pensive, her eyes shifting between us and back down to the wooden boards beneath her feet. Without hesitation, I dismount and throw Midnight's reins to Vincent. He catches them as I stride up to her, pulling her into a tight hug, hoping I can convey to her without words how much we love and support her. She wraps her arms around my waist in return.

"Dean, I love you, too, but you're crushing me," she mumbles a minute later, and I'm relieved to hear an unexpected lightness in her tone.

I give her one more squeeze for good measure before letting her go. "So this is it, huh? You're really leaving the old family ranch and flying away to Europe?"

"Yes. Is that okay?" Her green eyes lift to mine, uncertainty in their depths. I sense how much she wants my approval.

"As long as this is what you really want," I reassure her. "I just worry that you and Caleb—"

"And I want a future with him too," she interrupts. "But I don't want to choose my happiness over my calling. I think I can serve more people in need out there than here. It won't be forever. My contract is only for one year. I'll reassess then. But this is what I have to do right now."

Before I can reply, Knox's voice pipes up in the yard behind me. "Running away just when we thought we'd make a proper cowgirl out of you. We planned to get you on the range guarding the herd with us."

He's only teasing. Samantha leans around me and rolls her eyes at him. They are less than fifteen months apart in age and have been best friends since they were babies. A few weeks ago, Knox was especially upset to discover Samantha had accepted a contract to work in an orphanage in Spain after graduating from college this past spring. It's been a struggle to get him to understand that her life is moving in a different direction, away from our family fold. Things got tense between them, and then she left. By his teasing, I know he's trying to make amends.

"You'll never get me on the back of a horse again, Knox McCade," she calls back, shaking her head vehemently.

"You sure weren't saying that a few weeks ago when Caleb

took you riding," he counters.

Instantly, Samantha flushes. To spare her any more teasing, I turn toward the barn. "Do you guys mind grooming and feeding the horses while I check in with Mom and handle some business?"

Knox's hand flashes up to his temple in an enthusiastic salute. He taps his horse lightly, and the gelding jumps forward. "Tell Mom I'm as starved as a pack mule after a seven-day ride," he shouts over his shoulder, taking off for the barn at a trot as Vincent shakes his head and follows him at a more leisurely pace.

I throw my arm over Samantha's shoulder. "Come on. Let's sneak a piece of Mom's pie before he eats it all."

. . .

Our family has called Cascade Valley home for years. Nestled at the foot of the mountains just over a two-hour drive southwest of Bozeman, Montana, a small village sprang up a hundred years ago. When the village was incorporated, the town council meant to give it a new name but never could agree on one. Now, Cascade Valley has become synonymous with the lush grazing land that stretches below three dramatic mountain ranges, providing not only fertile ranching land but also exceptional fishing, hunting, and outdoor recreational activities, plus world-class skiing in the winter months. Over the past few years, the public discovered our hidden gem and began to descend upon it en masse. New building developments have popped up everywhere. Cascade Valley is growing, and there's no stopping the tide of progress.

Which has me worried for the peaceful, serene land on which I grew up.

It's no surprise to see our small mountain town abuzz with tourists every time I drive down Main Street. It's peak summertime, and the campers are taking full advantage of the nearby forests and lakes. You can always tell the tourists by their fresh, brand-new-from-the-outdoor-store clothing and unbroken-in hiking boots.

I'm already itching to get away from the hustle and back to the high mountain range.

I volunteered to drive into town this morning to restock our supplies. I may have also secretly wanted a break from Knox and Samantha bickering like a couple of teenagers at the house. Some things never change.

Parking the truck, I stride down the sidewalk, dodging oblivious tourists. Today, I plan to stop at Ammon's Gun Shop to pick up more ammo, the feed store to schedule a delivery for the farm animals and bulls still at the ranch, and Earl's Hardware. We've been planning a wetlands restoration in partnership with the Forest Service, and I need to buy a fresh hose and pump setup so we can water the herd far away from any areas where their hooves risk damaging the vulnerable ground as we approach the conservation area.

I also plan to make a stop at Mimi's Bakery on the way home to pick up something sweet and French for Samantha and Mom. The establishment is new to town, and everyone is thoroughly enjoying it.

I pass Mountain Realty on my path to Earl's and find my strides slowing as I scan the real estate listing printouts plastered all over the front windows. Shelby's listing catches my eye first. The house she owns sits on the edge of town with a "For Sale" sign in its front yard. She's already gone, packing up and leaving a week after she announced her departure.

I peruse the other listings taped to the windows. The real estate office is owned by a husband-and-wife team. It's the primary real estate service in the valley, and I imagine they've done well over the past few years.

Front and center, a flyer catches my eye with the heading: *"Quaint ski resort and mountain lodge for sale. Own a piece of Montana history and invest in the valley's future."*

Bear Creek Lodge.

I spent countless winter afternoons flying down the slopes of the ski resort nestled high in the mountains. Even during summer, the ski lanes cut through the forest are visible from the pastures of our ranch, and on clear winter nights, we can see the golden lights shining from the top of the slope. It was one of Dad's favorite places.

On a whim, I veer off the sidewalk and pull open the door leading into the office. Esther, one half of the dynamic duo who owns the company, lifts her head as the bell on the door jingles.

"Dean McCade!" she calls and beams toward me. Esther and her husband, Jeb, have gone to our church for the past two decades. Our family grew up with theirs. "What brings you in on this fine summer day?"

"How are you, Esther?" I approach her desk. "The Lintons finally decided to sell the lodge, huh?"

Her face falls as she brushes her long, straight, silver hair over her shoulder. Her eyes are the color of onyx, and I notice a glossy sheen coming over them as she replies, her tone husky. "It's a shame, isn't it? But they are ready to retire, and the kids aren't interested in taking on the management of the lodge or the ski resort. Everyone wants them to move someplace with a beach and a full bank account from the sale so they can enjoy their grandchildren while they are still young."

"How much are they asking?"

She names off a number that gives me sticker shock, but I

recognize that it's a good deal considering how popular the valley has become in the last few years. One of the big city investment corporations is going to snap the resort up without delay.

"The Lintons have always been good friends of ours, but even I think what they are asking is a bit steep." Her eyebrows rise to her hairline. "But Cascade Valley is growing. We are managing the sale for them, of course. And we already have a large real estate investment firm poking around, looking to make an offer. They'll probably build a condo development up there or a bunch of mini mansions." Her hands wave above her head in a dismissive gesture. "Frankly, the commission would be a game changer for Jeb and me. But you know Leslie and Jon. They wanted to open the sale to locals first. I think they want to keep it a part of valley history if they can, and they are willing to carry the loan if the right person shows an interest. And they are offering a discount on the price for locals only."

She names off a new number that, while still more money than I've ever thought about, is much more reasonable. Careful not to let my face reveal the thoughts instantly rushing through my brain, I ask, "Can you print a rundown of the listing for me?"

Esther's chair swings back toward the monitors on her desk. "Sure thing, honey. Are you interested in making an offer?"

As the printer spits out a stack of pages and she hands them to me, I shrug noncommittally. "You never know. One thing I do know—that mountain becoming crowded with overpriced homes and vacation rentals isn't what most of us want for our valley."

"I hear you!" She shakes her head.

After thanking Esther and exchanging goodbyes, I step onto the sidewalk again, tucking the now-folded stack into my back pocket. The afternoon sun is temporarily blinding, and I adjust the brim of my hat against the glare just as I feel someone bump my arm.

"Pardon me, ma'am," I say, automatically reaching out to steady the petite woman. Her sleek, black ponytail bounces as she looks up at me, and I recognize her immediately. "Jenna, hey. How are you?"

I don't know Jenna well, but she works as a full-time horse trainer at Caleb's ranch and is a darn good one from what I've observed. She's a few years older than Samantha and worked at Caleb's summer youth camp earlier in the summer with us, but I haven't seen her since.

"Dean!" she exclaims. Her teeth are bright against her olive skin. Her hands wave excitedly in front of her. "When did you boys get back into town? Are you here long? Oh, Dean, this is . . . my friend, Hunter. He's a real estate investor." Jenna gestures toward the office I just exited, the sentences spoken in a single breath. When she finally stops for air, she swings eagerly toward a stocky man standing stiffly on the sidewalk beside her.

During her ramble, I gave him a discreet once-over. I don't recognize him, which isn't saying much since real estate investors are becoming more and more frequent in the valley. Of medium height, with a muscular, tanned build that looks made in air-conditioned city gyms and tanning salons, Hunter's body language is tense. A thick, light brown beard covers half of his face, and the yellow specks in his hazel eyes resemble those of the gray wolves in the mountains.

Those eyes now cut down to Jenna as if he is annoyed that she has forced the two of them to stop in the middle of the sidewalk to talk to a strange man who might usurp his claim on her, but I have to give him credit for just as swiftly covering up his feelings and extending a hand in my direction.

"Pleased to meet you. Dean, is it?" I can't place his accent, but he isn't from Montana. "Happy to get to know Jenna's friends. She never introduces me to anyone."

Immediately, Jenna protests, a flush blooming across her cheeks. "Well, I haven't known you long enough to introduce you to much of anyone."

As soon as his hand drops mine, Hunter slides an arm around Jenna's waist and pulls her close to his side. His sharp incisors gleam against his tan. "Honestly, this pretty lady and I just met a few days ago. We're headed to get barbeque for lunch at . . ." Hunter looks down at Jenna. "What is it called, babe?"

Newly acquainted and we're already at *babe*? I lift a mental eyebrow.

"Full O' Bull." She laughs, her face all sparkles and smiles as she lifts it to look at him shyly. Her dark eyes gleam.

"You're welcome to join us," Hunter continues. "We'll probably end up playing pool and having a few drinks at the saloon later this afternoon."

I shake my head. "Thanks for the offer, but I have to get back to my ranch. We're having a small send-off for my sister tonight before we leave again, and I still have a lot of errands to run."

A shadow passes over Jenna's face. "Please send Samantha my best wishes," she says. "I hope she finds happiness in Europe."

"Yeah, I'll relay that message," I reply.

I don't know the full history between Jenna and my sister, but I do know there was some unspoken tension between them over the summer. The prospect of being brought into it instantly makes me uncomfortable, so I let the awkward pause linger as my gaze roams down the sidewalk behind the couple. My eyes alight on the figure of a woman exiting the general store across the street. She's both petite and shapely, and she's pushing a cart filled with paper bags. A dark cap is pulled low over her eyes, but something in the swing of her shoulder-length golden-blonde braid and the slight limp in the otherwise fluid motion of her stride triggers my memory. Staring, I watch her cross the parking lot, but before I can get a look at her face, Jenna pulls my attention away.

"I bet it's just gorgeous on the hills this time of year," she gushes. "Hunter, you and I should take a drive up to the mountains. Dean's herd grazes up there all summer, and it's just a dream."

"Except for the dirt, the bugs, the snakes, and not being able to take a proper shower or use a bathroom," I laugh. "Oh, and Knox's questionable cooking."

Hunter eyes me with amusement. "Home, home on the range, eh, Dean? I bet you see lots of weird things up in those woods."

"Weird? What do you mean?"

He shrugs. "Oh . . . you know, things like ancient burial grounds, abandoned backpacks, creepy cabins, somebody where they shouldn't be . . . You know what they say about serial killers coming up to live in the forest, right?"

The smirk on his face tells me I shouldn't take him seriously. City folks always misinterpret the pull of the forest.

"Oh, there's plenty of that out in our woods, Hunter." I clap a hand on his shoulder and wink. "The reality is, though, that wolf and bear attacks are probably the biggest threats we have around here. Carry a gun and be tough, and you'll probably survive."

Taking the chance to back away, I move toward Earl's, pointing a finger at Jenna as I glance one last time at Hunter. "Good to meet you, but I've got to run. Jenna, I'll relay your message to Samantha."

Once I've progressed down the sidewalk far enough, I swing back and scan the street, but the woman leaving the general store is gone.

Chapter Seven

Kasey
Late June

His voice trembles as he tries to be brave, asking the question again when I don't answer. "Where is Mama?"

The words strike my skull and reverberate. Finn stands and walks over to the boy, who flinches as the big dog sniffs his cheek, his black nose leaving a wet spot. When DJ lifts his hand to wipe it away, the motion jolts me into action. Swinging my legs over the side of the bed, I toss my hair into a ponytail and try to infuse a sense of confidence into my voice as I stall for time. The clock on the nightstand reads just after five. It won't even be light out yet.

"Your mom? Well, I'm sure she's around here somewhere, buddy." Gently, I herd him toward the stairs and away from the cold metal I shoved farther under the pillow when he woke me. I wish it were still in my hand or tucked into the waistband of my pajama shorts, but the last thing I want is to scare my nephew. Leaving it behind is a risk, but I can't grab it without him noticing. "Have you looked upstairs for her?"

When I gesture toward Finn, he falls into step at my flank, trailing me one step behind as I limp up the basement stairs. Getting out of bed too quickly aggravated my leg, and it flares with pain as we ascend to the main floor.

My eyes dart to every shadowy corner as we emerge in the opulent kitchen. "Where's Janie?" I say casually.

"She's sleeping," he replies. His rounded belly protrudes from his dinosaur pajama top as he leads me down the back hallway. "I always get up early with Mama, and we let Janie sleep in. We usually have hot chocolate."

His light brown hair flops as he cranes his head back to peer up at me hopefully. My stomach drops.

"Let's check on Janie first, and then we'll get a snack."

I'm on high alert as we approach the door to the nursery where Amy tucked her daughter in last night. I peek in, scanning for threats in the dark room. But it's clear. The sound machine hums in the corner. I creep across the plush carpet, my barefoot steps silent. My niece is fast asleep in her crib, her chubby baby cheeks pressed onto the mattress, a soft pink blanket tossed over her lower legs. Last night, Amy informed me that Janie is a good sleeper who usually sleeps in far past sunrise. In any case, she can't climb out of the crib, so I have time to check the rest of the house.

Backing away, I rejoin DJ in the hallway, where Finn stands guard at his side.

"Okay, now show me your mom's room," I whisper to him, giving what I hope is a reassuring smile in the dim glow of the night-light.

Without hesitation, he raises his hand and slips his palm into mine. His stubby fingers tug me toward the other end of the hallway. "It's over here," he says.

He drags me toward a darkly outlined doorway. The pitch-black interior of the room screams a warning as the hair on the back of my neck rises. My sister's frail form flashes before my mind's eye. Am I going to find her bound and gagged, trying to warn me before it's too late? Is this a trap? Are her husband's men waiting for me beyond that doorway?

Training that has been dormant since my injury reactivates, but I tamp it down, fearful of alerting DJ to my apprehension. My thigh throbs in response, the pain spiking my adrenaline more. Yet, I refuse to let myself limp into whatever waits for me in that room. The battlefield may have left me scarred and broken, but that doesn't mean I'll go down without a fight.

I whisper for DJ to remain in the hallway and motion for Finn to stay with him. The dog gives me a long look, but he obeys.

I feel the emptiness as soon as I push open the door. My heart pounds, a dark mist swimming over my eyes before I shake my head to clear it. The hallway barely illuminates the elegant cream envelope propped against the pillows and sitting upright on the undisturbed bed.

Checking all the corners first, I risk waiting to clear the en suite as I approach and lift the letter. I click on the bedside lamp. My name is scrawled across the linen envelope in beautiful handwriting. Before I open it, I take a breath, my eyes lifting and falling on Amy's wedding photograph. It sits in a gilded frame on the nightstand. I study the handsome, muscular man clasping his beautiful bride in the photograph. Behind them, a red sports car sits as a flashy prop. My sister's husband is visibly fit. His light brown beard is thick and full. His smile shows off sharp and pearly canines. He's handsome. I can see why Amy was swept away by him. On the outside, Dmitry looks like the perfect man, but even on the happiest day of his life, his narrowed gaze as he looks at the camera sends chills down my spine.

Shivering, I sink onto the edge of the mattress, a sudden surge of acid burning in my throat. Sliding a finger under the flap of the envelope, I pull out the single sheet of thick stationery:

Dearest Kasey,

I'm sorry I had to make this choice for the four of us. I wish I had been born strong like you. You've always been a warrior. I need you to call on that strength now to protect my children. If their father regains control of them before I'm well . . . the thought is too horrific.

I've gone away. Please don't try to find me. It'll only ensure that I fail in my mission. There is only a small window of time to protect them. I informed the security guards that we all came down with the stomach flu, so they won't expect us to stick to our normal routine for the next few days. Take them away, somewhere far, where my husband will never find you. I know you know what to do.

You'll find two bags in the closet with everything you'll need to disappear. I've left a burner phone inside. Once you reach your destination, turn it on, keep it charged, and wait for my updates. I'll reach out when I can. If, Heaven forbid, I haven't returned within six months and you haven't heard from me, go to the police and give them the letter I've left explaining everything. If I don't return, I've asked that you be made guardian over DJ and Janie.

Please pray that God strengthens me to walk through this dark valley and heals me from this affliction. I'll be praying for His protection over the three of you. I put it in His hands to reunite us safely.

- Amy

My heart seizes, and I pull in a deep and desperate breath. It's the first time I've known my sister to speak of God. I'm no stranger to prayers whispered in desperate hours, but right now, I feel alone. She ran away and left this mess with me. My emotions swerve from panic to anger. This isn't right. It isn't fair. I didn't ask for this. I never asked for any of it.

Except I did. I made a promise years ago that if Amy ever needed me, I'd be there for her. I can't offer her wealth or connections, but I can be the kind of family to her that I didn't have.

A rustling draws me back to the present and reminds me of my nephew's presence in the hallway. "Give me a minute," I call out to him softly.

I force myself to rise from the bed and walk quickly toward the grand en suite. I catch sight of my face in the mirror over the marble sink and startle at my pale, hollow-eyed appearance. In the spacious walk-in closet, I immediately spot two black duffel bags sitting on the center island. Ripping open the zippers, the last shred of hope that this is a nightmarish prank fades away.

Nestled atop the neatly packed piles of small, childish clothing is a gray prepaid cell phone, a thick envelope, and a manila folder. I flip through the folder first and discover a collection of documents that includes two birth certificates and social security cards, plus a letter from my sister stating her intention to have me care for the children in their parents' absence. She's included every bit of information I'd need to prove I didn't simply kidnap my nephew and niece and had it notarized. Grabbing the envelope next, I lift the flap. My stomach turns over when I see what looks like several stacks of one-hundred-dollar bills tucked inside. Amy inherited quite a large fortune after our father's death. Still, a withdrawal of this kind surely gets noticed.

I freeze for a moment, waiting for the nausea to subside.

Naively, I'd chalked up Amy's strange behavior last night to the effects of the withdrawal symptoms as she weaned herself off the prescription pills and tried to resist their call. Now, I see it. She told me what she was planning, and I'd let it go in one ear and out the other, never thinking she'd slip away and abandon her children.

Not abandon, my heart reminds me quickly. *Entrust.*

As if I'm suddenly submerged under water, my lips release a desperate gasp for air. The scope of Amy's plan spreads out before me.

"Is it possible? Can it be done?" I whisper toward the ceiling, my heart reaching out for comfort or guidance, something to get me through this trial.

She passed the torch to me. It's up to me to figure this out and protect my charges. Any missteps, and I risk failing them completely. I need to think and plan. My bum leg is stiff as I pull myself up from the floor, but I push the pain away as another side of me, one I haven't used since the desert, takes over. Tucking the phone, documents, and money back into the bags, I zip them up and leave them for now.

It's going to be tricky explaining Amy's absence to the children. I hope they don't cry. Hiding out in this mansion won't be any easier with the noise of two wailing children.

Slipping back into the hallway, I find DJ sitting against the wall with his short legs in front of him. Finn stands guard at his side, and I don't miss how the little boy's fingers dig into the dog's fur.

"Did you find her?" he asks me, the hope unmistakable in his eyes.

I squat in front of him, resisting the instinct to brush his smooth hair back from his forehead. My voice is pitched low.

"Can I tell you the truth?"

Solemnly, he nods, his eyes widening.

"Your mom has been sick, but she is going to get help from some special doctors so she can get better. She asked me to take care of you. We might go on an adventure to another place, but it'll be lots of fun."

"Is Mama going to be there?" He lifts his face hopefully.

I shake my head. "We won't see your mom for a bit, but she'll be back." I'm as honest as I can be with him, figuring that it's the best choice for the situation.

"Do you promise she'll come back?" His lip quivers.

"I promise." *Don't make me break this promise, Amy.*

"What about Janie?"

"What about her?"

"Can she come with us?"

"Of course. But I'm going to need you to be her big brother and help me take care of her. Can you do that?"

He considers what I've said for a long minute, his fingers smoothing the dog's fur. Finally, he nods and looks up at me. "Sometimes, Janie cries when she gets upset. But I'm really good at making her laugh, so I can probably help you."

I press a hand to his shoulder and squeeze gently. I can't help my gentle laugh. "I bet you are great at it. Thank you."

A soft whimper pierces the quiet hallway. Simultaneously, our heads swing toward the dark sliver of Janie's barely cracked doorway.

"That's weird," DJ says. "Janie never gets up this early."

I give his shoulder an extra squeeze. "How about we get your sister up and then go make that hot chocolate together? And maybe pancakes for breakfast?"

Chapter Eight

Dean
Mid-September

The tracks are imprinted deeply into the forest floor. We dismount quickly, tying up our horses on nearby, low-hanging branches. Vincent squats, the brim of his hat hiding his eyes as he examines the tracks. A low-pitched, irritating buzz echoes from the fresh yearling kill a short distance away.

"How many, Vince?" I ask tightly. Knox moves a few paces out, his head on a swivel as he scans our surroundings. I note his firm grip on the rifle in his hands. We're all on edge after discovering a yearling had wandered off after headcount last night. In the ensuing search, we stumbled across its half-eaten carcass in the woods, and the loss is hitting hard. It's the first member of the herd we've lost in several years, and I can't help but think it was preventable.

"No more than ten," Vincent replies tersely.

"Is it the same pack we heard a couple of weeks ago?"

"Could be. Hard to say."

"Are they headed up or down the mountain?"

"Up."

My brother is a man of thoughtful contemplation and few words. He's also an excellent tracker. I nod, processing the information, my brain scanning through everything I know about wolf behavior. I know a pack can range from two to fifteen wolves. Since the mid-nineties, when Fish and Wildlife reintroduced the nearly extirpated population into Yellowstone, the predators' numbers have grown. What I don't know is how to navigate the delicate struggle between conservation and protecting what we've worked so hard to build.

I'm all for bringing the majestic animal back to its homeland, but my muscles tighten at the knowledge of their proximity. It was one thing to hear their nightly calls. Deer and other wildlife are the natural prey of the gray wolf; however, should the pack get a taste for cattle, it will be a battle to balance the scales again. When we're stationed on the ranch, we have various methods of protecting the herd. But out here on the open range, it's us against the wolves. And with packs occasionally moving through the mountains between Montana and Idaho, we tend to be outnumbered. Financially, we can't afford to lose even one yearling to the mob.

This particular pack has grown increasingly bolder in trying to get to the cattle at night, but a few warning shots have been enough to scare them off until now. It seems we'll have to step up our security once again.

Solemnly, we remount and continue past the macabre scene. I urge Midnight into a brisk trot, wanting to get back to camp. Not that I don't trust the rest of our team, but assessing the security of our herd's position with the threat freshly in perspective will put my mind at ease.

When the pack first began to come around, I decided to stick with our original grazing path trajectory and reroute toward Fisherman's Gulch later in the month, hoping that if the pack was just passing through, we could successfully avoid them without changing our plans. As the season wanes toward autumn, we're able to graze the herd for longer periods of time in one spot. But now, we've worked our way to within five miles of the watering hole again, and we've discovered the yearling too late in the day to leave.

While we've worked hard to rekindle the herd instincts of our cattle, training mamas to stay with their calves and seek protection as a unit doesn't always pan out in the real world. Losing a yearling feels like a punch to both the gut and our narrow profit margin.

It's a harder hit since my brothers and I have decided to invest in Bear Creek Lodge. We're working with the Lintons to negotiate a deal. Mom is managing most of the initial paperwork on our behalf, but if we ever needed the ranch to perform well, it's this year. With the hope of diversifying our investments in the future, the three of us have set aside a portion of our wages for some time, but I'm holding my breath as we wait to find out what will happen next. Acquiring the lodge is a risky venture, but it could set us on a better financial path for the future. We can't afford any roadblocks.

As the moon rises, I'm on first watch when the howling begins. I jump at the sound as Midnight snorts with annoyance. The moon illuminates the meadow, casting the forest on the far edge into deeper shadows. We've set up our usual temporary electrified fencing around the cattle. Three riders patrol at all times. Montana law permits us to put a wolf down if they are an immediate threat. But the last thing I want is to come to the point of having to shoot one of the predators. My mission is to make the McCade herd a restorative asset to the mountain range, not take away from it.

Out of the darkness, Vincent rides up alongside me. "Edge of the tree line," he says in a low voice.

"How big is their territory?" I ask. "I scoured this side of Fisherman's Gulch backward and forward last month. There was no sign of a den anywhere in these woods. And we were encamped miles away when they first started coming around."

"Did you check across the fishing hole? They might be based there," he replies.

A flash of golden hair and fierce blue eyes surfaces in my brain. My stomach drops. Midnight, sensing the shift in my mood, stirs restlessly under the saddle. I haven't forgotten the expression on the woman's face as she lifted the rifle to point it straight at my head.

But, after all, the woman herself was quite unforgettable.

Her thick hair had glinted like spun gold in the sun. She'd thrown the fishing pole on the bank, those oversized waders drying swiftly in the summer heat as she stood among the grass, legs planted wide and strong. There had been no hesitation in her stance as she faced off against me. And those eyes. Brilliant aquamarine depths flashing up at me with a fierce, steely determination that was coupled with a deep wariness. She hadn't been afraid of the stranger approaching her in the middle of the wilderness. Her caution was grounded by something else: a wild and free determination to survive whatever threat came her way.

I've never seen a woman more beautiful.

And I may have put my herd at risk because of her.

"No." My reply emerges as a grumble low in my throat.

"There was a woman. She had a gun. I didn't go beyond the stream."

Even in the darkness, I can feel his gaze cut heavily to me, the edges of his frame highlighted by the red flicker of campfire behind us. "What woman, Dean?"

I shrug. "She was fishing in the river. Alone. I rode off the ridge to warn her to keep an eye out for wolves, but she got the drop on me before I could blink. 'Bout near shot me before I could convince her I wasn't a threat."

The shift in his mood is palpable. My brother is on instant alert. "Did you find out who she was?"

We ran wild across these mountains as boys, so I've never paid attention to the rumors of feral people living in the forest. People who—for whatever reason, by choice or necessity—have stepped away from society. Usually, it's for innocent reasons; sometimes, it's not. I've come across many questionable things in the woods. I always leave them be and redirect our grazing route. No reason to mess with things that aren't my business.

"She never gave me the chance," I mumble. "It was obvious she wanted me to leave. I offered her some extra ammo and rode out of there." I'm almost embarrassed to admit the next part. "I doubled back, but she'd already hightailed it across the meadow. The whole encounter was weird, Vince."

"I'll bet," he grunts. "We need to check those woods, though. If we've brought the herd into the den's backyard again, we've got to know. Might be about time to alert Fish and Wildlife before we lose any more cattle."

A heavy feeling of guilt sinks into the pit of my stomach. This situation is my fault. As the leader of the ranch and our conservation efforts, it's my job to juxtapose the needs of our herd while protecting the forest and its natural inhabitants. The last thing I want is to start shooting wolves, especially if there's an alternative.

The lone wolf howling beyond the timberline is joined by two or three others. Their cry sends a menacing chill down my spine.

"I'll go," I reply. "It's my fault for not assessing the situation properly. I'll scout it out in the morning. The rest of you can move the herd back a few miles to a different grazing spot just to be on the safe side."

. . .

Before dawn breaks in the sky, I'm up and saddled. The blue hour casts a misty haze around our camp. A chill permeates the air, a sign that summer won't last forever. Autumn will arrive soon, the snow soon to follow.

Knox slaps me on the back as he ambles in from the second night watch. "Sure you don't want me to go with you?"

My head shakes as I double-check the cinch of my saddle. "You're needed here. It's just going to be a quick trip in and out to see what we're dealing with."

He yawns. "Okay. But don't go looking for wolves and end up eaten by a bear out there." Dropping this cryptic bit of advice, he stumbles away toward his tent. He'll crash for a couple of hours and be up fresh as a daisy by the time the sun is still young in the sky.

The birds stir as I enter the woods and ride toward the gulch. In the growing light, I let Midnight pick his way along a deer trail. By the time we crest the ridge and start down to the other side, enough light has dawned to see the stream ahead. It's low at this time of year. My memory fills in the scene from the last time I was here.

No petite figure stands steady and strong in the rushing water, casting her line in search of a fresh catch. No one scrambles up the embankment at my approach. The beautiful woman is long gone, and I can't help but regret again that I didn't at least ask her name. That kind of fierceness should never be forgotten.

I dismount and lead my horse across. On the other side, we cross the meadow toward the line of trees in the distance.

I don't think there's any reason to fear for my safety, but I'm alert as the canopy of pines swallows me up. Very little except wildlife disturbs this side of the mountain. It feels as if I'm entering the Old Forest.

"'It was not called the Old Forest without reason, for it was indeed ancient, a survivor of vast forgotten woods . . .'" I murmur Tolkien's words, half expecting to see a wood elf with aquamarine eyes peeking around a tree as the first rays of light pierce the darkness.

The sun rises as the morning lengthens. Midnight picks his way through the trees. We move in a grid pattern, weaving back and forth as I keep an eye out for signs of a den. Various creeks and rivulets run off the mountain as we travel upward. I call out a few times to announce my presence. We've just entered bear hunting season. While it's unlikely any hunters have made their way this far out yet, I'd rather avoid the potential stray bullet meant for a bear.

Unexpectedly, a path opens on the forest floor, and I realize that I've stumbled across an old logging road, a relic of the nineties when the timber harvesting landscape changed in Montana. Though I suspect it's hardly been used since then, the dirt road is clear enough for a Jeep or a truck to get through, the tire ruts deep, promising a bumpy ride.

Just as the scene begins to look familiar, a sudden memory

drops into my brain.

"We found the road up to Danny's," I say aloud, the realization hitting me. Midnight's ears swivel back as if he remembers too. Danny Gardener may have been lost overseas in the line of duty, but the cabin he and his grandpa built together still stands downwind of this side of the mountain. Quickly, I orient myself with a glance up the hill. If I follow this road down and take the hiking trail when it branches off, I'll come across it. The cabin was built on BLM land with no plumbing or electricity—functioning with an outhouse out back and fresh, running water from a nearby creek—but Danny had been as proud of it as if it were a mansion.

A wave of nostalgia hits me. Tapping him lightly, I spur Midnight down the roughly cut road, intending to find the trail that leads to the cabin if I can. It might be lost to the forest by now, but I want to try. I think the memory of my friend deserves a moment of silence and reflection.

Years ago, Danny hacked a path from his cabin to the logging road for easy fishing access. He also tacked a "Private property of the Gardeners. No trespassing" sign on a tree. It was ironic because the Gardeners were the most welcoming and friendly family ever.

After doubling back a couple of times, I finally locate the worn, wooden placard nailed to a tree trunk. Danny's lettering is still bold enough to announce the entrance of the trail he broke. The trail is worn and covered with debris, but it looks like someone has recently kicked aside most of the larger fallen branches to make a decent walking path. I dismount and lead Midnight by the reins as we pick our way up the slope.

A few minutes later, a flash of log siding and a green metal roof catches my eye through the trees.

Pleased, I stride forward. As the trail bends, I can just see the edge of the cabin in a clearing. I'm guessing it's going to be damaged from years of neglect, but Danny would be happy I stopped anyway. Suddenly, the clearing opens up, and I'm in front of the cabin. The small, worn structure is nestled back into the trees as if the forest has decided to reclaim it as its own.

Immediately, the hair on the back of my neck stands up. My eyes dart back and forth across the clearing, an uncanny feeling that something isn't as it should be pounding with unrelenting force on my brain.

Then I spot what's out of place. Above the chimney pipe, a soft thread of gray smoke puffs. And there, where it should be empty darkness, I see slivers of golden light peeping around the edges of the window frames.

Acting swiftly, I guide Midnight back about ten yards down the trail. Tying him securely to a branch, I pull my rifle out of its case. Checking that its chambers are loaded, I step toward the cabin. It isn't unheard of for small drug laboratories to pop up in these woods from time to time. On occasion, we'll also get poachers traveling through. I have no intention of making my presence known, but if illegal activity is happening up here, I'll report it to Fish and Wildlife. I see no sign of a vehicle, but that doesn't mean a getaway car isn't stashed somewhere or hidden farther down the mountain.

Ducking and weaving through the trees on the perimeter, I approach from the side of the cabin to avoid being seen. Staying low, I creep across the overgrown ground, planning to peek in a side window. The salty scent of canned soup hits my nose about halfway. There's a window with a sliver of light around its edges on this side, too, so I make a beeline for it.

Placing a palm on the side of the log cabin, I lean forward, craning to see through the small opening of the curtains. The first thing I spot is several pairs of small boots stacked neatly on the floor and a pile of blankets on the old wooden bed. There are a few other things scattered over the floor, but I can't quite identify them, so I lean in for a second look.

The click of a rifle safety sliding back hits my ears before I feel the press of its icy-cold muzzle against the back of my neck. The stern but feminine voice that speaks in my ear is surprisingly soft. Yet, I don't doubt that she means what she says.

"Move even an inch, and it'll be the last thing you ever do."

Chapter Nine

Kasey
Late June

To my surprise, the first time I held the discharge papers signaling the abrupt end of my military career, I felt nothing but relief. Just that simple stack of papers meant no more dead-of-the-night missions, no more threat of roadside bombs, no more rushing to patch up the latest soldier cut to bits a thousand miles from home. No more danger.

It also meant the end of my career in medicine.

When I first decided to join the United States Army, it was in rebellion against my own nature. I wanted someone to teach me to be strong and courageous because those were qualities that seemed to elude me in real life. I couldn't even stand up to my own family, let alone effectively stand up for anyone else. I didn't tell a soul, except for Amy, that I had enlisted.

As soon as I went through basic training, I pursued a combat medic classification. I didn't think I could take a life or hunt for explosives, but I could use my hands to heal, and I'd thought of going into nursing anyway. When I moved on to the advanced training program, I leaned into every skill set it offered. To my surprise, I excelled in both my medical courses and marksmanship practice. It wasn't long until I was outshooting even Montana boys like Danny. All I knew was that when a gun was in my hand, my troubled brain went still, and I could finally think. I spent hours practicing, and eventually, the army felt like home. Finally, I'd found a sense of duty, purpose, and mission.

"This We'll Defend."

Until the day a careening blast of metal in my upper thigh shattered both my flesh and my career. I'd fought hard that day, saving some and losing friends, and I'd fought hard to keep myself together when it was all over.

When I held the discharge paperwork in my hand, I doubled over, clutching my stomach, silently wheezing from both pain and relief. As soon as I could, I buried the memories, the disappointment, and the heartbreak, picked up Finn, packed everything I owned, and set my face to the farthest western shores of the Pacific Northwest. Now, the only things left from my past are the scars along my torso and leg and a limp that flares up more frequently than I'd like, but I tell myself it's there to remind me that danger, like a quiet, stealthy snake in the grass, is never far away.

As I sip my third cup of gourmet espresso from the fancy machine on the counter, I sense it rearing its ugly head again. The children are playing in the kitchen. I'm looking over the folder stuffed full of papers that Amy left for me to find. For today at least, we're safe so long as we stay indoors and don't open the curtains. My phone sits on the counter near my hand. Every few minutes, I nearly reach for it to call the police and alert them to my sister's disappearance. The children will be put into foster care, but perhaps I can convince a judge to give me temporary custody until Amy is found.

After all, that is her express wish.

But with each hour that passes, the truth settles like a cold, hard lump in the pit of my stomach. I can't risk the lives and safety of my nephew and niece. I know the horror stories told about foster care. I can't let them experience that or end up with some stranger. Reality sets in. Truly, my only chance to protect them is to sneak out under the cover of night and pray I can drive far enough away that my brother-in-law's men can't catch up to us. I can deal with the legal consequences later, when I've had a chance to think and track down my sister.

But if I'm caught with two children who don't belong to me, their mother untraceable, their imprisoned father revengeful . . . I shudder.

Every decision I make from here on out feels like a gamble with the very lives of the small people entrusted to my care. A shadow settles over me. The desperate sense that I'm fighting a losing battle makes me want to freeze in place. There's no one I can turn to for help. I've never made friends easily, and even though I got along with my fellow soldiers, turning to any of them for help is out of the question. Danny had a cousin serving in the military, too, whom I got along with well, but I don't trust that he won't turn me in. And since I don't date or speak to my mother, that leaves no one. Once again, I'm left to pick up the pieces of a shattered life alone.

One thing I know for sure: We can't stay here.

As I move furtively through the house and make my preparations to leave, my sister's desperate pleas ring in my ears.

The memory of the raw fear in her eyes as she relayed her struggles and her fears causes a steely resolve to flood my being. I won't let Amy down.

At last, night falls, the last embers of sunset fading from the sky. I've fed, clothed, and entertained two children all day. I'm exhausted, but they are still alive and not crying, which I'm taking as a good sign. A deep, inky darkness settles over the neighborhood as the children sleep. The estates are spaced far apart, so unless they have cameras recording the street, we can move along the hedges almost invisibly. Since Amy covered the cameras by the service entrance, we should be able to pass through without a record.

Keeping the lights off, I wait silently in the sunroom. The only sound is the ominous ticking of the clock on the wall. It's after midnight when I gather the courage to rise from the plush rug and walk into the hallway, Finn's nails clicking after me. There will be only one chance to escape without getting caught.

DJ is easy to wake up. He's been on alert all day, preoccupied with helping me entertain his sister, but his watchful eyes kept darting toward me every few seconds. He slips on his shoes and tries to shoulder one of the bags. His fingers thread themselves through Finn's coarse fur, the dog stationing himself close to the small boy.

Part of my plan hinges on Janie sleeping through the whole ordeal. Amy left their car seats in the kitchen, and I already snuck out to install them in my Jeep.

Carefully, I lift the sleeping toddler. A moment ago, I shouldered the second bag, packed with extra supplies I gathered from the house, plus my own backpack. My hair is tucked into a trucker cap, the collar of my oversized jacket raised and hiding as much of my face as it can. I'm not naive enough to think there won't be plenty of evidence of our departure once it's discovered that Amy and the children are gone. I'm hoping against hope that my involvement will remain a secret. If I can keep them thinking Amy took the kids, I can keep them off our trail for that much longer.

In a silent whisper, I urge DJ to be silent. We depart the house by the secluded gate Amy led me through just two days ago. The trees and perfectly manicured hedges shield our passage. I'm on high alert, listening for any sounds of approach, my own ragged breathing filling my ears. Finn patrols at my flank, leading DJ as we emerge on the street.

Under the lush trees lining the street, the Jeep's green exterior gleams in the moonlight. I'm glad it isn't a full moon as I carefully buckle Janie into her seat. By some miracle, she hasn't awoken. Her head lolls forward, and I gently set it against the backrest. Earlier, I had to watch videos on proper car seat protocol. DJ climbs into his own. In a whisper, I instruct him to duck below the windowsill until I say it's okay.

Finn tries to jump in after him, but in a quiet voice, I order him to wait. He looks up at me mournfully but obeys. Once the dog is secure in the front seat, I put the gear in neutral. We're parked on a slight incline, so I use all my weight to push the wheels forward, running alongside the car as it begins to roll slowly downhill and away from Amy's house. As the car picks up speed, I jump in and steer it along the street, coasting in the darkness. Once we're a few hundred yards away, I turn the key. The engine comes to life with a rumble that has never seemed as loud as at this moment.

Turning to look over my shoulder, I breathe a sigh of relief that the noise hasn't woken Janie yet. Driving out of the neighborhood, I risk making a few unnecessary turns as we progress toward the highway, hoping to get lost in suburbia. Later, we'll have to stick to back roads, but for now, I just want to put as much distance between us and our starting point as possible. Keeping my head down, I pull my hat low, carefully maintaining the posted speed limit. It's only a matter of time before an APB goes out, and I become a fugitive with two small children in tow.

I'm not naive enough to think they won't eventually put two and two together and realize that Amy contacted me. Nothing stays secret for long in the modern world. It's a race to safety, and I intend to disappear entirely before that happens.

Though my heart longs for the tranquility of my coastal home, it's out of the question. We have to go where no one will think to look, and there's only one place I can think of to which I have no record of connection.

" 'The mountains are calling, and I must go,' " I murmur John Muir's words under my breath as the inky blackness of the asphalt ahead leads me northwest to the wild forests of Montana.

Chapter Ten

Dean
Mid-September

"Move away from that wall and start walking. I'd advise you to move slowly."

At her prompting, I lift my hands above my head, the rifle still gripped between my fingers. The barrel of her gun in my back pushes me to walk across the clearing, driving me away from the cabin. I hear her footsteps *thudding* behind me until I pause at the trailhead and chance a glance over my shoulder.

"I'm going to set my gun against this tree and turn around slowly, okay?"

The cold press of the muzzle doesn't abate, so I keep my movements slow and deliberate as I lean the gun against the trunk. Lifting my hands above my head again so she knows I'm not a threat, I take a step backward on the dirt, swinging my body around with it. My eyes fall on the petite woman whose rifle is now trained steadily on my face. She's a few feet away, and her brilliant eyes pierce mine icily, those full lips pressed together in a thin frown. I catch the moment she recognizes me.

"We have *got* to stop meeting like this," I drawl, allowing what I hope is a nonthreatening smirk to emerge. My attempt at levity will probably get me shot, but to my surprise, a flicker of amusement passes over her face.

But her voice is flat when she says, "You should really stop showing up where you're not invited."

"Catch any fish lately?"

"Are you here to make trouble?" she asks, ignoring my question.

"I could ask you the same question. Are you up here making drugs?"

It's a bold question, and her nostrils flare, a look of fire coming into her eyes. "I would *never.* And don't ever ask me such a thing again."

"Then why are you squatting in my friend's cabin?"

"It isn't squatting when you were invited," she retorts.

I shake my head firmly. "Now, I know you're lying."

Her expression goes cold. She tightens her grip on the barrel of the rifle. "I am not a liar. The owner of this cabin invited me to stay up here anytime I wanted."

I shrug. "Seems we're at an impasse, then, because the owner of this cabin passed away, and no one in his family lives in the valley anymore."

A flicker of pain passes tangibly through her eyes. "I know," she grinds out through gritted teeth. "I was there when he died."

"You're military?" I inquire without bothering to hide my surprise. If she's in the service, it explains so much of her wary nature and cool-in-the-face-of-danger demeanor. If she worked with Danny . . . My heart sinks, and I wonder about the limp I noticed that day at Fisherman's Gulch.

The question makes her take a step back, and she shakes her head. "A veteran, actually. Danny and I served in the same platoon for a while. I was the combat medic assigned to them. Look, mister—"

"Thank you for your service," I interrupt gently. Whatever she's seen to make her so distrusting of strangers, I'm guessing it's warranted.

My gratitude startles her. "Uh . . . thanks . . . but that's not the issue."

"May I lower my hands now? I'm starting to feel rather foolish with them raised in the air like it's worship hour on a Sunday morning."

She motions with the weapon, and I drop my hands.

"Mister, I'm not here to—"

"Dean McCade," I remind her.

She stares up at me like she doesn't know what to do with the situation, and we fall silent. The forest settles around us, the only sounds the trills of bird calls and the whisper of wind through the pines. As the awkwardness intensifies, her behavior the first time we met at the fishing hole makes sense. Her sturdy stance and alert, suspicious mind, the way she handles her weapon, the wary sharpness in her eyes—I recognize a veteran of war when I see one.

And if she's telling the truth about serving with Danny, she's seen more of this world than most and somehow lived to tell about it.

A look crosses her face as she lowers the rifle to her side, the barrel pointed toward the ground. To my surprise, a soft warmth blooms in her eyes. Instantly, I'm captivated by the change in her expression, but I wait for her to speak.

A demure smile lifts the corners of her mouth. "Look, Dean, I'm truly not here to cause trouble. Danny Gardener was a friend of mine for a long time. He was so proud of this cabin and invited me to stay in it if I was ever in the area."

"And you just happened to be in the area for several weeks?" My eyebrow arches, betraying my inner skepticism.

"Just enjoying a little R and R. Forest bathing, if you will." Her eyelashes flutter almost imperceptibly.

I can't concentrate on what she's saying. I must look like an idiot, staring at her the way I am. She was beautiful before, but she's radiant now. The lingering hint of a smile and the lightness in her eyes transform her face. But the haunted look of experience hiding in her expression doesn't escape me. With effort, I force myself to pull my gaze from her and make an assessment of the situation.

She's dressed in dark-washed jeans, a light gray t-shirt, a tan waterproof jacket, and hiking boots. Despite her toned build and military bearing, there's an exquisite refinement in her features. She's equal parts stoic and soft—strong yet with gentleness hiding below the surface. She looks like a woman who has witnessed pain and suffering but hasn't let it turn her coarse and hard.

I'm also fully aware that she's using the force of her feminine wiles right now to get me to leave her alone. It's working, but it's also sharpening my curiosity.

"It's just unusual to find a woman out here alone," I begin. "You are alone, aren't you?" I scan the cabin's clearing, looking for signs of anyone else's presence. Lazy wisps of smoke still puff from the chimney, and I think I catch a flicker of the curtains on the front window and the faintest sound of a voice emitting from the cabin before she draws my attention back to her.

Her shoulders rise in a shrug. "And what if I am? No law against women being hardy enough to survive in the woods is there, Dean?" The sarcasm is barely disguised.

"Actually, it's quite impressive." I lift my hands, palms forward. "Don't let me stop you from enjoying all that Montana has to offer. Do you have everything you need out here . . . I still don't know your name, Ms. . . .?"

"Miss," she corrects, conveniently ignoring my implied question. "And yes, I've got plenty of supplies, and the river always gives me fish for my fire. And I've still got the ammo you so graciously lent me. I promise I'll survive, and I won't starve." She winks. "I'll be moving along very soon, though. You won't even know I was here."

Another gentle flutter of those lashes. I decide it's time to take the hint she's not so subtly giving. "Well, Miss . . . I'm sure Danny would be happy to know you are enjoying his cabin. I'll leave you to continue your forest bathing."

Turning toward the base of the tree trunk where I left my rifle, I lift it gingerly. A rustle behind me is a warning not to move too quickly. Her eyes are watching me suspiciously as I turn back, her body hovering warily over her weapon.

"I get the feeling you are more than capable," I keep my tone even and friendly, "but if you do find yourself in need of anything, my ranch is at the base of the mountain. You can't miss it. Don't hesitate to come knockin'. The door's always open for a friend of Danny Gardener's."

At the mention of his name, her expression softens again, and the transformation nearly knocks the wind out of me. "He was a good friend and a good man," she murmurs with obvious sadness.

A wave of emotion pulses off her small frame. She looks tired, her shoulders caving just a touch despite her good posture, the circles under her eyes deep and dark. It's with a rush of clarity that I realize I want to know more about her. Who is this mysterious woman in the woods, and what has she gone through to make those velvet edges as sharp as steel? If she weren't bent on driving me away, I'd press her for more information.

"That he was," I reply instead, and the somberness of lives lost enters the clearing, neither of us acknowledging the weight of all that could be said.

An unexpected protective feeling washes over me for the woman in front of me. I hate the thought that she's witnessed the violence of war. Letting myself study her delicate face one more time, I don't bother to hide my curiosity and admiration. She seems to notice, her steady gaze unrelenting, but I see when the rosy blush finally creeps across her cheeks. I tilt the brim of my hat toward her.

"I'll be seeing you, ma'am."

Knowing I've outstayed my welcome, I turn and stride down the rough path back toward the forest. Her gaze burns into the back of my neck as I will myself not to look back. A voice inside tells me to stay, but I resolutely ignore it. Something feels off about her "vacation" in the mountains, but I won't let this woman feel threatened by my presence.

Midnight is a few yards down the trail. I've already reached him and slid the rifle back into its case before I remember what brought me into the woods in the first place. Maybe if I'm not armed when I go back to warn her about the wolf pack, she won't shoot me. Quickly, I retrace my steps and round the corner again. The small front porch of the cabin looms into view for a second time as I step into the clearing, and an unexpected scene unfolds before me.

She'd wasted no time in walking back to the cabin, and now,

the woman is urgently trying to corral two small children back inside. I hear her faint attempt to quiet them as they bounce around her, small hands reaching, high-pitched childish voices trilling across the open space. She's preoccupied with a little girl who lifts her arms to be picked up and doesn't notice my approach. But the large German Shepherd at her side spots me immediately. His deep, single bark rings out like a warning shot as he takes a few aggressive strides down the porch steps.

As the dog starts forward, one of the children—a boy—lifts his arm and points straight at me. His other hand tugs at the woman's pant leg. "Who is that man?"

Instantly, three pairs of eyes swing in my direction. I hear a sharp, "Finn, hold," before I raise my palms above my shoulders for the second time today.

Chapter Eleven

Kasey
Late June

As we escape down the interstate, I question every move I make.

Is this the right thing to do? Is it legal? Is it going to look like Amy abandoned her kids?

Am I going to get into trouble?

The questions form a whirlwind in my brain. One thing I know: I need time to figure out where my sister went so that I can take her children back to her and insist that she involve law enforcement if she feels threatened by her husband. Choosing me to protect them isn't the right call. But time is the thing I don't have at the moment. I'm caught between a rock and a hard place, and I don't know what to do.

I stay alert for state troopers who may already be on the lookout for us when the apricot glow of the sunrise peeks over the horizon. I'm well aware that taking my niece and nephew and leaving the state is at least a gray area of the law, if not outright illegal. Never mind that their mother has entrusted their care to me in writing and provided all the documentation needed to prove that she gave me at least temporary custody of them. But even from prison, I'm certain my brother-in-law can fight for his parental rights and ask to appoint a guardian of his own choosing.

And I don't trust him.

I glance back at the two sleeping children in the back seat. DJ tried to stay awake during the first part of our dark and quiet drive into the night. His face remained somber but brave, headlight flashes lighting it up occasionally in the rearview mirror, but he succumbed to sleep somewhere in Pennsylvania. The two of them look so peaceful and serene, cheeks red and hair sweaty from the warmth of the car. Finn has refused to relax, sitting ramrod straight in the passenger seat, staring straight ahead except for the times he swings his big head around to look toward the rear of the Jeep.

I reach across the console to pet him, his warm, steady strength as comforting as it always is. I wish to possess his loyal, determined resolve. Finn never fears anything or balks at performing his duty. If I could just absorb my dog's wisdom, maybe I would know what to do.

The sun has just fully risen when I realize that protecting these children is not only going to be hard, it's going to be almost impossible.

As soon as she awakens and realizes her mom is nowhere to be seen and she isn't in her bed, Janie begins to wail. "Mama," she screams over and over, her eyes red and squeezed tightly shut.

"It's okay, honey." I try to soothe her, my hand reaching back to pat her leg in the car seat behind me. "You're safe with Kasey."

Her sheer level of volume alone is distressing, even to an ex-medic who endured nights when grenades and rocket launchers roared across the sky in a sickening squeal before each inevitable boom. Each time I touch her, she wails louder and yanks her leg away. DJ leans in, trying to distract her with a favorite toy. Eventually, he succeeds in calming her a little by playing peek-a-boo with her. Her sobs subside, but it isn't long before I hear "thirsty" in a childish lisp.

"She's probably hungry," DJ informs me solemnly, his eyes meeting mine in the rearview mirror. "I'll help her drink some water."

His bravery nearly splits my heart in two and sends a wave of guilt crashing through me. Here it is, the first day of taking care of two little ones, and I've already forgotten something as basic as food and drink. Little mouths need to be fed. Little legs need to escape the cramped car to walk and play. Can children sleep in a car for more than one night? If it were only Finn and I traveling across state lines, we could make the trip to Montana in three days tops. With my two passengers in tow, how fast can I push us to our destination without doing more harm than good?

A heavy pit of fear takes up residence in my stomach. How many times will we need to pause for a break? Gas stations, restaurants, stores, motels—they all come with three things: cameras, financial records, and people who observe. Will anyone remember the plain-looking, thirty-six-year-old woman traveling on her own with two young children and a big dog? How long will it be before their father's cronies realize Amy has vanished and the kids along with her? How fast can they connect the dots to me and send all the forces of the law and their own measure of justice after us?

As soon as possible, I pull into a rest stop. It's still early. The grounds and buildings are monitored by cameras, so I'm careful to keep my hat pulled low over my face as we walk hand in hand toward the facilities. I hurry them along, awkwardly changing Janie's diaper and trying not to trigger her tears as we pile into the Jeep again. I give her crackers from the snacks I packed and toys to keep her occupied.

An hour later, fresh tears are shed when Janie gets hungry for real food. Taking the nearest exit, I pull into a fast-food drive-thru, ordering whatever the two of them ask for and a coffee for myself, my nerves too shot to think about food.

And that is how we continue for the next five days, my knuckles white on the steering wheel, holding my breath until the children fall asleep, my chest releasing a little until they wake again. Twice, I find a motel that takes cash and doesn't ask questions. The other nights, I find a rest stop where I can pull over and sleep fitfully for a few hours. I was trained to stay awake during combat, but the stress and chaos of two small children cooped up in a car while I watch my mirror carefully for red and blue flashing lights wears me out faster than I anticipate. With bleary, bloodshot eyes, I lean forward on the steering wheel, glancing at the road behind us every few seconds, pleading silently for the strength to protect them, whatever comes.

Even whispered in my brain, the prayer struggles to form. I'm not in the habit of talking to God. I'm not sure if He really even knows I exist. I certainly wasn't granted the blessing of an easy road in life. But if anyone can help as I walk through this minefield of disaster waiting to happen, perhaps He will find it in His heart to look down on us with pity. Again and again, I stumble over a prayer that He will spare my sister as she fights her demons and protect these children from harm until I can deliver them safely to her again.

As we cross state lines and wind through the highways, taking back roads as often as possible, I shake my head in disbelief that an APB hasn't come through for us. Surely, my sister's disappearance has been discovered by now. With every passing minute, I expect to see a cavalcade of men in pursuit behind us, ready to take back what belongs to their boss.

When we cross into Montana and the mountains come into view, I finally breathe a sigh of relief.

Danny's cabin is only a few hours away. There's still the matter of actually finding the log structure deep in the woods, but Danny loved to talk about it. Even then, I knew reminiscing about his hometown brought him comfort when peace was hard to find. I understood that he needed to talk about the memories to hold onto them, so I listened. He'd told me how to reach it a dozen times, describing every twist in the road and every landmark. In my sleep-deprived and terrified of shadows state, it almost seems as if my friend had a feeling that, one day, I'd need a safe place to hide from the world.

If we can make it to the cabin, we'll be safe for the time being. Hope begins to blossom in my chest, even as fear still struggles for dominance.

When we drive into Cascade Valley, I realize it's just the sort of town to come to if someone wants to disappear. It's still a small and outdated mountain village, but also touristy enough that strangers probably come and go often. No one will remember a quiet, single woman stopping for supplies at several local markets before heading off for a fishing trip. I can't leave the children in the car, so I pile them into a cart when we enter the store, bribing Janie with sweet treats. I keep my hat and eyes down, paying in cash pleasantly but in a straightforward way that I hope will be unmemorable.

Finally, I feel confident I've collected at least enough supplies to get us through the next few months. If our circumstances demand it, I can return to town, but hopefully, we'll have enough to last us for a while. I secure the children in their seats and toss the supplies into the back of the Jeep. We drive toward the mountain peaks in the distance. Over and over, Danny's descriptions repeat themselves in my brain.

"Straight up the western road leading out of town, past the cattle ranch at the base of the mountain. Drive up the main road, and when it forks, take the right one. It'll turn into a logging road. Follow it until you come across the marker me and Granddad nailed onto a tree. It's not hard to find."

He was killed in action less than six weeks after that conversation.

Nervous in case he oversimplified the directions, I study the road with laser focus as we travel past the rich ranching land. Wide, open spaces, roaming cattle, and wooden fence posts strung with barbed wire speed past along the shoulder. Houses are few and far between once we get out of town. We pass an equestrian center for Arabians, and then, a couple of miles later, a yellow farmhouse set back far from the road appears to be the last house for miles. After that, the road quickly winds up into the thick cover of trees.

"Home?" Janie whimpers.

"We're almost there," I reassure her, keeping my tone bright. "We're going to a super fun place for a vacation. You'll get to play outside. Maybe there will even be some games there."

The road leads up and up, curving around the mountain. Just when I think I must have gone where no civilized person has ever gone before, the pavement forks, and I veer off to the right, per Danny's spoken road map. The left fork continues winding even higher up the slope. It isn't long before the sound under the tires changes, and we turn onto an old logging road. It's rough and unpaved, though passable. I slow down to a crawl, trying to minimize the bumpiness. Janie cries. DJ tells her stories in a low tone. Despite the emergence of summer, there is still plenty of snow scattered in patches under the trees.

I almost rumble past the landmark before I spot it. The Gardener men nailed a small wooden placard to the trunk of a pine tree just at the entrance of an overgrown hiking trail that leads deeper into the forest.

"Private property of the Gardeners," it reads. "No trespassing." I know the cabin sits just up the trail.

But the passageway looks too narrow and treacherous for the Jeep. Twisting to look over my shoulder, I back the vehicle into a small clearing a hundred yards down the road, grimly accepting that I'll have to pack us in and out on foot. There's too much to carry now, so I'll have to hike down later while the children are asleep to disguise the Jeep and carry up all the supplies. Danny said the cabin wasn't too far up the trail, but I have two small children in tow and don't know how far up we will have to hike.

When I step out of the car, the air is crisp and smells of the sweet, heady scent of pine. The sun is beginning its afternoon journey toward sunset, but its rays are warm and comforting on the upturned skin of my face. Placing my hands on my stiff lower back, I stretch and breathe in the clear air before turning toward the Jeep.

"Janie, I'll carry you." I hold out my arms once she's released from the car seat, and to my surprise, she leans into them, her tear-stained face weary. When I lift her to my hip, she buries her head in my shoulder, clasping her tiny arms around my neck. Her exhaustion pulses in waves. "DJ, can you carry Janie's toy bag for her?"

Willingly, my nephew shoulders the small backpack. I grab a

bag of supplies, Janie's diaper bag, and extra blankets to get us through the next couple of hours.

"Let's go!" I sing in a cheerful voice that doesn't fit the setting . . . or my nerves. It only takes me a few steps before I realize that the shadowy forest is intimidating. The sunlight struggles to penetrate under the thick canopy, and every dark tree and unfamiliar sound is a threat I don't have time to assess. Finn strides boldly at my side, his pointed ears forward, alert, and eager. I keep an eye on him to sense any changes in his demeanor, and together, we step forward and begin the hike to the cabin. I hope we can all get some rest while I figure out how in the world I'm going to find my sister and ensure we survive until she returns.

. . .

And then, it's three months later, and we're still living in the cabin in the woods. To my horror, the nosy rancher just discovered our hiding place. Dean freezes at the head of the trail as Finn lunges toward him. Expression neutral, he lifts his hands above his shoulders, palms facing forward in a universal sign of nonthreatening intentions. A growl rattles in my dog's throat as he waits for my signal to rip the man to shreds.

"Finn, hold," I command without thinking. Slowly, Dean lowers his hands. He didn't return with the rifle, but my brain races as DJ tugs at my pant leg, trying to think of how to recover from the massive blunder. Janie whines for me to pick her up, her torso half in and half out of the doorway to the cabin. DJ flung it open seconds ago as soon as I stepped on the porch. He was supposed to wait until I told them it was okay to emerge from the safety of the log house. They were supposed to stay quiet and hidden while I convinced the unwelcome visitor that all was well.

But if I have learned one thing about children over the past couple of months, it's that they don't always make it easy to protect them.

I can't do anything to stop what's going to happen now as Dean takes a step forward, then another and another, his long strides bringing him ever closer. My fingers itch to grab my rifle, but I hung it back on the pegs above the doorway just moments ago, where I keep it out of the reach of small hands. A flash of intensity lights up the rancher's eyes as he appraises us with fresh perspective. I recognize his wariness because it mirrors my own, but outwardly, Dean is relaxed and casual as he walks closer. His bearded jaw works subtly, and I feel like grinding my teeth in protest.

A buzzing begins in the center of my stomach, running along my skin like electric sparks. My hands rise to smooth down my shirt. It doesn't make sense. His presence is a threat. I am *not* happy to see him again, so why do I suddenly feel so self-conscious?

As he approaches, I remind myself to balance my reaction to him. I can't show him fear, but I also can't show that there's something about him that sends electricity through my brain. I felt a spark of it at the fishing hole when he didn't back down, even when I threatened him with a loaded weapon. I felt the same spark again when I found him outside the cabin just minutes ago and watched his eyes light up when he saw my face. While his sudden appearance has startled me twice, not once have I felt threatened in his presence. He's too handsome, too tall, and far too inquisitive, but much to my dismay, there's something trustworthy about this man's open, genial face. My fingers itch to reach for my rifle as I hope I'm not completely misjudging his character.

Because I could use someone to trust right about now.

Cautiously, he approaches the porch steps. His eyes are filled with a friendly glow as he tilts his head down to greet the children. Finn growls again but stays put as I commanded.

"Big," Janie blurts out before he says anything. She points up to the sky. We've been working on her words, and she's begun to name everything. Boldly, she totters forward, her chubby hand outstretched. I reach to grab her, but Dean has already lowered his hand in response. His big palm swallows her tiny fingers.

"What's your name, little one?" He bends at the waist until he is eye level with her.

Protectively, I place my hand on top of her head, her bouncy curls springing up through my fingers. "This is Janie," I answer automatically before I cringe and remember that I'm supposed to give this stranger a fake name for my niece.

"And what about you, son?" Dean looks behind me.

I glance back at my nephew, who has backed into the doorway, hoping the look in my eye is enough to remind him of what we talked about. For three months, we've been cut off from the outside world. Once we'd been here about a week, and the fog in my brain dissipated, I realized the terrifying truth.

Searching for my sister was going to be impossible. Not if I hoped to keep our location a secret. Not only do I not have access to an internet connection, but I turned off my own cell phone and stashed the battery in my backpack, not daring to place a call or conduct a search for a possible location of a private drug recovery program. I have no way of knowing if news of my sister's disappearance has reached this far into Montana. If the FBI got involved, there could be a nationwide manhunt going on for a veteran and the two small children she kidnapped.

The gray prepaid cell phone stays charged and on my person at all times. Amy promised she wouldn't be gone more than a few months.

Surely, she can't stay away even that long?

Still, in anticipation of being discovered, I instructed my nephew to modify his name slightly. I hope he remembers.

He watches Dean with obvious apprehension, mumbling, "Junior."

"Janie and Junior, pleased to meet you. My name is Dean." He says it with a friendly smile. His eyes pan over to me as he straightens to his full height, Janie's hand still wrapped in his. My head tilts back a little to look up at him. "I can see the family resemblance. You both look just like your mama."

Now, I know he's lying because my barely wavy blonde hair and blue eyes look nothing like the rich luster of my niece and nephew's curly light brown hair and hazel eyes. They didn't even take after my sister, with her strawberry blonde locks, ice blue irises, and pale pink skin that burns in minutes. My gaze narrows. But when I speak, my voice takes on a relaxed drawl I don't feel.

"These two take more after their daddy, but it's nice of you to say. Say goodbye to Mr. Dean here, you two. We were just about to have an early lunch, and we don't want it to get cold."

Herding my young charges toward the door, my nerves are tense as I hope he gets the hint and leaves. Any thought that the man was going to hike back down the mountain and forget the unwelcoming woman he's encountered twice in the woods has effectively faded. All I can hope is that he leaves well enough alone and doesn't pry any further.

But Janie won't let go of his hand, and she tugs at it, pulling him toward the open door to the cabin. The scent of the soup I set to warm over the wood burning stove before Dean's unexpected arrival wafts out to us now. In the peak of the summer, I most often cooked outside on a small propane-powered camp stove I bought when I stocked our supplies on the way through town. But for the first time since we've been here, the morning weather has been cool enough to be able to use the stove the last few days. I wonder if the smoke alerted Dean to our presence.

"Something sure smells good," he says. When he steps fully onto the porch, his height and the breadth of his shoulders make it feel crowded.

I shrink away, trying to place myself between him and the cabin. But before I can block him from entering, Janie pushes around me, dragging the man into the cabin, which is dim since I only drew the curtains partially open this morning. Dean lets her pull him along, his head stooping as he ducks under the doorway.

"Um . . . please don't . . ." My words sputter out. As I lunge after them, I notice the way he glances casually right to left, his eyes sweeping across the space, no doubt quickly assessing it for threats even as he follows Janie, her voice prattling on with childish chatter.

She pulls him over to a wooden chair at the handmade table, pushing him into it in an unspoken command to sit, and climbs up into the chair next to him as he obeys. DJ and I are left lingering outside the door. The unexpected turn of events has floored me, and I wonder if I should demand that he leave immediately. I glance around, hoping there is nothing out in the open that would give us away. The duffel bags with the children's documents and the money are packed and ready, but they seem to stand out conspicuously from their station in the corner underneath the snowshoes hanging on the wall. With a sharp inhale, I gear up my courage to throw Dean out.

Instead, I hear myself saying, "It's just canned soup and crackers. Nothing special."

Janie is busy showing Dean her coloring pages, still spread out from the morning, but he swings his head to look over his shoulder at me. "Every meal shared by family and friends is special, Ms. . . .?"

I realize he is asking for my name . . . again . . . and I cast about for a fake name I can give him. But before I can respond, Janie squeals and points at me with a chubby finger.

"Kasey," she exclaims, looking up at me adoringly.

Instantly, my heart melts into a puddle at my feet. She's just a toddler, her words slow to come but gaining steadily. I've worked hard to get her to say my name. Summer was a struggle as Janie adjusted to life without her mother. It's just been in the last week or two that she seems to have accepted my presence as the current mother figure in her life. But it's the first time she's said my name willingly.

"That's your mama," Dean says with amusement. "She calls you by your first name?"

Like a fool, I find myself nodding, unable to stop myself from beaming at my niece. "She sure does." I hurry across the worn floorboards and press a kiss to the top of her fluffy head.

I should have corrected her and given him a fake name. But for the moment, when I see Janie's face light up as she shows him her coloring pages and I watch DJ edge closer, curiosity drawing him toward the newcomer, I realize I just want something— anything—in the midst of this nightmare to finally feel normal. There are so many things I have to keep secret that my name might be the least of my worries.

Dean flashes me a boyish grin that shouldn't be as attractive as it is. "Kasey." He draws out my name in that warm-as-honey-on-a-summer-day Montana drawl of his, that earnest gaze welcoming. Not for the first time, I notice how deep and pleasant a blue his eyes are. "It's nice to put a name to the face. I'd love a bowl of soup if there's enough to go around."

Chapter Twelve

Dean

Kasey draws the planked door shut behind her, murmuring a firm command of "stay" to the dark and imposing German Shepherd. His wary eyes are the last thing I see as he stands guard next to Janie and Junior. The little girl is babbling away in her pack and play, while the boy reads a book on the cot. As I ate the bowl of beef and vegetable soup Kasey set before me ten minutes ago, the dog watched my every move. While he hadn't lunged toward me again, he had strategically placed himself between me and the children several times, something I noticed his owner did as well whenever she could.

A whisper of wind blows a pine-filled scent as we trudge across the clearing together. I don't say anything as I follow her, our steps dull thuds on the trampled-down grass that forms a trail from the porch to the trees. I've found that silence will often bring out more raw honesty than pressing for the truth. And there's a lot of truth that hasn't yet been told. Of that, I am certain.

Just how bad the truth turns out to be remains to be seen.

"You were kind to the . . . my children back there." Kasey breaks the silence as we step onto the trail, and I move up to walk parallel to her. "You seem to know how to handle kids. Do you have children of your own?"

"Uh, no. None of my own." The question catches me off guard. "No nephews or nieces either. I guess I've just been around the kids at church enough to pick up a few pointers."

"It shows."

"They seem like good kids." I risk a glance down at her and am met with the full force of her intense gaze. The delay as she considers her response gives me a few seconds to recover. I watch as she visibly softens next to me.

"Yeah, they are good kids." Her voice thickens, and she turns her face away. "They've been through a lot, and I just want them to be happy and safe."

The roof of the cabin is still in sight behind us. It's only a few paces down the trail to where Midnight waits in the trees. He swings his ebony head toward us as we approach, tugging at the bridle looped around a branch with an impatient *whoosh*. He nickers at Kasey, his breathy sounds drawing her closer.

She pauses at his withers. Thoughtfully, she reaches out and strokes his mane while I unloop his bridle and check the saddle straps.

As I watch her out of the corner of my eye, I see when she opens her mouth to speak, pauses, then starts again. She studies a section of Midnight's silky mane as if it's the most fascinating thing in the world. "Dean, normally I wouldn't ask this of a stranger—"

"Do you think we're still strangers?" I interrupt. "You've fed me soup, after all." Chancing a lighthearted tone, I'm rewarded with her startled glance upward and a short, choked-off laugh.

She gives a tiny shake of her head. "Well, as close as sharing a bowl of soup makes us, we also don't know each other all that well. I just . . . The truth is, like I said before, the kids have been through a lot . . . I've been through a lot, and we're just here to decompress and get our bearings back. I'd rather not start getting a lot of visitors curious about the newcomers in town—"

"You mean visitors like me?"

"I just don't want to disrupt their daily routines or get them riled up too often." She takes a deep breath, then exhales heavily. "I guess I just hope you can respect our privacy."

"So I shouldn't send the Cascade Valley welcome committee up to meet you with their usual pies and casseroles in tow, then? Any friend of Danny Gardener's—"

Her expression reflects her horror. "I think it's for the best if you don't come back," she interrupts with a firm tone. "We'll be out of here very soon, so there's no reason to make a bunch of new friends or integrate into the community."

I pause and consider. "What you're saying is that you'd rather I keep my knowledge of your presence here to myself?" When I take a step toward her, reins in hand, she moves closer to the horse's head, and I hear her exasperation growing.

"Look, Dean, is it too much to ask? I just . . . I'm a really private person." Her fingers release the horse's mane, and she lifts her hands to wave them around. Her brow is furrowed, eyes narrowed, lips thinned.

I reach out to check the clasp on Midnight's bridle just as her hand falls back on his mane. Our fingers brush. Instantly, Kasey freezes. Her eyes flash up to mine, her irises darkening as she lifts her chin. She jumps back, and I see in her posture a fierce determination to fend me off if I suddenly decide to get handsy with her. Immediately, I soften my gaze, pulling my hand away and stepping back to put distance between us. But the burning sensation where her fingertips grazed my skin lingers like the kiss of a brand.

I try to reassure her. "Kasey, I promise I wasn't being serious about the welcome committee."

Still, that defiant, wary expression lingers. She pulls herself up to her full height, spine ramrod straight, like she's in front of her commanding officer. "Okay, because if you were . . ."

She leaves the words unspoken between us, but I hear them plainly in her tone. For whatever reason, she wants her presence on the mountain to go unnoticed, and if I threaten her sense of privacy in any way, she's gone.

And I realize I don't want Kasey to leave, so if my silence is required, then that's what it'll have to be. I'm intrigued by the mysterious, serious woman, and I hope to see her again.

Infusing my gaze with what I hope is an earnest look, I linger on her pretty, fine-boned face. "Your secret is safe with me."

She looks away, a touch of rosiness flushing her cheeks. "Thanks. I just need . . . we just need some time to ourselves."

If she's hoping to discourage my curiosity, she isn't succeeding. "Let me know if you change your mind. And Kasey," her gaze flashes back to me, "remember that my ranch is at the base of the mountain. If you and the kids need anything— anything at all—please go there first. Do you have a vehicle up here?"

If she does, it must be stashed down the logging road because no vehicle could make it up this rough-and-tumble hiking trail.

Her chin lifts, her shoulders going back again as she replies vaguely, "Yeah, I've got one nearby."

Something compels me to push her a little more. "I don't think I have to tell you how dangerous the deep forest can be. Our door is always open. There's usually someone around. Please, promise me . . ."

"Dean, we're fine. We've got ammo, water, and supplies—"

I lean forward, invading her space just a little, forcing her wary gaze up to meet mine. "Just promise me, so I don't worry about those kids you have up there." I point back toward the cabin.

Instantly, I see her soften. "I promise."

I believe her, and I'm relieved. Still, I wonder if she will hightail it out of here the second I leave, just like she did at the fishing hole. The sensation makes me oddly restless, turning into an uncomfortable nagging under my skin. But with a nod, I turn away. Kasey steps aside as I direct Midnight to face downhill. The horse takes a step forward, but I hold him back with a tug on the reins. Her chin turns up to look at me.

I stare down at her and let the urgency reflect in my tone. "That pack of wolves I told you about before may still be running somewhere in this territory. I haven't found their den yet, but they are hunting in these mountains. We lost a yearling last night. And it's not unheard of to spot grizzlies or black bears up here on occasion. Stay alert. Keep your rifle close, and don't let the kids wander far."

I lead my horse down the trail. When I look back over my shoulder, Kasey is still standing behind me, her expression unreadable and her eyes somber as she watches us walk away.

Chapter Thirteen

Kasey

I'm sorely tempted to pack every single thing we have into the Jeep and drive away during the night. My boots are loud on the worn porch planks as I pace back and forth in front of the cabin. I lift my head every few seconds to scan the clearing, paranoia about the wolf pack fully setting in. But the grassy space is just as peaceful and quiet as it always is.

The door is open. DJ and Janie are playing contentedly on the threshold with a box of crayons and a pad of paper I grabbed from the general store on the supply run I had to make last month. I had no idea two small children could go through so many snacks in such a short amount of time, and I was willing to risk the restock. Plus, I wanted to stock up on gas and battery packs since running out of fuel up here would be disastrous.

My rifle leans against the post within easy reach. Finn stands on the patchy grass, his eyes watching my every move with solemn focus.

We could leave the cabin and head out of Montana within a few hours. Despite the toys, books, and art supplies I bought for them, we're still traveling light. I've burned every scrap of trash I could, and our go bags are packed and repacked every night. We have loads of cash left, and we could just keep moving around until Amy contacts me. I would have left the primitive cabin months ago if I thought we'd be safe on the road, sleeping in seedy motels and living off fast food.

Now, I wish I'd taken the risk.

I have no reason to think Dean isn't a man of his word, yet my mind can't help but worry at the problem like a rat terrier with a mouse. The question of *what if, what if, what if* floats in my brain on repeat.

What if he gets down the hill and calls the sheriff on the unfriendly and suspicious woman squatting with two little kids in a cabin that doesn't belong to them? What if he gets curious and stumbles across a news story on the internet about the blonde, blue-eyed veteran who snuck out of her sister's home in the dead of night and disappeared with her niece and nephew? What if he puts the pieces together? What if there are photos of us? What if this all ends up horribly wrong?

On the edge of the porch, I pause to study the small clearing again. The trailhead is barely visible from here as the dark pines and leafy trees press in at the edges, their trunks growing so thick it's almost hard to see even a few feet into the depths of the forest. If I had any sense, the isolation and the darkness at nighttime would scare the living daylights out of me. The forest should frighten me to my core. I grew up in the city; the most trees I ever saw were in the park. Instead, during the long nights when I stand watch, the inky, velvety sky above our cabin dotted with a thousand stars, the hushed whisper of the wind caressing the pines, and the sense of being completely and utterly alone make me feel safe.

I didn't leave the cabin because I'm not afraid of what the forest holds. I'm afraid of what lies beyond it. I don't know if I can protect my small charges out there, yet I'm deeply aware of what will happen if anyone discovers our hiding place.

The press of the small, gray prepaid cell phone is hard against my hipbone. Slipping my hand into the pocket of my jeans, I follow its warm outline. I keep it charged on the solar-operated charger I brought to the cabin. Only two text messages have come through since Amy left for the drug recovery program, and I've read them over and over.

UNKNOWN ONE: I'm here. I'm safe. Forgive me. Please hug my babies and tell them I love them. I'm going to get through this as fast as I can.

That was less than a week after we arrived. Then, two months of silence later, another text came through late in the evening as I sat at the worn wooden table in the cabin.

UNKNOWN ONE: The doctors tell me I have to stay another month. I've begged to be released early, and they say I'm making progress, but it's not enough. I'm not supposed to have this phone. I'll reach out as soon as I can. I'm hating every minute I must be away from you, but I'm so close. I can feel it. Sending prayers and love to you all.

And then, silence. I've tried to call the single preprogrammed number in the contacts a dozen times. To my surprise, the cabin has decent cell service most of the time. There's never been an answer, though, and I'm plagued with so many questions.

Is Amy safe? How much longer until she can leave? Is she getting clean?

How long can we hold out here until we hear from her again? What's taking her so long?

And if we leave, where would we even go?

I pause and turn toward the cabin. Leaning against the post, I watch them. Ever observant, DJ's eyes travel up to mine. He regards me with thoughtful somberness, the worry evident in his young face. An idea hits me.

A month ago, we stumbled across the fishing hole by accident. It was the first time we'd ventured far from the cabin, and the sight of water was like a balm to my soul. The next day, in the early hours before dawn, while the two of them slept soundly and Finn stood guard, I went down to the spot for an hour to see if I could catch some fish to break up the monotony of our repetitive daily meals. Dean interrupted me that day, but since then, I've been teaching DJ to fish in the creek with the gear Danny left behind. He loves it, and having a new activity to focus on has brought a light to his eyes that hasn't been there since we left the only home he's ever known. He's questioned me a few times about his mom's whereabouts, and I've explained as best as I could without infringing on Amy's right to choose what to tell him. My reassurance that she will be returning soon usually seems to set his mind to rest.

Now, without speaking a word, I sense that he already knows I'm thinking of leaving, and he's worried. I've learned to paste a smile on my face in front of the children even when joy feels far away. But DJ is smart.

"Is that man coming back?" he says abruptly. "He was nice. I think he probably has horses."

I don't know how to answer this. I hope Dean never returns, and yet a facade of happiness tugs at the corners of my lips. I push off the post and clap my hands together.

"Do you know what sounds so good right about now?" A second pair of hazel eyes lifts to my face. "I sure could use an afternoon hot cocoa. Anyone else?" I can only make the drink from powdered packets and filtered and boiled mountain stream water, but there's little that cocoa powder and sugar can't fix, at least temporarily. On the hard days out here, the warm drink has become my comforting ritual, a moment to hold a steaming mug and sip a reminder of less troubling times.

Which have been few and far between in my life, if I'm honest.

Janie's chubby legs struggle to stand as DJ leaps up. They raise their hands as a chorus of "me, me, me" rings out in the clearing.

I mime the sweep of a broom, causing them to burst into laughter, and hustle them into the cabin. As I follow them through the doorway, I pause and turn back to grab the rifle leaning against the post. The hard press of its chilly metal frame in my palm is another kind of comfort, one an intruder will have to pry from my cold, dead hands if they threaten the peace and safety of our little world here.

As if the forest is trying to call my bluff, a shudder passes over me. My eyes dart around the perimeter of the timberline, as the eerie feeling of being watched sends shivers down the back of my neck. It's as if dark eyes are watching me from the shadowy depths of the forest, waiting to catch me off guard. The feeling isn't unfamiliar. It started about a month ago, and it's not lost on me that it coincided with Dean's approach at the fishing hole. I left that encounter with the uncanny feeling that he watched me from the cover of the woods after I brusquely sent him on his way. But I haven't been able to shake the sensation since, even though we haven't seen another person up here.

Turning on my heel, I whip my head around, my heart racing as I study the outlines of each trunk and bough. Nothing seems to have changed, but dread sweeps along my spine. The sensation builds, convincing me that a malevolent something—*someone*—is watching me from the cover of the forest.

But there's nothing there. It's all a figment of my overtired imagination and paranoia.

I don't know if I can protect us from every threat, but there's one thing I do know. Nothing in my life has qualified me to be the shepherd of these little ones while wolves creep in the shadows. If we make it through this, it won't be due to my strength, but due to the strength of something I can't even put into words.

"Please help us," I whisper heavenward as I step over the threshold and close the door.

. . .

My sleep since we arrived at the cabin has been fitful at best. It seems my body refuses to let down its guard as DJ and Janie breathe peacefully together in their cot against the wall. At least they are good sleepers, both falling asleep quickly and rarely waking until after the sun rises. Janie, especially, is a late riser. But every time I drift into unconsciousness, my brain nags at me, jolting me awake with shock waves of fear that something in the forest is waiting to strike the moment my survival instincts slip.

Lately, the nights pass with me sitting on the floor with my back against the far wall, my eyes drifting often to the door straight ahead. I have a sleeping bag, but I rarely use it. Instead, my fingertips rest on the barrel of my rifle. A single battery-operated lantern glows on the table in the center of the room as if its light source alone can keep the predators at bay. Its feeble rays cast eerie shadows on the tools, fishing equipment, and snowshoes hanging on the roughly hewn walls.

The night hums and chirps just outside the cabin door, inky

blackness pressing its fingers against the exterior walls and peeking in through the cracks of the wooden frame. Faithfully, Finn keeps watch with me, his furry head heavy on my thigh, an occasional deep sigh the only indication that he wishes his human would sleep so that he can too. But I can't sleep—won't sleep—not while the shadows of the unknown stalk us just outside.

If I fail to protect us, I'll never forgive myself.

And then, typically, the familiar memories come. They are the same ones I've fought since childhood, when Mom and I stood outside Dad's door as the dusk gathered its gloom like a scorned bride gathering her tattered gown, waiting for the checks that rarely came. I remember his shadow crossing the doorway when night finally fell and the darkness that crossed his face when Mom tried to convince him to let me stay.

But he sent us away every time.

Little did I know that an absent father wouldn't be the worst sorrow I'd face in life.

It seems Dean's visit has done something to me tonight, though, and I find myself falling into a deep and heavy slumber. I rest my forehead against my thin pillow for just a second, and the room begins to fade in and out. But when I sleep, it's punctuated by vivid and terrifying nightmares.

I'm on the battlefield with my platoon, the sweat and dust of the desert permeating every crevice of my very soul. I'm weary, sleep-deprived, and thirsty, but that is nothing new. Despite the heat and the hot slick of fear sliding down my spine, a steady sense of purpose punctuates every thud of my boots against the ground. I know why I'm here—my brain and heart beating in synchronized focus. For once in my life, I find myself wanted and even needed. And even though the threat of danger and death waits to pounce out of the dim corners in this valley of horrors, the steady press of my fellow soldiers at my back reassures me that whatever comes, I'm not alone.

I'm not alone.

We rumble down the sandy roadway, and I'm not alone.

Until the flash of light and heat and pain proves that to be a lie once more.

Chapter Fourteen

Dean

"Nothing? You didn't find any sign of their den at all?" Knox's expression is skeptical. "We were about to send out a search party for you. Thought you got lost."

In typical Knox fashion, his words are an exaggeration, so I don't bother to answer, choosing instead to tamp down the sudden feeling of annoyance his questions spark. My brain has been busy churning over the events of the day as I rode, and foolishly, I expected to be able to continue my quiet reflection when I returned to camp.

I sidestep my brother to finish wiping down Midnight's glossy coat. The heat intensified this afternoon, and we're both hot and drenched in sweat. It hadn't been my intention to return from my scouting mission with the afternoon halfway gone, the ride back taking longer than I anticipated. I still don't have any answers about the wolf pack, and it's too far along in the day to move the herd even farther away. We're stuck here for another night at least, and by staying, potentially opening ourselves up to another wolf attack. I just hope the team drove the herd far enough from their hunting grounds.

Stifling an annoyed grunt as Knox continues to chatter, I remind myself that my irritation is directed at myself, and my duty is to my herd and team. It was so easy to get caught up in the sweet, familial scene I stumbled across at the cabin this afternoon. To say it took me by surprise to discover the pretty woman from the fishing hole again would be an understatement, not to mention the shock of finding out that she is also a mother and a veteran. Her past makes her all the more intriguing, and her quick suspicion, wariness, and fierce protectiveness of those children . . . it all makes sense.

And yet, nothing about her makes sense.

Underneath the guarded facade, who is that woman? There is so much depth in those blue eyes, a soulful expression that calls me to explore.

She asked me to forget her, but how could I do that when I have so many questions?

My stomach growls with hunger as I add an extra scoop of feed to Midnight's bucket, but I ignore the urge, an undefined feeling nagging at my spirit. I try to turn inward to listen, but Knox's rambling voice as he fills me in on the day is distracting.

"Uh-huh," I mumble in response to my brother's deluge of words.

There has to be a deeper reason for Kasey's guarded behavior. She's right to be protective, alone as she is in the woods with two children, but something tells me there's more to her story than just a mother and her children out on a camping trip. They are in too primitive a setting to simply be on a vacation. A ripple runs across my skin, urging me to press for the truth about the mysterious woman.

Mysterious and beautiful.

This afternoon, I let my attention get pulled away by the three of them, forgetting temporarily that I was out on a mission, and my first responsibility is to my ranch and all who depend on it. But the little trio intrigues me.

Where is their father?

Or isn't there one in the picture?

And the most pressing question: *Why would a mother think the safest place for her children is alone in the middle of a dangerous forest?*

A quick, light punch in the shoulder from Knox's fist jolts me back to the present. "Earth to Dean? What happened out there in the woods? Are you sure you didn't see something?"

I shake him off and plaster a good-natured grin across my face. "Just tired from riding all day. You know, some of us actually do real work around here."

His laugh is loud and carefree, reverberating through the sloping hills as he falls into step beside me. Since my horse is fed, watered, and groomed for the rest of the day, I'm headed straight to the fire for some hot food. The air smells like spicy, rehydrated beef chili and cornbread. It's the third meal we've had of the freeze-dried rations this week, but I'm not complaining. At least we have plenty of food on hand to feed the crew, including the range riders we've called up as extra security. But the small bowl of canned soup I ate at the cabin expired long ago on my ride back to our base camp.

A flash of guilt hits me as we walk toward the fire. I didn't notice much in the way of food or resources around Kasey's tiny cabin today. She said she had supplies, but are they enough? Are the kids hungry? They looked well-fed and content, but maybe I missed some signs.

The thought makes me want to saddle Midnight up, pack a bag of our freeze-dried supplies, and ride back to her cabin before it gets dark. Kasey will probably be upset if I show up again, and even if I offer tangible help, will she take that as more interference in her desire for privacy? Before I can make any rash decisions, Knox lifts his arms and waves wildly to the cowboys gathered around the fire. They are already filling their plates with seconds of the fragrant chili, my arrival coinciding with a late lunch for the extra cowboys with us this week.

"Hey," he yells, "save some for the boss man over here. He's had a long day, and I suspect he saw a Bigfoot out in the woods but just doesn't want to admit how frightened he was."

Six faces lift to greet me, and six grins break out around the fire. In response, I reach over and give my brother a shove on the shoulder that sends him hopping away.

"The only Bigfoot around here is this guy." I point at him as we reach the fire, and he throws himself down on a log, still laughing. One of the men hands me a plate, and I dig in eagerly as the team teases Knox about the size of his boots.

. . .

Halfway through my meal, the thought of Kasey and those kids alone in the woods with only a rifle and the walls of a log cabin to protect them against every predator out there—whether animal or human—ruins my appetite. I hand the remains of my half-demolished chili-smothered cornbread over to Knox—who is the same bottomless pit he was in high school—and offer to take the first evening shift.

Deciding to give Midnight a break, I saddle up a spare horse and set out on patrols. Vincent joins me an hour later.

"You're probably tired after riding all day. Want to go take a nap?" His voice mingles with the soft *thump* of his horse's hooves as he approaches from the rear.

I shake my head as he ambles up next to me. "I have some things on my mind. Didn't think I'd be able to get any shut-eye."

My brother is quiet for a drawn-out minute, the only sounds the breathy *whoosh* of our horses exhaling and the soft rustles of the herd in the meadow. "Want to talk about it?" he asks. At first, I shake my head again, but then the day's events seem to come tumbling out without my intention. I tell him the whole story. My brother listens with his usual quiet intensity. There's no one in the world I trust more than my brother, and I know I can trust him even with secrets that are not my own. He'll take them to the grave and give me solid advice while he is at it.

After I relay the circumstances that first led to meeting Kasey at Fisherman's Gulch and how I happened to stumble across Danny's cabin today, Vincent considers the information quietly.

"And who is this woman?" he asks.

I shrug. "Someone who was friends with Danny Gardener. Worked with him in the army. She was there when he passed, and that's how she knew where his cabin was located."

"So she's been through some trials herself." Vincent's voice is heavy.

"I think so."

"Given her experience, it seems she's likely to be able to handle herself. Maybe you should honor the lady's wishes and let her be with her family."

With a sudden uptick in nervous energy, I shift in the saddle. The horse shuffles. With a quick palm to his shoulder, I calm him.

A protest rises to my throat, but Vincent continues, "If she's not trespassing or breaking any laws, it seems like the right thing to do might be just to let it go. I mean, no one in the valley cares if she uses Danny's abandoned cabin."

I exhale loudly, the protest taken out of me, and look around. The sun is on its downward trajectory for the night. As the shadows deepen, the forest seems to press inward, corralling us to the center of the vast meadow. The herd is rounded up for the night, with two cowboys on the other side of the meadow preventing any strays from wandering away. Another ranch hand is circling the group with the wire that will become their electrified paddock for the night.

The calves from this year's season are strong, thriving on the wild Montana mountain air and nutritious varieties of grass. We've got a fire going at the campsite, coffee hot and strong, and rifles at the ready in our saddles. There don't seem to be any threats against our livelihood at the moment, and if a predator, storm, or fire approaches, we'll handle it. My world is here, and I'm keeping it safe as the leader of our ranch. This is where I belong.

My brother is right. I do need to let go of the urge I feel to insert myself into Kasey's life. I need to ignore the whisper that tells me to go back to the forest to protect the small children and the petite woman with the vulnerable eyes that mask themselves behind a shield of steely resolve. A shield that I can see right through, her defensive walls only compelling me to become her protector.

She's not yours to protect, Dean. My own voice whispers the words inside my brain. The horse rustles again, moving restlessly over the earth. Vincent's ride does the same, bumping gently against my leg.

I understand the necessity of leaving well enough alone, but still, something nags at the corners of my heart, a feeling of urgency at war with my instincts to do the polite thing and leave behind the little family in the woods. Something tells me that Kasey needs someone in her corner, and I don't know if I can walk away.

Vincent's sharp eyes stare at me as the sunset crests the top of the mountains. "Unless the Holy Spirit is telling you differently. Then I'd say to ignore everything I just said and listen up."

I hear the smile underneath his mustache. I'm about to make a joke about ignoring everything he says anyway—which we both know isn't true—when a low, mournful howl pierces through the soft evening air.

The cry reverberates in my chest. I hear a yip and a cacophony of agitated growls emanating from the edge of the forest in reply. Vincent and I stare into the trees, trying to see the threat around darkened trunks and low-hanging branches.

"That's coming from the Fisherman's Gulch side." His voice is grim and low.

"Yeah, I know." I reach for my rifle as the glow of yellow eyes and hulking figures comes into view. The cattle in the electrified paddock start to rise, their instincts alerting them to the presence of the predator. They shuffle, and I pray that the wolves won't rush the temporary fencing. It'll only hold them off for so long.

As he rides away to guard the other side of the herd, Vincent calls over his shoulder, his words laced with worry. "Ignore everything I said, Dean. I think you need to warn her that the pack is officially still on this side of the mountain. She can't stay up there alone. And in the morning, you need to call Fish and Wildlife and tell them they need to get up here to take care of this before they start ripping apart our herd."

"My thoughts exactly," I call back, drawing my rifle as the first wolf strides onto the meadow.

Chapter Fifteen

Kasey

When the first rays of morning peep between the cracks in the log cabin walls, I wake to find myself leaning against the wood, my legs outstretched and pinned down by the big body of my German Shepherd.

I take it as a good sign we're still here. I didn't hightail it off the mountain in the middle of the night to disappear again. We've already disappeared and disappeared well. Leaving our safe space because one man has stumbled across our temporary home—albeit one slightly too handsome and very inquisitive man with piercing gray-blue eyes that give me the feeling he is looking right into my soul—would just be foolish.

I have to trust that Dean won't spread his discovery all over Cascade Valley. I've never lived in a small town—being a city girl until I bought my cottage in Oregon—and I haven't exactly been diligent about making friends with the neighbors there, but I've seen enough television to know of their reputation for gossip and suspicion of outsiders. All it takes is one person casually mentioning a nationwide manhunt for a veteran or one random news story on his social media feed . . .

I could be making a huge mistake by staying put.

Then I tell myself, who am I kidding? The chances of Dean having a social media account to begin with are slim to none. The man gives off classic old-school rancher vibes, anti-technology, ascribing to nothing but the back of a horse and the wind on his suntanned face.

And I find the quality strangely appealing. It's not like I have social media either.

With a sudden surge of anxiety, I nudge Finn off my legs. Stumbling a little as the blood rushes back, I stand, one hand leaning against the wall for support. My niece and nephew breathe softly in the cot as I creep across the floor and pause to look at them. Their hair is sweaty and pushed back from their chubby baby faces, arms flung above their heads. I brush a finger down Janie's flushed cheeks; her skin is hot to the touch. She rolls over without waking.

I'm unsure of the reason, but I've grown to love watching them while they sleep. Knowing they feel safe enough to rest deeply and well triggers an ache deep inside my soul. Despite entering their lives as a stranger, I've tried to earn their trust, and it seems to be working.

The ache I feel is the same one that makes my heart surge with another unfamiliar feeling as I gaze down at them. It's been steadily growing in the pit of my stomach over the past three months. It feels an awful lot like love, and it wars for dominance with my instinct for stoic survival. Something about these two small, precious souls activates an unshakable *knowing* within me. I would give my life to make sure they are safe.

Is this what it feels like to be a mother?

"Just a little while until your mama comes home and takes you away from all of this," I whisper, the words barely audible above the call of bird songs beginning to trill with the morning light. "She's going to be here soon. I promise."

If they stick to their usual habits, they'll sleep for another couple of hours. I motion to Finn and slip outside, pausing just across the threshold to survey the clearing and surrounding forest, wondering if the feeling of being watched will accost me again as soon as I leave the safety of our cabin. My bones feel extra achy this morning, and the lingering cough I've had for a few weeks is triggered by the crisp air. I try to clear my lungs quietly and stretch out the aches, reminding myself to get into my medical kit to find something to treat the cough later.

Every morning, I listen for movement through the trees and signs of anything out of place. In the light of day, I can't imagine that the wolf pack Dean mentioned is anywhere nearby. If there was one, surely, I would have heard their calls during the last few nights? We've seen very little wildlife up here, the extent of it consisting of a few foxes, some deer, and several rabbits.

If anything would drive me off this mountain, it's the presence of wolves or bears, but I don't believe they are a current threat. And surely not in the daytime.

If my thoughts keep drifting to the rancher, I might be tempted to leave, though. Dean is tall, lean, and broad-shouldered—an imposing man—so why is his presence equally gentle and nonthreatening? I remember how DJ and Janie lit up when he ate lunch with us yesterday. He kept turning to them, making bits of conversation that seemed intended to draw them out. By the time he left, Dean had managed to get DJ to talk about fishing. And Janie stayed close to his side, prattling in her baby voice, showing him pictures she'd drawn and the baby doll her mom packed for her.

The scene was adorable. It must have been something about Dean because, despite my tension that one of them was going to blurt out some secret to give us away, his presence had a soothing effect on me too. I can't get the pleasant feeling out of my head. My skin buzzes with the aftereffects of the strange feeling he sparked in me.

I shouldn't trust Dean. But I want to.

I jolt to the present with the realization that I'm still standing on the porch, frozen, my eyes locked on a pine straight ahead. The clearing is as quiet and peaceful as it has been since we arrived, with only the birds disrupting the silence. Standing out here in the cool of the morning has been my routine all summer. It seems to give me courage to face another day. These are the only moments I feel safe, when the screaming blackness of the impenetrable night fades into the soft, golden balm of morning.

I drop down to the porch, my legs hanging over its edge, my boots brushing the overgrown grass at the base. Finn patrols the perimeter for a few minutes and then returns to stand guard with me. His ears swivel as he assesses the threat level of each sound.

I alternate between stretching my stiff joints and petting him.

My thigh throbs, so I begin to work it, kneading my knuckles across the flesh and down to my knee, which aches as well. My jeans cover the puckered skin that hides along my femur. Lately, the nearly eight-inch scar that runs down my leg has been angry and dark purple. I ran out of my scar cream a month ago, and my skin is rebelling. I'm starting to reach a level of discomfort that makes me admit to myself that the primitive conditions of the cabin are quite miserable. I haven't even had a proper bath since we arrived.

I've managed to keep my hair and our clothes clean by washing them in a pair of buckets I found here. They also happen to be big enough for both children to take regular baths with the water I haul up, sterilize, and warm from the creek. Thankfully, they had a bath the night before Dean's visit, so they didn't look neglected. But the suspicion that I'm beginning to resemble the inside of a musty cupboard sends a flush rushing to my cheeks. Despite the dusty ride up the mountain, Dean had somehow managed to look (and smell) as cool and fresh as a daisy in spring.

A dip in the stream sounds revolutionary.

"Kasey," a soft voice calls from inside the cabin.

The sun is up, and my young charges are awake. Immediately, I pull myself up, limping a little, and open the door. DJ is half-risen from the bed, his hair curly and messy from the pillow.

"Good morning, buddy," I whisper when I realize Janie is still sleeping. "How did you sleep?"

He rubs his eyeballs. "Good. Is Dean coming today? He said maybe we could go fishing."

The man had said that as he walked out of the cabin yesterday afternoon. Immediately, I wished he hadn't. The last thing I need is for that man to come around us again.

I'm frustrated with myself for battling with the wish he could return, if only to amend both of the terrible first impressions I had to have made on him. I've pulled my rifle on him twice, and he didn't do anything to deserve it. Actually, he's been quite kind.

I refuse to admit to myself that Dean's presence has triggered a restless stirring that reminds me of the deep ache I carry within my bones. It isn't like I could permit myself to get to know him anyway. I think of my romantic life in three eras: pre-army, when I dated casually but nothing ever felt real—the army era, when I was too tired and focused on surviving deployment to do anything but push away interest as far and as fast as possible—and post-army, when surviving still seems like a daily struggle and romance is the last thing on my mind.

But Dean . . . it was difficult not to see his face in my dreams last night.

I pull myself back to the present and shake my head at my nephew. "Dean had to go back home to his ranch. He has a lot of work to do." When DJ's shoulders slump, I continue quickly, calling on anything I can to make the little boy happy. "But I was thinking, what's to stop us from going fishing together at the big stream today? I could use some good fried fish for lunch."

He perks up hopefully. "Yeah, I like fish a lot better than canned soup."

His instant elation at the prospect of eating something other than the canned foods that have been keeping us fed lately crushes me. I know the children are growing restless, both with our food and our living situation. My days are occupied with coming up with activities and lessons to amuse them. Sometimes, we explore the surrounding forest together or play in the creek. Often, we eat outside. But out of necessity, they haven't been able to venture much farther than the cabin clearing, and I feel like I'm letting them down.

I keep my voice light. "As soon as Janie wakes up and we eat breakfast, we'll go to the fishing hole."

Guiltily, I get the sense that I'm bribing him, but hopefully, it's the right thing to do.

. . .

As soon as DJ is set up with a fishing pole (not outfitted with a hook for safety) and Janie is settled on a blanket on the grass with a packet of fruit snacks I keep hidden for special occasions, I wade into the steadily moving water. My niece woke up tired, cranky, and flushed this morning. Immediately, I checked her temperature, which was slightly elevated. But since she had no other symptoms, I attributed her mood to teething, since her first molars have been coming in the past few days. Nonetheless, I intend to monitor her closely, but I'm hoping she is content to stay put on the blanket for just a few minutes.

I'll set DJ up to fish properly, but first, I'm in desperate need of a bath. The grime feels reminiscent of those long months on deployment, but I remind myself that it could be worse. At least I'm not dealing with the aftermath of battle.

My rifle is within reach on the bank. I doubt the wildlife will venture out during the day, but I find myself scanning every inch of the meadow. Perhaps venturing out here today was a terrible idea. Back at the cabin, I convinced myself that I remembered hearing that wolves hunt more at night than during the day, but under the open sky, surrounded by the dark edges of the forest, I'm suddenly not so sure. Both children are within sight of me as I float in the t-shirt and cotton shorts I pulled from the bottom of my bag and donned along with my hiking boots to trek out here. It isn't all that far, but it was a feat getting our gear and snacks down to the fishing hole, and I'm sweating with the effort of carrying Janie too. The clothes are technically pajamas, but they are as close to a swimsuit as I'm going to get. I didn't exactly pack for a summer stay at the lake three months ago. I make a mental note to drive down to Cascade Valley to pick up extra warm clothes and boots for the kids before the weather turns. They are going to need them if we are still here when the snow begins to fall, and DJ is beginning to outgrow his clothes.

With one eye on Janie to make sure she stays put and one eye on DJ to make sure he doesn't get too close to the edge, I pull my hair out of its braid and dip my head under the water. Over the summer, my hair—which I usually keep at shoulder-length—has grown. It falls in natural waves across my upper back. Danny's cabin doesn't have a mirror, but I suspect the sun has lightened it considerably too. With a bar of soap I picked up in town, I quickly scrub my locks and use the soap to reach as many places as I can before rinsing it all away.

As I climb up out of the water, it hits me that I forgot to bring a towel, and there's no way I'm leaving the children at the edge of the stream to go behind a tree to redress in dry clothes. I'll be forced to air-dry, as uncomfortable as it sounds. Shrugging, I wring out the material of my shirt and shorts as best I can, glad that at least the sun is still beaming with late summer heat. I should be somewhat dry quickly.

"Hang on for a minute, Junior, and I'll come help you," I call to DJ, reminding myself to use the nickname I've given him instead of his real name. I need to get into the habit so that if someone else discovers our cabin, I won't accidentally slip and give away his real name. I walk toward Janie, dropping down on the blanket to kiss her forehead. My lips burn as they press into her skin, and I draw back to look at her flushed face. The red on her cheeks has intensified, and her curls are sweaty. I kick myself for not thinking to grab a hat to shield her little head. I'll have to take her temperature again when we return to the cabin. She's fussy, and I wonder if she's getting sick. My medical kit is stocked with everything we could need for normal emergencies, but I'll have to reassess if we face anything more serious than a seasonal cold.

Opening a jug of water, I try to get her to drink a little, but she pushes it away, distracted.

"Wet," she says, pointing to my soaked t-shirt and shorts.

"I took a bath," I tell her, and she stares at me in surprise before a toothy grin breaks across her face.

"Catching any fish this morning?"

The familiar voice that calls across the stream freezes me on the grass, my wet clothes steadily dripping and creating a puddle around my knees. A ripple runs along my skin, raising goosebumps on my arms, but I tell myself it's just the soft breeze across the meadow causing the reaction.

Adjusting my facial expression into casual indifference, I rise slowly to my feet. When I turn, Dean and that black horse of his are standing on the other side of the water. How the two of them made it down the hill without giving themselves away is beyond me. DJ throws down his fishing pole and lifts his arms over his head, waving to both of them gleefully. I raise my hand, shielding my eyes against the sun to see them better, and catch sight of a strange expression on Dean's face. His eyes are turned away, no doubt trying not to acknowledge my makeshift swimsuit. Instantly, I'm conscious of the soaked fabric hanging off my skin and even more aware of the purplish scar running conspicuously down my leg.

I give my wet hair a little shake as I try to pull my dignity together. I'm confident the oversized fabric hanging off my frame is not a flattering look, but I reach up and wring some of the water out of my hair anyway.

Dean taps the horse's side and moves downstream to a spot where the banks narrow. I adjust my posture into something I hope looks like nonchalance as he approaches.

"Man!" Janie screams, rising to her feet and toddling forward, apparently not intimidated by the imposing horse whose hooves are striking the ground. I reach out to catch her and scoop her into my arms, grateful she can provide a bit of coverage to hide my dishevelment. Not that I looked any better the last time Dean was around, but at least I wasn't *dripping* with water.

He slows the horse and dismounts twenty yards away. His tan, wide-brimmed rancher cap with the white bill is pushed up on his forehead as he approaches, wisps of dark, collar-length hair peeking out around his neck, his blue eyes sweeping us and the meadow and the stream with alert vigilance before he settles on Janie with a wide smile. "Miss Janie, I didn't even see you there."

She reaches forward, chubby arms and hands outstretched for him, and before my shocked mind can catch up, he reaches out and she's in his arms. Without her to cover my torso, I feel exposed. Trying to shake off the vulnerable feeling, I pull back my shoulders, standing at attention, and cross my arms over my chest, hoping they can hide anything especially embarrassing. Dean's eyes meet mine, and I catch a flicker of something in them—a warning?—before he strides toward DJ, Janie prattling happily in his ear, her earlier fussiness forgotten.

"You decided to go fishing without me, Junior? Are you going to catch us something good that we can fry up for lunch?"

"That's what we're doing," DJ calls over his shoulder. "We're tired of soup."

Dean glances back at me, and I see the intensity in his eyes again. Inwardly, my defenses rise.

I rush forward as Dean squats next to DJ. My niece is secure on his hip, her arm thrown around his neck as if she's known him forever. Casually, the big rancher instructs the small boy in the art of casting the line. If he notices that I haven't placed the hook on the line yet, he doesn't mention it. Instead, Dean seems completely absorbed in the impromptu lesson, and I notice the gleam in DJ's eyes as he stares up at him with rapt attention.

"Now, you practice what I just showed you. Go ahead. I'll be watching." Dean rises.

I realize that Janie has fallen asleep on his shoulder. I don't know anything about childhood sleep schedules, but I've tried to keep her on a morning and afternoon nap routine. Her face is still flushed, and I remind myself to rehydrate some extra powdered milk for her later.

Together, Dean and I step away from the bank while DJ practices casting the line. As if by instinct, we stand parallel, facing each other, watching each other's backs. Our eyes turn frequently toward DJ, observing in case he slips on the embankment. I've always been a strong swimmer, and the military only strengthened my skills, but the stream's undercurrent is fast and strong in the deeper parts. If it caught the small boy and held him under, he could drown before I reach him, so I won't take any chances.

I'm focused on him, but a few times, I can't resist turning my head to peer up at the handsome man beside me. His cap shades his eyes, but I feel him leaning down toward me a little. Anxiety shoots through my stomach, but I tell myself it isn't Dean's presence making me nervous.

All I can think is that he knows.

Is he here to tell me he knows the truth, and he expects me to turn myself in? How did he find out so quickly?

My heart begins to race, and I wonder if its beat is audible outside of my body. The blood drains from my face. My mouth goes dry, my limbs hollowing as I prepare for the worst. I wait, but Dean doesn't speak, and the silence eats away at me until I need to break it, or I'll burst.

"I didn't expect to see you up here again today." My voice cracks. I speak softly so as not to wake Janie.

Dean's voice is only a husky rumble in my ear. "I'm very surprised to see you out here as well. In fact, I came back to warn you again. My herd was attacked by a pack of wolves last night, about ten miles from here."

I stifle the gasp that rises to my throat. My hand clutches the base of my neck. Without meaning to, I look him up and down, assessing him for wounds as if by force of habit. Quickly determining that he doesn't seem to be hurt, my gaze darts back to DJ and then up and around the meadow stretching out from the river's edge to the woods beyond the clearing. Ten miles suddenly doesn't seem very far away.

I feel exposed by the openness of the meadow. My limbs itch to snatch Janie from Dean's arms and run with my niece and nephew to the safety of our cabin.

"Are you . . . is everyone okay?" I stifle the tremble in my voice.

The brim of Dean's cap bobs in a slow nod. His arms cradle Janie's sleeping form. Her cheek is pressed to his shoulder, her eyes closed. "We didn't have any trouble fending them off for the night with our mounted patrols. It took a few warning shots, though. They left this morning, and we'll see if they return tonight."

The shadows under his eyes make sense. He was awake all night defending his cattle. His cotton t-shirt smells of smoke and ash and a musky scent of woodsy sweat that isn't exactly unpleasant. Underneath it all, I catch the fragrance of mountain pine, a smell that I noticed on him when he was at the cabin. It's as if the mountains have infused themselves into his very veins.

Dean continues, "Kasey, I rode back up this morning because . . ." he lowers his head an inch or two closer, his warm voice flooding my senses, "I'm even more worried about you three staying out here. These wolves were bigger than any I've ever seen around these parts, and I've never experienced an attack like that. Plus, the bears are preparing for winter, and they're the most aggressive right now. If any of these predators catch you unawares . . ."

"I haven't seen any bears. In fact, I haven't seen much besides deer and fox out here," I reply, and my tone is defensive even though my protest is beside the point.

He shakes his head. "That doesn't mean they aren't around. Clearly, the Lord is at work on your behalf to prevent one from lumbering into your clearing. If I remember correctly, there's a patch of huckleberries not far from your cabin, and they're in season."

He's right. We came across the patch of the dark, sweet berries late last month on one of our jaunts to the creek. We picked a bunch, and I cooked them down for our morning oatmeal. A shiver passes over my skin, and with it, a ripple of fear. My earlier feeling was right. I was an idiot for venturing out here this morning. My throat constricts, and my palms feel clammy despite the climbing sun. I feel shaky and tight and unstable all at once, as if I'm tumbling to the earth and floating away simultaneously.

The jarring spatter of gunfire and the dizzying spark of flashing bombs are what I know, what I was trained for, what I lived for a decade. I've waited for battle with less fear than the crushing panic I feel right now. I want an enemy I can see, one who fights fire with fire and isn't merely a ripple of fur and teeth waiting in the gloomy cover of the woods. I'm out of my element here, and I feel it deeply. A nauseous feeling settles in the pit of my stomach.

I don't realize I've leaned over and planted my hands on my

knees until I become aware of the warmth of Dean's hand pressing lightly on my shoulder.

"Kasey, can you hear me? Are you okay?" He doesn't raise his voice, but his deep tone rumbles gently in my ear, pulling me back from the dark valley at whose edge I'm teetering.

I grasp onto the strength of his voice and pull myself back to the meadow, back to sunshine and bird calls and the soft rustle of the breeze playing across the strands of grass.

I blink and reach for Janie. Dean seems to understand my unspoken plea. He hands her back to me, and I pull her into my arms, needing the comforting weight of her small body to ground me before I float away. Her sweaty head nestles onto my shoulder as she naps.

The meadow comes back into focus. There's DJ, still happily casting the line of his hookless fishing pole into the water over and over. There's the stream and the pines at the timberline. And there's Dean, standing between us and the unseen threats, solid, steady . . . safe. Inwardly, I startle as the word slips through my brain like sand running through my fingers and almost take a step backward in protest.

He's watching me with a concerned, thoughtful gaze. I prepare for the weight of his disapproval to feel as if it's crushing my lungs like I used to feel with my father on the rare occasions I saw him, but the sensation never comes. I probably look like a frightened deer caught between the hunter and the wolf chasing her through the forest, but I lock eyes with him anyway.

He's speaking, and I force myself to hear his words.

"I want you to come back with me to my house in the valley. You can stay there until we find you and the kids another place. You said you have a vehicle near Danny's cabin, right?"

I'm suddenly aware of Dean's fingertips hovering at my

elbow, as if he's careful not to touch me but is keeping a hand outstretched in case I go all woozy on him again.

I finally take a step back. My head shakes in protest. "No. We're not going to do that." Even I can hear the panic in the words as they spill out, and I fight to steady my voice.

"It's not safe until this pack has been dealt with." Dean pulls his cap off his head and runs his fingers through the dark, wavy strands of his hair. "We're going to get Fish and Wildlife up here to make an assessment. Maybe they can relocate them. It should only take a week or so. Come on, I'll help you get your stuff packed up."

An icy resolve replaces the fire burning in my veins. I lift my chin and straighten my posture. Janie feels heavier than ever as my tone carries a resolute edge I don't feel. "Thank you for the offer, Dean, but what I meant was that it won't be necessary. I was planning to leave Montana tomorrow anyway. The kids and I are going to visit my mother."

It's a lie, at least about my mother anyway. After nearly eighteen years of silence, I doubt she would have us even if I were willing to ask her for help. She made it clear I was on my own just after I turned eighteen. And, on the unlikely chance she would help me, Amy's children wouldn't be welcome in her home, not after my father left her to pursue Amy's socially connected heiress mother all those years ago. If I know my mother, she would see their plight as just punishment for our father's sins.

"You're nice to offer, but we don't need to be rescued," I continue firmly.

Dean shakes his head and begins to protest, but I don't listen to him. I call to DJ to gather his things—we're leaving. I don't know how I'm going to hike back up to the cabin with Janie, heavy and hot, in my arms, but I have to go now before I combust from the stress of it all. My lungs are burning, I feel a cough brewing in my strained chest, and I wonder if I'm coming down with whatever Janie has.

One thing I said to Dean wasn't a lie. We can't stay hidden on this mountain anymore. It's time to leave, and I've never felt so afraid.

Chapter Sixteen

Dean

Slapping the reins over Midnight's shoulders, I spur him into a faster gallop up the hill. He bucks forward in protest, his ears going back, but he picks up the speed of his stride. Normally, I'm patient with the gelding, but at this point, I just want to get back to my team and assess the cattle after the terror they experienced last night. I should have been with them this morning or already on my way to get Fish and Wildlife involved, but no. I've been riding all over the mountain trying to rescue a woman who is as stubborn as a mule.

A really cute mule trying to hide her . . . did she go swimming in her pajamas? And where did she get that scar?

I fume to the air. I should have known Kasey was going to continue being a handful when she aimed that rifle at me for the second time. The first time it happened after I startled her at the fishing hole, I can understand. *Fool me once.* The second time should have been my clue. *Fool me twice.*

"We don't need to be rescued."

Then why am I dead-to-rights certain that Kasey-whatever-her-name is in desperate need of rescuing? From what, I'm not sure, but I know it's something. And the sight of the long, puckered, purple scar running down her thigh has sent my brain into overdrive. Realizing she was uncomfortable being seen in her wet shirt and shorts, I tried to avoid looking at her too much. But that scar was hard not to notice. The thought of what she's probably been through to earn a wound like that is infuriating and devastating all at once. I barely know her, but I'm confident that no one has ever given Kasey the protection she deserves.

I grunt in frustration, the wind across the hillside whipping the sound right out of my throat. That stubborn, aqua-eyed woman in the woods has rattled me thoroughly.

She refused to let me help her hike with the kids back up to the cabin. She refused my offer to stay at our ranch until the wolf threat is handled. She even refused to allow me to arrange a vacation rental or a motel in town for her and the kids to stay at for the next few days.

And now, she claims she's leaving, but there was a ring of falsehood even in that. Was what she's told me about the reason for the three of them being up here even the truth? What if I never see her again . . .? That would probably be for the best.

"What is that woman so afraid of?"

Midnight's ears turn back toward me. I lean down and pat his shoulder as a sign of goodwill.

Abraham sees me coming from far away, and his arms lift above his head. His voice is lost in the wind until I almost reach him. His long, gray beard trails across his chest as he fills me in on the latest progress report.

"The boys are with the herd. About two dozen already tried to wander off, so a couple went to round 'em up." His voice is as calm as his demeanor.

My boots thud on the dry grass as I give him a nod. It's typical for one or two riders to have to go after at least a couple of dozen strays to round them up for the night, but given the circumstances, we'd rather the herd stay together even during the daylight.

I hand my horse's reins off to Abraham. "Will you see that he gets fed and watered and brushed down?"

"Sure thing." Abraham leans forward, leading the black gelding back toward our campsite as Vincent and Knox approach from the north.

I pace toward my brothers. They dismount fifty feet from me, walking their horses, leads loose in their hands.

"So are we riding out at dawn to hunt this wolf pack down?" Knox exclaims. He slaps his cap against his thigh. "It's time to show these dogs whose mountain it is." Throwing his head back, he howls at the sky like a wolf.

"You know this isn't a joke, right?" I retort sharply as a greeting, not in the mood for his exaggerated banter, no matter how lightheartedly he means it. "Are you going to take this seriously, or are you going to goof off like you normally do?" Regret for my harsh tone hits me as soon as the words leave my mouth.

Knox is immediately subdued, his chin dropping. "I know it's not a joke. I'm worried about the calves, too, you know. Some of the wolves in that pack could carry them off in a second, and I just want to stop them."

I clap a hand on my brother's shoulder, shaking my head. "I'm sorry. The situation is getting to me, I guess."

Knox gives me a single nod in reply, avoiding eye contact, and as his silence continues, my regret grows.

Vincent draws in a deep breath, lowering his eyes toward the grass, lips pressing together under his dark mustache. The toe of his boot scrapes across the ground, tracing patterns in the grass only he can see. The move is classic Vincent: reserved, thoughtful, and patient.

"More realistically," he breaks the awkward silence, "it seems the best choice we can make here is getting the game warden involved. I say we graze in this pasture for the rest of the day, then move the herd tomorrow when we won't risk losing strays in the dark. We've got enough ammo for a couple of nights, maybe three tops if they get aggressive."

Thoughtfully, I nod. "I'll stay and manage the relocation with you tomorrow. Then I'll ride down and contact Fish and Wildlife. I'll bring up more ammo on the way back." I make a sweeping motion with my hand. "Let's get a perimeter set up and have each head accounted for well before dark. Start a few fires around the camp but watch them. The grass is dry this time of year, and the last thing we need is to start a forest fire on top of all this."

My brothers are silent as I lay out my instructions. When Knox hurries away to relay it to the rest of the team, Vincent walks beside me.

"How did it go?" he asks.

Grimly, I press my lips together and shake my head. "Let's just say it didn't go at all. Something's up with that woman, Vince, and I don't like it. It doesn't matter anyway, because she says she's leaving tomorrow."

There isn't time to go into the details, as we both feel pressured to finish preparations for the rest of the day, and two days go by before I feel we've placed enough distance between ourselves and the immediate wolf threat that I can be spared from the team. I saddle up one of the pack horses, a chestnut gelding, choosing to leave Midnight behind to rest, and gather a fresh canteen of water and some jerky and dried fruit for the ride down the mountain.

It's before noon when I set off, and my pace is brisk as I retrace the path we made as we led the herd up to the high pastures over the summer. We've been running the same pasture route for three years now, steering the cattle clear of any areas where their hooves could damage the delicate ground. It takes us all summer to make our way to the high ground and work our way back around and start the trek down the mountain.

Focused as I have been on managing the cattle and making sure we don't lose another one, I haven't allowed my mind to wander to Kasey and whether she left the mountain like I advised her to. I regret that I didn't ask for her contact information before we parted ways, but I'd rather they were somewhere safe.

The past few days resurface as my mind cycles through the situations troubling me. Darkness creeps at the edges, pressing into the corners of my consciousness. It's not just the threat to the herd that is troubling me. The fate of Kasey, Junior, and Janie lodges like cement in my throat.

They are strangers to me, but I feel an inexplicable need for them to be safe and sound. Whatever the circumstances that brought them here, they are vulnerable and deserve to be protected. But the spikes of anxiety I keep feeling highlight the fact that I'm not in control in this situation.

I'm used to being the one in control, the one everyone turns to for leadership.

If only the flighty woman with the haunted eyes and the wary mistrust would let down her guard long enough for me to protect her . . . to protect them. If only my duty wasn't split between the little family in the woods and my family's legacy. As it is, I feel the weight of responsibilities fulfilled poorly.

As frustration rises in my chest again, I do the only thing I know will calm me. I pray aloud, casting my voice through the trees.

"Father God," I begin, "I feel wedged between a rock and a hard place right now, like I'm being dragged down into a ravine of anxiety and worry I don't know how to get out of. But if I follow Your truth, then I have to stand on the words, 'Whenever I am afraid, I will trust in You.' This isn't about me riding in to save the day just to look like the hero to this woman; this is about Your promises of protection. Please protect Kasey and those kids right now. Please protect my herd from the threat rising against it. Please help me to trust You even—"

The stock horse stumbles on a patch of rocky terrain as we pick our way down, and I refocus as I help guide him along the path. I decide that I've either put this situation in God's hands or I haven't, and my attention needs to be on the biggest problem at hand right now: getting home, restocking our ammo, and dealing with this wolf pack.

The miles take me through the morning and into the afternoon. The hot sun's rays beam overhead by the time I ride across the back pasture leading up to my childhood home. The horse's hide is glistening with sweat, and I'm eager to get him fed, watered, and groomed. Our barnyard comes into view first, then the farmhouse. I didn't feel like pausing to call ahead to warn Mom, so she'll be worried by my sudden arrival, thinking one of us must have had an accident on the range.

She is standing on the back porch as I ride up. "You all right?" she calls.

"Everyone is all right, Mom. Be up at the house in thirty

minutes. You all right?" I return the question.

"Always," she replies.

Reassured, I head straight to the barn and make swift work of grooming and feeding the horse, doing a quick walk-through of the space afterward to check on the rest of the farm animals. My inspection of this season's steers and the bulls on the back pasture will have to wait until evening. They've been finishing for the last few months on grass and forage and are going to market soon, but I already know that Charlie, our ranch foreman, takes looking after them seriously. When I enter the house through the back door, slipping off my dusty boots and leaving them on the porch, I walk into the kitchen in my socks. I'm dog-tired, and my bones ache from riding all day, but the smell of bacon grease and coffee hits my senses and gives me a jolt of energy.

"It's good you came down this week. I have the lodge sale agreement ready for you to look over. But you three are going to need to come down together to sign the paperwork." Mom turns from the stove with a plate just as I walk in. "And I fixed you something to eat. Figured you would be hungry if you've been riding all day." Her face lights up with a smile, even as her familiar dark blue eyes appraise me carefully.

"Starving. Did you have the lawyer look over the paperwork? How have the inspections gone?" I drop into a chair at the worn wooden dining table and dig into the plate of fried eggs, crisp, salty bacon, and warm biscuits lathered with homemade butter and honey she places before me. It's stick-to-your-bones, old-school country food, and I couldn't be happier to have a break from Knox's freeze-dried reheats. He tries, but it's not Mom's cooking.

She slips into the chair across from me, palms wrapped around her own mug of hot coffee. "Of course," she replies. "He says you boys have everything in order on your end, and nothing should prevent the sale from going through. Everything came back as expected with the inspections; there's no structural damage, but cosmetic repairs are needed, of course. And the lift and the ski lanes are a mess. The Lintons just want to get the paperwork signed and the deal closed before the season, so they are pushing to get escrow going."

Last month, when Vincent, Knox, and I decided to pool our savings and invest in Bear Creek Lodge, we underestimated the hoops we'd be required to jump through and the sheer amount of paperwork we'd have to read and sign. Since we've been in the mountains with the herd, things almost fell through until Mom stepped in to be our mediator.

Despite her outwardly calm demeanor, I know she is anxious to hear why I rode down ahead of schedule. Between bites, I fill her in on the situation, and her shoulders visibly lower as her tension eases. I push away the plate when I'm three-quarters of the way through and rise to my feet.

"I've got to give Jeff at Fish and Wildlife a call before it gets any later. Thank you for the food." I lean over and hug her. She is wearing the same comforting scent of lavender that she always does.

"Go," she says, squeezing my hand. "I'll clean up and bring you a fresh cup of coffee."

Jeff Humphreys is the on-call game warden serving the Cascade Valley region. We've had a good working relationship since I took over the ranch, but he answers the phone in his usual gruff manner. I try to impress on him the urgent need for a wildlife assessment and potential investigation into our yearling's death. He grunts and reassures me that they will take our concerns seriously.

After I've answered all his questions and emailed the photographs we took, I hang up and sip the last of the coffee Mom brought me. There isn't much else I can do until morning. I could probably make it back up to the herd by late evening, but I still need to restock our ammo and pack up some nonlethal deterrents we've decided to add to our arsenal of defense against the predators. I glance at the clock. The farm store just closed, so I'll have to wait until morning.

Looking over all the lodge paperwork keeps me occupied until the sun goes down. "You should sleep." Mom sets her hand on my shoulder. "I'll wake you early and have some sandwiches made for your trip back."

"Thanks, Mom."

My bed is already turned down when I enter my room upstairs, with fresh clothes set out and folded, ready to be placed in my pack in the morning. My mother's dedication to her family never ceases to amaze me. A twenty-minute shower later, I collapse onto the bed. I'm dead to the world as soon as my eyelids close.

Ten minutes or ten hours later, a commotion awakens me. It sounds like someone is pounding on wood, then Mom's voice echoes with an urgency that carries up the stairs and pushes me to listen. Lifting my head and still only partially conscious, I struggle to comprehend what is happening. And then I realize that Mom's soft tones aren't the only female voice I hear.

Instantly, I'm awake and on my feet, moving down the hallway and taking the front stairs two at a time. The hair on the back of my neck stands on end, my senses now at full alert. Anyone familiar with country life knows it's either a desperate move or a stupid one to bang on the door of a dark farmhouse at the end of the driveway in the middle of the night. I'm wary of the potential threat. As the foyer comes into view, I see Mom standing at the front door in her robe. It's already cracked open a few inches as she converses with someone standing on our porch.

"Mom, who is at the door?" My voice comes out strong and deep, so our visitor is aware of my presence.

She glances back at me. Stepping aside, she lets the heavy wooden door swing open. "It's for you, Dean." Her surprise and confusion are obvious. "This woman says she knows you and needs help."

As the opening widens, I look over the top of her head, and my heart drops into my feet.

"Dean?" Kasey peers into the house. Her face is as white as a sheet, her wavy hair sweaty and plastered around her face. Janie is passed out on her shoulder, and Kasey looks as if she's about to let the child slip off her hip any second. Her breath comes out in gasps as she speaks. "You said we could . . . if we needed . . . help—"

I spring forward to catch her and the toddler as her eyes go blank, and she crumples to the floor.

Chapter Seventeen

Kasey

There's nothing like the comfort of your own mattress and sheets, everything worn down in just the right places to cradle your aching muscles and tired bones. When I was discharged from the army and handed a lifetime one hundred percent disability assessment from the VA, I bought my cottage, and I bought a new mattress.

In the months since I left the army, both have been a safe haven in their own way. I nestle deeper into the softness now, needing the comfort to ease the throbbing pain in my head. It feels like a railroad spike is being driven through my temple. My upper thigh is throbbing, too. My lungs feel weak, and taking each breath is a struggle. Squeezing my eyes shut, I tell myself I'm just going to stay in bed a while longer before I get up to face another day.

The sound of a woman moaning in pain hits my ears. My eyes crack open in alarm, instincts on high alert. The light from the window across from my bed hits me first, then I catch sight of unfamiliar, buttery gingham curtains studded with tiny blue flowers hanging in front of it. Trying to lift my head, I look around, taking in the sight of a decidedly girlish room that is most definitely not my sparsely decorated bedroom back in Oregon. A feeling of panic spurs me to lift my heavy head. But I can barely turn my neck, and I realize the tortured sound is coming from my own throat as a pain-filled whimper echoes again throughout the space.

With a rush, everything comes into focus. Gasping, I fight to pull myself straight up in the comfortable bed, my thoughts frantically downloading with question after question.

Where are the children? Did Amy come back? Did her husband find us?

My eyes catch on the man a few feet away, and I gasp again, and then my racing heart slows its pace. Dean is sitting on a chair at the end of the bed, one ankle propped across his knee. Finn rises from the rug and strides over, planting his muzzle on the edge of the mattress for me to touch. I reach for my dog, threading my fingers through the soft fur under his ears, all the while staring at Dean as if he is an apparition. I can't deny that the sight of him sends instant relief washing over me.

"Where are we?" I croak out.

Surprise lifts his eyebrows toward his hairline. It's the first time I'm getting a good look at him without a hat, and I stare at the softness of his dark, wavy hair. He's pushed it straight back, and something in the hazy fog of my brain makes me wonder wildly if it would feel as soft as it looks if I ran my hand through it.

"Kasey, you came to my family's ranch," he answers my question.

We made it.

"Thank the Lord you're awake. We've all been praying. How are you feeling?" His voice washes over me with a raspy timbre as he adjusts and leans forward, planting his forearms on his knees.

"Junior? Janie?" I barely manage to groan out their names.

"Mom is taking care of them." His reply is quick, correctly interpreting my desperation. "Janie was running a fever when you arrived, but between Dr. Burke and Mom, they both managed to agree on the proper way to bring it down. It was a pretty bad flu, but she is already on the mend. Junior has been all over the barnyard helping Charlie tend the animals and garden this morning."

He rises, and the movement makes me startle, pressing myself away toward the wall as he approaches the side of the bed. Despite forcing myself to endure the rough-and-tumble life of a soldier, I don't mix well with big men who make quick movements. They remind me too much of my father, an unpleasant association. Finn scuttles to the side as well, watching him warily but with a friendly demeanor that I realize is new.

Dean squats down until he is eye level with me, his expression filled with so much concern that a painful lump rises in my throat. His eyes are so full of compassion and concern that it catches me off guard.

"Don't worry, Kasey," he says. "The kids are safe. You are all safe here."

I want to believe him, but I can't help but remember that there's so much Dean doesn't know. *How can we be truly safe anywhere?*

Pushing away the emotions that his words spark, my voice comes out sharper than I intend. "I don't want the kids left alone with strangers. They will think I abandoned them. I need to get up to take care of them."

But with gentle pressure, his warm hand pushes my shoulder back down to the mattress. At first, I struggle against him, the fight rising up in the center of my chest as he prevents me from getting out of the bed. But I'm too weak, and my efforts are like the pitiful beating of a moth's wings against glass. I collapse, the struggle leaving me with a sudden gasp.

Dean checks my temperature by pressing the underside of his forearm to my forehead, and I feel his fingers gently attach to my wrist as he takes my pulse.

"Just rest," he says. "You've been very sick. And there are no strangers when you are in as tight-knit a community as Cascade Valley."

Aghast, I stare up at him. "How long have we been here?"

He seems satisfied with my temperature, dropping his arm from my forehead. But he doesn't move from the bedside, his warm palm still encircling my wrist. While the unsolicited touch would usually make me feel stifled, in my weakened state, it's strangely comforting.

"You've been fighting a fever and have been pretty out of it for almost two days," he informs me.

My jaw drops in horror at the same moment I realize how thirsty I am. I try to moisten my lips with a tongue that is too heavy and thick. Dean seems to read my thoughts, immediately reaching for a glass with a straw on the nightstand. He holds it to my lips and uses his free hand to help lift my head so I can drink. It drops heavily back to the pillow after I've sipped the water greedily.

"What's wrong with me?" I croak out.

A half-smile twists up Dean's lips. "Just good ol' walking pneumonia. You had a bad case of it."

"How is that possible?" I groan. "I'm healthy. I'm strong. I never get sick. I was in the army, for crying out loud."

"I don't think the army is a magic immunization against ever getting sick again, as tough as I know you G.I. Joe . . . *sephines* are." Despite my misery, the way he phrases it amuses me. "That drafty cabin probably hasn't done you any good," he concludes.

"Hey, don't insult Danny's labor of love like that," I manage to rasp out in protest.

Dean laughs, and I decide it's a singularly pleasant sound, like sitting around the campfire on a perfect summer night, roasting marshmallows and telling stories until the sky dances with starlight.

"Junior seems in perfect health, but Doc almost airlifted Janie to the nearest hospital the night you arrived," he continues.

I gasp and struggle to rise again. "Why didn't you tell me immediately? I must go to her! What hospital is she at? Where are my keys?"

My breathing is ragged with the effort to scoot myself off the bed. I'm panicking not only at the thought of my niece alone and sick in a cold, sterile hospital room but also at the realization of the mess we've just landed ourselves in. There's no way I'll be able to prevent the truth from coming out now. Hospitals mean paperwork, documentation, and questions that demand answers. Answers I can't afford to give.

Everything is lost.

But I'm too weak to rise. I collapse and glare up at Dean as if he is single-handedly keeping me from my niece. I'm prepared to physically fight him if he prevents me from leaving, even though the effort would probably knock me to the floor right now. And realistically, Dean is many times stronger than I. The man could simply scoop me up and prevent me from going anywhere. As desperate as our situation is, maybe there is some way I can avoid the hospital finding out that Janie is one of two children who disappeared in the middle of the night from their home in Greenwich months ago. I know I'm being delusional, but I have to hope.

Please. Help me. Desperately, I hope the plea doesn't fall on deaf ears.

"We've got her. He didn't take her from the house, and Mom hasn't left her side." Dean's voice soothes me as he pulls the soft sheets over me again, his hands gentle as he settles me back against the pillows.

"Who are *we?*" I demand, feeling a desperate need to exert some kind of control over the situation. Tears spark in my eyes as the chaos in my mind intensifies. "Who lives here?"

Dean sinks onto the foot of the bed, his weight pressing the end of the mattress down. His voice is patient. "Right now, just Mom is here full-time. But usually, all of my siblings and I live here."

"And just how many of you are there?" I grumble.

"I've got two brothers and two sisters: Vincent and Knox, Demi and Samantha. My brothers are currently protecting our cattle against that pack of wolves I told you about up there in the mountains." He motions over his shoulder at the dark green peaks rising beyond the window. "Demi works for a modeling agency in New York City, so she doesn't make it home often. And our little sister, Samantha, left a few weeks ago to work for a non-profit adoption agency in Spain. She's our jet-setting, wanderlust-filled, adventurous one."

The corner of his mouth lifts as he smirks at me, his ruggedly handsome face suddenly lighting up with amusement. The impish expression does something to my insides, sending an involuntary ripple through my stomach as Dean continues, "Too bad you weren't around during the summer when she moved home after graduating from college. Something tells me the two of you would get along. It might be your stubborn sass, but I don't know."

"I'm not stubborn," I protest, a wave of exhaustion washing over me. My eyes flutter, their edges filled with gritty sand. I try to stay awake, to gather the strength to go to Janie, but it's a futile struggle.

The last thing I hear is Dean's voice rumbling in my ear as he leans over me to tuck the sheets around my shoulders. "Oh, darlin', you are the very definition of stubborn."

. . .

When I come to again, I'm alone. The room is almost dark, and I can see the last rays of sunset beyond the window. I'm thirsty and a little hungry, my bones are still achy, and my lungs are strained. But I don't feel as if I'm on death's door anymore, so I suppose that's a good sign.

The night we stumbled up to the porch and pounded on the farmhouse's door, I felt like I might not make it. I didn't even know if we were in the right place, but I couldn't drive any farther. Now, I remember how comforted the single golden light shining in the window made me feel, like it had been placed there just to draw me home.

Janie and I had gotten sick so fast. In retrospect, I'm kicking myself for being woefully unprepared for emergencies. I know better. I've been trained to do better. As the fever boiled my insides, and Janie grew fussier, I knew we needed help. All I could think about was getting to the one person I knew would be there for us.

Gingerly, I peel back the sheets. To my surprise, I'm not in the jeans and t-shirt I was wearing a few days ago. They have been replaced with a blue cotton nightgown, the type I remember seeing during late-night binges on shows like *Little House on the Prairie*. My muscles tremble with weakness as I lift myself from the mattress and place my feet on the floor. My lungs are leaden, each breath a struggle.

Finn sits patiently, watching me with alert eyes. If I call to him, he'll be at my side in an instant. But I stand on my own, the nightgown pooling around my ankles. The woman it belongs to must be at least half a foot taller than I, because I have to gather several inches of it in my hand to get it off the ground. I'm swimming in the fabric, but I don't see my own clothes anywhere in the room.

My lungs feel as if they are about to collapse, but I push through, my initial amusement at my new clothing shoring me up for a moment. Then my lips twist into a grimace as the thought of Dean potentially being the one to put me into this getup.

He'd better not have dared. Did he seriously think it was okay to take that kind of liberty with me?

Instantly, I'm annoyed, the emotion giving me a temporary burst of adrenaline, enough to take my first steps. I assure myself he'll be on the receiving end of my wrath if I find out he undressed and redressed me.

Shaking, I take one step at a time as I cross the room to the door. When I pull it open, there's a hallway on the other side. I make my way through the upstairs hallway, pausing frequently to catch my breath as I descend the staircase with painful slowness. Finn paces with me, his big paws matching me step-for-step.

I hear the light, boyish laugh first, followed by a deep, familiar rumble. When I find the living room, Dean and DJ are settled on a comfortable-looking sofa, their eyes glued to the classic cartoon playing on the television screen across the room. A cat chases a mouse, and the story never ends. I lean on the doorframe to watch, my strength already drained.

His body turned toward the doorway, Dean sees me as soon as I enter. His eyes zero in on me, and a flush warms my limbs as the fabric of my borrowed nightgown swims around my legs. Since my dignity is already in shreds, I try to pull myself to my full height and lift my chin as DJ spots me for the first time.

Flinging himself off the sofa, my nephew races to me. "You're awake!" His voice is thick with instant tears. He throws his arms around my waist when he reaches my side, hugging me so tightly I wonder if he'll ever let go.

I register the look on Dean's face as I bend over the little boy and hug him with every ounce of strength I have. We're both crying when we finally release each other. I peer into his face and brush the light brown hair away from his eyes, reminding myself that I should probably give him a haircut before his mom returns and catches him looking like a feral child raised in the backwoods.

"Let me look at you," I exclaim in a raspy voice. "Are you all right?"

DJ nods, tearfully mumbling something about me, being scared, and Janie.

"Where is she?" I lift my head, looking at Dean sharply, my words coming out with an accusatory lilt.

He rises and strides toward us. I keep my expression tight and stern, trying not to flinch as he towers above us. Not surprisingly, in the confines of the charming farmhouse, Dean seems even bigger and more imposing than he is in the great outdoors.

"As I told you, Janie is safe," he reassures me. "How are you feeling?"

"I'm fine," I snap, my heart beginning to pound as my desperation to see my niece with my own eyes builds. "Tell me where Janie is. If you took her away from me without permission . . ."

Dean knows it's an idle threat and doesn't bat an eyelash at my hostile tone. He points in the direction from which I just came. "She's upstairs and at the end of the hallway, tucked into bed, watching cartoons with Mom. We were hoping you could sleep a while longer before bringing her to you."

I glance upward, the thought of making the trek back up the staircase I just descended nearly sinking me to my knees. I barely had the strength to make it down the steps. When I look back at Dean, a look comes over his face. His expression softens.

"Let me help you up to see her," he says.

Feeling a flash of stubbornness, I almost shake my head, but then I relent and take the arm Dean offers. I clasp his tanned forearm, which is warm and sinuous under my fingers. DJ hurries and tries to support me from the other side with my arm thrown around his little shoulder. I only make it to the foot of the staircase before my knees are so shaky they almost give out. I try to lift my foot to place it on the first step but stumble over the hem of the nightgown pooled around my feet instead.

Without a word, Dean bends and scoops me into his arms, lifting me effortlessly off the floor and walking up the stairs. The instant heady rush the movement creates is enough to prevent me from protesting and demanding that he put me down immediately. Frantically, I wrap my arms around his neck and squeeze my eyes shut, clinging to him as the spinning feeling makes me afraid I'm about to tumble to the floor.

When I recover enough to open my eyes, I'm staring straight into his gray-blue pupils, and all I can think is how long and full his dark eyelashes are. The rising protest dies in my throat as I am caught up in staring at him. As if the details of his face are the anchor that will keep me from floating out to sea, I memorize his features and notice there are laugh lines around his eyes when he smiles, his short, dark beard frames his wide, rugged jawline, and his lips are full, covering attractive, pearly teeth. The man is absurdly handsome in the most rugged, Montana cowboy way, and I am sure I currently look like a cave troll.

He speaks, the rumble of his voice buzzing in my chest as he explains apologetically. "If we wait for you to make it up the stairs on your own, the clock will strike midnight before we reach the top. I wouldn't want you to turn into a pumpkin on me." His tone is teasing and light, eliciting an instant laugh from DJ, who trails behind us. I only shake my head, not mad about the effort he saved me.

We're striding down the upstairs hallway, and we've walked through the doorway of a softly lit room before I get my bearings. Janie is sprawled in the middle of a massive four-poster bed, her head on the lap of an older, very pretty, cocoa-haired woman who glances up inquisitively when we enter. A soft smile blossoms across the woman's mouth, and instantly, I know this is Dean's mother. She lifts her pointer finger to her lips and indicates that we should be quiet.

I realize Janie is fast asleep as Dean carries me over and places me gently against the pillows next to my niece. My heart pounds as I stare at her chubby, baby cheeks for a moment, my eyes darting up again a second later, full of questions and worry. The soft glow of the bedside lamp reveals a pair of familiar eyes regarding me from across the mattress.

"She fell asleep again about half an hour ago," Mrs. McCade whispers, "but her fever hasn't come back. She's got a bit of a cough, but she'll be up and chasing the chickens around the yard in no time. So don't worry; your baby is going to be fine."

Her smile draws me in, and my heart feels as if it drops ten pounds as relief floods through it. She knew exactly what I needed to hear, and I'm filled with immense gratitude as I smooth a hand across Janie's forehead, caressing her soft brown curls.

"Thank you," I breathe, unable to choke out more at the moment.

DJ clambers onto the foot of the bed to join us.

"It seemed touch and go there with you for a bit," the older woman continues. "How are you feeling?"

"Better but weak," I admit, glancing between her and Dean. "I'm sorry we put you through so much trouble. Please let us know how we can repay you."

She smiles again. "Not an ounce of repayment is necessary, darlin'. How's your appetite? Do you think you could eat a bowl of chicken noodle soup?"

"I think I could eat a little bit," I reply, and she slides off the bed, moving with quick, smooth strides across the floor.

"Why don't you three share this room tonight?" she calls back over her shoulder in a soft tone. "That'll give me a chance to get your room cleaned up, and I think this mattress is more comfortable than the one in Samantha's old room anyway."

The mattress on the four-poster bed is like a cloud. I sink into it gratefully, her gentle motherliness stifling any instinct I feel to protest. I haven't had a mother for a long, long time. For just this once, I have a bizarre willingness to let her take care of us. Against my better judgment, I admit how safe this old farmhouse feels. It's as if within its friendly walls, there's a peace and a stillness I've never experienced before. Though I know I should keep my guard up and get us out of here before our secret gets discovered, I find myself wishing with wistful angst that we could stay here forever.

Dean starts to follow his mother out of the room but pauses, his broad shoulders filling up the doorway. "You three rest up for the next couple of days. I have to leave at first light to check on my cattle, but I'll be back in a few days. Kasey, will you and the kids be here when I get back?"

He stayed to make sure we were okay. The realization hits hard. His eyes study me so intently, I wonder if he can see into my soul. I nod once, unsure if I'm telling the truth. I know we shouldn't stay for long, but I don't want to disappoint or lie to the man who has been so kind to us. I've already kept the truth from him about so many things. My stomach twists with guilt at the same time it thrums with gratitude.

He studies me a moment longer, then mirrors my single nod. "Good. When I return, I want to sit down with you and have a conversation."

And then the doorway is empty, and the guilt twists painfully in my stomach a little bit more.

Chapter Eighteen

Dean

In the darkness at four in the morning, I'm not enthusiastic about saddling up the chestnut gelding again after being grounded for three days at the ranch. My reluctance to leave is unlike me, and I know it's all due to the petite, golden-haired firecracker currently sleeping upstairs in my mother's bed.

At least, I hope she is sleeping. If Kasey needs anything right now, it's rest and a few solid meals. She was as light as a feather when I carried her up the stairs last night, the hem of my sister's ridiculously long nightgown trailing over my arm, her slender arms clinging tightly to my neck. As if I would ever let her slip out of my grasp. She's leaned out since I first caught her at the fishing hole, and the hollows under her eyes have deepened. Whether that's due to scarce resources, stress, fear, or all three, I'm unsure.

Hopefully, though, by the time I make sure the herd hasn't been decimated by the wolf pack and return to the ranch, Mom will have fattened her up a little on biscuits and gravy, rich quiche made from our farm-fresh eggs, and homemade huckleberry pie, the pastry filled to bursting with the ripe berries Mom picks warm from the bushes and tops with vanilla ice cream churned from butter-yellow cream from our milk cow.

If anything can tempt a woman as flighty as Kasey to stick around, maybe Mom's cooking can do the trick. Whatever has spooked that woman and made her think she has to fight all her battles alone, I'm determined to find out what it is.

I want to stay with her, but right now, my duty is to my herd.

Riding back to the range today is a strategic choice. Mom and I have had several intense conversations the past couple of days, in between Dr. Burke's visits, entertaining Junior, and pacing the hallway outside Kasey and Janie's sick rooms. We've agreed that the best thing for Kasey is to feel safe while she recovers. Dr. Burke has us on strict orders to make sure that she and Janie rest undisturbed. Plus, Mom thinks that she'll have a better chance of getting the wary woman to let her guard down if it's just the two of them—woman to woman.

"There are walls ten feet thick built all around that woman, but she seems like a sweetheart," Mom murmured to me last night after we descended the stairs and sat in the living room together, our three guests fast asleep in her room. Her quick intuition isn't a surprise. "There's no telling what trauma she's been through to drive her that deep into the woods. She's not at peace; that's plain as day. But she sure loves those children."

As I ride across the back pasture toward the gate that leads up the mountain, I pray for protection to surround my ranch and a peace like the stillness of a quiet mountain brook to touch all who are within its borders.

As I ride, I make a quick call. The sun hasn't even begun to rise, but I know my friend will be awake. I don't think he has slept much the past few weeks . . . not since Samantha left for Spain.

"Hey, are you good?" I ask by way of greeting when Caleb answers on the second ring.

His voice is weary but light. "I'd be better if you weren't calling me in the middle of the night while I'm trying to sleep."

"Finally working to improve that haggard, hangdog look you've been sporting lately, huh?"

"Not all of us get to go camping all summer, roasting 'mallows and singing campfire songs with our buddies. Some of us actually put in hard work."

Our ribbing is all good-natured. Caleb Kane owns the Arabian horse breeding operation down the road. He's only a couple of miles away, and I've counted on him many a time to keep an eye on my family's ranch while we're away with the herd over the summers.

We've been friends for many years, as both of us spent most of our youth in Cascade Valley, but it wasn't until the past couple of months that our friendship reached another level. During the summer, I discovered that Caleb has been secretly harboring a slow-burning flame for Samantha for a few years. But ever since we lost our dad while he was riding a spirited colt that came from Caleb's ranch, my sister has declared that she despises Caleb and will never stop blaming him for the tragedy. They didn't speak for years.

I never thought the two of them would reconcile, but a secret romance blossomed between them when Samantha offered to coordinate the marketing program for Caleb's charity summer horse camp. We were all shocked when we discovered their budding courtship.

When she chose to break off their relationship and follow

through with her plans to move to Spain, it crushed him.

"Will you keep an eye on the ranch the next couple of days?"

My tone turns from lighthearted to serious. "We have some unexpected guests, and I want to make sure Mom knows she has backup if she needs it."

"I'll make my presence known. Everything okay?" Caleb's tone shifts with mine.

"All good for now. Just taking precautions."

"Roger that. See you when you get back?"

"See you then."

We end the call, and I concentrate on leading the chestnut gelding up the slope as I wonder what I will find when I reach my team.

. . .

Three days ago, in the chaotic hours that followed Kasey's sudden arrival, it became obvious that I wouldn't be going anywhere anytime soon. I put in a call to one of our on-again-off-again ranch hands, Ian Summers. The young cowboy was more than willing to ride up and let my brothers know that a situation was holding me up in the valley, and I'd be up as soon as I could.

I instructed him to reassure them that the situation had nothing to do with our mother or the ranch but was something that required my attention. He also carried up the restock of ammo and nonlethal prevention methods I'd intended to bring.

Ian's lanky figure sitting astride a tall, gray horse is the first thing I see as I crest the ridge hours later and spot the grass-fattened shapes of our cattle spread across the meadow. The fact that I didn't see any mutilated cow bodies along the trail as I rode up already put me at ease, but I feel another weight come off my shoulders at the calm sight before me. Due to my early start this morning, the sun is still high in the sky as I ride down the slope. Ian spots me from afar and lifts his arm in greeting, his shout alerting the rest of the team to my arrival.

Vincent and Knox break off from the rest of the riders, urging their mounts into a gallop as they thunder across the grass. They meet me halfway. Before he even speaks a word, I see the annoyance on Knox's face. He throws up his hands as they approach.

"Fine time to go off and take some R and R," he calls, his tone gruff. "I know you're the boss and all, Dean, but we need all hands on deck right now."

I stare at him, resisting the urge to snap back in response to his unexpected attack. When I look at Vincent, he's watching the two of us with his typically impenetrable expression. I already know he won't get involved unless it gets physical. After a moment, I manage to grind out, "R and R? Didn't Ian fill you in?"

His eyes cut back toward the man in question. "Yeah? That some situation with a woman had you tied up at home. She must have been really pretty to leave your brothers hanging for three days just to go on a date."

His sarcasm triggers my ever-present guilt, the weight of the responsibility I bear toward our family's legacy rising in my throat like bile. Instantly, I realize what the team must have thought of my unexpected absence, and I know this isn't the moment to let my pride prevent me from making things right.

"Knox, I'm sorry," I apologize. "I should have made sure you and the team were better filled in on what was going on. A friend and her kids had an emergency, and I stayed behind to make sure they got through it okay. I promise you that shirking my responsibilities here wasn't intentional, and my presence was genuinely required."

His dark blue eyes inspect me thoroughly, as if assessing the sincerity of my words. I see the moment he relents. "At least tell me Mom sent you up with pastries?"

I hand over my saddlebag. "She sent a bunch of stuff. Why don't you take it to the rest of the team? And don't worry. I'm on dinner duty tonight."

"Darn straight you're on dinner duty. Least you could do," he retorts, but I'm relieved to hear a smile underneath his words. His horse gives a little jump when he taps its flank. "I expect to be filled in on all the juicy details about your girlfriend later."

"She's not my girl—"

But he's already gone. Vincent lingers with me, our horses ambling toward the herd.

"You good?" he says in a mild tone.

"Yeah. Fish and Wildlife make it up here yet?"

Vincent replies in the affirmative and fills me in on their visit. Since I'd called Jeff several times while I was grounded on the ranch, I'm already aware that two conservation agents were sent up a day and a half after I first informed him of the issue. My brother informs me that when they arrived, he did his best to show them the evidence of the pack's presence, but the skeletal remains of our yearling were thoroughly picked over. They hadn't seen or heard from the agents again, and ever since we moved the cattle farther away, there hadn't been any further attacks during the night.

"Are you going to fill me in on what kept you in the valley for three days?" he finally asks, and I catch his inquisitive glance in my direction.

"That woman at the fishing hole, the one I told you has been staying in Danny's cabin . . . she showed up at the house the night

I arrived. She was sick, and one of her kids had a fever. They are finally on the mend now, though, so I figured I could be spared to come back. Mom will work her magic to help them recover."

Normally not one to break his cool, calm demeanor, this news catches my brother by surprise. He sits up straighter in the saddle, his voice turning gruff and disapproving. "You mean this family is there now, staying alone with Mom? Dean, what if she's—"

"She isn't," I cut him off quickly before he accuses Kasey of anything nefarious. "If you saw this woman, you'd know immediately, Vince. She's guarded and suspicious and scared-to-death to let anyone get near her, but she's no danger to Mom. Besides, Charlie is on the property most days, and I called Caleb to ask him to keep an eye on things until I return."

Vincent scrubs a hand through the scruff on his face, smoothing down his dark mustache, slightly mollified. "When are you headed back?"

"I'll stay a couple of days and go back to check on things," I reply. "Will you be able to hold down the fort here? I think Ian will stay and take my place for a bit."

"You got a real interest in this woman beyond neighborly kindness?" One of my brother's eyebrows lifts as he studies me thoughtfully.

"Well, she certainly is easy on the eyes." I grin despite myself. "It's not just that she's attractive, though. There's something about her and those kids that I strongly feel I'm meant to protect. She needs peace more than anyone I've ever met. Yet, her fears haven't diminished her fire. She's like a wounded doe that is cornered but still puts herself between the threat and her fawns despite the odds stacked against her. And something just seems . . . off about the whole story of how she and those kids ended up there."

Vincent's eyes sharpen. "Do you suspect her of something illegal?" He grimaces. "Or do you think she's avoiding an abusive ex? Especially considering she has kids . . ."

I shake my head. "I don't think it's anything illegal. She's a veteran. I can't see this woman being involved in a crime." I shrug, knowing it sounds like I'm inserting myself too much into a stranger's life, but I'm unable (or unwilling) to back off. "It certainly could be an ex, but I don't get the feeling that's it. Whatever it is, I'm going to get to the bottom of it before she up and disappears on me."

My brother nods. "Do what you have to do. But, Dean, be careful. Don't get hurt yourself in the process."

My horse trots alongside his until we part ways to take our respective posts around the herd. "Believe me, I'm trying not to."

Chapter Nineteen

Kasey

The temptation to pile all our things into the Jeep and run far, far away almost chokes me a dozen times over the next couple of days.

As Janie fusses and DJ runs wild across the barnyard with the older man who helps out around the ranch, I'm still too short of breath to do much more than keep my niece entertained. But I feel my strength returning as the hours tick by. Whatever elixirs and tinctures and warm, comforting drinks Mrs. McCade keeps bringing up to me seem to be working their magic.

If only she could heal my troubled heart, too, while she is at it. Our hostess tends to us like we are valued guests instead of the sickly pests that I know she must secretly think we are. I can barely handle the guilt I feel deep in the pit of my stomach.

Guilt for abandoning my duty to Amy years ago and letting her marry that piece of garbage husband in the first place.

Guilt for not going to the authorities immediately after my sister disappeared and pushing them to do something to prevent my brother-in-law from getting out of prison, then tracking her down and convincing her to return.

Guilt for housing my niece and nephew in an old, drafty cabin.

Guilt that they've probably been bored and longing for their real mother for months.

Guilt that I've withheld the truth from the one man who has tried to protect us with such kindness. And now, we're taking advantage of his mother as well.

I'll never be able to repay either of them for their generosity, and when they find out the truth or I disappear with the kids again—whichever comes first—they'll regret everything they've done for us.

Dr. Burke stops by a few times to check on us. He's a kindly man, middle-aged, and just the sort of person I'd expect to see practicing medicine in a small Montana town. In addition to medicine, he prescribes a dose of sunshine and my feet on the grass, plus plenty of warm, nourishing broths and tea.

On the second day, I feel strong enough to sit outside on the front porch with Mrs. McCade—or Emma, as I learn is her name. Finn stretches at my feet, ignoring the happy-go-lucky border collie named Shadow who keeps bouncing around the yard, trying to tempt him to play. Instead, my faithful dog refuses to leave my side for even an instant.

Janie is well enough to sit with us, and she insists upon Emma holding her, which she does, cradling her on her lap and talking softly to her the way I imagine a loving grandmother would. Not that I have any precedent to know what that is like. My mother was never on speaking terms with her own mother, and I never met my father's mother, since he didn't take my existence seriously enough to make the effort.

The sight of Emma and Janie together makes an unwelcome lump rise in my throat. I look away and stare toward the mountains, their dark shapes promising to hide me from all the emotions I've been feeling lately. In the woods, it's just you and nature and the will to survive. It's easy to hide from the things that are too painful to look at. But here on this idyllic farmhouse porch, with its worn wicker furniture and charming swing hanging from the ceiling, I'm exposed. I've got nowhere to hide from the feelings that threaten to crush me.

As much as I've grown to love DJ and Janie, I am not foolish enough to kid myself into believing I'll ever have children of my own. Before I joined the army, I realized that a husband, a family, and children couldn't be in the cards for me. There's still too much scar tissue from my dad's brutal childhood abandonment for me to ever be vulnerable enough to trust a man and marry him, let alone birth innocent children that I could fail and disappoint.

And who am I kidding? The army not only shaped me, it broke me. I went into it as an angry young woman with no sense of purpose, ready to prove my right to exist in this world. I came out a broken woman, battered and bruised, with the physical, mental, and emotional scars to prove it. I am convinced that bringing children into this world would pass my brokenness down to another generation, and I'm not willing to do that.

But the sight of the kind and gentle woman before me sparks a feeling I'm not quite sure what to do with. It makes me wonder how my own mother fares. It's been years since we've spoken. She blamed me for Dad leaving; I blamed her because he never came back. Inexplicably, I feel an urge to call her just to hear the voice I remember.

"It wasn't him, by the way." Emma's voice breaks into my thoughts. When I turn to look at her, she continues, "The nightgown. It wasn't my son who dressed you in it. I just thought you would want to know." Her grin reminds me of Dean's impish expressions.

"Oh." Instantly, I blush, the heat scorching my cheeks. I've been in countless barrack showers, intrusively examined by dozens of doctors, had multiple surgeries, and lived in a zero-privacy battlefield for months on end, but the idea of Dean slipping a nightgown over my head is too much for me to bear. "That's kind of you to tell me. I didn't know what to think, and then I forgot to ask."

Her eyes regard me kindly. "You were sweating so profusely, and the items needed a good wash, so I took the liberty of giving you something more comfortable, and my daughter would have told me to lend it to you."

She's being polite. Laundry at the cabin has been more challenging than I expected, even with buckets, soap, and creek water. The clothes needed more than a good wash. The other night, when she brought up a bowl of the most delicious and comforting chicken noodle soup I've ever tasted, my clothes, soft and fragrant with laundry soap, had accompanied it. I have to admit I was tempted to stay in the cotton nightgown but decided a trip-and-fall-down-the-stairs scenario on the too-long hem would be a disaster I couldn't afford.

"It was very comfortable," I admit. "I've seen pictures of your family around the house. Your daughters are beautiful."

Her sons are exceptionally handsome, too, but I'm not about to admit that out loud. There are three brothers, just like Dean said. There's a dark-haired brother who looks close to Dean's age with a mustache and the kindest, navy blue eyes I've ever seen. And there is a brother who looks to be in his early twenties, all goofy and floppy, with a wide grin and eyes bearing hints of stormy green mixed in with their blue, his expression giving away that he is perpetually pulling the funniest pranks ever devised. And then there is Dean, his smooth beard and gray-blue gaze always a comforting anchor. He looks so much like the woman before me, except he oozes a strong, confident masculinity that I wasn't sure I liked at first. But now, despite how much he's tried to meddle, I associate Dean's protective demeanor with a sensation of safety that I've never really experienced before. It's new and unfamiliar but not unwelcome. Even in the short time I've known him, he's unlike any man I've crossed paths with in all my life, except perhaps Danny Gardener. I've known good men and bad men and men who fell somewhere in between, but I've never met one like Dean.

He is one of the good ones; of that, I'm sure. There is something about him that says he would move heaven and earth to protect the people under his care.

A light turns on in Emma's eyes at my compliment. "That they are."

I feel timid asking my next question. "How old are they all?"

"Dean is the oldest; he's almost thirty-three. Vincent is also in his early thirties, Demi is twenty-eight, Knox is twenty-four, and Samantha is only fifteen months younger."

So Dean and I are over three years apart, I have time to muse before she continues, "I am very proud of the treasures Dan and I raised. Dan is . . . was my husband," she adds in response to my confused expression.

There isn't any Mr. McCade around the farmhouse; that much I know. "What happened to him, if you don't mind me asking?" I venture.

Her face falls, and her voice grows thick. "Several years ago, Dan was out checking fences on a young colt he was training for the ranch. We think a snake may have spooked the horse. We found Dan later that day in the field, and he was already gone."

"I'm so sorry," I murmur. It doesn't feel as if there is anything else I could say that would be sufficient for such a great loss.

Tears glisten in her eyes, but she smiles. "We still miss him every day, but we know it wasn't goodbye. It was only see-you-later."

I don't know what to say in response to this statement, so I watch DJ happily swinging in the tree just beyond the porch. Of course, I believe in heaven, but the idea of deserving to go there when this life is over is foreign to me.

"Junior seems to be loving farm life," Emma breaks the silence a moment later.

I nod, my lips twisting up in a half-smile. "Every little boy's dream."

We fall into silence again as a mounting sense of worry takes root in my stomach. We may be emerging from our valley of sickness thanks to the kindness of unexpected friends, but a mountain of obstacles still rises formidably before us. Not only do I have to make decisions about our future, but I can't think of any place where we are better hidden than Cascade Valley. Leaving puts us at greater risk, but do we have a choice? I have no legal ties to the valley. It's as out of the way as one could get. I haven't used a bank card or checked my email since we arrived. Even my personal cell phone is turned off, battery removed and locked away in my bag. There aren't many people in my life who would call anyway, and if I never return their calls, it isn't that unusual for me.

My only connection to technology or the outside world is the gray cell phone that sits in my pocket, waiting for the day another text message or a call comes through.

And of course, there is the small matter of my brother-in-law's release from prison. I've had no opportunity to check the internet to see if he's still awaiting parole. He isn't powerless from behind bars by any means, but it would be a small modicum of comfort to ensure he isn't moving about free in the world. The only problem is: I don't know if he has a way to monitor who searches for him online. Can someone do that? It seems like something I've watched on a crime investigation show at some point, flagging searches and tracking their IP addresses. Would searching for Dmitry Valkov risk leading him straight to our door?

Despite the danger, I realize I have to try. I need to know what we're facing if we surface in the real world again.

"I need to run an errand tomorrow." My words break the cicada-filled evening air before I can stop them. "Would you be able to watch the children for a couple of hours until I return?"

Emma glances at me. There's a question in her eyes, but she nods without hesitation. "Of course, dear. It would be my pleasure, but are you sure you feel up to it? You're still recovering, you know."

"I'll be fine," I reply. I'm not fully back to my old self, but I will force myself to do what I need to do. "I appreciate everything you've done for us, Emma. I appreciate everything you and Dean have done." I can't make sense of the hot flush that seems to rush across my cheeks every time I say his name.

"We wouldn't have it any other way," Emma reassures me. "You've got two really precious charges here," she nods toward DJ and Janie, "and whatever you need from us—no matter how big or small—I want you to ask. Promise?"

I could never ask them to do more than they've done. But I don't know what else to do except promise and reassure her several times that I won't hesitate to seek their help again if we find ourselves in need.

"I don't know why the two of you have been so nice to me." I lower my gaze and wonder how much Dean has told her about the circumstances of our meeting. "You had to think I was crazy, banging on your door in the middle of the night."

Emma's expression reflects her curiosity. "I was startled at first—country folk don't get a lot of middle-of-the-night visitors---but Dean knew you immediately, and then it was all hands on deck to get you two better." She cuddles Janie closer, my niece's head relaxed against her chest as she sucks her thumb. Emma continues, "I have been curious, though, what made you come to the ranch in the first place?"

That horrible night flashes through my memory. "I just didn't know where else to go." My face pales with regret. "I don't know if you are aware that I was an army combat medic." Emma shakes her head. "I've got the training . . . I should have known what to do . . . I should have seen the signs. But when Janie fell sick and then I did," I shiver, "I just drove down the mountain and hoped and prayed. Dean told me his family's ranch was the first property at the base of the hill, and I thought if I could just make it here . . ."

"I'm so glad you decided to take the chance." Emma smiles at me. Her hand stretches out. "We're here for you, Kasey, for anything you need."

I feel the lump in my throat rising again.

Chapter Twenty

Dean

"Where is she?" My voice is agitated as I step into the farmhouse and see Mom at the sink scrubbing a basket of carrots.

She glances over her shoulder, a smile lighting up her face. "There you are, darling. I wondered if we'd see you today. Did you already groom your horse?"

"Where is she?" I ask again.

Midnight is currently in the backyard tied to the post on the back porch. When I rode up and saw that the Jeep Kasey drove to our ranch the other night wasn't parked in the yard, my heart dropped into my boots. There will be time for grooming after Mom answers my question.

She turns, wiping her hands on a towel. "Do you mean Kasey?"

"Yeah. Where are the kids?"

When she walks away, I follow her into the living room. At

first, I don't see anyone, even though the television is on and playing a cartoon. Then I spot Junior and Janie, cuddled together on the sofa, their eyes focused on the show. The relief is palpable but short-lived. Kasey has been on my mind since I left the other morning. I can't get her out of my head.

The fear that Kasey would take off and run as soon as I was out of range nagged at me for days. I expected to come home to find her gone like a puff of smoke dissipating into the atmosphere. And somehow, I've been in doubt that she would head back to the cabin. I've been around enough wild animals to recognize when something is going to run for its life.

The prospect of losing sight of her sent my brain into immediate overdrive, and I'm startled to realize that the thought dominating my consciousness is: *I'm not about to lose someone who belongs to me.*

Except she's not mine, and I need to get myself under control.

I lean against the doorframe, trying to calm my breathing and rein in my reaction. Her children are safe and sound under my roof. Her missing car triggered my fear, but it's going to be okay.

The thought of Kasey abandoning them never even crosses my mind.

"Kasey went into town about half an hour ago," Mom says, walking back to her task. "She said she won't be more than an hour or two."

Walking through the kitchen, I grab my hat off the table where I threw it when I walked in the door. "I'm going to take the truck and run an errand, Mom. Be back soon."

I don't give her the chance to answer me. Making quick work of grooming, feeding, and stabling Midnight, I give the horse a final pat on the shoulder and grab a pair of keys hanging on the hook in the tack room. Forty minutes after arriving home, my dusty boots are pressing the accelerator to the floorboard as the truck roars down our old country road. I barely glance at the white gate that leads to Caleb's ranch when I pass it. I keep my eyes on the road, alert for whitetail deer and elk crossing the asphalt.

For the sake of the sheriff, who would have a heart attack if he saw the truck hurtling down the road at the speed of light, I slow down when I get within a mile or two of Cascade Valley. The town pops up around the bend. There are plenty of new houses going up on the outskirts, but my guess is that I'll find Kasey in the center of town, where the majority of the major shops and wilderness supply outfitters are located. If she's planning to make a run for it, I imagine she'll need to restock her supplies.

Cutting to the right, I park the truck in the first open space I see on Main Street. Throwing it in park, I'm out and striding down the street before the engine has stopped. But I grind to a halt on the sidewalk a second later, my head on a swivel, eyes darting between the grocery store, the mountaineering shop, and the outdoor supply chain store that took up residence in Ammon's Gun Shop when they moved up the street to a bigger facility last year. She could be in any of them, and chances are I'd pick the wrong one and miss her completely.

I'm frozen in indecision when, by pure chance, I catch sight of her golden blonde locks and the muted colors of her olive green cargo pants and basic black t-shirt as she slips through the doorway of the internet cafe that has somehow survived the evolution of the internet and cell phone technology and managed to stay alive in town. It was a useful place to frequent fifteen years ago when we didn't even have dial-up at the ranch, and it seems to have been useful to Kasey today as well. She is headed up the street in the opposite direction, her head bent, a baseball cap pulled low over her eyes, her focus on the piece of paper in her hand rather than the sidewalk.

I cross to the other side, making my way toward her and gaining ground as my longer, faster strides overtake her short, hesitant ones, her slight limp noticeable today. I get a look at the paper over her shoulder and see a jumble of words and numbers, but before I can identify any of them, Kasey looks back and jumps. Immediately, she shoves the piece of paper into her pocket, the troubled expression on her face wiping itself clean. In less than a second, she goes from petite, fragile, and visibly disturbed to sturdy, stone-faced, and fearless. She even seems to grow an inch or two as she pulls her back up ramrod straight.

"Are you following me?" she demands before I can get out a word, her tone surly and unwelcoming. Her stance is wide-legged, as if she expects me to attack her, and she is determined to stand her ground.

I didn't expect her to be thrilled that I showed up in town, but this reaction is more than I bargained for. To put her at ease, I raise my palms to chest height and grin down at her, leaning back against a post as I do. "Fancy running into you here. Did you find what you were looking for back there?" I tilt my head toward the internet cafe. Her eyes narrow.

"How did you know where I was? Aren't you supposed to be way up in the mountains babysitting a bunch of cows?" She tries to hide her suspicion with dripping sarcasm, but I see how she shifts on the balls of her feet, and her eyes dart around to look for an escape.

"That's really boiling it down to a nutshell there." My tone matches her sarcasm, and I think the shift startles her.

The grin stays on my face as I push off the post and take a step in her direction. She matches my step with a backward one of her own. Archery season has just started in Montana, so the street is full of tourists and hunters milling about. It's noisy and impossible to have a private conversation without shouting. I move toward Kasey, using my approach to maneuver her into a small alcove between shops where the noise is partially blocked, and we can have our conversation with a degree of privacy. Fortunately, I don't see anyone I know walking down the sidewalk. To onlookers, we probably look like a man and a woman staring deeply into each other's eyes. Which we are, except hers are full of defiant fire, and mine are growing increasingly serious behind my amusement.

"What are you doing?" she hisses.

I lift my arm and lean it against the brick wall above her head. She's backed into a literal corner, and I'm pressing in, holding her there but also shielding her from the view of the rest of the street.

"What are *you* doing, Kasey?" I counter. "If you needed to use a computer, we have one sitting in the kitchen at home. You can use it anytime."

The rosy color drains from her cheeks, sharpening their edges. Her eyes are too bright, too intense an aqua even in the shade. I stare at them in fascination as she stares back at me with wary apprehension.

"I . . . I just—" Something comes over her features. She quivers once and gathers herself, her expression clearing.

She starts to continue, but I'm almost leaning down to her level, so our noses are only inches apart. Our breath mingles. It would be a vulnerable moment if not for so much tension crackling in the space between us. I see the labored rise and fall of her chest, and I forget why we're here.

"I just came into town for a few supplies and wanted to look something up. I didn't even think about using the computer at your house because it's not *my* house, Dean. Some of us have boundaries."

Her words barely register, caught up as I am studying the details of her exquisite face. Before I can catch myself, my eyes dart down to her lips. They are parted slightly as her words fade. Though the color has drained from the rest of her face, her full lips are a deep pink, smooth and soft, standing in sharp contrast to the rest of her skin. My gaze lingers on them for a moment, forgetting that she's still getting over walking pneumonia, and that probably accounts for her haunted look. When I glance back up, I'm glad to see her glare of angry suspicion has been replaced by a startled shyness. Suddenly, I don't care to talk about her computer usage anymore.

"I just want to know if you and the kids are in danger." The words thrum in my throat.

"But that isn't any of your business," she hums back, her voice throaty and rich.

Drawn as if by a magnetizing force, I lean down a little more, closing the space between us. She looks startled but doesn't back away. "And what if I want to make it my business?" I murmur, locking her gaze with mine.

Her head gives an emphatic shake, her eyes darting between mine with frantic energy. "Dean, please. There are things . . . circumstances . . . I can't . . . Keeping the kids safe is my only priority." She stumbles over the words.

"You don't have to protect them alone. Tell me what you are so afraid of. What were you looking for back there?" I motion toward the cafe.

She closes her eyes, fluffy lashes fluttering over her cheeks. She's vulnerable, and we both know it. Ever since I stumbled across her at the fishing hole, she's been equal parts frightened deer and ferocious wolf, coming at me with both softness and strength. But I feel the call of every masculine instinct within me, telling me to protect her and set her free from her fears.

When she reopens her eyes, I see the look of steel has returned to their depths. She shutters her expression, placing her hands on my chest with a gentle but firm pressure. Immediately, I step back and let her pass. She walks out a few steps in front of me, and I catch the telltale protrusion of a concealed handgun under her shirt against her back, the fabric just loose enough on her slim frame to hide it. The sight of it startles me, though I'm carrying too. Taking a gun everywhere is a force of habit from ranch and mountain life because you never know when danger will strike. A lot of the women carry around here, but something about the fact that Kasey feels she needs her gun even in the middle of sleepy, peaceful Cascade Valley sets off alarm bells in my head. I file the information away as she swings around to face me.

"You're wrong," she insists. "As much as I appreciate your concern, this is something I have to do alone. Things are at stake that I can't reveal. Please . . . just accept that this is the road I must walk."

I shake my head, and she looks ready to bolt. But instead of running, she stands on the sidewalk, staring up at me. I realize I'm going to lose her if I can't show her that she can trust me. Sighing, I reach down and cover her hand with my own, twining her fingers with mine. To my surprise, she doesn't pull away.

"Fine," I sigh, although this most certainly isn't over. "We'll table this discussion for now. Come with me. I want to show you something."

I think she is too startled by my sudden pivot to protest. Despite her slight limp, she trots along next to me as I keep her hand tucked securely in mine.

"Are you planning to just drag me around town all afternoon against my will?" she grumbles. "Wait, why are we going to the gun store?"

We've crossed the street and are approaching the large, standalone building that houses Ammon's Gun Shop. The business moved last year when it became obvious that Cascade Valley is going to keep growing. They added an indoor shooting range and a wider selection of hunting weapons. Kasey tries to slow me down, digging in her heels on the snow-worn pavement.

"If you are going to carry that thing around my town, I want to see for myself that you can use it," I say in reply to her question.

"What are you talking about?" she sputters. "What thing?

I stop just before we get to the door and reach around to her back like I'm pulling her in for a hug. My hand descends lightly on the handgun, and her face instantly goes pale. The defiant expression dims.

"I support your right to carry, and I think every woman should," I say in a low tone only her ears can hear. "But I'm thinking of my mom, not to mention Janie and Junior. You're going to show me that you can handle that weapon, or I'll have to ask you to keep it in your Jeep until you and the kids leave."

"You didn't seem to care at the cabin," she protests.

I remain silent, watching her with an open expression. It isn't a trap. Gun safety is something to be taken seriously. She stares up at me with a mixture of discomfort, anger, and . . . something else. I see when surrender hits her, a tired look washing over her features.

"Fine," she snaps. "Let's go, then. But you're going to show me how *you* handle *your* weapon, too, so *I* feel comfortable having *you* in the house around *my* kids." She emphasizes each pronoun sarcastically, each word a finger in my chest. Then she leans forward, her arm slipping around my back, her hand clamping onto the handle of the weapon tucked into my holster belt. Her movement is so quick that my arm is trapped and still looped around her back. And all at once, we're frozen, locked in an embrace neither of us expected. I stare down at her, and something passes through her eyes as she looks up at me. It's the most tension-filled hug I've ever experienced.

Abruptly, Kasey pulls herself away, yanking open the door. I follow her into the building, the cool air a relief against the simmering emotion that was building outside. The men behind the counter greet me warmly and give me grief for the length of time since my last visit. I get us set up for a stall, purchase some extra rounds, and we proceed without speaking toward the rear of the building.

The range is full, even at this random time of day. The sharp retort of gunfire accompanies us down the line. We find an empty space, and I hand her a pair of goggles and ear protection. Kasey takes them from me. Her lips are set in a straight line, the skin around her eyes drawn and shadowed. She's angry that I implied I don't trust her with a weapon in my house, but that isn't even the case. If my suspicions are correct and she is afraid, I'd rather know she can handle herself than worry about hurt feelings. Feelings won't protect you in a fight.

At our station, she widens her stance and crosses her arms, staring defiantly up at me with a look that dares me to question her again.

"You first." Her tone says I'd be better off not arguing.

Obliging her willingly, I go through the steps of preparing to shoot the target. Drawing the handgun out from behind my back, I rack the slide to release the bullet in the chamber, then go through the process of releasing the magazine and reloading the clip. With Kasey just to my rear, I send the paper target the farthest distance away, move my legs far enough apart to steady myself, raise my arm, adjust my sight line, take aim, and fire.

I unload the clip into the target, centering all but one of my shots. I put the last round through the target's left eye socket.

When the target returns, Kasey and I step forward to inspect it. My spray was a little wild, but there's a general circle in the center of the paper figure. The last shot put a decent-sized hole in the dummy's head. Not a bad showing for someone who hasn't been to the range in a while.

She flicks her eyes up at me, and I get the sense that she is not impressed.

"Your turn." I nod at her.

With a dexterity that tells me she's familiar with the practice, Kasey swiftly sets up another target. She reaches behind her back, pulling out the handgun and unloading it in a swift motion that is almost seamless. She reloads the clip, her fingers quick and nimble, and is just about to take her stance when a melodic voice at my elbow startles us both.

"Well, Dean McCade, fancy running into you here. What are you doing in town this time of year?" Jenna's bright voice is unmistakable.

Kasey and I pivot simultaneously to face her, and I see that the horse trainer is not alone. Hunter is on her heels, his hands carrying two unopened boxes of ammo. Jenna leans forward to hug me, but I think it is just a pretext for her to peek around and get a closer look at Kasey, who seems to shrink back into the shadows of the stall.

"Are you on a date?" Jenna exclaims as Hunter and I exchange a nod.

His beard has grown even thicker since the day I met him,

covering most of his face. The yellow specks in his eyes glisten underneath his trucker cap. I can't tell if he's happy or irritated that Jenna has interrupted their progress down the aisle as his gaze flickers, taking in each of us in turn. At Jenna's question, his nostrils flare.

I don't take the time to analyze his mood.

"Not a date. Just a friend," I hasten to clarify before Jenna interprets the whole scene wrong, causing a dozen people to come up to me the next time I'm at church to congratulate me on my upcoming nuptials. I know how gossip works in this town, well-meaning as it is. "Jenna, this is Kasey. Kasey, this is Jenna."

With obvious shyness, Kasey steps forward, the bill of her cap pulled low over her eyes. She extends her hand to Jenna, who shakes it, then eagerly pivots around to pull Hunter forward.

"Kasey, meet my boyfriend, Hunter." She beams at him, her eyes sparkling. "He's taking me shooting for the very first time. Can you believe I've never been?"

Hunter fumbles with the ammo boxes, fitting them into one palm to reach forward and shake Kasey's hand with the other. He lingers briefly for an extra second, his eyes sharpening brightly, staring down at her with a sardonic smile peeking out from under his beard.

"So the most eligible bachelor, Dean McCade, has finally found a woman to tame him, huh?" he says. He leans forward, peering at her intently. "What'd you say your name is? Cassie?"

"Kasey," she murmurs as I jump in to protest with a hasty, "Nope, still a bachelor."

"Kasey, ah," he repeats, then turns to give me a funny look as Jenna laughs and shakes her head.

"We don't believe you. Word on the street is that you are going to win Cascade Valley's Bachelor of the Year award—again.

Watch out, Kasey; the ladies are going to be gunning for this man." She throws her head back, elbowing Hunter in the side and laughing at her pun. "Better snap him up while he's still on the market."

Kasey twists her hands together. I notice that her weapon is on the table behind her, magazine discharged and safely off to the side. "I'm just passing through town, honestly," she protests with clear discomfort. "Not trying to take anybody's future husband."

"Oh, you're not a local?" Hunter interjects.

Kasey gives a brief shake of her head, her eyes darting toward me. "Nope."

"I'm not either," Hunter continues. "I'm up here scoping out some real estate investments." He laughs. "We city slickers have to stick together. I'm not sure we're entirely welcome in Cascade Valley."

Jenna slips her arm through his. "Oh, you're welcome," she beams, "but don't try to change our way of life."

Hunter winks at her but continues, "Kasey, where are you from?"

"Here and there," she replies, shifting her footing uncomfortably. "I've moved around a lot."

He nods. "Same, but I've mostly lived back East. There's just a vibe in New York City that can't be found on the West Coast."

I must bring out the worst in his personality because the maximum brilliance of his charm is on full display. I can see why Jenna seems so smitten with him and why her features have morphed from happy to annoyed as he continues making conversation with Kasey, plying her with small talk. I have to give her credit for at least attempting to hide her disapproval.

Wanting to save Jenna from further mortification, I interrupt. "We were just about to finish our practice round. I know Kasey probably needs to get home to the kids."

"You have kids?" Jenna blurts out. "Is your husband out here too?"

Eagerly, she steps forward again, eyeing me with a smirk on her face. Hunter steps back as if the mere mention of children sets him on edge.

Reluctantly, Kasey nods, shuffling her feet in the universal language of *let's get this over with*. "Guilty as charged. But no. No husband."

No husband, I take mental note. An official confirmation, to my relief.

"How many? How old are they?" Jenna presses. "I love kids. I even work at a youth horse camp in the summer, and I wish I could do it full-time."

"Oh, I think they are probably too young for that," Kasey hems. "Under six years old seems a little young to be at a horse camp all day."

"Yeah, ours is for teens," Jenna replies. She seems to have quickly released her reluctance to embrace Kasey as part of the community at the news that she's a single mom. She turns to Hunter, grabbing his forearm to prevent him from leaving and batting her eyelashes at him. "Let's stay and watch her shoot. Maybe I'll get some pointers from Kasey. She looks like she knows what she is doing."

"I don't think—" Kasey begins.

"Please, Kasey! I don't want to look like an idiot my first time shooting," Jenna pleads.

"I'd like to see you give it a go," Hunter adds.

Kasey looks at them first, then turns to me with a bitter expression, and I grimace in silent apology. If I'd realized how introverted she is, I wouldn't have forced her to come in here. I've spent enough time with Vincent to understand how quickly an introvert will run from being the center of attention.

But Kasey turns away from us toward the target. She squares up her shoulders and hips. Despite her discomfort, her stance is no less professional and controlled than it was earlier, and her experience with the weapon is strikingly obvious. Her breathing becomes deep and steady. She checks the clip, reloads the magazine, pulls back the chamber, slides back the safety, raises her arms, and takes careful aim at the target. Despite my guilt at causing her discomfort, I watch with rapt attention. When she pulls the trigger, the shots ring out in rapid succession. Even from a distance, I can see that the target is instantly decimated. Mimicking me, she saves the last round for the headshot.

When it's over, the four of us are silent as the paper target flies across the cable to us. We stare as it flutters to a stop. Fourteen holes are grouped neatly in a tight circle, center mass, each shot placed far more precisely than mine. The final shot is placed directly in the center of the forehead.

"Whew," Hunter whistles under his breath, leaning forward for a closer look. His eyes cut over to Kasey, looking her up and down as he seems to take fresh stock of her.

"That's . . ." Jenna's lower jaw drops open.

"Impressive," I finish her sentence, flashing a look of admiration at Kasey. "I see your time in the military served you well."

She doesn't seem to notice our admiration. Instead, she keeps her head down, quickly disassembling and reassembling her weapon a third time.

"I'm sorry, but I need to go," she says, turning toward the exit.

"Don't leave on our account," Hunter says.

But we part as Kasey pushes past our group. limps down the aisle. and disappears from sight.

"*Whew*," Hunter whistles under his breath.

"Was she . . .?" Jenna turns to me with a questioning look. "Her leg?"

"Army veteran," I offer the only explanation I can.

"Wounded or not, I wouldn't want to face her in a gunfight," Hunter declares before he and Jenna meander away.

Quickly, I slip past them and follow the path Kasey took. When I reach the street again, the golden-haired soldier is nowhere to be seen.

Chapter Twenty-One

Kasey

Within ten minutes of my return to the farmhouse, a truck pulls into the driveway behind me.

When Dean walks into his home, he finds me trying to tidy the messy evidence of our presence, which seems to have scattered itself all over the house. Watching me with solemn focus, Finn jumps aside when I cross his path yet again. Emma observes from her desk in the corner of the living room. She says she is catching up with her correspondence, but I suspect she is just trying to stay out of my way. Janie keeps running up to her, grabbing toys from the bin and taking them to show the older woman.

"Janie," I chide gently, stopping her from grabbing yet another rag doll from the toy chest. "We have to put our toys away now. It's time to go home."

"No." She jerks her arm out of my hand, shrieking in a high-pitched tone and running back to Emma. "Mama? Mama?"

Emma wraps her arms around her protectively, looking up at me with an apology written across her features. Janie begins to sob, her wails filling the room. I sit back on my heels helplessly, completely at a loss for what to do, and tears sparking in my own eyes. Janie has broken down many times since I've been taking care of her, but she seems to have reached a new level of comfort with me over the last couple of weeks. Now, I'm wondering if Emma's motherly nature has triggered her memories of Amy.

I can't imagine how confusing this whole situation has been for both kids, their father disappearing first, then living happily with their mother one day, and being whisked off with a stranger the next, with no explanation. All summer, they've had to stay close to a cabin that is light-years away from the luxury of their own home, and now, I've brought them to a farmhouse with more strangers. DJ has been quietly playing with a pair of plastic horses while I run around the house, but he slides off the sofa now. He glances at me as he walks over to Janie, his tender, brotherly arms surrounding her comfortingly.

"Don't cry, Janie." His boyish voice soothes her. He tries to turn her face to look at me, but she screams and buries her face deeper into Emma's breast.

"No. Mama!" she cries.

I've got no business raising these kids. *Amy, please come back.*

Dean's frame takes up the doorway, and I wonder if I'm going to have to push him out of the way to leave. He watches as everyone seems to descend into tears simultaneously.

I struggle to my feet, the ache in my leg intensifying with the effort. I feel completely and utterly defeated, and the weight of my failure crushes me. How am I supposed to protect these children if I can't even keep them happy?

"I'm sorry, Janie, but we have to leave now, sweetie." I try one more time, but she cries harder the closer I get. My eyes sting with tears that I valiantly try to hold back.

Then I'm enveloped in a strong, tender embrace. Dean's arms wrap around my shoulders, and he turns my head into his chest. I struggle against the instant urge to let myself rest against him. I'm so tired and so sad, and I just want my sister to come home for her babies because I don't think I can carry this burden alone anymore.

"Kasey," Dean whispers in my ear, "let's let Mom put Janie down for a nap while you and I talk. She probably just needs to sleep a little."

With a glance at Emma, who nods at me to go, I let him pull me outside, and he shuts the front door behind us. The volume of Janie's wails grows faint as he leads us toward the old tree in the front yard. Its branches stretch toward the porch like the outstretched arms of a hug. I hold back the tears as best I can, unwilling for Dean to see me descend into a sobbing mess. I'm a soldier. Soldiers on a mission don't cry, and this is the mission I signed up for.

Dean paces under the tree for a moment before he halts in front of me. His expression is serious. "Kasey, I'm so sorry for what happened in town today," he begins. "I never should have forced you to go to the shooting range. Please don't leave because I made you uncomfortable."

I wave him away, shaking my head and dabbing at the water leaking from the corners of my eyes. "You had every right to make sure I was a safe person to have in your home." I hesitate, unsure how to say what I need to say. "But Dean, we can't stay here. This isn't our home. You have your own life to worry about."

"I'm perfectly happy to make worrying about the three of you part of my life."

The words are too kind, too heartfelt. I can't take it, the tears welling up and beginning to spill down my cheeks. My hands lift, flailing about my head in a circular motion. "Oh, believe me, this is one hot mess you don't want anything to do with."

He tilts his head to the side, his gray-blue eyes narrowing slightly. "Now that you mention it, you actually are quite attractive. Especially when you unloaded an entire clip center mass into that paper dummy. Do you want to talk about that little display of marksmanship?" His arms cross over his chest.

Something about the absurdity of it all draws out a laugh from me, but it chokes off as I begin to cough, wheezing a little as I try to catch my breath. When I dare to look up at him, I recognize the undeniable admiration in his face. It beams at me, echoing in the huskiness of his voice, and I feel my skin flush. He's too handsome to look straight at, but I can't pull my eyes away from him either. The flush runs up and down my limbs, tingling in my fingertips and toes. He doesn't break our eye contact, and neither do I.

Somehow, Dean knows how to say all the right things.

"Not really," I finally murmur with a dismissive shrug. "The military teaches you a lot of useful things. I happened to like marksmanship, and I did well in it."

The admiration in his face only deepens. "That was more than just training. That was years of practice and dedication."

Forcing myself to break eye contact, I look away, trying to hide the fluttering that is beating wildly in my chest. Only the former members of my unit knew how many hours I spent practicing my shooting skills. Part of the reason I practiced so much was because I was terrified that, as a combat medic, I'd end up in an emergency on the battlefield that required me to jump into the fray and end up freezing from fear . . . or worse, missing my mark entirely.

But it didn't take long for the noisy shooting range to become the one place that could drown out all the hurtful voices in my head, the voices that said I was just the black sheep of the family, the unwanted child from a betrayed relationship with no prospects and no future. Over and over, I would take aim at the target, the reverberating shock of the discharge a jarring counterbalance to push out the memory of it all.

Dean may feel admiration for the skills I so carefully developed, but I wonder what he would think if he knew what a broken, scarred, and unwanted woman I've always been.

The only worthy things I've ever undertaken were in the service of my country and now taking care of my niece and nephew. And even those things I've failed miserably.

While I try to formulate a response, my inner consciousness inconveniently reminds me that I don't know what to do with the feelings Dean stirs in me. The admiration on his face is reflected in the beating of my own heart. He's so kind and so generous with his trust that it makes me want to lean into him, to rely on him, to let him lead. But the reality is that I *can't* do anything with how I feel. Whatever comes, my sister's battle is just beginning when she returns from rehab, and it will be my duty to stand by her side. Even if there's a possibility of keeping her struggles hidden from the outside world, Dean won't want me when he finds out I deceived him.

But it hurts because he's everything a man should be. Kind, strong, gentle, protective, and excellent with children, and his broad, lean rancher's build, dark raspy beard, and those gray-blue eyes that seem to look straight into my soul certainly don't hurt. Yet, it isn't just his looks that make me want to curl up in the pocket of his t-shirt—the one sewn over his heart—and live there forever. He makes me feel safe—like I belong to something good—and he doesn't even truly know me.

The guilt surges in again. This man has done nothing but do his best to take care of us from the first day we met. He's had every right to be suspicious, but he has only been kind to us. And in another lifetime, I could fall hard and fast for Dean McCade.

Maybe in another version of life, I could let myself soften toward him. Maybe I could let myself dream of what it would be like to be wrapped in those work-hardened arms of his, safe from the wolves that always feel as if they are just outside my door.

But every day I withhold the truth from him is another day I've driven another nail into the coffin of our future, dead relationship. When he discovers what I've been forced to hide, he'll turn me over to the sheriff, or worse, over to my brother-in-law.

I must protect DJ and Janie at all costs. If my service in the military taught me one thing, it's that duty comes before the longing of my heart. I steel my resolve, and my heart crumbles a little more.

"We have to leave. I'm sorry," I whisper. "But I want you to know, everything you've done for us, everything your mother has done, I can't ever repay you. And I'm so grateful." Reaching out, I press my fingers to his forearm, curling them around the warm, sinuous muscle, hoping the touch conveys how thankful I am.

"You'll never need to repay me," he replies, leaning closer and narrowing some of the inches between us. His hands move toward me as if he's about to take me in his arms.

"Why are you being so kind to us?" I blurt out the question I've been wanting to ask for days.

He draws back a little, the question bringing a thoughtful look into his expression. "Why wouldn't I be kind to you?"

"Because people aren't kind," I reply. "They do things for you, but their kindness comes with conditions." I don't know where the words come from, but they've been on my mind since I arrived.

"I'm sorry you've experienced people like that," Dean says. "That isn't how the Lord calls us to treat others."

It doesn't surprise me that Dean is a man of faith. Danny was too.

His response generates something else, a protest from deep within. "But they do," I continue. "And then they go to church on Sundays and sit in the front row and make everyone think their life is perfect when really, they—" My voice cracks, and I stop abruptly.

He nods thoughtfully. "The flock is damaged, Kasey. Did you know that sheep will lead each other right over a cliff? They are hardwired to instinctively follow the leader and will even follow each other to their own destruction. While the church is filled with just as many sinners as the rest of the world, and hurting each other happens all too often, our eyes have to stay fixed on the Shepherd. Unfortunately, we can't look to the sheep to be our guide because we'll be disappointed every time. Our guide through life has got to be Jesus because He's the only one who will love you unconditionally and bring you safely into the fold."

He leans down, closing the distance between us again. His voice takes on a husky timbre. "And who's to say I don't have a slight ulterior motive? I would really love to get to know you more, and how can I do that if you insist on being an antisocial hermit living deep in the woods?"

The words draw a laugh out of me even as his tone brings out a shiver across my skin. I laugh. "But I am an antisocial hermit. I like being alone."

His echoing laugh is deep and full of starlight. He looks earnestly at me. "I respect your decision to go, but can you stay one more night? The kids aren't ready to leave yet, and you look exhausted. Mom and I will gather some extra supplies to send with you, and you can drive out in the morning."

His gaze lowers, and I watch as it seems to land on my lips, lingering there for only an extra beat before he meets my gaze again. I wish I could respond the way my heart wants to respond right now. Distracted, my brain struggles to process his request, shutting down as a sense of exhaustion sweeps over me. All I want right now is a soft place to sit and a piece of Emma's huckleberry cobbler. The thought of the long drive back to Danny's cold, dark cabin—which I'm not sure I could even find after the sun goes down—fills me with dread. With two cranky, tired kids in tow, forget about it.

I nod, my voice raspy. "Okay. We can stay one more night."

"Good." His warm fingers intertwine with mine again, and we walk back to the welcoming yellow farmhouse together.

. . .

The nightmares hit me with their usual force, but rather than dream of the day Danny died, I dream of my father and the day I realized he didn't love me. He looms before me, larger than life and intimidating, just as he always was. His lips are turned into a disapproving frown, his aquamarine eyes—so like my own—distant.

He was never a significant part of my life but rather a shadowy figure that my mother occasionally guilted into giving us a modicum of begrudging attention. I thought it was normal for fathers to wear nice clothes and drive around in a fancy car with a chauffeur while Mom and I slept in the same bed to stay warm in the winter.

Many times, I've comforted myself with the thought that, perhaps, I was the test run. A failed experiment to push him into being a good father to his second daughter when he couldn't be good to his first. At the very least, Amy grew up safe and happy, and I've never resented her for it. Perhaps I was given more strength to endure the hardships, and that's why I didn't need parental affection.

I was probably six or seven when I first understood I had a half-sister—that I wasn't alone in the world—that someone out there smaller and more fragile than me belonged to my family tree. It took me much longer to understand why we couldn't live together.

My nightmare is predictable.

I dream of the day Mom and I took the bus to the stop near my father's house. It was late when we arrived. Mom was trembling, her hands shaking the way they had begun to shake a couple of years before. I'd only seen my father's house a few times since I wasn't allowed to go there. It was on a wide and pretty street on the Upper East Side, a heritage brownstone that had been passed down through his wife's family. The windows cast golden light onto the pavement, music tinkling out into the night.

It was my tenth birthday and Amy's fifth, our arrival on earth ironically having coincided down to the day, five years apart.

I stood awkwardly to the side as Mom knocked on the door until someone answered. She demanded that Kenneth Carter come out to wish his daughter a "happy birthday," until someone interrupted the party long enough to get him to come to the door.

He came striding onto the landing, his face angry and red, his finger wagging in Mom's face, his voice seething as he told her never to come to his house again or he would call the police.

"We're not married," he seethed. "We never were. I don't owe you anything. Can't you see I have another life now?"

He only glanced my way once.

When he slammed the door, we were left on the cold, empty street.

I knew that day that my father never loved me. We'd been merely a stopover for him as he worked his way to his real life. But inside that house, there was someone who could love me, who might love me, if only I could prove that I was worthy of it.

A small, familiar bottle fell out of Mom's coat pocket as we walked toward the bus stop, the glass breaking into a million tiny shards as it shattered on the sidewalk.

A whimper startles me awake. I sit up shivering and covered in sweat in Emma's comfortable bed, the moon gleaming beyond the fluttering curtains. I look around frantically for the source of the whimper, but the children are sleeping peacefully beside me, their warm bodies pressing into my sides. I hear the familiar sound emitting from my own throat again and quickly swallow it back.

Immediately, I feel stifled and trapped. I need fresh air and the open skies. Gingerly, I ease off the mattress, taking care not to disturb the children. Although, once I'm standing, I can't help but stop to look down at the two of them, studying their silky light brown hair, golden skin, and fluffy eyelashes that stand out even in the shadows. So much like each other and yet perfectly unique. How anyone could leave them for so long is unfathomable to me.

"Come on, Amy," I breathe over them. "Please come home."

Slipping into the upstairs hallway, I limp down the stairs in my bare feet, my scarred leg and knee stiff and sore after sleeping. I take care not to make any noise. Dean is sleeping in one of the upstairs rooms, but I'm not sure which one is his. Emma is in her daughter's old room.

The back door squeals a little on its hinges when I open it, but then I'm standing outside under the canopy of stars that you can only see when there aren't any city lights to pollute the night sky. I stand in the yard barefoot, the sharp wind chilling my arms, the country night sounds surrounding me. The air is fresh and clean and chilly with the rapid descent of autumn. Deeply, I breathe it in, trying to fill my lungs to their full capacity as my mind processes what I found today during my quick stop at the internet cafe in town. After months of hiding and avoiding any digital footprint, I knew I had to at least try to assess what looming threats we could be facing.

According to the Federal Bureau of Prisons, Dmitry Volkov is still safely contained within the walls of a prison in New York, but the clock is ticking. If Amy's insider information about his parole hearing is correct, he'll be out within a matter of months instead of years.

Gathering more information on him wasn't hard. Dmitry was a notorious East Coast playboy, and his fall from grace took the internet by storm when his case first went to trial, with article after article about the infamous owner of Club Thirteen and its companion clubs. Feeling as if it was taking a huge risk to search for any information about my brother-in-law, I kept my queries brief and to the point, but my breathing still grew shallow as my chest tightened with worry over being traced.

I'm not tech savvy enough to know if anyone could track searches on Dmitry's name and inmate status, but I'm wise enough to know that in the modern age of the internet, it's possible if you know the right people. Just the thought that the IP address of the computer I used today could be used to trace a search on my brother-in-law back to Cascade Valley makes the bile rise in my throat again as I let the chilly night breeze cool my skin.

Dmitry and Amy were once the golden couple of the Manhattan social scene. My search brought me across dozens of photographs of them, always pictured with a few muscular bodyguards wearing dark sunglasses and black suits. Needing that level of protection should have been a sign. Other than a cursory glance, I ignored the bodyguards and studied my sister.

It was clear to me when Amy's trouble with addiction began, as her slim face grew more and more gaunt over the past year, her eyes increasingly hollow and wild. Fortunately, she must have insisted on keeping the children out of the spotlight because any photographs of them are from over a year ago and have a faraway, candid vibe. In the few I came across, Janie is only a baby.

To my shock, I don't find any articles related to Amy, DJ, and Janie's disappearance. I scroll through pages of search results, but most of the articles about Amy are related to gossip tabloids published around the trial. Can it be possible that no one is looking for them? Does everyone think they are simply vacationing in California as she planned? With Amy's money, it isn't implausible that she could disappear to a quiet retreat.

But no. I shake my head. It's not possible. I must believe Dmitry is searching for his wife and children. And by extension, me, since I've committed the unforgivable sin by removing his ability to control them from prison.

Under the stars, my panic rises. I limp forward a few steps. My muscles shake, and it takes me a minute to realize it's not raining, but the dampness on my face is from my own tears. I dash them away with the backs of my hands.

Desperate to regain control of my emotions, I cast about for something to calm me. My brain latches onto the memory of a painting hanging in Emma's room on the wall across from her bed. The scene is of a beach, with so foamy waves flowing in toward the shore, upon which a double pair of footprints can be seen. Except that the farther away the footprints get, the more they narrow to just one set of footprints in the sand. There are words printed alongside them, and I've read them so many times that I have them memorized.

My heart echoes the words of the poem now: *"I don't understand why when I needed you most you would leave me . . ."* Frantically, I repeat the final line aloud, seeking to understand its comfort.

"My precious child . . . when you see one set of footprints, it was then that I carried you," I whisper into the night.

What does it mean? My mother didn't raise me religious, but I went to church regularly with one of the neighborhood girls when I was young. I've never doubted there is a God. Given the vastness of the universe and the complexity of humanity, His existence has always simply made sense. There was even a time when the pastor did an altar call, and I went forward. But then we moved, and I didn't go to that church anymore. My doubt in His sovereignty didn't waver, but my faith was something that existed because my neighborhood friend invited me to Sunday school. Just because God created me, does that mean He wants anything to do with me? Am I just a disappointment, a disgrace? I've lifted feeble whispers to heaven more in the past few months than I ever have, but how can I know if God is listening? Is help on the way?

A sob ripples through me, and even as I choke it back, another rises to the surface. I bury my face in my hands and walk farther into the yard, moving away from the house. The night closes in, the once-comforting canopy of stars now a terrifying menace. I can't see, can't think, can't breathe as the sky descends, and I stand under it, utterly and desperately alone.

Just when I think my cries will bubble out of my throat despite my best efforts to hold them back, I'm surrounded by a pair of strong arms and pulled against a chest that feels as solid as a wall of stone. His signature scent of fir trees and moss, and a faint hint of barnyard, fills my senses. I cling to it, leaning in and pulling strength from him as the tears consume me.

"Let it out, darlin'. I've got you." Dean's breath is warm against my ear.

I don't hesitate. Wrapping my arms around his waist, I hold onto him as if the very winds of the earth are trying to rip me away. He cradles me in an embrace so secure it feels as if no matter how strong the storms get, he'll never let me go.

I press my cheek into his chest, and my voice emerges, weak and muffled. "Dean, I can't do it all. I can't protect them and raise them and provide food and chop firewood and watch for predators and wash the laundry and do all the things I have to do to give them a good life so they don't end up totally damaged."

I'm saying all the things I shouldn't be saying, mumbling and whispering and blubbering into his white cotton t-shirt. It's growing damp with my tears.

Gently, his hands smooth over my back, tangling in my hair at the nape of my neck. "Then don't. You don't have to carry this burden alone. There are people who want to help you. I want to help you."

The tears come slower now as I fight to pull myself together. "I know you do. But you can't. No one can."

"Don't go back to the mountain, Kasey. Stay with us," he whispers, drawing me up, his arms wrapping tightly around my lower back. His breath caresses my neck, brushing the skin peeping above the top of my collar.

I want to let go, to release the burden of everything I'm carrying into his capable hands. My heart urges me to tell him everything. If caring for my sister's children while she is away getting help and their father is in prison is illegal, then so be it. If Dean rejects me once he hears the truth and throws me to the mercy of the legal wolves, at least I'll have saved myself the heartache of falling in love with him.

Because falling in love with Dean McCade would be so easy. And it would also be the worst mistake I've made yet. I can't let the carefully woven cloak of secrecy I've drawn around us be torn down. My mission trumps the cry of my heart.

I try to pull away, but my effort is weak, and he only draws me closer. My voice trembles. "I have to fight my battles alone. We're leaving tomorrow. And I don't want you to try to stop me."

Hopelessness sets in, and I feel the tattered remnants of my stoicism settling back into place.

"If you won't let me fight them for you," Dean murmurs against my hair, "then let God. I know you may not feel it now, but He is with you on the mountaintops, and He is with you in this shadowy canyon of trouble. There is nowhere you can go that His love won't find you."

"I don't know how to believe that," I admit honestly. I lean back to look at his face, the stars lighting up his chiseled features.

There have been moments at the cabin during the long nights when just the small battery-powered lantern burns as I keep watch, that I've reached for the dusty Bible left behind on the table. Danny's name is scribbled inside, as are the names of a couple of other generations of Gardeners. I've tried to understand the things that I read, but the only words that make sense are in the Book of Psalms. I feel a kinship with the outcry of the poet king, a solidarity with his desperation to right his wrongs. I've tried to pray, stumbling over words muttered into the stillness that feel foreign and strange. On a few occasions, when I'm sitting, staring at the black cracks in the cabin door, an inexplicable peace washes over me. In those moments, I think to myself that, somehow, it's all going to be okay because it feels as if we've been protected and provided for in the most unexpected ways on this journey.

Still, my relationship with God feels as rocky as ever, not that it has ever been very good. I wish I understood where Dean gets his faith.

"Faith takes time," he replies in a calm tone. "There are days when it feels strong and days when it feels attacked from every side. But it doesn't matter how weak we are. God is strong, and if we allow the Good Shepherd to guide us, He'll lead us by waters still and sweet, where we can rest peacefully no matter what battle rages around us."

"I want that. I want that so badly," I whisper, clinging to the strength he offers.

Leaning back, I stare at him, memorizing his features. I trace every line of his bearded face, searching the depths of those deep-set eyes, finding the lips hiding within his beard. As if in response, his head dips only ever so slightly. And in that moment, I know that if he thought he could, Dean would kiss me now.

But he doesn't, and I'm glad. Instead, he lowers his forehead to mine, our breaths mingling as if by his nearness alone, I can draw from his strength. I know I have to let go. I have to push him away. Yet, even though I'm losing him and walking back into the dark forest of my own accord, I feel that inexplicable sense of peace washing over me again.

The sensation calms my racing heart, and there under the canopy of stars, for the first time, it feels as if I'm telling Dean the truth.

Chapter Twenty-Two

Dean

Only Mom could convince a woman as determined as Kasey to stay for a hot and filling breakfast the next morning. Blueberry pancakes, scrambled eggs with the homemade cheddar that Mom made last year, loads of fresh butter and maple syrup, and coffee cups filled to the brim.

And then only Mom could, by some miracle, convince her to accompany us to church service so the kids could go to Sunday school. "It'll do them so much good to play with the other kids and sing and play games," Mom exclaims at the kitchen table. "Won't take more than an hour or two, and then you three can go wherever you need to go."

Kasey swallows the bite of pancake she is chewing, her eyes darting first to the kids, then to me, then back to Mom, her head shaking all the while. "I was hoping to get an—"

"Just an hour or two's delay, dear."

"Mom, maybe some other week—" I interject.

"I want to go to Sunday school," Junior's small voice interrupts. He's sitting across the table from me, and his eyes are fixed on Kasey's face. The boy is usually quiet, watching the goings-on at the farmhouse with serious, greenish-brown eyes. From what I've observed, he seems to have enjoyed running around the barnyard with Mom and Charlie, feeding the chickens, and milking the cows.

The uncertainty drains away from Kasey's face, a new sense of resolve strengthening her features. "You want to go to Sunday school, Junior?"

He nods, and her shoulders visibly relax. "I guess we'll go then."

So we lead the way down the back road to the church, where the McCade family has attended since we moved to the valley. At her insistence, Kasey drives with the kids in her own Jeep—to have an escape vehicle handy, I'm sure.

With curiosity, I watch her as we file into the same pew we've occupied for years. Our conversation as she cried against my chest under the stars last night is still fresh in my mind. My heart hasn't stopped praying for the beautiful but haunted woman who has somehow landed under my roof—and it feels like—under my protection. Something . . . or someone . . . is still troubling her. I can see it in the way she startles and jumps every time a voice breaks the silence unexpectedly, in the way her eyes are constantly scanning the windows as if waiting for some threat to appear, and in the way her nervous energy doesn't ever allow her to rest.

It's to my shock that she allows the children to go into their Sunday school classes by themselves. But she keeps glancing toward the doorway leading to their classrooms, her foot bouncing as if she is contemplating a mad dash back the way we just came.

I struggle to get my heart into the right place for church, overwhelmed by the frustration of knowing she is holding something back from me. Pushing her won't do any good. She'll just cut and run, like she's been trying to do since we met.

I am fully aware of several dozen eyes on our seats as the worship team asks us all to rise and begins to lead us in song. Dean McCade doesn't bring women to church, and the whole town knows it. I've asked only a few local women out on dates over the years, Shelby being the most recent, but all those women already attended our church, mostly with their families. Any newcomer to our small, tightly knit community is cause for curiosity, but by the boldness of the looks cast our direction, I am beginning to wonder if the whole town has secretly taken out bets about the length of time the McCade brothers will stay single.

Malia DeWitt, the valley's primary event coordinator and caterer, throws a smirk in our direction. Esther and Jeb beam at us from their seats, and he gives me a confidential nod, no doubt because of the pending deal on the lodge. A couple of other bachelors from the valley don't even try to hide the fact that they are checking Kasey out. I'm surprised to see Jenna and Hunter in the row parallel to ours. Hunter's eyes cut to Kasey, and his nod is accompanied by a subtle wink and a pistol motion with his hands.

Caleb is the only one who seems to keep his eyes fixed on the words of the Gospel song as they appear on the screen.

The attention is distracting, and I almost wish Mom hadn't convinced Kasey to attend with us because I am sure I will be mobbed by a crowd of our friends after church, everyone curious about the newcomer.

The inward agitation grates on me until I realize how still

Kasey has gone at my side. With a subtle glance at her, I see that her eyes are fixed on Pastor Miller, who has begun his morning message on the pulpit.

"Good morning, friends," he greets the congregation with a welcoming smile. "This morning, we are going to continue our study of the twenty-third psalm. Will you turn to the passage in your Bibles with me?"

Kasey doesn't have a Bible, so I let mine rest on my knee, open to the passage, and turn it toward her. She bends her head to read as Pastor quotes it aloud, her blonde waves shifting across her shoulders as she leans over the open pages.

"He makes us lie down in green pastures," Pastor says. "My, doesn't that sound nice? We've got a few ranching and farming families here. How happy does it make you to see your livestock just relaxing out in the fields, green, lush grass growing all around, not a sound except for their contented noises?" He looks around the room. "Whether you've got one chicken or a whole herd of sheep under your care, you know that those animals will not rest if a predator is around. The animals will alert you if you just pay attention to the changes in their behavior. They will stop eating, they'll be nervous, they'll tighten ranks, and they won't be at rest."

He pauses, his kind eyes surveying us. "What if, in the Lord's presence, you could find rest even when the very wolf himself is knocking at your door? What if you didn't have to carry the burden of protecting yourself? What if you gave that burden to the Good Shepherd, and instead of fighting and striving and trying to control everything on your own, you simply settled in green pastures for a rest and let Him do the work for you?"

He flips the page, looking down and studying the passage for a moment. "A little later, the psalmist tells us that even if we walk through a valley so terrifying it is like the shadow of death is looming over our heads, we don't have to be afraid. We don't have to be afraid of evil because our Shepherd has already proven Himself trustworthy with our safety. We know He'll protect us in the pastures, beside the waters, and through the valley because His Word tells us so."

Kasey is utterly still next to me, her eyes fixed on the pulpit.

Emotion thickens our pastor's voice. "He'll supply all our needs because that's what He promised to do. He'll heal our souls and guide us in the paths that lead us to Him because He already sacrificed His life for us. It isn't a question that the Shepherd will protect His flock. It's simply His nature. The more we let Him lead, the easier it gets to trust that no matter what the threat, He is with us.

"When you find yourselves in that valley of terror, you'll have to release all the doubts holding you back from resting in Him first. Then let Him do the rest."

Pastor Miller closes his Bible and places his palm upon it. "What burdens do you need to lay at your Good Shepherd's feet today? Church family, can we bow our heads and seek the Lord together this morning?"

At my side, I finally feel Kasey's feet shuffle. She sniffles as Pastor leads us in prayer, and with a quick glance downward, I see her head bowed and a trail of tears slipping down her cheeks. I find her hand, wrapping up her fingers in my own. With a gentle squeeze, I hope she understands what I want to say. It takes a few moments, but I feel her fingers readjusting. She threads them through mine, giving me a return squeeze as the worship team leads us in a closing song.

. . .

The stillness of the farmhouse after Kasey, Junior, and Janie pack up their things and leave to go back to the cabin is disquieting.

Before they left, Dr. Burke gave the family the all clear, sending them with some medicine and care instructions. Mom seems discombobulated, starting a book, then putting it down, getting up to make tea, then forgetting to strain the leaves. I find her staring out the front window more than once.

The McCade ranch has always been chaotic. When the five of us siblings were young, it was our friends from town coming out to visit. The house was always packed, and Mom often kicked us outside to run wild across the property. As time has passed and the five of us have built our own lives, the house has grown quiet when we're away. And since none of us have settled down and started having children yet, that means Mom is without the grandchildren I know she longs for.

And for a few days, Kasey's kids brought a fresh burst of energy to the house, and I welcomed it, for Mom's sake as well as mine.

"I just don't know why it feels like they were here forever," her voice breaks the silence. She laughs, and I hear the sadness underneath. "They were only here a little while," she trails off.

I look at her, feeling the intensity behind my gaze. "They'll be back someday, Mom. I promise."

Her eyes are glassy with tears. "Thank you."

"The question is how we'll make that happen," I continue with my own short, humorless laugh. "Their mother is exceptionally stubborn."

"Not unlike someone else that I know around here." Mom smiles at me before her face grows serious. "I'm worried about her, Dean. Do you think she's going to be okay?"

I sigh and run my hand over my beard. "I don't know. I think she needs the Lord's grace and a soft place to land when whatever she is running from catches up to her."

"So you do think she is in some kind of trouble, then?"

"I do." My nod is slow and thoughtful. "I have no idea what kind of trouble, but I suspect it has something to do with the kids' dad."

Mom lifts an embroidery hoop from the basket on the seat next to her and picks at the threads thoughtfully. "Whatever it is, I don't want her going through it alone."

"She's got to accept a helping hand first." I shrug. "I just don't think she trusts anyone enough to let them in."

Mom peers over her reading glasses and points the embroidery needle at me. "Then you keep showing her you are a safe place from the storm of whatever she is facing. I don't want those children spending Thanksgiving or Christmas alone in that dingy cabin."

"So you're saying I have until the holidays to get them back down here?" I stare at her in amused shock at the seriousness of her tone.

"You heard me, son. They belong with us until Kasey finds her footing again. And that's all I have to say about it." She rises, turning toward the kitchen. "I don't know about you, but I think I need a cup of tea and a piece of that huckleberry cobbler to soothe my nerves."

"Mom," I call out, and she looks over her shoulder, "thank you. For everything you do."

She smirks. "Don't thank me yet. I'm aiming to have you marry that girl and get me started off with two ready-made grandchildren to pamper. I declare I've never seen a man look so frustrated yet so enamored with a woman at the same time."

She turns and walks away toward the kitchen, leaving me

sitting open-mouthed in complete and utter shock.

Chapter Twenty-Three

Kasey

Danny's cabin is cold and dark when I finally carry Janie into it after we leave the McCade family's farmhouse. She rests her head on my shoulder as we hike the rocky trail, and, before too long, falls asleep.

DJ trots along beside me, surprising me with his quick willingness to hoist his own bag on top of his shoulders. I have to handle our other bags, and there are too many to take in one trip with a toddler on my hip. I'll have to put Finn on guard later and hike back down the trail when they are asleep to hide the vehicle and get the rest of the supplies Emma sent with us.

Wearily, I drop into a chair at the wooden table, Janie still asleep on my shoulder, and survey the small space. The log cabin with its rough floors and hand-cut walls looks nothing like Emma's bright and comforting farmhouse. Already, I'm regretting my departure from her welcoming home.

Home. A word barely familiar to me. I haven't felt at home anywhere since my tenth birthday, the day I realized my existence was a disappointment, and I was a meaningless pawn in the bitter game the grown-ups played.

But I didn't feel meaningless while I recovered at the McCade family's home. I felt valuable, cared for, and worth something.

Despite my conviction that I had to put distance between us, I already miss it . . . them . . . him.

Dean stood at the bottom of the front porch steps, his arms folded across his chest, his brow low and heavy, watching us as we drove away. Leaving him felt like a mistake, but it was a mistake I had to make. No matter how much it broke me.

I've been broken a thousand times before, and I've survived every time.

I stare at the cold, dark stove, the wood box empty beside it, and realize how behind on chopping firewood I already am. The days are shortening as the calendar ticks ever closer to October, the entrance of autumn bringing with it the first frost and chilly nights.

We'll need more supplies than what I was able to gather on this trip to town and the extras Emma sent with us. Every survival instinct I have yells at me to stay away from people, but however reluctantly, I'm going to have to go into Cascade Valley again before the snow falls. Briefly, I wonder if Emma will be willing to watch the children once or twice this fall while I go into town to purchase enough to get us through the winter here.

Because we have to stay.

Halfway through my internet search for my brother-in-law, I realized that running away would only risk exposing us more. If the Volkov goons haven't shown up yet, chances are good that their boss has no idea where his wife and children are, but they are almost certainly looking. Cascade Valley is almost off the grid, and tracing Danny Gardener to Kasey Carter would be nearly impossible. Not totally impossible given our shared military service, but improbable. After all, we may have served our country together for several years, but would anyone think to dig that far into Amy's estranged sister's past? Doubtful. For all anyone else knows, she and I haven't spoken in years. I can only hope that when Amy did contact me, she covered her tracks so our clandestine communication is in the clear.

Unless a security camera recorded me driving out of her posh neighborhood and caught my license plate. In that case, trouble is already breathing down our necks.

Winter is coming and coming fast. Even if I wanted to leave, there isn't enough time to set up a safe house anywhere else. Amy is due back any day. The last I heard from her, she said the doctors wanted her to stay another month. If she's going to reach out to me any day, I don't have a safer location to give her the space and time she needs to make plans once she returns.

A heaviness presses down on my eyelids as I think. Dr. Burke said I was recovered enough from my walking pneumonia to resume semi-normal activity, but my chest still feels weak with a lingering cough. I just want to stretch out for a few minutes to rest my eyes. Then I'll plan. I'll figure out what we need to do to keep surviving until Amy returns.

Rising, I half-stumble, half-walk, carrying Janie over to the small cot against the wall. I put her on the mattress, and she rolls to her side. There's just enough space on the cot for me, so I grab one of the extra blankets Emma packed for us and snuggle in next to my niece.

Glancing over my shoulder toward DJ, I see he has thrown himself onto the floor with a comic book Dean lent him. There is plenty of light for him to see with the miniature battery-operated lantern Dean also sent him home with. He's turning the pages slowly, studying the illustrations, his brow furrowed in concentration.

"Will you be okay for a little while, buddy?" I ask him. "Auntie just needs a short nap, then I'll make you a sandwich with that bread Miss Emma sent with us."

I barely register his affirmation. My eyelids can't stay open any longer. They flutter closed, and I'm instantly lost in a dreamless sleep.

. . .

"Heyo! Anybody up in the cabin?" A deep, male voice penetrates my slumber, waking me instantly. My heart leaps into overdrive, pounding in my ears, my senses on full alert. I spin out of my sleeping bag, landing in a crouch on the floor, my eyes adjusting to the light streaming through the cabin windows. I reach for the rifle hanging above the door, far out of reach of little hands. We've been back for less than a week, but I don't feel ready to face the human threat that has just landed in our clearing.

The morning isn't new, but the children are still asleep. It's amused me more than once how late they sleep, like tiny teenagers. Nothing seems to disturb them.

I stay low and creep toward the window, peeping around the curtains to get a look at whoever is outside. My adrenaline spikes, sharpening my senses, but hiding isn't an option. The smoke rising from our stove into the frosty air of morning already gave us away.

The sight of the big man wearing the familiar trucker cap in the clearing almost causes me to collapse to the floor with instant relief. It seems Dean has learned from our past experiences, waiting at the edge of the trees and sending out a loud call to alert me to his presence. He is probably tired of me pulling the rifle on him.

My heart flutters at the sight of him, and I force it back down, hardening it resolutely against the instinct to run to hug him. I'm so glad to see him. I wish he would scoop me up and tell me that he'll keep us safe and never let anyone harm us, but I can't allow myself to want that.

"He already did that, Kasey. And you told him to let you fight your battles on your own," I mutter to myself, anger at myself rushing in to replace the grief I feel.

I realize now I never should have let Dean get as close as he has. His presence isn't safe, either for him or us. The more he pursues us, the more opportunities there are for us to be discovered out here. I should have made it clearer that we don't need his help instead of nearly kissing him under the stars like a fool. I blame myself.

My frustration fuels me as I pull a sweater around my shoulders, shove my wool-socked feet into my boots, and yank the door open. Finn tries to follow, but I motion him back. Mindful of the sleeping children, I close it quietly behind me and step onto the porch. I don't bother to hide my displeasure as I stride across the clearing, noting the whispers of frost still on the morning grass.

Dean leans against the trunk of a tall pine, leisurely threading the straps of Midnight's bridle through his hands while he watches my approach. The smirk on his face spikes both my adrenaline and my annoyance. I stop five feet from him and plant my fists on my hips, boots wide, and heels digging into the earth. Glaring at him, I try to ignore how handsome he is or how soft and full his beard looks in the autumn morning light.

"Hey there." His voice is husky and low, eliciting an involuntary tremble from me. "You're still here."

"Hello. We are. For now." For all my inward bluster, the short phrases are all I can manage to squeak out in response. Resolutely, I pull myself together, determined not to let his masculine charm distract me from my purpose in stomping out here. "What are you doing here, Dean?"

"Well, Kasey," he drawls dramatically, "I thought I'd come by to see how you are and ask if you'd like to go get an ice cream sundae with me after the drive-in theater next Friday." The smirk deepens.

I feel a twitch at the side of my mouth. "Do they even have drive-in theaters anymore?"

He shrugs. "Perhaps we can find out together? I took a morning away from my herd to check on you."

"Well, isn't that just so sweet of you," I reply with soft sarcasm.

He shrugs again. "It's a pretty ride. And a pretty view." There is no mistaking the admiration in his expression as he stares down at me.

At this, a laugh tries to bubble up from my throat, but I choke it back. Somehow, I doubt that my bedhead and current uniform of shabby sweats and a grungy sweater that I should never have packed—but is my favorite piece of clothing—qualify me as a pretty view. I cross my arms across my chest and frown at him, narrowing my gaze with the same level of intensity my instructor used to floor me with in basic training. I don't speak, letting the silence stretch on.

My tactics don't seem to faze Dean as he tilts his head, his gray-blue eyes staring right back at me. "How are the kids?" he asks.

The gentle question catches me off guard, and I reply without thinking. "They miss you and Emma. I haven't heard the end of it for days. 'Where Dean? Where Mith Emma?'"

My imitation of Janie's toddler speech causes a full-blown grin to spread across his face. "I've missed you too."

He steps forward, arms reaching toward me. I've been craving another of his hugs since the moment I drove away from the farmhouse, so I almost let myself be drawn into his arms. But I come to my senses long enough to jump back and out of the way.

"No, Dean." I lift my palms to keep some distance between us. "This isn't right."

He closes the distance anyway, not touching me, but his gaze holds me in place, nonetheless. "What's wrong with a man visiting a probably lonely friend who is squatting in a cabin way out in the middle of nowhere? Surely, you three need some company."

I shake my head and desperately try to call back my annoyance from earlier. I glare up at him. "First of all, it's not squatting when the owner invited you. And everything is wrong with it. I told you: We don't need your help."

Immediately, Dean grows serious. "I'm just a friend—"

"I won't allow the children's emotions to be yanked around like this." Firmly, I shake my head. "You can't be here. They are going to get their routine totally messed up, and I won't have that." My voice cracks as I choke out the last sentence. "I'm grateful to you and your mother, but you need to leave before they wake up and see you."

A shadow passes over his face, darkening his features. "Nobody's routine would get messed up at all if you would simply give up the craziness of staying up here all the time and at least come down to interact with people now and then. This level of isolation isn't good for you or the kids."

He's right, but I can't tell him that, so my temper flares. I narrow my gaze. "So now, you're calling me crazy? Right now, we're where we want to be, and it's none of your business. Who are you to tell me how to live my life, Dean?"

"It's not where you want to be; it's where you think you have to be," he retorts.

My eyes widen. "Maybe you should just leave."

"Is that what you want?"

"You know what, right now, I think it is what is best for all of us. I need to think before I see you again."

Before he can answer, I spin on my heels and march straight for the cabin. With each thud of my boots onto the earth, I feel the knife I just stabbed into my own gut twist a little more. The look on his face as I spat out the words was pure shock. Hurting him was never my intention, but it was necessary to protect him from the awful truth. The last thing I want is for such a kind and good man to get caught up in the sordid mess I suspect is going to come crashing down around my ears before the waking nightmare of this whole ordeal is over.

I don't look outside again until I'm sure he is long gone.

. . .

As the onset of fall pushes away the summer warmth, I don't have nightmares in my dreams anymore because each night I fall into the cot too tired for anything other than the deepest of slumbers. The last time I was in town, I bought a few supplies to make some improvements and repairs to the cabin, and they occupy most of my time for the next couple of weeks. I work on my projects and chop loads of firewood to keep the cabin warm all winter. My muscles have never felt as tired as after a day spent dragging fallen logs out of the forest, chopping them into usable pieces, and stacking the wood under the open-sided woodshed behind the cabin, but as the days pass, I sense my strength increasing.

Most of my work has to be completed during the morning hours before Janie wakes, or during her naptime, or after I've put her to bed for the evening. Keeping up with her busy, curious, often fussy toddler self is a full-time job. We read books, we color pictures, we play with her dolls, and we make castles out of blocks. We dig in the dirt, we splash in the creek (even though the water grows icier with each passing day), and we pick the falling leaves from the trees and make mini piles for her to jump in. There are days we practice lessons—she's learning the alphabet. I help DJ with his reading and arithmetic skills. Then there are mealtimes, bath times, naptimes, and bedtime routines. The days pass in a hazy blur, and three weeks have gone by before I've had time to blink.

Relentlessly, I keep myself occupied with as many tasks as possible to prevent the ache of loneliness and regret from taking root in my chest. Since I told Dean off and ordered him away, he hasn't come back to the cabin. I don't blame him. But now, everything reminds me of him, and I keep wishing his strong hands were here to lighten the workload that threatens to topple me over before the heavy silence of winter descends.

For his sake, I hope I scared him off for good.

The McCades sent us out with several bags of the freeze-dried meals they prepare for the team of cowboy range riders who guard their cattle all summer. The food is simple but hearty, nonperishable, easy to rehydrate, and warm up over the stove. It's plain, but anything would beat the over-salted canned soup and vegetables, chili beans, oatmeal, dried fruit, and crackers we've made the bulk of our diet for the past few months. Emma showed me how to make homemade bread and easy biscuits while we were recovering, and I keep wondering if I should haul up a bag of flour and pick up some yeast before winter hits.

Janie and DJ welcome the change in menu fare, scarfing the hot meals, freeze-dried fruits and vegetables, and bags of cookies Emma packed into sealed bags for us. Every now and then, I find chocolate bars that she stashed away for me. Somehow, she guessed my deep love for milk chocolate and the power of something sweet to make the hard days a little less hard. My niece's and nephew's eager enjoyment of the food makes me cringe with guilt, even as I eye our rations nervously.

I'm keenly aware that the food will only last us so long. I need a way to provide more protein and fat to fill their bellies during the coming months. I don't trust my ability to hunt and dress a deer in the field, so that option is out. Even if I could manage it, we have no way of freezing the venison all winter long. And even if I had the skill set to hunt a deer, I don't have a hunting license, and I'm not about to turn into a poacher.

So far, not a single threat has come through the clearing. I know there are probably bears making their final preparations for winter in these woods, but I've never seen one. The wolf pack Dean warned me about is still a concern, but after hearing eerie howls for a few nights in a row, I haven't heard them in a couple of weeks. Our forest clearing is quiet and peaceful, with only the occasional deer making her way through.

Yet, these growing children need calories to thrive, and they never seem to get full. At the rate we're blowing through our supplies, we won't have enough left for the winter. When it arrives, the snow is going to come in hard and fast. Hot, easy-to-heat meals rich in protein are going to be essential when we're snowed in. I can stock up on our supplies again, but realistically, how much protein can I store away for us? Without refrigeration or the ability to freeze meat, we'll be relying on beans, jerky, and peanut butter for most of the winter. Not particularly appetizing choices for two growing children.

The only way out will be by snowshoe, and that won't be happening often with Janie and DJ in tow. Danny hung a couple of pairs of snowshoes in the corner of the cabin, but attempting to use them wouldn't be a fun excursion. Not to mention, I'll need to keep the hidden Jeep cleared of snow. The main road is only a couple of miles away, but getting out if the snow dumps and cuts off the logging road could be trouble.

I still haven't received another message from Amy, and as the weeks pass, my worry grows with each passing day. She's found a way to contact me more than once. Why haven't I heard from her again? And what's taking her so long to return?

As the leaves on the aspens by the creek fade into the golden kiss of autumn, I remember the fishing hole and the plentiful Kokanee salmon currently making their yearly run in the chilly depths of the stream. While we ate the bland rations the army handed out to us, Danny told me about the years he and his grandpa would come up to the cabin in autumn and spend days catching the blue-backed fish. Since the cabin has no electricity, their only option for preserving the fish was to cook it over a low, smoky fire until a dried and long-lasting jerky was the end result. The American Indian tribes that once roamed the region were the original inventors of the useful method of preservation. Danny described the process to me during the long, sometimes dull, night watches on patrol.

An idea blooms in my mind as I make yet another small repair to the cabin. If I could catch and dry enough salmon, we would have a plentiful protein and fat source to get us through the winter, or at least until my sister returns. The jerky can be eaten plain or thrown into soups and stews to soften and rehydrate. It won't spoil or go stale, and I can reuse the preservation bags Emma sent with us to protect our supplies even more.

The biggest hindrance to the plan is not having a babysitter. Given the potential presence of wildlife, bringing the children along isn't the safest option, but leaving them alone for any length of time during the day is also out of the question.

But then it hits me, and my tired brain latches onto the idea as if it is our saving grace. Danny told me that he and his grandpa often went out fishing at four in the morning because that's when the salmon were biting best. The possibility brews in my mind, and I wonder if I can take the chance. It's a risk, but I think I can make it work this one time.

Chapter Twenty-Four

Dean
Late October

Climbing out of my tent, I stretch and try to work some of the kinks out of my back. A fine sheen of frost covers the ground, and the scent of fresh coffee wafts through the gloom of first light.

I shrug on a thick, long-sleeved flannel shirt. Autumn is creeping across the mountain, and each day that passes brings us closer to driving the herd back down the trail to the ranch for the winter. Snow season is coming.

I have to admit that I'm looking forward to the change.

Striding over to the fire, I grunt a "good morning" to Abraham, who is stirring a pot of thick oats for our breakfast, and pour myself a cup of the black sludge Knox insists is the ideal grounds-to-water ratio for the ultimate caffeine boost. We tolerate it because life without caffeine isn't something we want to navigate.

"You with us yet, boss?" Abraham inquires with amusement.

I grunt again. "Dirt floor beds seem to get harder every year. That sleeping pad isn't cutting it anymore."

The older man chuckles. "Imagine being my age."

We fall into silence as I sit on a rock and sip my coffee.

This time of year brings with it as much anticipation for the season ahead as regret that another summer on the range is over. I'll be glad to return to the valley for Mom's sake. Lately, she seems extra lonely. In early October, with the threat of the wolf pack seemingly abated, Vincent, Knox, and I left the herd with the cowboys and rode home to harvest this year's steers. Slaughtering and preprocessing our own cattle is an unusual choice for a rancher—the task often being outsourced—but it's a responsibility we believe rests firmly on our shoulders. Since we allow our stock to spend more time on pasture and reach a higher level of maturity than most beef ranchers, we're keenly aware of the sentience of our animals, and giving them dignity and extra care in their final days is prioritized.

After harvesting and initial processing, we turned the meat over to our fulfillment partners for freezing and distribution to the families who will be nourished for the next year. When all of that was over, we stayed on the ranch to help Charlie put up the hay for the winter, hundreds of bales gathered, rolled, and stored. As regenerative ranchers, our goal is to feed as little grain during the winter as we can. Almost a hundred percent pasture-raised beef is a lofty goal, requiring a great deal of planning and effort during the warm seasons. But so far, the quality of our cattle has only improved year by year.

It took us nearly a month to rejoin the herd and take over to give the rest of the team a break. Abraham stayed behind, claiming that he needed to keep an eye on us youngsters. It's good to be back, but as our time on the mountain draws to a close for the season, I'm aware of a growing sense of foreboding in the back of my mind.

I've turned my focus onto the herd, my team, and getting everything into place for the start of escrow on Bear Creek Lodge. The property isn't currently operational for the upcoming snow season, but it will give my brothers and me a project to bond over during the winter as we do the remodel and prepare it for next year. I'm staying focused on my family's legacy, both present and future, but my attention keeps slipping away to that cabin in the woods.

I haven't returned in a couple of weeks.

When Kasey told me she wanted space to think—space away from me—I rode away angry. It was a feeling that quickly shifted into a sense of disappointment that I've had to frequently remind myself I have no right to feel. Offering her a helping hand was the right thing to do, though I'm honest enough to know my goodwill has no doubt been influenced by the attraction I feel toward her. The vulnerability she hides behind that wall of toughness sparked an instinctive response in me from the beginning.

But I can't protect someone who doesn't want it. Kasey's stubbornness frustrates me to no end. As much as she tries to hide it, I see right through her ruse of being the tough loner.

But until she trusts me enough to let me in, my hands are tied. Unless I'm willing to risk her ire and insert myself into her life unasked, I can't protect her. If I cross her boundaries and make her feel trapped again, I can almost guarantee she'll disappear.

Losing contact with her is the last thing I want. Knowing she is still hidden away in the forest is better than never seeing her again.

In the distance, Knox and Vincent are walking up the slope together, thermoses of coffee in their hands. I missed our walk this morning because I slept in, but my currently sour mood wouldn't have contributed much value to the conversation.

For much of the season, we've had a routine of walking together at first light to do rounds, checking on the health of the horses, discussing the herd, and comparing notes on the nightly watch activity. We are often spread far apart during the days as the cattle wander across our current grazing range, so the mornings are our best time to catch up. Sometimes, one or the other of us will be on environmental restoration duty as we assess areas of our grazing path that need either protection from the trampling of our herd's hooves or more of it, the cattle's heavy hooves tilling the ground, and their droppings fertilizing it. We're seeing the fruits of our labor, as many areas we've grazed in the past are thriving with new growth when we make our way back through.

My brothers eye me as they stride up to the fire with an ease that I wish I shared. My shoulders feel tense, and I'm well aware of the grumpy expression I can't seem to stifle on my face.

Per usual, Knox is the one to speak, drawing out the words in his teasing manner. "So . . . what are your plans for today?"

Quietly, Vincent lowers himself to the log next to me. His face is introspective, but I can feel his sharp observation.

My eyes lift to Knox, but I don't move my head. "I don't know, Knox. Maybe the usual: Guard the cattle and keep as many of them safe and healthy as possible so we can scrape by with just enough profit to keep the ranch running for another year while we simultaneously protect and restore an entire mountain while not disturbing the local ecosystems and wildlife? What are your plans for the day?"

He snickers. "Somebody is in a mood this morning."

I shake my head and try to avoid acknowledging the wave of guilt his words trigger. I've been in a mood for weeks, and I'm well aware that my team has noticed.

"Sorry. I just have a lot on my mind, and I'm feeling the pressure of the end of the season," I reply.

"Oh, I'm sure you are. And you must be missing your pretty lady friend and her kids something awful too?" Knox's tone is serious, but his eyes dance merrily.

When I glance over to Vincent, he lifts his palms in a surrendering motion.

"It wasn't him," Knox continues. "You already know Mom told us all about your future wife while we were home. Why didn't you tell us the lady you are courting is both feisty and pretty? That's a win-win. Mom said she gave you a run for your money."

"I'm not courting anyone," I grumble. "But I suppose the whole western half of Montana now thinks I am?"

Knox places his hand over his heart. "Brother, I am *shooketh* that you would think such a thing of me. As if I would betray such confidential information about the love life of the most eligible bachelor in all of Cascade Valley." An expression of faux dismay crosses his face. "Do you think I want all those ladies running to my arms for comfort because they missed their chance?"

I swipe at him with my empty coffee cup, and he dances away, narrowly missing the campfire as he bellows out a laugh. While I know he is only teasing me, the words are painful as they hit their mark.

"I didn't let him tell anyone," Vincent says to me in an undertone, "though he was rarin' to go whenever we went to town."

I'm grateful that he was able to hold in check Knox's dramatic love for a good story, but my irritation persists. Of course, my brothers were already aware of the reason for my extended stay at the ranch weeks ago. I didn't keep any of it from them. I just left out the part about Kasey being gorgeous, stubborn as a mule, and capable of outshooting half the men I know. Leave it to Mom to fill in the details for her sons, but to be fair, I never told her to keep anything private beyond not talking too much about her around the valley to respect Kasey's wishes.

Vincent isn't done. "Sounds like Mom was pretty taken with her and her kids. She wants them to spend Thanksgiving and Christmas at the ranch. You'd better pass that onto your lady friend . . . Kasey . . . Do you know her last name?"

"No, I don't," I admit. "Did Mom really ask you to tell me that?"

"Yeah." And that's all my brother says about it, rising and dusting off his jeans before he strides off to saddle up his horse for the day's shift.

I'm left to ponder this new information, and it stays with me as I go about the day's duties. Within the next couple of weeks, we'll be driving the cattle back to the ranch as the first snowstorms begin to hit the mountains. While the cattle are hardy against the cold temperatures, the grass they've been feasting on is slowly diminishing, so wintering them in the hills is pointless.

Winters on the mountain can get dangerous fast. There are three key elements to survival as a cattle rancher: shelter, heat, and food. And daily prayers for protection against illnesses or emergencies. If even one of these elements goes awry, the consequences can be deadly.

And my stomach sours at the thought that there is a woman and her two small children planning to winter in a cabin Danny only built to be a hunting and fishing lodge. It's stupid and foolhardy and completely unnecessary.

By nightfall, I've made up my mind.

When I rise from the fire and turn toward my tent, I pause to look back at the trio of men gathered around the flames. The days are still warm, but the nights are growing chillier. We haven't been back from the valley for long, but what I need to do can't wait.

"In the morning, I'm going to head back," I say to the group. "I need to check on our winter preparations and handle some personal business. Escrow on the lodge is commencing soon, and I want to make sure it's wrapping up smoothly. I'll send Ian up to cover me. You boys good here for a day?"

Three pairs of eyes turn toward me in the gathering darkness, each head nodding in acquiescence. Knox and Abraham lift their hands to their temples in salute.

"Right-O, boss. We've got it covered here," Abraham speaks, ever the faithful cowboy. "You do what you need to do."

I give him a nod and a grateful look before turning in for the night, hoping that what I have to do isn't a mistake.

. . .

Morning is cold, and I'm in no less a troubled mood when I wake the next day than I was the night before. I grumble to myself even as I wonder if my priorities are misplaced.

After Dad's accident, I didn't know how I'd ever live up to the standards I knew he'd expect. Without letting my family see my inner struggle, I fought for our future. I fought to keep Dan McCade's memory alive. I fought to temper my need for control, to let the growth of our ranch be a collaborative effort. I struggled against my protective older brother instincts when Samantha chose to move her whole life overseas this summer.

I haven't been the perfect brother and rancher, but I've tried.

It's been over four years under my leadership, and right now, we're surviving. I can't predict the future, but so far, things are going well.

Which is why my failure to protect Kasey, Junior, and Janie stings so much.

Long before the sun comes up, I gather a few supplies, saddle my horse in the dark, and leave our camp. Midnight's long, steady strides cover the miles quickly. I head in almost the opposite direction of home. From our current grazing position, it would be easier and faster to take the back shortcut to the valley. I'm taking the most direct route to my destination on purpose. An urgency claws at my gut, cementing my resolve that I'm doing the right thing.

When the trail that leads toward the back of Fisherman's Gulch looms in the distance, I don't hesitate as I lead Midnight into it. We pick our way across the familiar forest floor, stepping over fallen logs and debris. Tapping his flank with my heels, I spur him up the slope that leads toward the fishing hole. It's peak hunting season, so I stay alert for signs of anyone else in the woods.

There are a couple of ways to get to Kasey's cabin, but those are easiest to access from the valley itself. I'm headed straight through Fisherman's Gulch to get to Kasey's cabin from the backside, the more direct approach from our current camping position. It's still dark, but I have no intention of delaying my visit. I'm going directly to the source of all my recent frustration. She might want to shut me out, but sometimes, cornering a wild animal is the only way to get it out of harm's way.

I keep Midnight at such a quick pace that the morning hasn't even dawned when we crest the ridge. Only the lingering light of the moon and the stars illuminates the meadow as we ride down.

I'll wait until the trio awakens, but at least the smoke of their stove will let me know they are still here.

I don't realize that I'm actually smelling the smoke of a campfire until the glow of the flames catches my eyes.

Even in the darkness, her figure is easy to spot as she moves in and out of the firelight. I have no doubts about who is on the other side of the water. She is moving around, her back to the gulch. I linger for a moment on the frosty grass, studying her, noticing how Kasey's usually smooth, controlled demeanor seems to have been replaced by a stumbling uncertainty. Her limp is more noticeable, and her hands flail. She seems to be grabbing frantically at whatever is hanging over the fire.

The sight of her and the realization that she is completely alone out here and unaware of my presence triggers a response deep within me. A fire builds in my chest. It's too bad that scooping her up, putting her on top of my horse, and carrying her off the mountain is out of the question.

My brain races. *Why* is she out here alone before dawn? *Where* are the kids? *How* could she leave them alone? If something happens to her out here, no one will ever know. There are a hundred ways to get injured, or worse, alone in the wilderness. The water, a random wolf or bear wandering through, falling and breaking a leg on the trail, or hunters tracking down a deer and accidentally shooting her all represent threats that could end her life. The kids would be left alone with no one around for miles and miles.

A flash of pure, hot anger runs across my limbs, and I feel it work its way up my throat, bursting forth in a harsh shout of "Kasey!" that echoes across the meadow.

She whips around, freezing momentarily at the sound of my voice. Standing in front of the fire, her hands ball into fists, and she plants them on her hips, her feet spread wide in a stance that is becoming all too familiar.

This isn't going to be a fun conversation, and I'm ready for it. I spur Midnight and ride toward the water, splashing across it recklessly.

She doesn't flinch when I dismount and throw my horse's reins to the ground. I stride straight up to her and stop mere inches away. My fury grows as she stares up at me, and the frown across her full lips doesn't do anything to cool me down.

"Do you want to explain what you are doing out here?" I shout, the words gritty and forceful as they leave my mouth.

"Do you want to explain what *you're* doing here?" she counters in an equally loud tone, those lips tightening when she's done.

"I was riding up to your place to check on you because I was fool enough to feel guilty that I let you drive me away," I snap out. My jaw clicks. "I'll ask you one more time, Kasey, and I want a straight answer: What in the world are you doing out here in the dark?"

"I'm catching fish to smoke and preserve for the winter," she says through gritted teeth. "What does it look like I'm doing?"

Glancing past her to the small smoking station set up over a crackling fire built on the sandy embankment, I have to give her points for creativity and ingenuity. Strips of Kokanee salmon are folded over the green sticks she's used as a hanging rack. It's a creative setup and a good idea.

But my anger isn't even close to burning out. "And you're doing it way out here, why?"

She throws up her hands. "So bears and wolves and mountain lions don't smell it and start hunting around the cabin for it."

I'm slightly impressed. "You have the right idea, but do you realize it takes days to cold-smoke meat and fish to a level that is safe for preservation? You'd be out here for days keeping your fire going at just the right temperature."

"Is this cold-smoking?"

"This is hot smoking. What you should be doing is packing the fish in salt for a few days and then air-drying it. You're running the risk of botulism with this method."

Her face pales, her expression immediately turning aghast. Her stubborn demeanor fades, but she doesn't seem ready to stop fighting just yet. "I thought I told you I don't need any help."

The words make my temper flare again. I throw my hands out to my sides, encompassing the entire meadow and the woods beyond with the gesture, staring down at her incredulously. "Don't need my help? Kasey, where are the kids? How in the world could you leave them alone like this? I've told you time and time again how many threats are in these woods at any given time, but you won't listen."

I see when the weight of what she's risked hits her with full force. "But I left Finn with them," she stutters. "He's on guard. The door is locked. The fire is out. There's nothing they can get hold of that they shouldn't. Janie is sleeping in her pack and play. She won't be up for a couple of hours. She can't climb out, and Junior knows not to open the door."

Her excuses hold no weight with me. "You'd be surprised at what a small, determined child can climb out of." I fold my arms across my chest. "What if Junior tries to light a fire because he's seen you do it so many times? What if someone with evil intentions happens across the cabin and realizes two small children are alone inside? How could you leave them so unprotected?" I raise my voice again and hear it echo across the meadow.

Her face blanches, but her voice comes out shouting. "Evil? I'm doing everything I can to protect them from evil." Her hands flail out to her sides, her eyes flashing with fire. "You want to talk evil, Dean? I've already seen it. I've stared it straight in the face in the shape of a roadside bomb that took the life of my friend and several other soldiers in my platoon and nearly took mine." Her chest heaves with the effort of her breaths. "And before that, I saw evil in the shape of a father who abandoned the daughter he chose to create—and I had to watch him choose everything else over me."

Her voice falls to a whisper. She chokes out the words. "I'll never let anything happen to those children because I know what it's like to face the terrible things in life alone."

I'm at a loss for words. Before me stands a woman who has been shattered in a thousand places. Somehow, she's pieced herself back together, but the cracks are still there, a vulnerability in her armor, clear despite all her blustering. My heart hurts for the battles she has faced by herself with no one to protect her. I feel my anger fading. The urge to pull her into my arms and promise her that I'll never let anything happen to her again is immediate and hard to resist.

With a superhuman effort, I gather my self-control. My hands come up to hover at her elbows as I whisper over her. "But Kasey—you're not alone anymore."

Chapter Twenty-Five

Kasey

Tears well up in my eyes, an instant reaction to the words falling from his lips. I have a fleeting wish he would raise his arms a little higher and hold me close. I've never felt a need for hugs, but the memory of the strength of his embrace last month under the stars has convinced me that true safety exists in Dean's arms.

But if I'd let him keep getting close to us, it was the surest way to put him in danger too. And once I hear from Amy, we're gone for good. Leaving no trace of our presence here is the only way to ensure that the secret of her addiction and her recovery in rehab stays a secret. She's supposed to be enjoying a relaxing vacation in California. I've imagined the outcome of her eventual court case against my brother-in-law a thousand times. There's no way he can admit to committing illegal acts—especially if he's been using less-than-legal means to track her down—but the only way to truly guarantee that she gets full custody of her children is to make sure no one ever knows that she sent the children away with me in the first place. Out of pure survival, it must be as if this all never happened.

There's no coming back to Cascade Valley once the burner phone rings. Better that the good man before me thinks we simply got up and moved on one day without a word. The thought of treating him that way makes my heart ache.

I have to convince Dean to forget about us.

And that's going to be hard to do after he just caught me out here being a complete and utter fool.

Whirling around, I stomp back to the fire, realizing how delusional I was to think surviving the winter would be as easy as smoking some fish. Catching the salmon wasn't the hard part. They were biting like mad this morning when I hiked down here at three o'clock to get set up. I convinced myself that I could catch a few fish, smoke them, and then return before my niece even awakened.

It turns out all of this was a colossal waste of time.

I'm just going to have to try again with salt. I'm kicking myself for not thinking of that before. I'd already be back up the hill with my catch by now, and this entire fight with Dean wouldn't have happened.

I kick dirt and water over the flames to smother the fire before snatching up what is left of my fresh catch from the morning. The waders I donned in the dark are too big and uncomfortable, the rubber slapping around my legs as I try to hoist the bucket of fish, the fishing pole, and all the supplies I brought onto my shoulder. If Dean weren't here, I would strip down to the jeans and flannel I'm wearing underneath for the hike back, but there is zero chance of me doing that with him standing ten feet away.

He's watching every move I make with those too-perceptive,

too-inquisitive eyes of his. The fury pulsed off him in waves minutes ago when he first rode up. In hindsight, I realize how well-placed his anger was, but at the moment, his gaze is sad. I feel as if he can see right through me to the painful thoughts swirling through my mind, and I hate it. But mostly, I hate myself for putting my niece and nephew in danger. They were sleeping when I left, and I thought I could be back before they'd even woken up. What a fool I was.

What a fool I've been over and over. And it just goes to prove what I already believed: I will never deserve to be a mother.

Ignoring Dean, I limp toward the forest, my knee shooting pain, the purple scar puckered and painful as the rubber pants slap against it.

God, please let them be okay. I would never forgive myself if anything happened to either of them.

Trying to pray at such a desperate moment feels foreign. I wish I had the assurance of faith that Dean so easily witnesses. But I'm trying . . . trying to trust the God I've pushed away for so long. Because it's glaringly obvious that I need intervention from the Hand of Divine Providence right now, as failure seems to cloud every attempt to protect these kids from harm.

A spike of fear shoots through my stomach—fear that I won't get back in time to prevent something terrible from happening— and I break into a stumbling run toward the line of trees at the edge of the meadow, dragging my supplies with me. Filled with shame, I can't even look back over my shoulder at Dean in farewell. I hate that he can now hold such a huge blunder against me.

What if he calls child services? What if he reports me? What if . . .

My focus is solely on reaching the shadowy line in the trees, where I can disappear at last. But when I hear the snort of the big, black horse he rides coming from only a foot or two behind me, I jump and spin around. Dean is walking just to my rear, his long legs shortening their stride to keep up with mine, the reins looped through his hands. I stop, the supplies nearly tumbling out of my hands as I face him with shame.

"Why are you following me?" The tears are close to the surface, evident in the thickness of my voice. I hear the edge of frustration, too, the emotion rising instinctively to protect me from the desperation I feel.

"You don't think I came all this way just to leave you to fend for yourself," he replies. The gentleness in his tone when I'm expecting condemnation guts me. He extends his hand. "Kasey, here, let me carry some of that for you."

I can't muster up a reply. Wordlessly, I hand off the bucket of salmon to him. He takes it, and I turn and continue my rush into the forest.

In silence, we climb the trail. It winds eastward toward the cabin. In the months we've been up here, we've worn what was once a very faint deer trail that led directly to the meadow into one that is at least somewhat comfortable and quick to hike. Anxiety spirals in my stomach, its intensity growing along with the pain in my knee with each step. Relieved of the heavy bucket, I force myself to ignore the discomfort and quicken my pace. Dean trails behind, letting me outpace him as he guides Midnight's steps.

I'm breathless by the time the trees thin and the pitched roof of the cabin comes into view, the sun just beginning to furl its light across the sky in the distance. I almost drop to my knees at the sight of it, my nerves working double time in a terrified frenzy that, somehow, in my absence, the cabin will have disappeared into thin air as if it never existed, taking my precious niece and nephew with it.

But there it stands, peaceful and serene in the quiet clearing. There's no smoke pouring from the chimney; the windows and doors look closed. I reach the porch and drop everything I'm carrying with no regard for how it lands. Shoving off the cumbersome waders and leaving them in a pile on the floor, I reach for the doorknob and throw it open, the chaotic flutter of adrenaline in my stomach reaching a fever pitch.

Please let them be okay. Please let them be okay.

The silent plea is an echo straight from my soul.

Janie is still fast asleep in her pack and play. DJ is awake and looks up when I enter. His battery-operated lantern is on, and he has spread the water-based paints and markers Emma sent with us all over the floor. Finn is alert and on guard at his side. His big ears turn forward, and his posture stiffens when I enter with a rush of air and soft, morning light, but he quickly relaxes when he recognizes me.

"I woke up early to watch over Janie," DJ whispers as I enter. "But I'm glad you're back now."

Janie begins to whimper and cry from her bed, no doubt woken by the frantic clatter of my boots. It's the most wonderful sound I've ever heard.

Stumbling, I walk forward and pick her up. I collapse on my knees beside my nephew, reaching for him. I hug both children, kissing their cheeks and the tops of their heads, realizing how stupid I was to leave them alone. No matter how much I justified it in my head, nothing could be more important than being here to protect them.

"I love you both so much," I say over and over.

Janie wraps her arms around my neck. She stares with a

confused expression as the tears stream down my cheeks. "You sad? No sad. I love you," she prattles, her hands coming up to touch the tears on my face.

The sudden declaration catches me off guard. "I'm not sad, baby girl. I'm happy," I assure her, hugging her tightly until she wiggles away and totters over to the wooden box that has become a makeshift toy chest to pull out the doll Emma gave her. I rise to turn on another lantern to give us light until the sun fully rises.

"I'm hungry," DJ declares.

"Me too," I reply with a clap of my hands. "I'm going to get some firewood and make us a big ol' breakfast."

When I rise, Dean is in the doorway, his frame darkening the space. Normally friendly with the rancher, Finn senses that something is off. He rises onto all fours and stares him down until I mutter a quiet release. Only then does he trot toward the door, his fluffy tail wagging as he approaches Dean, who squats to pet the big dog, scratching the sides of his face and ears with friendly camaraderie.

When the children notice him in the doorway, Dean takes my silence as unspoken permission to enter. They run to welcome him, and he bends down to their level, his arms outstretched for hugs. They chatter to him, and laughter from all three fills the room. For a few minutes, it feels like we are one happy family with no monsters waiting in the shadows.

But the sight of their enthusiasm gradually breaks my heart. There is no denying that they love having Dean around. Yet, all too soon, he will have to leave, and we'll be alone again. How can I explain his absence in a way they can understand? They've already had so much taken away. My eyes sting with tears again, but I swallow them ruthlessly.

The firebox is empty, so I grab the canvas bag I use to carry logs from the woodpile, skirt around the small group in the middle of the floor, and head for the still-open doorway. When I step off the porch, I hear Dean rising, speaking to the children in his deep voice, telling them to color him a picture to take back to Miss Emma.

I wish he wouldn't follow me. I just want a moment to be miserable all by myself, but I don't say anything as I hear his boots in pursuit of my retreating form. I know I deserve whatever harsh words he has for me.

The cabin door clicks shut as I round the corner of the house and head for the woodpile. In a few weeks, I've managed to stockpile a decently sized fuel source for winter. It sits about the height of my waist and took me hours to chop and stack, but now, in the soft light of morning, it seems like nothing at all. Is it enough to get us through the winter? How can I even predict what we'll need? If I only had to fend for myself, I could get through the snowy season with ease. I don't need much; army life ensured that. But the two tiny souls back in the cabin? They deserve safety, plentiful food, warmth, entertainment, learning opportunities . . . things I can't fully guarantee we'll have if the winter is particularly harsh.

Against my will, the tears run in salty streams down my face. I feel heartbroken and heart weary, defeated and beaten down. My knee throbs, the skin tightening along my scar, and my limp grows more pronounced with each step. My body seems as if it is suddenly shutting down. Can I even go on with this charade anymore? Maybe I should just turn myself in, leave my fate in the hands of the authorities, and pray that the legal system is fair when my sister returns to find her children. Surely, even foster care would be better for them than the place I've brought them to.

Once, I couldn't save my team and was left with dead friends, painful memories, and a disability that will stay with me for life. And now I'm failing my pretense at motherhood.

When I reach the woodpile, the canvas bag falls at my feet. I bury my face into my hands as the tears fall, trying in vain to choke back the sobs. I'm waiting for his condemning words to fall around me like missiles, hitting their mark and shredding me to pieces.

"Kasey, talk to me."

Instead, his hands are gentle when they land on my shoulders. He turns me around, and the next thing I know, his arms are wrapped around me, and my face is buried in his shirt. For the second time since we've met, I cry out the pain into his chest, clinging onto him for dear life. And once again, he holds me as if he'll never let go.

"I'm so sorry, Dean." My voice is muffled against the thick cotton fabric of his navy t-shirt. "I didn't mean to mess up so badly. I'm such a terrible person for leaving them alone."

His fingers bury themselves in my hair as he cradles my head. His voice whispers against my ear. "No one is calling you a bad parent. You're a single mom trying to make this work out here on your own. The environment isn't exactly the easiest. Don't beat yourself up. They are okay."

Except I'm not a mom, and all of this is a lie.

The tears dry up, and my sobs slow as the despair returns to my chest. Anger surges in, pushing away the pain, fortifying me with the only strength I seem to have left. Slipping away from Dean, I step under the overhang that protects the stacked wood from the elements, breathing in the scent of pine. When a shadow passes across the far wall, I whirl back to face him. His expression is unreadable.

My breath comes heavily as we stare at each other. I can hear the children laughing a few yards away from the windows in the cabin.

"What aren't you telling me, Kasey?" His voice carries a husky timbre that tingles across my skin. The words hit too close to home.

Stubbornly, I set my jaw. If the ire in my gaze doesn't throw him off, maybe my silence will.

He doesn't falter, taking a step closer, ducking a little under the sloped overhang. "Why are you really out here?" The question isn't a request; it's a demand. "And don't give me any lines about it being a vacation. No one chooses to live off the grid in these primitive conditions unless there's a good reason."

I lift my chin, pretending his words don't set off alarm bells in my head. He's getting jarringly close to the truth.

Dean steps closer, his boots crunching across the feathery pine needles. He reaches up and whips off his cap, running a hand through his messy hair. Frustration pulses off him in waves.

"Are you married? Divorced? In a relationship?" The gruffness deepens.

"What?" I exclaim. "No, no, and no."

"Then what kind of trouble are you in? Because I know you're spooked by something; don't try to deny it."

A cold shiver breaks out across my scalp, and I'm not sure if I can take another breath. I call up what little fight I have left and warn through gritted teeth, "I've told you to leave it alone, Dean. What I'm going through is none of your business."

I dart around him and start toward the cabin, my arms flailing, my limp causing my leg to drag. The porch is just around the corner when his hand captures mine. He spins me around, both hands alighting on my shoulders. Without giving me time to react, Dean backs me into the logs of the cabin wall. My back hits it with a soft thud. He holds me in place, his face only inches away. His narrowed eyes capture mine, and I stare back. I'm terrified of the truth, but I don't want to run.

"And I've told you," he says through tightly pressed lips, "I don't care what you're dealing with. I fully plan to make it my business. Because whether you like it or not, you're mine to protect."

At his fiercely spoken words, I try to call back my anger, but there's nothing left. My fight dissipates, replaced by an urgent flutter in my stomach. My legs become jelly, and I wonder if I will collapse in a puddle against the cabin if Dean releases his hold on me. Just on the other side of the log wall, DJ says something that makes Janie giggle, reminding me of why I'm here in the first place.

"But why? Why won't you let this go?" My voice is thick. "Don't you understand I don't want you involved in my mess? Why do you care so much about what happens to us?"

He leans over me, his arms slipping around my back, drawing me close. My hands rise to rest against his chest, my fingers closing to bunch the fabric of his shirt between them. His eyes go dark, their gray tones deepening to a perfect storm.

"You speak as if caring for you is hard," he rumbles. "But Kasey, it's not. It's easy. And maybe I care so much because I'm hoping that one day, I can kiss you without a dark cloud hanging over your head."

"I think I was born with that dark cloud." I shake my head. "You don't want me, Dean. I've got scars and baggage like you wouldn't believe."

"If you're referring to that scar on your leg," his gaze won't let me go, "all I see is the woman who must have put her life on the line to earn it."

"That's just the one you can see," I admit. "The others . . . some of them go more than skin deep."

His arms tighten with gentle pressure around my waist. "Then each one serves as a reminder of what you've gone through to make you into the incredible woman you are, and they're beautiful to me."

Every word echoes its truth in the pulse of my veins. Head back, I stare up at him, unable to break the hold his gaze has on me. And I don't want to; I want to stay in this moment here with him forever. Because being with Dean is the safest feeling I've ever known.

My mind spins, and when his head finally dips, I'm not prepared for the moment his lips claim mine. A startled gasp emits from my throat. But his touch is gentle, his lips pressing only lightly at first. The soft rasp of his beard brushes my skin. Instinctively, I know that he is giving me ample room to push him back, to demand that he walk away and leave us alone forever. But I couldn't escape his kiss if I tried.

Instead, I melt into him. I feel the murmur of incoherent words rumbling in my throat, lost somewhere in the deepening of our kiss as I lift myself onto the toes of my boots and wrap my arms around the back of his neck. His low muttering echoes mine. Everything goes still, the sounds of the forest fading as a blast of warmth shoots along every nerve ending in my skin. His hands press around my waist, drawing me in as I simultaneously pull him closer. We're wrapped up in each other, and I feel a precipice looming, but this time, it doesn't feel like I'm the only one hanging on for dear life.

For the briefest of moments, there's no danger breathing down the back of my neck, no terrifying, faceless men hunting us down, no sorrow for the terrible choices my sister has made, no regret for the part I played in it by my abandonment of her. For a moment, there's only fire at the ends of my fingertips as they curl into the soft hairs at the nape of his neck.

He's the first to break the kiss, and I groan, wanting to pull him back. If this moment never ends, maybe, just maybe, he'll give me the strength to survive another day. Maybe if Dean never lets me go, the shadowy ravine that lurks around every corner of the forest won't swallow me up in its depths.

But as if it is just waiting for him to release me, the darkness presses in at the corners of my mind again. The stoic mask I've fortified myself with for years slips back into place as he stares down at me, his eyes hooded and glossy. My lips sting from our kiss. The almost painful beating of my heart slows its rapid pace. I see the moment he leans down to claim my lips again, but I stop him, placing my fingers lightly over his mouth.

"I don't want to keep the full truth from you, Dean," I murmur. My hand drops to his chest, and I place it over his heart. Its steady rhythm gives me the strength to say what I must say. "There are things I can't reveal just yet. Secrets that must be kept for the safety of Junior and Janie. I need you to trust me for a little while longer. Can you trust that every decision I make is for their benefit?"

He pauses, studying me, not loosening his grip at all. I'm still wrapped safely in his arms. My fingers curl into the fabric of his t-shirt.

"I can," he finally replies, the words slow and thoughtful, "but only for a short time longer."

Relief washes over me. "I don't need long. But I'm scared," I whisper. "It feels like I'm walking through an ever-deepening ravine, trapped between sheer mountain cliffs on both sides. I can't climb out of it. It's pitch black behind and ahead of me. One wrong step and I could plunge forever into the abyss. I just want to see the light again." The bitter words spill out from someplace deep within. It's the most truthful I can permit myself to be with him.

I expect him to push me away, but there's only tenderness in his expression. "I think you know by now I would take it all away for you if I could," he says. "Though I don't have all the answers for you right now, Kasey, there is One who does. Others have walked in your shoes. King David once wrote, 'Yea, though I walk through the valley of the shadow of death, I will fear no evil; For You are with me.' I know you are still on a journey of faith, but I can promise you this: No matter how alone you feel, God is with you."

"It feels like something evil is right around the corner, and I'm powerless to stop it," I whisper.

He pulls me closer. "But He's not powerless to stop it. He's with you, your Good Shepherd. You may not realize He's guiding your path, but His staff is next to you, preventing you from walking unwittingly into the darkest places." A fierce urgency rings through his words as his arms tighten around my waist. "All through the valley, He walks with you, and when the trail gets too narrow and treacherous, He picks you up and carries you to safety. Cling to that truth, and don't let it go."

Dean's chest rises and falls with a deep breath before he continues, "And God also provides help along the path that it's up to you to take. How can I help you if I don't know what we're up against?"

My heart leaps. Since when have he and I become a *we?* Somewhere along the way, despite all the times I've rejected him, this man and I have slowly morphed into a unit, one that I desperately wish I could lean on forever.

"Honestly, I don't know," I whisper. "If I'm doing anything wrong, I promise it's not intentional. I'm not involved in anything illegal. Please don't ask me any more questions."

He shakes his head. "If not pressing you for the truth is the right choice, then I'm sorry, I can't do it. In this case, I'd rather be in the wrong."

I nod, a regretful smile creeping across my face. "I'll be honest, if this experience has shown me anything, it's that life isn't all black and white. Sometimes, I wonder if you have to do what might be perceived as the wrong thing for the right reasons."

We both know I'm not talking about his meddling anymore. He stares at me, his mouth pressing into a somber line.

"Kasey, I'm going to ask you a question, and I want an honest answer. Do you have legal custody of those two?" The words are unexpected and gruff, spoken as a sharp glint enters his eyes.

"Yes!" My protest is immediate, loud, and vehement. Quickly, I pull myself together and repeat the word. "Yes. I promise. I have legal custody of those children."

It isn't a lie, though it's not the full truth. I recall Amy's express and notarized letter of guardianship sitting securely in the duffel bag. Withholding even a fraction of the full truth from this man feels so wrong. But what can I do? It isn't my life and future at stake. It's Amy's. My sister's life and freedom hang in the balance, and the scales are precarious.

He gives me a deep, searching look. I try not to crumble, feeling the chink in my armor widening. If he keeps looking at me like that . . . A few seconds more and I may not be able to keep myself from telling him everything.

Finally, he nods, his mood somber. "I trust you. But pushing me away and shutting me out stops here. Whether you like it or not, something brought me to your cabin door, and I'm not walking away. I care about those children, and I care about you. Let me in. Let me help you."

The chink widens. I want nothing more than to permit myself to lean on him, so I nod. My hands slip behind his neck again. "Okay. I'll let you help us. But it has to be on my—"

He pulls me up before I can finish the sentence. For a moment, the forest brightens as the sun rises above the trees. The press of Dean's lips against mine becomes an anchor in the turbulent tempest of my soul.

And I can't help but wonder if this is the calm before the storm.

Chapter Twenty-Six

Dean

Kissing Kasey didn't do anything to help me walk away from her. The way she leaned into me—her soft breath coming out in little huffs as she nestled into my arms like she'd only been waiting for me to make the first move—told me that I might have saved us a world of frustration if I'd just made my feelings known sooner.

I only left after she promised she would drive down the mountain to stay with Mom soon. If she plans on wintering at the cabin, the easiest place to prepare is at the ranch. Our deep freezers are well-stocked, and Mom is an expert at canning and preserving. She'll ensure that the family has at least several months of food, herbal tinctures, and natural remedies before the snow sets in. To successfully get through a deep Montana winter, Kasey will need whatever supplies she can gather . . . or that I can convince her to accept.

I suspect that no matter how many times we offer her the

ready-made provisions from our root cellar, she'll insist on doing everything herself.

It's fine with me if she wants to work herself to the bone drying, canning, smoking, and preserving, because I have no intention of letting them go back to Danny's cabin. Somehow, I'll convince her to spend the winter on the ranch with us. She can stay at the foreman's cabin on the back pasture rent free if she wants her privacy. That's the only way I can convince myself to temporarily leave her behind on the mountain again.

One way or another, I'm going to get her to tell me why she's so dead set on living like a hermit. I tell myself it won't change the way I feel about her, but I need to know her secrets, even if that means I have to do some digging into her past without her knowledge.

As Midnight eats up the miles—his steady trot keeping pace down the mountain toward the ranch—the truth seems to linger around each corner, darting just out of sight as we approach the bend. A hundred scenarios play through my head, each worse and more sinister than the last.

She's not married, and she's not divorced. I'm glad both of those possibilities have been eliminated. My attraction to her isn't forbidden. I'm free to pursue her, and that's what I intend to do. So what is it, then? What could be so terrifying that a woman moves as far away from society as she can get? Ever since we met, there's been something I couldn't put my finger on, but without anything definitive to investigate, it's left me forced to accept her explanations. A growing sense of trouble makes me wonder if my attraction to her distracted me from something I should have seen already.

Perhaps she isn't a divorcée, but those children probably have a father. Where is he? That's what I want to know. Because that changes everything.

My hands grip the reins tighter, and Midnight responds with a concerned jolt. His ears swivel, glancing around to see if a threat is waiting for us. His metal shoes clatter sideways, kicking up sparks on the rocky path. I force my heart rate to slow, and in response to the change in its beat, my horse calms too.

Whatever Kasey's secrets, I want to uncover them. If only to put my mind at ease. What I'm even suspicious of, I don't really know. That a self-reliant, stubborn-as-a-mule, beautiful-as-the-sunrise woman won't let me be her knight in shining armor?

I scoff aloud, realizing how ridiculous I sound.

When we reach the valley floor, McCade ranch land stretches before us, and we cover the last few miles quickly. After tucking a freshly groomed, watered, and well-fed horse into his stall, I make a quick sweep of the barnyard before heading into the house. Mom isn't home, so it gives me the chance to shower and change and jump into my truck without feeling guilty that I can't stay to fill her in on the week.

A few ranch hands are working on some winter preparation projects in the pastures as I drive out. A twinge of regret hits me for not stopping to help, but I have my own work to do.

When my truck roars down Caleb's driveway, he strides out of the barn as I pull in front of the stables, his chin tipping up in greeting.

My friend is carrying a saddle. He throws it easily over the fence and waits for me to exit the truck. A white colt trots over to the fence line in the paddock next to the stable, his regal neck arched as he makes a beeline for the rancher. Caleb reaches for him and strokes his mane.

"Didn't expect to see you here again until you brought the herd down in a few weeks," he remarks as I approach.

"Everything good?"

"Yeah," I draw out the word hesitantly, "everything is good. I needed to get some business done before we bring the herd in for the season." I cut right to the chase as he eyes me. "Do you remember Danny Gardener?"

He nods in his thoughtful manner, his dark eyes observing me with curiosity. "Yep, I do."

"Do you remember which regiment he served in?"

"Can't say that I remember it off the top of my head, but I can make a call to find out. I still talk to his cousin now and again. He's stationed in South Carolina."

"Can you reach out to him and let him know that I have a few questions for him? Check that it's okay for you to pass on his number to me."

"Something going on that you care to share?"

"Not yet. I just need to dig up some information about Danny's time in the service."

Caleb observes me keenly. I attempt to keep my expression light and unbothered. We've been friends for years, and there isn't much that gets past his quiet, stoic exterior. He's snarkier and more vocal than Vincent, but they both conduct themselves with the same trustworthy, carry-your-secrets-to-their-grave steadiness. I trust Caleb with my life, and more importantly, with the lives of my family members. And, as it turns out, with the future happiness of my youngest sister . . . if she ever decides to stop being stubborn and let him put a ring on her finger. I've no doubt Caleb would give up everything and move to Europe to pursue missionary work if it came down to it. The two of them are just too mule-headed for either to make the first move.

"I'll get in touch with Jared," he finally replies.

"Thanks. Heard from Samantha yet?" I redirect the

conversation casually, noting how the abrupt change in subject causes his suntanned face to pale under his dark beard.

He shrugs. "A few texts here and there when she first left, but we haven't spoken in a while."

"Have you tried reaching out to her again?"

Caleb reaches for the white colt. Beau is his name, and the horse prances away, bobbing his head, dancing sideways before lumbering back to the fence. "If your sister wants to talk to me, she has my number," he mutters.

There's a hint of bitterness in his tone, for which I don't blame him. Samantha's decision to move to Europe to pursue a career at an orphanage surprised us all. Even more surprising was her willingness to walk away from Caleb.

Extending my hand, I grasp his shoulder. "Don't lose heart. God wants the best for both of you."

A light that was missing reappears in the depths of his eyes. One corner of his mouth lifts into a smirk. "You know, you're pretty good at this counseling thing. Ever thought of making a career change? Life coaching might be right up your alley."

I laugh. "And who would you suggest I offer my services to first?"

He turns serious. "Knox sure could use a reality check. That kid is something else. Did he tell you he came over and tried to convince me to let him ride Beau when y'all were down here last?" He nods toward the prancing colt.

I shake my head in disbelief. "You're kidding?"

Knox is an excellent horseman, but Beau is Caleb's most prized possession and an exceptional representation of the Arabian breed. He may end up being the future of Caleb's breeding program, so the only people allowed near him are Caleb, Griff the ranch foreman, and Jenna.

We turn toward the house and fall into step next to each other. The spirited horse trots alongside us down the fence line, trying to catch our attention with his antics. I know there's work to be done at home, and I need to stop by the bank to make sure the transfers are in place for the close of escrow on the lodge, but something about the weathered porch that I've sat on a thousand times in the company of my friend calls to me. The thrumming of the crickets fills the air as the afternoon winds down.

Out here in the country, time slows and worries fade. There's only the earth and the sky and the mountains as far as the eye can see. Soon, autumn will change out her light coat for her heavy winterwear, and the pleasant evenings will be replaced by cold, snow, and ice.

It's been a long time since I just sat and sorted through all the thoughts troubling me, so when Caleb offers me a cold soft drink and a seat on the porch, putting off my errands until tomorrow seems like the right idea.

Chapter Twenty-Seven

Kasey
Late November

"Kasey, do you need to grab a coat for tonight?" Emma's warm tones break into my thoughts, and I feel the heat of the ceramic mug of hot tea I've been clutching since the last piece of Thanksgiving pie was scraped off Knox's plate still warming the palm of my hand as she continues, "The tree farm will be chilly, and we're about to leave."

As her voice fades and her eyes meet mine keenly, I startle and realize it's expected that the three of us will join the family for their annual tree-cutting expedition. I have to admit I'm shocked we're still staying at the farmhouse. I was too reluctant to disappoint Emma to refuse her hospitable offer, so we've been guests at the ranch for the past two weeks, and it feels as if we are settling into a routine that is both terrifying and comforting. The thing that has surprised me the most is how much I enjoy life with the McCades.

When we first arrived, Emma insisted that I take Samantha's room for a few days until the empty foreman's cabin on the other side of the ranch could be tidied up for me. DJ has his own cot, and Janie and I snuggle on the comfortable mattress of the bigger bed. She and Dean keep saying the cabin only needs a little more fixing up to be ready for us, but oddly enough, I'm not finding myself in a hurry to separate us from their gentle family life.

Out of the corner of my eye, I catch sight of DJ and Janie already bundled into the warm coats I bought for them. A sense of panic stirs in my chest. McCade family outings are a brand-new hurdle that I never thought to mentally prepare for. I certainly didn't expect to join them for Thanksgiving. I should have insisted that we go home before the festivities began, but here we are. And now, it's obvious we're expected to accompany the family to the tree farm.

But I don't think it'll do me any good to protest, so I don't bother, instead rising meekly to grab my coat from upstairs.

I'm not used to observing holidays, rarely having anyone with whom to celebrate them. Now, the house is filled with people, including Dean's two brothers, Knox and Vincent, and his sister, Demi, who flew in from New York City to spend the holiday weekend. Their youngest sister is in Spain, but I've been assured several times that Samantha would love to meet me.

Friends of the family have also flitted in and out of the house all day. To my dismay, I've been introduced to everyone who stops by. Their looks of surprise as they glance between me and Dean aren't lost on me, nor are the searching looks Dean's siblings gave me upon their arrival. I'm guessing they were already aware of my existence. Meeting them was more terrifying than my first deployment.

Vincent simply shook my hand, giving me a long look that felt as if he were looking into my soul, but his greeting was as quiet as he appears to be.

Demi stepped forward and folded me into a warm hug at our introduction. "It's such a pleasure to meet you, Kasey," she said.

Something in her gentle, husky voice made me think she walked into the house determined to make me feel welcome.

Knox, on the other hand, swept me into an unexpected bear hug, a grin plastered across his boyish face. "I can see why Dean keeps going up to that old cabin to visit you. You're pretty. I have to admit it's been nice not having him around base camp as much. Maybe you can keep him away more so he can't order us around like he's the boss or something."

Other than the furious blush that set my face ablaze, that was that. No one has questioned my presence in the valley or interrogated me about my past. No one has even asked me where the children's dad is. It's clear I'm welcome here just as I am.

I don't know what to think about the fact that his family members assume something is going on between us and are happy about it. I tell myself that nothing is going on, but the butterflies that erupt in my stomach every time Dean catches my eye and that frustratingly appealing smirk creeps over his lips as his eyes warm and crinkle at the edges whisper that my internal protests are very much a lie.

It's all making me as jumpy as a jackrabbit.

And now, we're headed to the tree farm to pick out a Christmas tree like one big, happy family, and I'm questioning how I got myself into this position in the first place. Dean appears at my side as I buckle DJ and Janie into their car seats. I should take my Jeep just in case we need to make a quick escape, but somehow, we've wound up climbing into Dean's truck. The rest of the group is already pulling out of the driveway in another truck, Knox's deep laughter and Demi's smooth, melodic tones carrying loudly into the crisp, starry night. There are snow clouds on the horizon, and I wonder for the dozenth time today if the kids and I should head back up to our cabin this weekend. If it snows, we could be headed for some rough road conditions. I don't want the snow to get so bad that we can't get up the logging road. As peaceful as things have been on the ranch, I'm determined not to spend the entire winter here. It's just too risky. Emma has been teaching me to can, preserve, and freeze-dry, and we have gathered just about enough food and fuel reserves to get us through the winter.

Still mulling over how I'll make my escape, I shut the back door of the truck. Dean is standing behind me when I turn around. Lifting my chin, I stare up at him silently, leaning against the truck with my hands tucked behind my back.

His broad frame blocks my view of the yard, the fog of his breath leaving a smoky trail in the air. When he steps forward and rests his hands against the truck on either side of my head, my heart drops into my stomach at his proximity, but I don't want to escape. For the moment, he is all I can see, and rather than feel stifled and trapped as would be my usual default, I feel content, safe, and protected. I'm hedged in, but I don't want him to step away. It's a strange feeling and one I know I should resist, but I can't because I'm caught up in memorizing how dark and stormy his eyes look in the chilly darkness of the winter night.

He stares down at me, a familiar twitch working the outer corner of his lips under his beard.

"You look pretty cute in that coat, but are you going to be warm enough tonight?" He breaks the silence.

At the moment, I feel as if I'm on fire underneath the puffer just from the intensity of his gaze, so I simply nod with more enthusiasm than I intend.

His smirk deepens. He leans closer until his breath brushes across my chilled cheeks. "Good. But if you do get cold while we're at the tree farm, let me know. I'll share my coat with you."

I swallow hard, my words catching, and all I can croak out is, "Thank you for everything you and your family have done for us. I want you to know how grateful I am. Spending Thanksgiving with you all has been . . . special."

His eyes darken, their gray-blue depths smoldering like a storm. A sense of relief washes over me when he leans down, and his lips finally brush mine, their heat a stark contrast to the frosty night. I lean into him, stretching up on the toes of my boots to close the gap between our heights.

We haven't kissed since that day in the woods, and I've wondered if he would want to do it again.

Dean has been away most of my visit, his work for the ranch occupying the majority of his time. I've spent the time scurrying after Janie and assisting Emma in various tasks for our winter preparation anyway, but it occurs to me now that I've been holding my breath since the last time Dean and I were alone. A breathy *whoosh* rushes out of me along with a contented sigh as I lean into his embrace with hungry fervor. Though I stay awake at night, dreading the day this bubble breaks and nothing is ever the same again, the moments Dean is nearby make me feel as if, even though all the odds are against us, we'll never be safer than we are right now.

When he breaks the kiss, I sigh again but this time in frustration. I'm breathless when he opens the passenger door and extends his hand to help me climb into the lifted truck. Janie's animated babbles greet me from her car seat. When I clumsily catch the toe of my boot on the running board, Dean's strong hands warm the sides of my waist as he gently helps me into the seat. He waits until I'm buckled in before giving me an approving smile and shutting the door. I have all of three seconds to gather my composure before he steps in on the other side and starts the truck.

With a knowing glance at me, he turns to look at the back seat. "Who's ready to find the prettiest Christmas tree on the farm and drink gallons of hot chocolate?" he says.

Two little voices clamor, "me," and when Dean reaches across the console and twines my fingers in his, I grip them tightly. As foolish as allowing the daydreams is, I can't help but wonder if there's a future in which the laughter of children and the deep soothing tones of a good man are commonplace in my life—if I manage to stay out of prison for kidnapping, that is.

My free hand falls on the cell phone tucked into my pocket, and I think of the last message I sent Amy.

UNKNOWN TWO: Sis, where are you? I'm so worried. We haven't heard from you in so long. Are you coming home?

There's been no answer, and I'm painfully aware that the clock is ticking down the days until I have to go to the police and confess what I've done.

. . .

I've never searched for the perfect Christmas tree on a tree farm. Growing up, Mom's ideal holiday decoration was a pre-flocked plastic tree that she could put into a bag fully decorated for the next year. I've never seen a reason to pick out a tree for myself since I've always lived alone or been on base.

Tonight's new experience is punctuated by learning just how

fast Janie can run. Dean is tramping up and down the rows of pine-scented trees with DJ on his shoulder, the little boy having been given the task of scouting ahead, though I doubt Dean's towering height needs his assistance. I'm on Janie-duty, struggling to keep up with the tiny toddler as she sprints around the trees, grabbing at every fluffy bough she can reach and laughing as if she's discovered the funniest activity in the world.

It seems everyone in Cascade Valley has gotten the memo that Thanksgiving night is tree-picking night. The farm is tucked back among the lower mountains on the other side of town, rows of trees extending all around. We haven't ventured this far away from the cabin in months, and I find my nerves creeping up as I try to avoid any encounters with the locals. Down the rows and rows of Christmas trees, I catch sight of several faces that I recognize from my few excursions to the shops around town and the couple of times we've been at church with the McCades. I do my best to avoid eye contact with anyone. With my wool beanie pulled low over my forehead and my hair tucked into my oversized coat, I'm hoping I can pass for a tourist just in town for the holidays. Though I'm acutely aware that my anonymity won't help me to avoid notice if I'm seen with the McCades. My best hope is that we can find a tree and leave sooner rather than later.

On a few occasions, the woman from the shooting range—Jenna, if I remember correctly—crosses our path as I chase after Janie, with her burly boyfriend only steps behind her. When we pass each other the first time, I see the recognition in her eyes. She lifts her hand to wave, a bright smile across her face. Her boyfriend seems to recognize me, too, but as he opens his mouth and steps forward, Jenna grabs his arm and hauls him away to inspect another fluffy Christmas tree. They must not find what they are looking for because, to my annoyance and despite my efforts to avoid them, they seem to be lingering on every row we venture down, and I get the feeling of eyes on the back of my neck more than once as I pursue my niece.

Finally, I recognize Dean's voice calling for us a few rows up. I scoop Janie into my arms and attempt to hurry across the cold ground, my weak knee reminding me of its presence with a dull ache. The McCade family has gathered around a magnificent-looking tree with perfectly spaced, fluffy limbs and a straight branch at the top.

Dean's eyes gleam at me as we approach. "What do you think? Is it the perfect tree?" he asks.

DJ pokes his head around, his eyes sparkling and voice exuberant. "Is it perfect, Kasey?"

I cringe as he blurts out my name. Since returning to the ranch, we've talked time and time again about not calling me by my first name, but I don't expect him to remember in his excitement. Squatting down to his level, I use my free arm to pull him close.

"It's perfect, buddy," I whisper in his ear, hoping no one else caught his slip.

But no one says anything, and after Vincent and Knox make quick work of sawing the tree down, Dean scoops up Janie and ruffles DJ's hair. "How about we go get that gallon of hot chocolate I promised you?" He casts a wink over his shoulder toward me, his long legs striding away. "You coming, Kasey?"

Wordlessly, I trail after them, Emma and Demi walking arm in arm along with me. The ladies are lost in their own quiet conversation, and the wind brings snippets to me, phrases like "come home" and "acting weird" whispering across my ears. I'm glad they are occupied and don't expect me to make conversation, but when we exit the trees, I can't help but emit a startled gasp. I was expecting a tiny hot chocolate stand in the middle of a clearing, but the winter wonderland spread out before me exceeds all expectations. There has only been minimal snow in the valley so far, but there must have been enough moisture in the air for the farm to create its own. Fluffy, white piles cover a big section of ground. In the center of it all is a towering and brightly lit Christmas tree. It's surrounded by a large ice skating rink, and I can't help but let a delighted laugh ring out at the magic of it all.

DJ is already gustily consuming a hot chocolate that is bigger than any little boy should drink mere hours before bed. Dean hands me a cup piled high with whipped cream and crushed candy canes. I blow on it and test it with a careful sip before sharing it with Janie. It's delicious and everything a hot chocolate should be, immediately sending a rush of warmth along my limbs. I sip it just as eagerly as the children. When I catch sight of Dean staring at me with a delighted grin on his face, I freeze with wary suspicion.

"Why are you looking at me like that?" I hiss in his direction.

He lifts a hand and motions at his face. Chagrined, I hastily swipe at my own mouth, certain I'm sporting a chocolate mustache. When Dean shakes his head, I stare up at him in frustration as Janie pulls at my hand for another drink. Deliberately, he steps forward and closes the space between us. The Christmas lights twinkling everywhere reflect in his gleaming eyes as he reaches up and ever-so-gently dabs the tip of my nose with a napkin. He holds it up so I can see the remnants of peppermint-candy-studded whipped cream he just removed.

"Thanks," I mutter, embarrassed.

"You're welcome." The words rumble in his chest. He bends down to me. "But I should be thanking you. The sight of your adorable nose frosted like a Christmas cupcake is a sight I'm glad I didn't miss."

The statement is ridiculously absurd, like a cheesy line from a sappy Christmas movie, but it warms me right down to my toes. My face grows hot, and I feel a heady rush, but I busy myself with Janie until the gentle pressure of his hand cups my elbow. Still trying to regain my composure, I look at Dean. His gaze is more intense than I'm expecting, and it catches me off guard.

"Kasey," he begins somberly, "will you do me the honor of . . ."

My breath freezes in my chest. It feels like the world is about to come crashing down around my shoulders.

"Of ice skating with me," Dean finishes, and my breath releases in a rush of foggy air. He leans over me with a smirk. Butterflies riot in my stomach. "And if you don't know how to ice skate, you can hold onto me."

Rolling my eyes, I suppress the urge to laugh. "I do know how to ice skate and quite well, thank you very much." I click my tongue regretfully, letting a bit of sarcasm creep into my tone. "But I'm afraid Janie is enjoying her hot chocolate too much right now for me to step away. So sorry."

"Mom," Dean's voice booms out, "will you hold Miss Janie for a bit while Kasey and I skate?"

He's called my bluff. Emma calls out her acquiescence, but it's Demi who steps forward gracefully to take Janie from my arms. I find myself handing my niece over before I realize what I'm doing. Dean's sister is one of the most beautiful and elegant women I've ever met, and it isn't a surprise that she is a sought-after model in New York City. From the short time I've interacted with her since she arrived yesterday for Thanksgiving, I can also see that she inherited her family's unwavering sense of kindness. Her gentle hug when she first greeted me was warm and heartfelt. Of course, next to her, I feel like a lump of clay in my oversized, bulky coat, which I bought for myself at the thrift store in town. I've never had many friends, but my heart whispers that it would be easy to be friends with Dean's sisters.

He clasps my hand in his and leads me toward the skating rink. We're quickly fitted with rental skates and step onto the ice together. Ice skating was something my mother loved. She'd grown up taking lessons and practicing at the neighborhood rink as often as she could. Her big break came when she got the chance to tour with a theatrical company. She met my father during a production in New York City when he was just a low-level stockbroker on Wall Street. Their romance was passionate, intense, and quick.

My subsequent arrival put an abrupt stop to all hopes of her continuing her figure skating career. Still, it was the one thing she insisted I have lessons for in middle school, working an extra shift every week for a few months just to pay for them. I think she hoped I'd make a profession of the sport so she could live vicariously through me, but she stopped paying for them when I didn't show as much enthusiasm as she wanted.

Still, I'd picked up the skill easily all those years ago, but I haven't skated in years, so my first few minutes on the ice are a struggle to find my balance. I cling to Dean, threading my hand through his arm as his other arm slides around my waist, supporting me. Immediately, my knee acts up with the added pressure to support my weight, and I find myself having to compensate for its drag.

"Whoa there, now," he rumbles in an amused tone when I nearly fall on the ice. "Am I going to have to pick you up and carry you back to stable ground?"

"I know how to skate," I insist, gritting my teeth. "It's just this leg of mine." My ankle twists, but his arms quickly firm, and he holds me up. When I glance into his face, I catch his eyes flashing to my thigh, right where my scar hides underneath my jeans.

"At some point, you'll have to tell me how you got that," he says gently.

My heart constricts, and I shake my head. "Maybe someday. I have a few others too. But believe me, you don't really want to know."

"There's nothing I don't want to know about you," he replies quietly, and the truth in his tone brings a lump to my throat.

When he pulls my hand through his arm, I lean on him heavily, feeling like a spindly foal just learning to walk again. When I figure out how to move in a way that doesn't trigger the shooting pain up my leg and regain my confidence, I don't pull away from him. We begin to glide across the ice in near-perfect sync.

At the edge of the snow, a live band is playing Christmas songs that carry through the night. The air snaps with a crispness that isn't unpleasant. The spicy scent of pine fills my senses, and whether it's coming from Dean or the trees, I don't know, but I breathe it in greedily. Golden Christmas lights have been strung everywhere, twinkling off the gilded decorations of the tree in the center of the rink, and the stars twinkle far above in the inky night sky. For a moment, I don't know if a more perfect scene has ever existed, and I draw closer to the man beside me, wrapping my fingers around his forearm, blissfully content in his presence.

Chapter Twenty-Eight

Dean

Kasey wasn't lying when she said she knew how to skate. Once she regains her balance, her feet glide confidently across the ice, and to my surprise, the open, happy expression on her face tells me it's also an activity that she is thoroughly enjoying. I feel as if my invitation has just peeled back another layer of her personality. I can't recall a time I've seen Kasey relax, and the sight warms my heart.

But it also twinges guiltily when I remember I need to get in touch with Danny Gardener's cousin in Fort Jackson. I'm going to ask for a list of the soldiers he worked with during deployment. To have any chance of helping her, I need to know more about Kasey's past. I keep meaning to remind Caleb to reach out to him for me, but I have been putting off following through. I'm not sure why.

I'm distracted from my thoughts by the feeling of Kasey's

small hand grasping my arm as we skate across the ice. She moves in sync with me, her short strides keeping up with my pace around the Christmas tree in the center of the rink.

We glide for another few minutes, then I deliberately slow us down and guide us toward the inner edge of the ice. I position her in front of me against the barrier set up around the brightly lit tree and place my hands on either side, shielding her from the view of the other skaters and the townspeople mingling about the venue. I'm sure the Cascade Valley gossip cup has already been filled to overflowing tonight. If they haven't already seen us at church together the past two weeks, by morning, everyone will be speculating about the mysterious blonde woman skating with the oldest McCade brother.

"It's almost like you've skated before," I tease her quietly.

Her aqua eyes sparkle up at me. "I told you I could."

"Maybe I was just hoping you couldn't so that I could put my arm around you," I reply, and her eyes darken dangerously.

"Funny. I seem to recall you already doing just that," she replies.

Just as I'm considering the consequences of sneaking a kiss in front of every townsperson in sight, I realize another couple is lingering nearby. Off to our right and slightly around the curved barrier, Hunter has his lips pressed to Jenna's neck, and she's laughing at something he's whispering in her ear. I've heard from both my mother and Esther at Mountain Realty of the very public and rapid relationship that has developed between the horse trainer and the newcomer since late summer. According to Mom and Esther, no one in town seems to know what to make of Hunter's sudden appearance upon the scene. One day, he and Jenna were simply eyeballs deep in a whirlwind and very public romance. He doesn't live in town, coming and going often, and so far, there's no public knowledge of him making any real estate investments around the valley.

But they seem enamored with each other, though it surprised everyone that she would even be interested in the smooth-talking city slicker since she's a Montana girl, through and through. But since he has been seen exiting Jenna's small cottage on the edge of town on more than one early morning, everyone hopes for a proposal any day now.

At least, according to Mom, Esther, and Knox—my brother never one to turn down a chance for a good story.

Ignoring them and turning back to Kasey, I smile at her, relieved to see the brightness still lingering in her eyes. The Christmas tree lights reflect behind her, surrounding her frame with a charming glow. Her cheeks and nose are red from the frosty night air, and my brain goes back to the prospect of another kiss.

A sudden commotion drags my attention away from Kasey's adorable, beanie-topped face.

Jenna emits a high-pitched squeal, and I turn just in time to see Hunter step back to kneel on the ice in front of her. The excited woman's outburst quickly draws the attention of everyone skating, and glancing back over my shoulder, I see many of the people lingering around the clearing already turning their attention toward the couple. Jenna's hands are pressed dramatically over her mouth as Hunter proposes in a loud tone.

"Jenna, my sweet, sweet Jenna," the man begins, "ever since the first moment I laid eyes on you, sparks flew between us. And after getting to know you, I wanna keep this roller coaster running all night long. How about we get married and let the good times roll?" His hands lift together to present a ring box.

Jenna gasps out a "yes." Even from a distance, the oversized diamond ring flashes brilliantly against the lights strung everywhere. She slips it on her finger and throws her arms around Hunter's neck as he rises and presses his lips to hers. The crowd bursts into cheers and applause, many of the skaters approaching to congratulate the couple and hug Jenna. Hunter pulls away as she accepts the showering of compliments. He stands off to the side, his arms crossed over his chest, head bent as he watches the commotion. When his gaze shifts over to us, I look away.

I turn back to Kasey and see that her lips are twisted, one eyebrow lifted in a skeptical expression I'm not sure she realizes she is making. She catches me watching her, and I bend my head in time to hear her quiet words.

"Shall we skate a bit more?" she says.

I nod and take her hand, the sharp clash of our blades cutting across the ice with swift precision. We take a few spins around the ice rink, our conversation lighthearted, casual, and filled with frequent laughter, never dipping into anything serious. Finally, Kasey motions toward the tree lot.

"I think I'm done skating now. You've about filled my cardio quota for the day. My knee is hurting, and I still need energy to chase after Janie."

"As you wish," I reply, and she smirks up at me. We've nearly reached the edge of the rink when a voice stops us in our tracks.

"Oh, Dean! Wait a second, will you?" Jenna's voice trills across the ice.

"Please don't stop," Kasey whispers.

"Sorry," I mutter, pulling her to a halt and turning to see the newly engaged couple skating toward us. The ring on Jenna's hand flashes again as she holds it up for us to inspect.

"Well, aren't you going to congratulate me?" She giggles.

"Congratulations to you both. We're happy for you." I take the liberty of speaking for Kasey, too, as she seems to have positioned herself slightly behind me and fallen into a dead silence.

"Can you believe it?" Jenna doesn't seem to notice Kasey's lack of response.

Hunter does, though, and I take note of the frown on his face as his eyes linger on Kasey for a moment before drifting to the outer edge of the rink. I follow the direction of his gaze, but I can only see Mom and Demi lingering near the hot chocolate stand with Junior and Janie.

"My brain is already spinning with everything that needs to be done," Jenna prattles on, "but there's one thing I know for sure. I want to talk to you about having the wedding up at the ski lodge."

Her announcement catches me by surprise. Jenna flashes a wide smile. She lifts a hand to wiggle a playful finger in my face.

"I know all about your family purchasing the lodge, Dean. Everyone in town is happy that it's going to stay local instead of being sold off to a corporation, and I want to be the first to throw a wedding there—"

"I don't know, Jenna. The deal isn't even closed yet," I interrupt.

Jenna glances at Hunter and follows his distracted gaze before turning back to me with a pleading expression. "Please. It would mean everything to me. I spent half my childhood at Bear Creek, and I want Hunter to experience it with me in all its winter glory on our special day." She reaches back for him, and he takes her hand, lifting it to his lips for a kiss.

"I'll talk to my siblings," I acquiesce, unsure how to put off her pleading.

Jenna squeals and throws herself into Hunter's arms. "Oh, goodie. Thank you, Dean. I want to drive up tomorrow to take a tour. Will you meet us there?"

I'm caught off guard again. "Tomorrow? Like I said, the deal hasn't even closed yet . . ."

"Please, Dean!" Jenna doesn't accept my answer. "I know the Lintons. They won't care if we look around, and I'm sure you have keys now."

I glance around to Kasey tucked behind me and notice she is already edging away. Seeing an opportunity to pull her into the community, I turn back to Jenna and agree. "Sure, we can meet you up there. But only if it's okay that Kasey tags along."

My request seems to catch everyone off guard. Kasey's hissed protest is thrown at me in an undertone as Jenna and Hunter exchange a glance. But Jenna quickly smiles.

"Sure, of course. The more, the merrier. Shall we meet at one o'clock?"

Plans are confirmed, and we part ways. Kasey and I turn in our rental skates in silence, and she still hasn't spoken to me as we make our way across the frozen ground to rejoin the others. When Janie reaches out for her, she takes the little girl in her arms and holds her tightly, pressing her nose into the toddler's cheek. Her chest rises and falls with heavy breaths, and suddenly, I realize I may have just put her in an uncomfortable position.

Kasey has avoided becoming part of the fabric of life in Cascade Valley—I was surprised she even came to the tree farm tonight—but I'm not sure my brilliant plan to get her out of her shell was the right move after all.

"I'd like to get the kids home and to bed," she breaks her silence, glancing at me.

Without hesitation, I nod, and she turns and limps toward my truck at the entrance of the farm, calling Junior to follow her. With a farewell glance at Mom and Demi, I trail after her. By the time I reach the truck, she's struggling to secure Janie in her car seat. I help Junior climb in and buckle him into his booster seat, which we just transitioned him into, having outgrown his previous car seat over the fall. Kasey's frustrated energy fills the space between us all the while. When she finally gets Janie snapped in, she climbs into the front passenger seat, her movements jerky and stiff.

I keep my hands safely on the steering wheel as we drive back to the ranch in silence. Or as much silence as there can be with a hot-chocolate-stuffed five-year-old and a fussy toddler up past her bedtime. A chill enters the warm farmhouse as we pile in, and the trio heads straight upstairs.

I offer to help but receive a curt refusal, which I can't blame her for. I give Kasey her space as she performs the usual bath time ritual and prepares the kids for bed amid loud protests and plentiful tears. At some point, the rest of my family piles in and finds me sitting in the dark living room alone. My siblings go to the kitchen to filch pieces of pumpkin pie before bed while Mom heads upstairs to assist Kasey. She returns a short time later and joins the others in the kitchen.

As the second floor grows quiet, I realize that Kasey isn't coming back downstairs. Briefly, I wrestle with the best course of action. It doesn't feel right to let the night end while I still owe her an apology. With hesitant steps, I walk upstairs and down the hallway to her room. The space under her door is dark.

"Kasey," my knuckles rap softly against the wood, "are you asleep yet?"

The silence stretches on for so long that I think I have probably missed my chance tonight. It takes a few minutes until I hear feet shuffling across the floor. The door opens a crack, and an aqua eye peeks out at me.

"Hey," I whisper, "can we talk?"

The crack widens a centimeter. "I'm going to bed, Dean," she says. "Can it wait?"

I shake my head. "Honestly, no. We need to talk."

A heavy sigh reaches my ears from the other side of the door.

There's a muffled shuffle, and Kasey slips out to join me in the hallway. Shutting the door quietly behind her, she leans against the doorframe, one socked foot propped up against the wood, her hands hanging loosely at her sides. She's pulled a worn, knitted sweater over a pair of casual gray sweats. Her hair is piled into a messy bun at the top of her head, and for a moment, I'm taken aback at this unfamiliar, relaxed look. I pause to soak in the sight of her. I've rarely seen her in anything other than jeans, a basic t-shirt, and heavy hiking boots, except for the one occasion I caught her at the swimming hole.

In her cozy pajamas, she's utterly adorable, and I suddenly lose all the words I came up here to say as I stare at her in fascination. Kasey's typically serious demeanor and fixed posture always indicate she's alert and ready for anything. Now, she looks somehow both younger and more tired, her vulnerability giving her unique beauty an ethereal quality.

"What do you need?" she breaks the silence, and I realize I'm staring at her. Echoes of laughter and conversation drift up the stairs, a reminder that we aren't alone in the house.

Extending my hand toward her slowly, I run my thumb along the soft skin of her wrist. "If I grovel, will you forgive me for putting you on the spot with Jenna and Hunter tonight?"

Her chin dips toward her chest, eyes on the floor. But a hint of a smile lifts the corners of her lips. She heaves a resigned sigh. "There's no need to grovel, Dean. Technically, you didn't do anything wrong."

"But I realized afterward I made you uncomfortable, and I'm

sorry." I pause, hesitating briefly before continuing with, "And I'd like to understand why. You live in Cascade Valley now, and you could make so many new friends if you would just let the townspeople have a chance to get to know you."

Her chin pops up, and I see a flash of her usual defiance in her eyes. "But we don't live here. Our stay is temporary. At some point, we'll be moving on." Her arms draw up and cross in front of her chest. "And I don't want any new friends."

I'm used to hearing such declarations from Vincent, so it doesn't dissuade me. I reach out and tug one of her hands free, surprised when she allows me to twine our fingers together.

"There's no denying that you are one of the most fiercely independent women I've ever met, but that doesn't mean you don't need a strong community the same as the next person. Fellowship doesn't make you weak, and it doesn't automatically lock you into a place forever." I hate giving any weight to even the idea of her leaving, but it doesn't make my statement untrue.

Her lips purse, and she shrugs. I venture to press her a little more.

"I wanted you to come with me so I could show you the lodge. My brothers and I have a lot of plans for it, and I'd like to get your opinion."

She stares up at me with skeptical eyes.

"And I thought Jenna might want you to join us." I test the waters again. "I think you might like her."

Kasey shakes her head, the messy bun bobbing a little with the motion. "There must be at least ten years between us. I doubt that young woman wants to be friends with some antisocial veteran who has nothing in common with her."

"She's at least twenty-six," I protest.

"Yeah, we're not even close in age."

"How old are you?" I ask, suddenly inquisitive. Our respective ages have never come up in conversation, and now I find myself wondering how old Kasey herself is.

"Thirty-six," she replies. She eyes me with an amused expression. "Even you're a youngin' compared to me."

Leaning down, I close the gap between us, our warm breath mingling. I wait until she looks me straight in the eyes. "Oh, I don't know," I mutter huskily. "Younger or not, I think I've got the maturity to handle a woman like you."

Her pale cheeks turn a rosy pink, and I watch in delight as the amusement fades and she blusters.

"Stop it. You're ridiculous. Will you stop looking at me like that?" Her free hand comes up to cover her face.

"What did I say?" I protest with wide-eyed innocence.

She shakes her head, changing the subject. "Is it going to become a whole thing if I don't go up there with the three of you tomorrow? Am I going to end up being the talk of the town as the grumpy hermit of the Cascade Valley mountains?"

My thumb traces small circles on her palm. "To be honest, I think that's probably already your reputation around here."

Her eyes widen in horror. Her free hand lifts to lightly smack me on the chest. "How could you say that? I'm a very nice person."

"Who said hermits aren't nice people?" I shrug. "Weird and unfriendly and secretive but still nice as a general rule, I'm sure."

She tries to suppress it, but a grin breaks out across her face. "Fine," she rolls her eyes, "I'll go with you tomorrow. But only to protect my delicate reputation and prevent the rumors."

"Good." With a grin, I release her hand. I turn and start down the hallway but pause to call softly over my shoulder. "Oh, and Kasey. There will still be rumors. But at least they will be the good kind."

Her exaggerated gasp echoes in my ears as I disappear around the corner.

Chapter Twenty-Nine

Kasey

As soon as we get to the top of the mountain, I can see why Dean and his brothers wanted to buy the lodge. I step out of the truck, and a blast of frigid air hits me. Shivering deeper into my coat, I draw the collar up higher on my neck, burrowing the lower half of my face in it. It seems that overnight, Montana has officially turned the corner into the winter season. A sheet of blue-gray altostratus clouds covers the sky, a promise of a snowstorm soon to descend.

The lodge that looms above us is a marvel of wood and grand architectural design. But it isn't the building that catches my eye. Without thinking to wait for Dean, I stride eagerly toward the lookout that was formed long ago from a natural platform of rocks in the distance.

The previous owners, no doubt wanting to capitalize on the photogenic quality of the view, reinforced it with a guardrail of rocks hewed from the mountain to act as a wall. The valley spreads out before my eyes; the river far below is a ribbon glistening through it. It seems like the richly textured land stretches out as far as the eye can see. Trees, farmland, and grazing pastures blend like they were splashed on a canvas by an artist.

Dean's apology last night hasn't left my mind. It meant a lot to me that he cared enough to try to mend things after his blunder at the ice skating rink. I dreamed of walking with him hand in hand through the forest and woke with a strange feeling in my chest. I felt a twinge of fear as we traveled up the mountain and passed the turn off for the logging road that leads to my cabin, but it was quickly displaced by something almost reminiscent of hope.

Up here among the clouds, it's hard to believe what dire circumstances brought us to these mountains and everything I've faced to learn to mother my young charges. I've made countless mistakes, but somehow, we're making it through. And right now, the threats hanging over our heads feel very far away. The beauty of it all sparks tears in my eyes. If only I could let myself be happy living here. If only we could stay. If only Amy would tell me she's on her way home, and we could put all of this behind us. Despite the darkness that lingers in my peripheral vision, there's something about the view of this valley that almost makes me feel at home.

"Isn't it beautiful?" Directly at my side, his deep voice melts me.

I twist my neck to look up at him, a soft smile rising easily to my lips. But Dean's eyes aren't focused on the breathtaking view; instead, they study me with a softness that doesn't take away from the power and force of his masculinity. I'm probably just imagining it, but the gray-blue shade of his irises seems to turn into a stormy sea whenever he looks at me.

A shiver—not of fear but of delight—runs down my spine. Suddenly, the view from the lookout pales in comparison to what's in front of me. His face has been chiseled and tanned from the sun and the wind, his lean, muscular form shaped from years on horseback and sheer grit. There's no doubt that Dean could be dangerous if circumstances called for it, but with him, I feel fully and truly safe.

I turn all the way around to face him and realize a startling truth—I want to be held. The independent, pushes-everyone-away-because-I'm-too-scared-to-get-hurt one wants his strong arms to comfort me when I'm weary and hold me up when I'm weak. I've reached a point where I'm tired of pushing away the good because I'm terrified of the bad.

I stare up at him, my tongue trying to twist sounds into words. Should I reach for him, twine my arms around his neck, and cling to him until he promises never to let me go? Without moving a muscle, Dean waits, only the smoke of his exhale evidence that he is breathing.

An inexplicable urge to tell him everything, to spill every bit of the sordid truth that brought us here, comes over me with a rush. Could telling Dean what we're dealing with be the rescue we need? Maybe he'll know what to do. My mouth falls open.

"Dean," I swallow painfully, "if I tell you something, will you promise not to hate me?"

He seems to draw closer, his shadow encircling me. "Hating you is never going to be an option." His lips draw up in a smirk. "Why? Did a tiny thing like you murder someone?"

I shake my head, rolling my eyes. "Nothing like that. But I can't say I'm proud of everything I've done."

"Tell me, Kasey," he urges.

But then I'm terrified. "I'm afraid that once you know everything, you'll send me away."

The brush of his warm palms over mine is rough with calluses. "Trust me," he urges, his voice a whispered growl as he leans over me.

My lips part, the truth on the tip of my tongue.

The blare of a horn makes us jump apart. A red Ferrari roars to a stop next to Dean's truck. I stare at the car, the hairs on the back of my neck prickling as I register a flash of relief at the interruption. Jenna and Hunter emerge from the sports car at the same time and look in our direction.

"Okay, you two," Jenna waves, "one wedding at a time around here."

"Go on up," Dean calls. "We'll be right there." He turns back to me.

My breath rushes out painfully, and I realize that I just received a warning. Disclosing everything my sister has fought for on her self-imposed exile would be a mistake, no matter how deeply I trust Dean.

"We'd better go." Ignoring his outstretched hand, I outpace him and stride ahead toward the grand entrance of the lodge.

. . .

"Kasey," Dean turns to me and motions through the windows, "you'd have no way of knowing this, but there's a trail that leads down to your cabin out there. Your cabin is about a half mile off the trail once you hit the ridge and start going down. In the summer, you can hike, and in the winter, you'd have to snowshoe, of course, but it's possible to get down to the main road from here. We used to do it all the time when we were teens. Park one truck up here, hike, then drive back up with a second truck we'd left at the bottom."

Surprised, I stare in the direction he indicates for a moment. And here, I thought Danny's cabin must truly be in the middle of nowhere. Of course, I knew that the main road led up here, but just the ski lodge's proximity, regardless of how many miles up the mountain it is, sets me on edge.

I stare at the lookout before trailing after the group as he walks ahead with Jenna and Hunter. If I were to judge the strength of Jenna and Hunter's relationship based on today's impression alone, I'd say Jenna is giving more than 50% to their future at the moment. She chatters to Dean as we tour the lodge, her excited voice throwing wedding ideas around like confetti. It's clear that Jenna is very enthusiastic about the prospect of having her wedding up here. Hunter, his expression bored and feet dragging, doesn't seem as excited.

I can relate. I wish I could be anywhere but here.

Hunter lingers behind the pair, his stocky frame filling my peripheral vision. Still angry with myself for nearly spilling everything to Dean earlier, I try to ignore him, not wanting to give him any encouragement to start a conversation. His presence is heavy, though, his steps loud as we wander around the lodge. Despite myself, once or twice, my eyes flicker toward him. The second time, I catch him looking at me from under thick eyebrows. His ensemble is all black except for his boots: a black Stetson, Levi's, a button-down, and shiny, silver cowboy boots. The few times I've seen Dean in a cowboy hat have given me flutters. Hunter looks like he put on a costume that barely fits.

My brain registers instant alarm when he bares his teeth and his unnaturally sharp and pearly canines flash at me, but then, I realize he's just smiling. He nods toward Jenna ahead.

"My fiancée's wedding ideas are probably inspiring you, huh?"

I'm confused. "Excuse me?"

"I bet all her ideas are making you think about your own wedding." His Montana twang gives the impression he's just trying it on for size. He nods toward Dean's tall figure.

"I'm not . . . we're not . . ." I frown, trying to get the words out. "We're not getting married."

He glances toward Dean, whose head is bent toward Jenna, a patient expression on his face. "I just naturally assumed, with you two being so close, and living at the McCades' ranch and all . . ."

I sink my teeth into my lower lip, biting back my annoyance. I knew the Cascade Valley gossip chain couldn't hold back for long. It's all I can do to avoid vehemently protesting. "That's all temporary. The McCades have been kind enough to let us visit for a while. We'll be going back to our own cabin soon."

His hazel eyes flicker in my direction. "Is your place around here?"

I don't know how to answer. "Not too far away, actually," I reply after deliberation, already regretting allowing this conversation to start.

"Oh yeah, Dean said you could hike to it from here," he remarks with indifference.

"Yeah, I guess so," I mumble. "I didn't know."

"Must be nice to have your own little piece of the Montana mountains," he says.

"It's not ours," I blurt out. "Just a friend's cabin."

"Oh!" He looks surprised. "Is your friend staying there too?"

My heart sinks. "No, he passed away a while ago."

"You've got a couple of kids, don't you?" Hunter redirects the conversation. His tone makes me think he's already getting bored.

"Two," I confirm.

"Lotta work taking care of small children by yourself." His gaze turns toward the snow-dusted pines that rise outside the floor-to-ceiling windows in the great room.

While the valley seems to be late on getting its first snow, the top of the mountain already sports a dusting of white. It makes me wonder if the cabin has snow too. Jenna's voice almost drowns his as she enthusiastically describes her vision for the ceremony, her hands flailing wildly about.

"Your kids don't have a dad who can help out sometimes?"

I realize Hunter has turned back to me, the hat casting a charcoal gloom over his eyes. He stares at me until I feel compelled to respond.

"Uh, no, actually," I reply with reluctance. "Their dad isn't in the picture."

"Pity." Hunter's mouth twists in a grimace. "It's hard for a boy to grow up without his father. And a daughter . . . well, every princess needs her daddy to protect her. I hope you gave their father a chance before you took them away."

I shake my head, my inner hackles rising silently for Amy. "Their father . . . he isn't a good guy."

"Oh . . . ?" He shakes his head with a mournful expression. Suddenly, he leans closer. My nerves spike. "Was it a domestic violence case?" he asks in a low tone.

I shake my head. "Not exactly."

"Was he unfaithful?" The words flip off Hunter's tongue with a casual air.

I shake my head again. "Not that I know."

He looks at me, his expression hidden behind the beard that covers half of his face. "He must have been a poor provider? Did you not have a roof over your head and food on your table?"

The questions are throwing me off. My agitation rises. "He just wasn't a good man."

Hunter shakes his head this time, his lips twisting up into a teasing smirk. "Maybe you didn't see his good qualities. Perhaps you were ungrateful."

My defenses rise at the implication. I want to defend Amy, to protest at any hint that her decision to remove herself from her husband's control is unjustified, but I can't. I don't know every detail of what she experienced. Abuse, infidelity, manipulation— they all come under the range of the trauma my sister endured, but I'm unsure, and I'm hesitant to either confirm or deny.

But I have to say something. "He was abusive, okay?" I hiss. "Emotionally manipulative, a charlatan, toxic . . . and he was involved with shady people and business dealings. When he finally got what was coming to him, I left the first chance I got."

The truth, the lies, and the uncertainty of it all blend together as the words slip out before I can stop them.

A soft gasp startles me. I look away from Hunter and realize Jenna and Dean have approached us and are staring at me with surprised expressions. A confused frown flickers across Dean's face.

The weight of my foolishness descends on my shoulders like a millstone. Instantly, I'm sick.

"Excuse me," I mutter, my voice weak. "I'm not feeling well this morning. Dean, I'm going to wait in the truck."

The heaviness of their gaze follows me through the lodge as I stumble down the staircase and burst outside into the frigid mountain air.

Chapter Thirty

Dean

When Kasey descends the stairs the next morning with her bags in hand, her jaw is set in a determined line.

I lingered behind after breakfast, sitting at the table, coffee mug in front of me, legs outstretched, with a suspicion that this moment had already been brewing for a couple of days. It's like our trust level takes two steps backward for every step forward. When she barely spoke to me yesterday after leaving the lodge, I knew she was about to make a run for it.

I'm frustrated and annoyed that despite how far we've come, this is what we're facing again. The woman is like one of the wolves whose territory we accidentally grazed into over the summer. She's cagey and easily triggered, her energy tightly coiled and ready to pop off like a spring if she's cornered. I want to make her sit and tell me the truth, but hedging in a wild animal is asking for trouble. The only way to make my she-wolf come back to me is to stand aside and let her go.

Plus, after overhearing yesterday's exchange with Hunter, it's clear that whatever brought Kasey up here is worse than I thought. The man she's running from sounds dangerous. I saw the way talking about him snuffed out the light in her eyes, and I have no intention of waiting another day to find out more.

She'll fight me to keep her independence, but I won't let her face her fears alone.

She drops the bags at her feet on the kitchen floor and squares off in front of me as if preparing for a fight. Her posture is upright and stiff, her back straight as a ramrod, her military training evident as she observes me keenly but keeps a stoic look on her face. Keeping my own expression serene, I lift the mug to my lips and sip the black brew, looking at her over the rim.

I win. The uncomfortable silence forces her to speak.

"It's just time, Dean," she begins. "I can't keep putting it off forever. We've got plenty of food and supplies to get us through the winter, but I need to make sure our woodpile is adequate. And I . . . can't . . . we just need our own space, okay?"

I take another sip from the mug before I nod and reply. "There's a perfectly good foreman's cabin sitting at the back of the property. Yours for the taking. No need to run away to bury yourself in the woods just to have a little space, Kasey."

Her lips tighten, the wispy hairs around her face shivering as she protests. "Not running. Just leaving."

"What happens if you three get snowed in? Janie's getting to the age that she wants to be on the move all the time. It's not fair to keep her cooped up all winter. How are you supposed to manage all by your—"

"I can take care of my *nie* . . . daughter," she snaps. "I've got a phone, batteries, and solar chargers. I'll call you if there's any danger."

"Didn't know you had a phone," I reply casually.

She drops her eyes. "Well, I do, okay?"

Swiveling my head, I glance through the kitchen windows toward the gray skies. "It's supposed to snow tonight." When she doesn't reply, I continue, "Mom'll miss you."

She and Demi drove to town right after breakfast to do some shopping. Kasey's timing doesn't escape my notice.

"We'll miss her." Her voice is somber and sincere.

"You sure about this?"

The blue of her eyes is as clear as the sky on a summer day as she stares at me for a drawn-out minute before her breath huffs. "I'm sure, Dean."

I rise, and the way she flinches at my movement rankles deep inside my bones. At my height, I tower over her small frame. In all her determination to be strong, she's forgotten how delicate she truly is. She stares up at me as the happy chatter of Junior and Janie echoes from the living room.

"Okay, then," I acquiesce. "I'll help you get the Jeep packed."

An hour later, I watch the dirt-stained vehicle retreating toward the mountains until it is out of sight. Only when I'm sure she hasn't changed her mind and turned around to come back do I pull the keys from my pocket and take determined strides toward my truck.

. . .

"I need to talk to Danny's cousin in South Carolina right now." I don't waste time exchanging pleasantries when Caleb comes strolling out of his barn, wiping his hands on a rag.

He takes my brusqueness in stride, drawing his cell phone

from his back pocket in his usual leisurely manner. I wave at Griff, Caleb's ranch foreman, when he walks across the yard. Scrolling, my friend pulls up a number and holds the phone aloft for me as I copy it onto my phone.

"His name is Jared," he reminds me, preemptively answering my next question.

"Thanks."

Caleb doesn't follow me when I turn and stalk toward the porch of his house, my thumb already pressing the call button. I pace as the call connects, my boots thudding on the worn porch treads. When a deep voice answers at the other end of the line, I exhale. Danny's cousin is still active duty, so I remembered too late that chances were high he wouldn't be stateside.

Jared Gardener didn't grow up in Cascade Valley but spent most of his school summers with Danny running wild in the mountains. He remembers my name as soon as I say it.

"Yeah, Dean McCade, how are you, bro?" he says in a friendly tone. "Caleb texted and said you wanted to talk, but I've been busy, sorry. What's it been since I last saw you? Twelve years."

"Something like that," I reply.

"Had some good times camping with you and your brothers and Danny. Miss those summers." His voice goes husky, but he recovers quickly. "What can I do for you?"

I clear my throat. "I've got a question for you. You were stationed with Danny for a while, weren't you? Did you ever meet any of the members of his platoon?"

"Sure," Jared replies promptly, "plenty of them over the years. We deployed together a few times as well."

"Do you remember a woman who worked with him sometime within the last few years? Short and petite but athletic, golden blonde hair, bright blue eyes. Kind of antisocial."

"That's probably Kasey Carter." He doesn't hesitate, her name falling from his lips with ease. "I only served with her once, but it's difficult to forget that woman, despite how hard she tries to fade into the background. Haven't heard her name in a while, though." His voice grows emotional.

Before I can reply, Jared continues, "I've never seen a more dedicated combat medic, that's for sure."

"Do you think she saw a lot of action out there? Could it have affected her when she came back?"

"Oh yeah. She's retired now, but the last one . . . well, they had a tough assignment. And then, she was there when . . ."

I know what he's about to say, but my heart still drops, thudding painfully. "Yeah, I know she was there when Danny . . ."

Neither of us can say the word aloud. The heavy silence on the other end of the line echoes my thoughts. His breath comes out ragged.

"She shouldn't have had to do what she did," Jared mumbles. "It shouldn't have happened to someone like her. She was never like the rough-and-tumble army crowd. Kasey was different. Driven. She just wanted to help people."

I hold my breath, dread growing in my gut.

"I wasn't on deployment at the time. I wish I had been. Danny was the squad leader, you know? He requested that Kasey be stationed near us anytime he could because she was just the kind of medic you wanted in your corner." His voice cracks.

"Did the two of them ever . . .?" I ask, prepared for the truth if Kasey had withheld it from me.

"No," Jared replies immediately. "Nothing like that. But they were friends; he'd taken her under his wing. And Danny knew she was loyal. She'd move Heaven and earth to serve her platoon."

"Can you tell me what happened out there?"

Caleb appears in the barn doorway and looks in my direction, but I only vaguely register the sight of him. Every cell of my being feels intensely locked onto the words that spill hesitantly from Jared's lips.

"Not all of it." Jared pauses. "Where is this coming from, McCade? Calling me up out of the blue and asking about Kasey Carter. Maybe I shouldn't even be talking about this."

"She's here," I blurt out. "She's been staying in Danny's old hunting cabin."

Jared draws in a deep breath. "I wondered where she'd disappeared to, all these months. I tried calling her a few times, but no response. Is she okay?"

I hesitate. "I think so, but then again, I haven't known her long. We just sort of stumbled across each other, and she's . . . intriguing." I pause before my next question. "Do you know anything about her kids' dad?"

"Uh," Jared draws out the word, "kid . . . I didn't know anything about her having a kid. As far as I know, she was never married and never had anyone. She didn't even date. I can't see her as a mom, to be honest. Kasey was loyal and good at her job, but she was a loner. Quiet. Standoffish and unfriendly until you got to know her."

"That tracks," I reply with a twinge of amusement.

I recognize the snap of fingers on the other end of the line.

"Though . . . there was a sister," Jared continues in a brighter tone. "We were stationed on base together at one point about five or six years back, and I remember her getting an email saying her nephew had been born. I remember because it was the only time I ever saw her get emotional. I think her sister wanted her to come meet the baby at some family reunion that was happening, but

Kasey was estranged from her family—"

As he speaks, I suck in a sharp breath. "Five years, you said?" I interject when Jared pauses.

"Yeah, or six years. Sometime, a few years back. So if there is a kid, it could be her nephew."

"There are two kids," I reply without thinking. "A boy and a girl."

"Hm, yeah, I don't know anything about that. All I know is she didn't have any kids when she was medically retired, and that wasn't too long ago."

My brain races with the new information as my stomach roils with discomfort. Something doesn't feel right, but I don't want to acknowledge it. I have one more question.

"Can you tell me what happened out there when Danny . . .?" I repeat the question.

"Not all of it. There are parts of it that haven't been released." Jared swallows, the sound thick and heavy. "But what I do know is that what was supposed to be a fairly routine assignment in a territory our guys had already patrolled and cleared turned quickly into a hostile situation.

"They were ambushed. It escalated fast." Jared hesitates. "When the explosion happened and took out their vehicle, Kasey was with them. She pulled five soldiers back inside the Humvee while under fire—despite taking a nearly fatal wound to her own leg—and risking her own life in the process. Danny was one of the guys she pulled back inside. She tried to save him. I don't know how she was physically able to do it . . . Well, you've seen her."

My breath catches. I can't breathe. The gravity of every word he utters lands like a punch to my gut. With a wound like that, her limp makes sense. My mind roils with anger that she went through an event so traumatic. The fact that she survived is a miracle. She walked through the valley of the shadow of death and lived, but the trauma left its scars.

"She held them off and performed what medical aid she could to all five until reinforcements arrived. She always was a good shot . . ." His voice trails off, and the heaviness of his tone lingers in the miles between us.

The scope of everything I still don't know weighs on me. "Do you know who her family is or where they might be located?" I ask.

"No," Jared replies. "The only thing I ever heard about her family is that her dad was some big shot in Manhattan. Wall Street, I think. But she didn't have anything to do with him. Her sister lived out that way, though, too, and they spoke occasionally. That's all I know." He hesitates briefly. "Is she in some kind of trouble?"

"I don't know," I reply. "That's what I'm trying to find out."

I thank him and end the call, wasting no time pulling up a search engine on my phone. Hastily, I type in "Kasey Carter: Manhattan, New York," my stare blank as the results load.

There's nothing. I scan through pages and pages of results, but my Kasey Carter is a ghost. Or she simply doesn't have social media. I plan to search for her father next, but I need a minute to process the implications of what I've just learned.

The truth still waits to be discovered. Shadows of it, hazy and undefined, flit through my mind. Getting up to pace the porch, a restless anxiety comes over me. My peace has been disturbed, the unknown staring at me from an abyss of mystery. I want to venture into it, but I'm afraid of what waits on the other side.

Caleb approaches the porch slowly, his leisurely, loping stride giving me plenty of time and space to compose myself before he climbs the steps. He throws himself down in a porch chair and looks up at me.

"Did you get your questions answered?"

I grimace in his direction, tracking the flight of a lone bird of prey across the cloudy sky. "The answers just created more questions."

He nods. "Tends to work that way most of the time. Want my advice?"

I glance at him. "Probably."

"Whatever answers you're looking for, make sure you really want them before you go digging. There's no coming back from the truth."

"So you're saying I shouldn't try to find out why a woman who practically flinches at shadows is going to be living in our buddy's cabin in the middle of winter with two small children who may or may not belong to her?"

A single snowflake drifts down from the sky.

His expression registers his surprise, but he only shrugs and resettles the trucker hat over his head. "Give her a chance to explain before you make any moves. The woman you love deserves that much."

My eyebrows lift. "The woman I . . .?" I straighten my shoulders and shake my head. "It's not like that."

He just stares at me. "Yes, it is. I've known you a long time, remember?"

I look away, and a few minutes later, Caleb's voice breaks the silence. "Have you heard from your sister?"

I know he means Samantha, and I turn to him sympathetically. "We got a call from her on Thanksgiving, and I've texted her when I'm down here to see how she is, but that's about it."

A look of resigned misery passes across his face. "Is she happy out there?"

I'm not going to lie to my best friend. "She says she is. She's doing a lot of good with the kids she's working with."

After a minute, he nods toward the other porch chair. "Want to sit a while?"

"Can't. I have something I need to do," I reply.

Stepping off the porch, my stride is determined and unerring as I cross the yard to my truck.

Chapter Thirty-One

My arms swing the axe over my head and bring it down on the chunk of wood with a dull *thwack*. I've been hacking away for what feels like hours at the pile of discarded branches and random pieces of wood I pulled from the forest weeks ago and placed under the woodshed's roof to dry. My arms are exhausted, my fingers cramping around the handle of the axe, blisters smarting. Despite the sweat I've worked up underneath my coat, the deep chill of winter is settling into my bones. My leg aches as I shift my weight to take pressure off it. For the hundredth time, I glance over my shoulder, scanning the timberline with tired but focused eyes before I lift the axe and swing again.

I might be able to make some progress on stocking up our woodpile if I didn't stop every five minutes to check on Janie and DJ. At least, I've set up a small baby fence around the stove, since

Janie is on the go constantly. After months of being their sole caretaker, Emma's help had taken much of the burden of responsibility off my shoulders. I didn't realize how little I knew about caring for children until I watched her expertise. Now, it's been less than two weeks without the McCades, and it's taking more and more creativity to keep my niece happy and occupied.

I'm only around the corner at the shed, but I'm terrified to leave the two of them alone inside the cabin for too long while they are awake.

The first snowstorm hit a few days after we returned. The dark gray clouds finally fulfilled their promise, and the fluffy flakes fell silently through the night, muffling the world in a blanket of alabaster that shimmered in the moonlight. I stood just outside the door and watched as our clearing became an iridescent landscape of rolling mystery shapes. When morning came and the snow stopped, I shoveled a trail, desperate not to allow it to trap us in the cabin. So far, not enough has fallen to fully snow us in.

We burned through a quarter of the woodpile in the first twelve days. I worked hard to replenish our supply. Then, a few days ago, the howling began. I hadn't heard it in months. It was distant at first, a mournful, muffled cry echoing through the deep forest. But every night since, it seems to have grown closer. Finn won't leave the children's side. He's taken to sleeping across the foot of their cot, his furry body pressed against their small feet, his dark, expressive eyes rarely fully closed.

We keep watch together.

When night falls, I barricade us inside the cabin. And during the cold, ever-shortening days, we stay close to its safety. I keep my handgun in its holster and my rifle within reach. Perhaps it's the poor sleep or the eerie, snow-blanketed quiet, but for the second time since we've lived here, I get a sensation as if eyes are watching me from the dark shadows of the forest, the hair on the back of my neck suddenly prickling. I've scanned the trees again and again, searching for the yellow orbs I keep expecting to see, but nothing except darkness greets me. Even the trees don't feel as friendly now, their welcoming boughs sagging with the weight of the first snowfall.

The question of whether I made the right decision in coming back is never far from my mind. I check the cell phone again and again, holding it up to the sky to make sure it still has service, the small bars my only beacon of hope.

My messages to Amy are like a diary of my desperation, their count building into the dozens.

I've never before needed help like I need it now. The plea for guidance echoes through my brain at the same time another voice echoes that it's futile to ask for it. I've needed help plenty of times, but help never seemed to arrive until it was too late.

I needed help when my father refused to acknowledge me, leaving my mother to struggle to raise me alone.

I needed help when I turned eighteen, and she told me that I'd ruined her life for long enough and that I wasn't to bother her anymore.

I needed help when I had to watch my friends die in a Humvee under enemy fire, and despite my medical training and the hours I'd practiced at the shooting range, I couldn't save them.

Thwack. The axe sinks its teeth into the wood with a little more angst.

I don't want to do this anymore. Where is my sister, God? Why haven't You brought her back to me? I only have the strength to say the words inside my head, but a guilty feeling at my silent, accusatory tone singes my skin. I try again.

I see how You've kept us safe up here and sent us help when we needed it. I don't doubt Your presence. But I need more. I'm sorry if I'm asking for too much. I need my sister returned to me safely, I need those precious children to be with their mom again, and I need . . . Dean to forgive me for how unfair I've been to him.

I pause, wondering if I should continue. Something tugs at my heart, pushing me to ask for what I really need from the God I'm slowly learning to trust. There was a moment during a quiet evening at the farmhouse when Emma and I were alone for an hour or two. She was reading her Bible on the sofa, and suddenly, she looked up at me and said, *"Kasey, is Jesus your Lord and Savior?"*

I'd stuttered, replying that I'd said the sinner's prayer once when I was very young, but I never really knew where to go from there. *"I've been trying to read my Bible, though,"* I admitted, *"and I'd like to know more."*

"You could always rededicate your life to Him now and start afresh," she suggested.

I'd nodded then, feeling something well up in my heart that I didn't recognize, but it'd felt as though it had been lost and was finally found. And there in the McCade family's living room, she held my hand and led me in the age-old prayer again.

Now, I knew I could say what I needed to say to the One who always hears. *Please give me a sign that we're going to come out of this mess okay. Because I'm starting to lose hope.*

The gray burner phone never leaves my pocket, my ears always alert for its ring. We're approaching six months, the maximum length of time she said she could potentially be in the recovery program. I'd thought, surely, she'd get through it quickly, but after months without messages . . . if Amy doesn't make contact to tell me she is headed here soon, I'm going to have to alert the authorities and get the children into protective custody until their father's rights over them can be sorted out through the legal system. It's not what my sister wants, but we can't hide out forever.

A crack reverberates through the quiet clearing.

"Hello," a deep voice calls, the sound muffled and far away.

Tossing the axe down against the shed wall, I reach for my rifle and move cautiously toward the front of the cabin. When I round the corner and see him step off the snow-covered trail, my heart drops, but it's with relief and not fear. I stand and stare at him, watching as the clumsy snowshoes flip up sprays of snow that sparkle like glitter in the midday sun.

His gaze meets mine unerringly, but he doesn't speak.

My hesitation lasts only a moment. Leaning the rifle against the cabin, I run along the path I dug out, my boots thudding dully on the ground. I fling myself toward him, and Dean's arms come up and around me immediately. Thick coats fill the space between us, but I can almost swear I feel the beating of his heart.

"I thought you abandoned us," I mumble into his coat, tightening my grip around his neck, knowing I'll shatter if he pushes me away.

He doesn't answer, so a minute later, I risk leaning back and glancing into his face. He's staring down at me with a strange look simmering in his stormy eyes. His voice is a husky rumble when he speaks.

"I'd never abandon you."

Tears well up in my eyes, and I'm unable to do more than whisper. "I thought you were mad at me after the way I . . ."

"Well, you've been a little feisty, but I've got two sisters and a mother. I'm used to feisty, stubborn, hardheaded women." I realize his lips have twisted up into a grin, and my heart lightens when he continues with a quiet, "I don't abandon the people I care about, Kasey."

You're not alone anymore. The soft-spoken words whisper in my soul.

"I take it you're not mad at me still?" His voice vibrates with amusement.

"I was never mad at you," I whisper in reply. The truth feels as if it's been waiting at the surface for just this moment in time. I can't stop myself from continuing, "There's just been so much that I wanted to say, so much that I couldn't tell you, no matter how much I wanted to. I'm so scared of failing those kids, Dean."

He doesn't reply, and the silence stretches between us.

"I know they aren't your children," he finally says, the words low and quiet.

I feel as if I've just been punched. Dropping my arms, I step back, my boots crunching on the snow, and stare up at him in horror. My head swirls with fear. His expression is solemn, the crow's feet around his blue eyes deeper than they were the last time I saw him.

He takes a deep breath. "I came up here to . . . I think it's time to talk, Kasey."

I cross my arms, trying to widen my stance and straighten my shoulders, hoping I don't look as terrified as I feel. I glance behind him, wondering if a team of sheriffs or the FBI is about to step out of the woods behind him.

He anticipates my thoughts. "I came up here alone."

"You've been checking up on me?" I demand. "What do you think you know?"

He studies me. "It took me a while to figure all this out. I know your father was Kenneth Carter and that he made a fortune on Wall Street back in the nineties. I know he was never married to your mother, and you have a sister who was born five years after you. A sister who married a glamorous nightclub owner with notably sketchy business dealings, who is now serving a five-year sentence for assault and battery. A sister who gave birth to two children: Dmitry Junior and Jane."

The lump in my throat nearly prevents me from choking out a reply. "That's quite a lot to know."

Dean continues, "I also found out that you fought to save Danny and your team when you were ambushed." He pauses for a breath. "I don't believe a person who commits such acts of bravery suddenly goes rogue for no reason."

He takes a step closer, and I fight the urge to run.

"Tell me this isn't what it looks like, Kasey."

Guilt floods my limbs, crushing me under its weight. My shoulders slump; my fight dissipates. "It looks pretty bad, doesn't it?"

"Did you kidnap those kids?"

"Of course not," I protest, a flash of fierce energy welling up within me, "or at least, that's not what I intended to do. And I know you don't think I did, or you wouldn't have come up here alone."

His face doesn't soften. "Where is their mother?"

"I don't know," I admit in a whisper.

Dean's face is half covered by a wool cap, but I can still see his eyebrows shoot up.

"Any day now, I'll hear from her," I hasten to add. "She needed time to . . . get herself into a better place, to heal an addiction that was preventing her from being the mother she needs to be. As soon as she contacts me, this is all over. I'll bring the children back, and after that, it's up to her to make things right."

He eyes me skeptically.

"My sister is an addict, Dean. She couldn't break it on her

own, so she went to an immersive treatment program somewhere in the States."

"Why not just take you and the kids with her and have you stay nearby?" Dean is right to question me, but I can't help the sting.

"I don't know," I admit with reluctance. "I have so many questions too. I can only think that she was desperate and not thinking clearly. My sister is afraid of her husband. If he found out that she's trying to get help so she can break his hold on her, or if he discovered her location and then tracked us down while she was cut off from outside contact . . . I just want them all to be protected until she can prove to a judge that she is the best person to have custody over them after he gets released."

"Keeping a father from his kids is circumventing the legal system at the very best," Dean replies. "At the worst . . ."

I nod, barely able to choke out the words. "He was still in jail a few months ago when we left. There was no one else to give guardianship of the kids to without compromising Amy. I promise we were both just trying to do what is best for Junior and Janie." I swallow painfully, knowing what comes next. "You should probably turn me in, but can you just give me a few more days? If my sister calls, it can be like none of this ever happened."

"Kasey," DJ's voice calls to me from the direction of the cabin.

Sighing, I turn away from Dean. "I never leave them alone in there this long. Do you want to come up to say hello? They'll want to see you."

"I want to talk more about this," he replies.

"I'm sure you do," I shrug, feeling any fight I have left washing away in the exhaustion of it all, "but right now, they need me more."

I don't wait for him to follow, but the thud of his boots is heavy as he strides down the snow-scattered trail after me.

Chapter Thirty-Two

Dean

It takes me a couple of days to dig up enough information on Kasey's family to be able to make an educated guess at the circumstances that brought her to Cascade Valley. While I still don't know the details of how she came to be living alone with her nephew and niece, once I found her dad's name and connected him to her sister and her imprisoned husband, an idea of what the woman in the woods is facing fell into place. There aren't any articles about the situation or warrants out for her arrest, so I'm hopeful but cautious as I finish my research.

I put in calls to the National Personnel Records Center to verify Kasey Carter's service record and photograph.

But my informal investigation comes to a screeching halt when it's clear the snow clouds gathering above the mountains again aren't just passing through. Getting the herd back onto the safety of our land becomes a pressing matter that can't wait any longer.

I ride up to the team the next morning.

The open trail and the cold, biting wind clear my head. Even Midnight seems eager to be saddled up in the hazy fog of early morning, the thick strands of his mane dancing as he prances along the frost-covered ground. Caleb rides up with me as he often does when we are scheduled to bring down the herd. Whenever we've needed an extra ranch hand over the years, he fills in. His presence doesn't disturb my racing thoughts, since neither of us is in the mood for much talking. As Christmas approaches, I know his mind is on Samantha, and I'm thinking of how I'm going to convince Kasey to let me help her out of this mess she's gotten herself into.

I use the walkie-talkie to alert the crew when we are a couple of miles out.

"Halloo, is that you, oh brother dearest?" Knox answers my call melodiously. "Wherefore art thou? Hark, do I hear thy worthy steed approach?"

I can't help but snicker despite my mood, rolling my eyes toward Caleb, who rides at my flank. He lifts an eyebrow in response, clearly not fazed by Knox's shenanigans.

"Reading Shakespeare again in your spare time, I see?" I say into the device.

Knox scoffs on the other end. "I'll have you know that, though short and steeped in tragedy, there's no love story like Romeo and Juliet's."

"I don't know about that," I retort. "Seems a love story that ends like that isn't much of a romance at all. We are coming up the hill behind you. Tell the boys to get everything but the essentials packed up. We're riding out as soon as we arrive."

"Already on it," Knox snarks. "Figured the snow clouds

would remind you of your duty. Sorry to drag you away from your girlfriend."

My brothers rode up the day after Thanksgiving, so they aren't aware of Kasey's departure.

"Did Mom and Demi leave for the airport yet?" he continues before I can counter.

"They were driving there a few hours after we rode up."

Demi is headed home to New York City, but back in the early autumn, Mom booked a flight to Spain for the week after Thanksgiving. She wanted to visit Samantha before the chaos of the holidays. I'm glad she is going to see my sister in person. While I know Mom talks to her via FaceTime almost daily, and we've chatted over text whenever I have cell service, there's nothing like an in-person visit to reassure us of her safety and well-being. I know she's busy serving her calling at the orphanage, but Mom will have the chance to make sure she's also taking care of herself. Plus, Mom loves to travel. As much as she loves the ranch, she and Samantha seem to share the same adventurous spirit.

Once we arrive, I focus completely on the herd. For the next week, we make a slow trek back down the mountain as the snowflakes fall and the drifts gather on the trail. For the few years we've been running our grazing program, we don't rush the herd off the mountain before the first snowfall descends. The cattle are hardy, able to withstand the gradually lowering temperature as we lead them home. They'll spend the rest of the winter on the McCade ranch, with shelters protecting them from the worst of the Montana winters, eating a blend of hay and the dry forage we work tirelessly to gather while the weather is good.

The journey gives me the chance to prepare for confronting Kasey, and by the time the herd is settled and we've completed all the last-minute chores needed to finalize our winter preparations on the ranch, I'm ready for what must come next.

Mom returns, slightly tanned and glowing from her trip to Spain. She reports that Samantha is homesick but happy and focused on her mission in Europe.

Despite the urge I feel to get up the mountain, I'm obligated to spend a couple of days handling closing inspections and banking paperwork for the lodge as escrow enters its final stages. Our purchase of Bear Creek Lodge is scheduled to close on Christmas Eve, and I can't skip out on what we've worked so hard to negotiate. The investment wasn't a decision my brothers and I made lightly, but I find myself having many conversations with Vincent and Knox about what the future holds. The lodge itself is in fairly good condition, albeit out of date, but the lift and ski trails are going to need professional help before we can reopen for business.

After Mom's return, she proposes we throw an impromptu holiday party on Christmas Eve to celebrate our new business venture. After years of hard work and history in the valley culminating in the takeover of this local landmark, inviting our entire community to a holiday open house sounds like a blast. Since we've been hoping to surprise her when everything is finalized, we plan to call Samantha during the party with the lodge decked out for Christmas to tell her the good news. She and Dad made countless trips up there to ski, so it'll be a special moment to share with her.

As a flurry of preparations commences, the identity verification request I put in for the National Personnel Records Center is confirmed. When the accompanying photograph downloads, I'm temporarily caught off guard. It's Kasey all right, the firm set of those full lips and the piercing stare of those aquamarine eyes unmistakable in the green and brown army-issued uniform.

But the woman who served her country and risked her life for her teammates isn't my Kasey. My Kasey is softer, time and loss and experience blurring the lines of her defensive nature. There's something different in her eyes now, perhaps a spark of life or a sense of hope that didn't exist within her before. I realize I don't ever want to see that light fade away.

As I puzzle together the final bits and pieces of her life, a story unfolds that settles like a heavy weight in my stomach. What I have to do can't wait any longer. There's work to do on the ranch, but I put it off, unwilling to go another day without the full truth. It's time she and I had a conversation.

But when I drive the truck up the steep, snowy mountain road as far as it will go, I'm hit with the very real possibility that she's already hightailed it out of Danny's cabin. Has she flitted away, disappearing into the mist like a doe in flight? Each thud of my boots as I hike up the trail feels like a resounding confirmation that I'm about to hit a dead end.

I dread the truth, and I dread the lies.

But the faint wisps of smoke coming from the chimney lift a weight from my chest that has lingered like a dark cloud for days.

When she rounds the corner of the cabin and runs to me, I can't help but pull her into my arms and wonder if it's possible that all my suspicions, the half-formed explanations in my head, are completely wrong.

And now, inside the sparse cabin that somehow feels warm and homey, her eyes are pleading with me to give her more time. In furtive whispers, she fills me in on her sister's battle with addiction, her determination to recover, and her fear that her husband's retaliation will turn on her and the children if she can't prove that she's clean. She ran away into the night and left her older half-sister to pick up the pieces.

"She said the addiction treatment center is somewhere in the States, but I haven't been able to do much digging given the circumstances," Kasey mumbles. "With the money she inherited from our father, I've no doubt it's as secretive and exclusive as they get."

I watch the children as she confesses it all. Junior—DJ—is practicing his numbers on a pad of paper, and Janie's head nestles on my shoulder. I can't deny that they are healthy and happy children.

Kasey shows me the gray prepaid cell phone her sister gave her, programmed with only a single number. There are dozens of outgoing text messages, but only a couple of incoming ones. She also shows me the notarized letters and paperwork Amy sent with her.

If anyone has ever been stuck between a rock and a hard place, faced with an impossible choice and a dangerously uncertain outcome, it's the woman before me. Six months. If her sister hasn't called by the six-month mark, she plans to go to the authorities herself and take the consequences.

I can't say I wouldn't have made the same choices if faced with such a desperate situation and the chance to protect my family.

I pull in a deep breath, feeling the metaphorical rock and a hard place closing in on me too.

"Three weeks," I begin firmly, the mist in her eyes immediately weakening my resolve. "We'll get through Christmas and the New Year so the kids can enjoy the holidays, and then we're going to set up an appointment with Pastor Miller and a lawyer. They'll help us figure out where to go from there. Okay?"

Her narrow shoulders slump inward. "Okay," she whispers,

her eyes landing first on her niece, then on her nephew.

We fall silent, the crackle of the wood stove and the cheerful chatter of the children the only sounds to break the silence.

I wonder if I'm taking a risk by giving her the space and time to run away. I can't force her to come back to the ranch with me, and I can't stay up here to watch over her all the time. But the truth is hitting me differently than I would expect. Maybe my moral center is off-kilter, but I can see the situation from her perspective. In a moment of desperation, she made what she believed was the right decision to protect her small charges and her sister at the same time. When I return home, I plan to dig more extensively into her brother-in-law to see what she's up against.

"I'm guessing I can't convince you to come back to stay at the ranch with us until Christmas?" I'm the first to speak again.

Her expression is sad, and she pulls her lower lip between her teeth. I see the battle waging in her head. "Not yet. It's better for us to be up here."

I know what she's not saying is that she feels safest up here, away from prying eyes and their curious questions.

"Christmas is coming," I remark, and at the word, DJ and Janie look up at me with eager expressions. "Mom would like you to be at the ranch to celebrate with us." I clear my throat. "We all would, actually."

I watch her bite her lip again.

"I just don't know if it's . . ."

I extend my free hand across the table. "You're the safest when you're with us, Kasey. When you're with me . . ."

The soft light from the lantern makes it seem like there are twinkles in her eyes.

"And we're throwing a Christmas Eve party at the lodge," I

continue. "The lodge isn't that far away, you know." I motion upward, toward the mountain slope that rises above the back of the cabin. "It's not far from here if you keep going around the mountain. There will be lots of food and games and presents for the kids and a Christmas tree."

"Presents!" DJ exclaims, jumping to his feet. "Can we go to the party?"

Kasey glances up at me from under fluffy lashes, her cheeks rosy, her expression almost shy, but the light is still sparkling in her eyes. She looks at me, but her words are directed at her nephew. "Maybe we can, buddy. We'll just have to see."

It isn't much, but it feels like it's enough for now.

Chapter Thirty-Three

Kasey

My hands shake a little as I tie the laces of my boots and reach out to straighten the bow in Janie's hair, but the tremor originates from a shiver of excitement and not from fear.

Somehow, two chubby-cheeked children have cajoled me into attending a Christmas Eve party where half the town will be in attendance. A Christmas party we have no business showing our faces at. By some miracle, my brother-in-law hasn't turned us in, no one has sounded the alarm over Amy's disappearance, and somehow, we're not on the public's radar . . . yet . . . and I can't help but think it's a stroke of good fortune too good to be true.

But I can't deny DJ and Janie the chance to have a good Christmas. I've tried to make our cabin festive with foraged pine boughs and battery-operated lights, and we've been making paper snowflakes to hang around our primitive home for weeks now. Back in the fall, I bought a few gifts for them on a trip to town that I tucked away in a hiding spot. The glee on their faces when Dean described the impromptu Christmas Eve celebration was undeniable. So I tell myself we'll keep a low profile and leave if the townspeople start getting too nosy.

Flurries of snow are falling like powdered sugar sprinkled across a cake when we leave for the party. I'm pleasantly surprised that the snow on the trail down to the Jeep isn't too deep for us to walk in, somewhat protected as it is by the tree boughs that stretch over it. According to Dean, snowfall has been uncharacteristically light for the season, but he wants us off the mountain before it descends with a vengeance in the new year. He hasn't insisted that we move down to the ranch to stay with his family quite yet, but I know his deadline is coming.

I carry Janie down the trail, bundled in her puffy coat, and choose my steps carefully with DJ at my side. Finn follows in our rear. He'll stay in the Jeep until after the party. On my shoulder is an overnight bag since I've promised Dean we'll spend Christmas Day with his family. The snow on the logging road is already scraped and packed down, my Jeep's tires dug out of the snow. Dean's doing, and I'm so grateful.

On one of several visits up here over the past couple of weeks, Dean gave me careful directions to the lodge, but I don't think I could have missed it if I tried. Taking the logging road back toward the valley, I follow the same route Dean and I took to the lodge the first time. Even with the incoming snow flurries lowering visibility on the road, it's easy to find.

When we reach it, Bear Creek Lodge is lit like a beacon on the hilltop, golden lights shining brilliantly across the snow. The untouched ski lanes stand out, bold lines running like ribbons down the mountain.

From the looks of it, half the town is already here. Christmas music and laughter float from the lodge into the night.

Everyone I see has turned up in their holiday best. I didn't have anything to wear that said, "festive Christmas Eve celebration," so I'm dressed in my usual dark-colored jeans, a white t-shirt, hiking boots, and a coat. I shake the snowflakes off my shoulders, tuck my hair behind my ears, and try to smooth down my rumpled shirt as we walk upstairs to the second floor, the railing strung with fresh garland and strands of lights. The prepaid cell phone is tucked, as always, in my pocket.

I feel the warmth of his presence before I even reach the top step. Dean spots us as we ascend the stairs. He strides over, and I catch my breath at the sight of him dressed up like a model who just stepped off the cover of *Montana Cowboy Magazine*. I've determined previously that the McCades are a very good-looking family. The three brothers are exceptionally handsome, the daughters are gorgeous, but there's something about Dean's magnetic strength, combined with his dark features and those gray-blue eyes, that takes my breath away.

When he reaches us, he extends his hands to Janie, and she practically leaps into his arms, a happy, toothsome grin on her face. His gaze is bent on me, though, as I step fully onto the second floor.

"You came," he says, and with an approving gleam in his eyes, adds in a slightly husky tone, "and you look beautiful."

A warmth that is now familiar crosses my face, and I drop my eyes. It isn't like me to be fluttery around a man, and somehow, Dean McCade has me blushing every time I'm in his presence.

"I look just as I always do," I reply dryly, clearing my throat, "and we're here because the kids wanted to come."

"Didn't you?" His low, deep tone is for my ears only.

I finally gather the courage to look at him again. The grin that creeps across my lips is genuine. "Oh, I did too. But they were a little more enthused about the prospect of presents than I was."

He returns my grin, his lips parting under his full beard. He looks down at Janie, who peers back up at him adoringly. "Speaking of presents, come with me."

We follow him into the second-story great room, weaving through chattering townspeople toward the wall of windows that looks out over the hilltop. My breath catches a second time as golden light spills out, illuminating the snow-capped pines.

Dean leads us over to the towering Christmas tree in the corner, and I pause to admire it, wondering how they managed to carry the massive specimen into the building. It's strung with lights and a popcorn and cranberry garland, with piles of presents nestled under the lower boughs.

When my eyes widen, Dean laughs. "Everyone who came brought a gift to share. However, I do happen to know that there are a few presents for two small children under there."

DJ's face brightens. He tugs on my pant leg and asks permission to look for his name under the Christmas tree, which I readily give. Not to be outdone, Janie wiggles down and toddles after him. As DJ helps Janie search for her name, I finally have the chance to take in the rest of the space.

A pair of buffet tables stretches across the other end of the room, surrounded by round tables decorated with poinsettias and candles. A tall, redheaded young woman in an eye-catching forest-green dress catches my eye as she carries in trays of food through a pair of swinging doors that I assume must lead to a kitchen. She pauses to speak to an older couple lingering nearby, and I notice when she freezes, her eyes lifting toward the grand staircase.

I follow her gaze and recognize Caleb, one of Dean's friends, just as he reaches the top of the grand staircase. His arm is supporting a tiny and frail white-haired woman as she totters up the steps. As he steps onto the landing, the man's gaze sweeps across the room and lands on the redhead. Even from under the black cowboy hat shading his eyes, I observe the expression of surprise that crosses his face at the sight of her. Drawn into the exchange, I look back and forth, observing their silent communication.

And then I see Jenna, her hand wrapped through the crook of the man's other arm as she steps onto the great room floor. I expect to see Hunter trailing behind her, but he doesn't appear, and I feel a sudden rush of relief. After feeling like he pushed me too far during our last encounter, I'm not eager to interact with the nosy man again. Jenna catches sight of the young woman, too, and her diamond ring flashes as she lifts her hand in an eager wave.

When I look back toward the buffet table, the redhead has disappeared.

"That's my youngest sister, Samantha," Dean says from behind me.

I turn to him and smile. "I thought I recognized her from your family photos. She's beautiful. But that's true of all the women in your family."

He stares down at me with an appreciative expression. Just as he begins to say something, Knox calls him over to help move around some of the tables. Janie has begun to tear the wrapping paper off as many presents as she can reach, so I step forward and scoop her into my arms, looking around for something else to entertain her. As more townspeople arrive, I try to stay in the shadows along the outer edge of the room until the assembly line for dinner forms.

I'm staring toward the picture windows, trying to see beyond my own reflection in the darkened glass, when an icy chill whispers across the back of my neck. My shoulders tremble with an involuntary shiver. The hairs on my arms stand up as goosebumps pebble across my flesh, an undeniable sensation that I'm being watched flashing over me again.

My head whips around, and I scan the townspeople mingling throughout the great room. But no one seems to be paying us any attention, though the sensation continues to buzz in the back of my skull.

DJ and Janie are hungry, so I slip into the line and fix plates for them, trying not to make enough eye contact to initiate a conversation with anyone.

Emma and Demi stand on the other side of the table, dishing out delicious-smelling food. They both greet me warmly, Emma's eyes especially lighting up at the sight of us. I remember guiltily that I need to apologize to the older woman for my unannounced departure. She deserved at least a goodbye.

Samantha rejoins them to help serve as we leave the buffet. When I turn away, Dean beckons me over to one of the tables set up across the floor and helps me get Janie settled to eat as a few of his friends, including Caleb and Jenna, wander over.

Jenna sweeps down to coo over Janie, her expression bright. "I hope Hunter and I have babies right after we're married," she exclaims. "I'll give up horseback riding for a few months for that."

I help Janie lift a spoonful of mashed potatoes into her mouth. "Where is your fiancé tonight?" I ask Jenna casually.

"He had some business come up out of town," she replies, "and he wasn't going to be back until late. I caught a ride with Caleb and Mrs. Jensen. Hunter should be here later, though, to take me home."

I recognize the starry-eyed look of a woman in love, and a

part of me feels bad for disliking her slick city boyfriend. I'm distracted from the thought when I feel Dean's warm, strong hand slip over mine. His eyes are deep and stormy, and I feel the strangest sense of something mysterious and new striking my heart, something that feels like a dizzying rush of certainty that I'm almost out of this valley of shadows and into the light. Deep in my bones, there's a conviction that despite the odds, there can be a future for me here if I want it.

"I want to introduce you to someone," Dean says.

"Go." Jenna grins. "I'll watch these two while they eat." She makes a shooing motion with her hands.

"I'd really rather not," I protest, but I rise from the table and trail after Dean.

Samantha walks out of the kitchen, carrying a tray piled high with sugar cookies to the dessert table.

"Dean," she exclaims, "can you grab the cake Malia brought and bring it out? It's a little heavy. Oh, who is your friend?" Her smile beams like a gentle ray of sunshine onto my face.

"Sure," he turns to me, his fingers closing gently over my elbow and leading me forward, "but first, I'd like you two to meet. Sammie, this is Kasey. Kasey, this is my youngest sister, Samantha."

Automatically, I extend my hand to her, and her long fingertips brush mine. She's much taller than I and built with a curvier frame than Demi. Given her striking mahogany hair and freckled complexion, she doesn't look much like Dean at first glance, but then, I start to see him in the shape of her nose and intelligent expression. Instantly, I feel myself drawn to her.

"I'm so pleased to meet you, Kasey," she says, her green eyes darting back and forth between me and Dean.

"Likewise," I reply.

"Sammie decided to fly in from Spain tonight and give us quite the Christmas surprise," Dean says. "We were planning to surprise *her* with the news that we'd bought the lodge, but she arrived just before we left. I suspect she timed her arrival perfectly to get out of cooking and setting up for the party tonight."

I peer up at him in time to catch the wink he gives her. She rolls her eyes and laughs in return.

"Hence, why I'm doing all the hard work and slaving away in the kitchen now while the rest of you enjoy yourselves out here," Samantha says. She looks around the space, and her voice thickens. "I can't believe you bought this place. So many memories—" I see her eyes glance toward the table where Dean's friends are sitting. She gives a little start. "Oh my goodness, the hot cocoa! It's on the stove. I'll be right back."

She darts away through the swinging doors into the kitchen, the thick waves of her hair flowing in her wake, leaving us staring after her.

"She is lovely," I say with admiration.

Dean's eyes roam my face until they land on my lips, and his reply warms me. "Have I told you how glad I am that you're here?"

Maybe it's the Christmas lights reflecting like twinkling stars in his eyes or the scent of pine that always seems to linger on his clothes. Maybe it's the Christmas music echoing through the lofty rafters of the great room doing things to my head or my heart. I don't understand the choking rush of emotion, but I feel the urge to speak come over me.

"Dean," I begin softly, lifting my hand to touch the shirt button over his heart, "there's something I want to say—"

The buzz of the phone in my pocket nearly causes me to jump out of my skin. My eyes widen, and I gasp, my hand flying to my pocket. Shoving my hand in, I draw out the small phone. Instantly, Dean understands what is happening.

"Hurry," he directs me toward the staircase, "we'll watch the kids." He waves to Emma from across the room.

I'm too startled to do more than nod and speed walk away. Looking toward the table, I catch a glimpse of my niece and nephew finishing their Christmas dinner. My heart aches to see them reunited with their mother again and to know once and for all that love can knit a family back together piece by piece until it is whole.

My boots thud on the staircase, my heart pounding to the beat. I fly down the steps and burst into the night. The brisk winter night nips at my face as the phone buzzes in my hand. I don't even know what I'm doing, my steps turning toward the lookout as I slide open the call and press the phone to my ear. The light snow flurries have completely stopped by now, and my boots crunch over the frozen, freshly dusted earth.

"H-h-hello?" My voice trembles.

"Kasey?" Her voice—at once so familiar and yet so strange—is studded with tears. The sharp spark of my own emotion pricks my eyelids. I gulp back a sob as I reach the lookout.

"Amy?" I can only manage a whisper. "Where are you?"

"My babies," her voice breaks on the other end of the line, "DJ, Janie . . . please, tell me . . ."

"Safe." I try to pull myself together, and the words rush out. "We are all safe. They are healthy and growing so big, and Janie is saying so many words. You won't believe it . . ." I pause, realizing my tongue is tripping as the words tumble out of me, and Amy sobs loudly in relief.

"I can't wait to hold them," she chokes out.

"Where are you?" I ask again. "Why haven't you contacted us

in months? What's happening?"

She breathes deeply to calm herself. "I'm in Florida. I was just off the coast at a private facility. They released me this morning, and I already rented a car," she replies. "Oh, Kasey, it's been awful. They wouldn't let me leave before now. They found the phone after I sent the last update, and they took it away. The doctors said I had to start the program over because I'd broken trust. I've been so scared. I couldn't communicate with you. I just did whatever they said to get out of there. Where are you?"

"We're in Montana. Just outside a small town called Cascade Valley." I almost dread saying the next words. "Do you want us to come to you?"

"No," Amy replies quickly. "I'll come to you. I'd rather not drag my babies all over the country . . . especially if things don't go as planned."

"Where is Dmitry?"

She hesitates. "He's out. They released him two weeks ago." Her voice trembles. "I've already been in contact with a lawyer to make sure the kids and I are protected no matter what comes next."

There's a long pause before she speaks. "Kasey, I'm going to try to work things out with him."

"What?" I'm taken completely off guard. I scan the inky horizon over the treetops, unconsciously counting each glow of light from the town in the valley. "Why would you do that? He's abusive. He's dangerous. You said so yourself. Why?"

She sighs heavily. "For so many reasons. But mostly because I've had the chance to work on myself while I've been in recovery. I've made so many mistakes, and yet, God has forgiven me of them all and walked with me even in my darkest places. Perhaps Dmitry has come to know the Lord while in prison. Perhaps he's ready to be a better man. I think it's the right thing to do to give him a chance to correct the wrongs he's done."

My boot toes a loose stone at my feet. The night presses in, and a familiar tingle tickles the back of my neck. Glancing around, I search the dark forest, looking for anything to indicate why it feels as if I'm suddenly being watched. But just like every time before, there's nothing visible, just the trees and the wind and the sound of laughter and Christmas music echoing down from the lodge.

I don't speak. I can't. My heart rebels at the thought of my niece and nephew anywhere near their father again. Does he deserve the chance to make amends? Can a man change?

"I'm taking precautions," Amy seems to read my thoughts, "and we won't go back unless Dmitry takes actionable steps to change his ways. I don't want to break up my family if I don't have to, Kasey." Her soft voice pleads with me to understand.

And as the child of broken trust and broken hearts, I do.

"I know you'll do what's best for them," I finally find my voice, "and that's what matters. When will you be here?"

"I don't want to take a flight in case he's watching, so I'm going to drive. I can be there within the next three or four days," she says. "Tell me where you are."

Carefully, I give her detailed instructions to the cabin. At this point, we could go stay in a motel in town to make it easier for her to reach us, but my heart is screaming at me to keep up my guard, even though all of this is almost over. I want my sister to see the safe haven we've created for ourselves up here before she makes the decision to break the peaceful bubble we're living in.

"I love you," she says after writing it all down.

"I just want to protect you," I whisper in reply.

"I know," she says, and we end the call.

I hold the gray phone to my heart afterward, willing my breathing to calm, reminding myself to think, and realizing I need to plan out what comes next.

"This is in Your hands now," I whisper toward the inky night sky before I turn away from the lookout. I need to find Dean and make an excuse to take the children home before my trembling hands give the truth away to everyone. As I begin the slight ascent toward the glowing lodge, my peripheral vision catches the outline of a dark figure twenty feet away, stationed under the trees. I startle and take a second look, my instincts and training pressing me to investigate the presence of this unwitting intruder into my solitude.

Was I talking loudly? I wonder but quickly reassure myself that there was no way anyone could have overheard my conversation with Amy over the music spilling out into the night.

Besides, the shadowy form is already retreating. It disappears into the tree line just as the moon glints off a pair of shiny silver boots.

Chapter Thirty-Four

Dean

When Kasey appears in the great room again, her eyes wide and her expression a cross between grim and hopeful, I know things are going to change quickly. She makes her excuses and prepares to take the children home.

She promised to come home with us after the Christmas Eve party, but she won't risk not being at the cabin when her sister arrives. I know the trail to the cabin is perfectly safe since I cleared it myself after scraping the logging road. After she tucks Janie into her car seat and helps Junior into his booster seat, I shut the Jeep door and pull her into my arms. She stares up at me. Even in the moonlight, I see the concern etched across her face.

I stroke the space between her shoulder blades. "You know that I'll take you back up there in a couple of days to receive your sister. Then she can come back with us, and we can make a plan to go from there. Or better yet, have her come to the ranch.

Mom'll take good care of her."

Her cheek lowers to nestle against my flannel shirt, and her arms go around my waist. "I hope you know that when you say 'we,' it makes me feel as if everything is going to be okay." Her voice is muffled by the fabric.

"Because it *is* going to be okay," I assure her.

Her arms tighten. "There are a lot of unknowns, but the way you've supported us and protected us means everything to me, Dean." She leans back, and I see the glisten of tears on her cheeks. "I've never really had that before, and I'll never forget it."

When she lifts onto her toes to press her lips against mine in a kiss that is pillowy soft, I draw her closer, leaning over her when she finally breaks away. "Hey, you're talking like I'm never going to see you again."

Her smile is pained. "I'm just not sure what's going to happen, and I have to make sure Amy gets through this okay."

I can't pretend I don't understand her protective instincts. I'd be the same if one of my siblings were in a similar situation.

Still, it takes every ounce of self-control in me to let her drive away. She'd go to the edge of the earth to protect her family, but I'd go to the edge of the earth and back again to protect her.

I just wonder if I'll ever get the chance to prove that to her again.

"She's in Your hands now, Lord," I mutter. "Please give Kasey wisdom and protect that family from harm as they figure out the future."

The prayer soothes my troubled heart, and I find the strength to let Kasey walk into this final valley with the One who will pick her up and carry her through it.

I'm thankful the weather app indicates we're not supposed to get much more snow for the next few days because I wouldn't have let her go back to the cabin if a storm was about to roll in. We'll see if the meteorologists get it right this time. The snow was coming down in light flurries just a few hours ago, but the sky is now cloud-free and inky black. An amused sound escapes me when I realize I'm a newbie ski lodge owner and operator who is glad the season has been unusually mild for this time of year. The snow can come, but only after I know Kasey and the kids are safely back in the valley.

Two days later, I'm still thinking about her as I walk into the kitchen at the ranch. It's midafternoon the day after Christmas, and all of us have been taking it slow and soaking up our time with Samantha before she leaves for Spain again. The scent of a bottomless pot of coffee and warm shortbread cookies leftover from Christmas Eve warms the room.

"My truck isn't outside," I announce to no one in particular.

Mom looks up. "Did Sammie borrow it?"

I shrug. "I guess she could have. All the other trucks are outside."

Mom rises from her devotional study at the worn kitchen table to glance into the yard. "Did she leave when we were all in here earlier?"

"Beats me." I refill my mug with fresh coffee and stare out the window toward the barn on the other side of the yard. It looks like the weather app has gotten it wrong again. We weren't expecting snow, but what started as a crisp winter morning without a cloud in the sky has turned into stray nimbostratus clouds sporadically layered across the valley. The sky above the mountains is slowly gathering the gray and gloom under the weight of a pending snowstorm. The weather app predicted its arrival tomorrow night at the earliest.

"Did you need your truck for something? Take one of the

boys' trucks instead," she presses.

"It's fine." I glance toward Mom. "I'm planning to drive up to visit Kasey."

The room is quiet for a moment.

"Good idea. Get up there before the storm hits later," Mom says softly. "If you do, please give her and the kids a hug for me. Get them to come back with you if you can."

When I announced after the party that Kasey wouldn't be joining us for Christmas Day, she was visibly disappointed. So disappointed that it made Samantha express her curiosity about the trio, and her questions launched an inquisitive discussion of the current status of my relationship with the reserved woman. I avoided my family's questions as much as I could because, after all, what is there to say? What is my relationship status with the beautiful woman in the woods?

We're not dating. To date, she'd have to first be willing to go on a date.

We're not together, but it feels in some way that our fates are twined together as one.

Yet, after her sister's return, will I ever see Kasey again?

The future is completely uncertain.

In short, our relationship is complicated.

And once her sister is back, it's going to get all the more convoluted.

But for now, colorful wrapped presents for Junior and Jane are still waiting under our tree. There are a few for Kasey too. And Mom is missing her adoptive grandchildren. Of course, she has no idea that Kasey is waiting for her sister's arrival and may never return. I don't feel it's my place to break the news.

I walk over and squeeze Mom's shoulder. I'm about to grab my coat and boots, planning to finish a few chores before heading up the mountain, when I see a flash of metal through the window as Caleb's truck pulls into the driveway. Another flash—this time of familiar mahogany hair—and I stare as Samantha and Caleb tumble through the back door together. Caleb is grinning like a fool. Samantha freezes at the sight of us, her eyes bright and a brilliant smile lifting her cheeks. Caleb snakes an arm around her waist and pulls her close to his side.

I feel Mom rise behind me, the ticking of the clock on the wall loud as the seconds pass in an unbroken silence. She inhales sharply.

Samantha's smile turns shy. As her eyes drop to the ground and a rosy flush brightens her freckled cheeks, she says softly, "We're . . . we came to say . . ." The words begin to tumble out of her in a rush. "Caleb and I are engaged!"

A delighted cry emits from Mom's lips, and she gives me a gentle shove in her rush to throw her arms around her youngest daughter. I'm close on her heels.

Caleb draws me into a hug. I slap his back enthusiastically.

"Welcome to the family, brother." There isn't an ounce of hesitation in my words.

The gleam of joy in his eyes says it all.

The room erupts in laughter and shouts of congratulations. It takes only a minute or two before Vincent, Demi, and Knox come tumbling into the room, drawn in by our loud celebration. I look their way with a grin plastered across my face and beckon them closer.

"What in the tarnation is all the ruckus about?" Knox shouts in an exaggerated drawl, his heavy boots loud on the wood floor.

"We could hear you all clucking like a flock of hens from upstairs," Demi teases in her softer tone.

Only Vincent is characteristically quiet, his quick, perceptive eyes scanning the four of us. A grin breaks over his face before the other two finish speaking. He strides over to Caleb, hand outstretched. "Congratulations."

Caleb takes his hand and shakes it heartily.

"What?" Demi and Knox shout together, rushing forward.

"We're engaged!" Samantha exclaims again.

There's a fresh eruption of joyous laughter as a chaotic tumble of questions, hugs, and congratulations ensues. Everyone wants to know how this turn of events came to be. No one seems surprised by the news—Caleb and Samantha's quiet, budding romance this past summer has already been discussed within the family many times over. But we were all collectively disappointed to know they hadn't really spoken since she broke things off with him and left for Europe. Our hope of officially adding Caleb Kane to our family seemed to be at a standstill.

The news of their engagement infuses fresh life into our old farmhouse. Mom rushes to pour chilled sparkling cider for everyone, and a series of enthusiastic and joke-filled toasts ensues.

Amid the commotion, I pull Samantha aside and wrap her up in a hug. "Happy for you, sis," I whisper against her hair.

She draws away and smirks up at me. "Sorry for taking your best friend. Hope you can forgive me."

Twisting my lips, I pretend to consider. "Hm, it might take me a bit to accept that my best friend is now going to be contractually obligated to pick you first, but I think I can get over it." I grin. "I expect you to keep that rancher on his toes at all times, though, and give me first dibs when you plan to pull a prank on him."

Tossing her head back, Samantha's hearty laugh rings out. But when she stops, her green eyes are wet with tears. She drops her head into her hands.

"Hey, hey, what's wrong?" I bend my knees, trying to see into her face.

"I just wish Dad were here to celebrate with us," she whispers throatily.

Just his name brings a lump to my own throat, but I clear it quickly. When Dad passed, he took many traditions with him, including walking his daughters down the aisle. She's the first of the McCade siblings to get engaged, and he isn't here to see it.

I squeeze her arm. "Me too. But he'd be so proud to call Caleb his son-in-law."

She nods and gathers herself. The corner of her mouth lifts. "I'm sorry I left your truck at Caleb's in our rush to come back to tell you all the news. I'll have to drive back with him to get it for you later."

"Don't even worry about it," I reassure her. "I'll have Knox or Vince drive me over in a bit."

But my plans are scrapped when the flurries start, the storm descending all at once. What starts only as flurries quickly turns into a full-blown blizzard. My plan to drive up to see Kasey and the kids is shut down without warning. As the storm builds, Caleb interrupts their engagement celebration early to make sure his horses are well buttoned up for the night. His departure prompts the rest of us to scatter around the ranch to tend to the herd and the farm animals. Years ago, Dad built roofed tin shelters big enough to give the cattle at least some protection from the pelting snow and freezing winds of the Montana winters. Rushing to beat the worst of the snowstorm, we distribute extra hay among the pastures and double-check the water troughs, though they'll probably be frozen over with ice come morning.

By the time everything is battened down and we're all assembled in the house again, I can't see the end of our driveway.

Swirling snow has turned the yard into a dizzying landscape of white and black. I stand at the windows and stare toward the mountains, which have all but disappeared. Under my breath, I pray for Kasey's safety as the storm pummels the forest. I wonder if her sister arrived before it hit, and I begin to pray for her as well.

Vincent appears silently at my side and watches the storm with me. The rest of the family chatters loudly in the kitchen while dinner is prepared.

"You thinking about your girl?" My brother breaks the silence in his calm tone.

"Yeah."

"Is she prepared for a storm like this?"

"Yeah," I reply. "I made sure of it the last time I was up there."

"They should be good, then." Vincent nods.

His steady reassurance isn't doing anything to calm my anxiety. "I just wish I'd made it up there before the storm started today. It hit earlier than they predicted."

His hand lands on my shoulder. "They've got a better Shepherd than you watching over them, brother. Besides, I'd put money on Kasey being able to keep them safe, warm, and fed for the next couple of days."

Grins break over our faces at the same time. I know Vincent approves of Kasey's resourceful, fine-on-her-own, leave-society-behind personality because it so accurately echoes his own.

Personally, I'd prefer that she lean on me a little harder.

At the very least, the storm ensures she can't go anywhere for a bit. There's nothing I can do until it slows enough for the snowplow to clear the main road up the mountain. I can attach a plow to my own truck, but chances are good that it would be too big of a job, and I might get stuck in a drift myself. For now, I'll wait and pray and hope that by the time I reach her, Kasey hasn't already packed up and disappeared.

Chapter Thirty-Five

Kasey

I check the cell phone for the dozenth time, knowing full well that the snowstorm has temporarily knocked out service on the mountain. If Amy tries to call again, she won't be able to get through. She kept me updated through the first leg of her road trip to Montana, but I haven't heard anything since late yesterday. I can only hope I gave her adequate directions to the cabin, and she's able to find it despite the snowy landscape.

If anything goes wrong . . .

Christmas Day passed with as much cheer as I was able to muster. We hung our woolen socks on the wall for stockings, and the children were delighted with the small presents and candies I gathered for them.

As for me, I've been pacing the cabin for the past three days, peeking through the windows every thirty seconds, and peering toward the head of the trail as if my sister is simply going to walk through the snow and emerge from the forest any minute.

I don't even know if the road is passable.

Finn senses my volatile emotions, rising frequently to pace the worn floor with me for a minute or two before his protective instincts kick in again, and he returns to Janie's side. He nuzzles up to her, and she laughs, grabbing onto his coarse fur.

Since I don't have any way of checking the weather, the only warning I had of the impending storm was the gray clouds that quickly took over the sky and began dumping their contents all over the mountain. On his last couple of visits, Dean helped me get well-stocked on firewood and brought extra blankets from the ranch to keep us warm. And every time he visits, he hikes up with a box of treats from Emma, so we're in no danger of going hungry.

When the snow falls enough to cover the path to the woodshed out back, I expend some of my nervous energy by shoveling it clear again, though the thick falling flakes erase my progress almost as quickly as I make it. Off and on, I work on the path that leads to the trail, too, carving out the entrance, knowing we'll need a way out when Amy arrives. I can only work for longer periods when Janie is down for her naps. And only with my rifle slung across my back and my pistol on my hip. The midnight howl of the wolf pack ceased a few days before Christmas, and I wonder if the pack is making the rounds of its territory again and moving farther and closer away periodically as a result. But I won't take any chances on getting caught outside without protection.

I just want to hear from my sister that all is well. Staring through the small cabin windows, I chew at my fingernails until they are stumps. After months of waiting, Amy is finally returning home, and I'm terrified. My mind is filled with a thousand what-ifs, and I'm struggling to hold onto any hope that this will all turn out okay. I fight against the fear, a feeble prayer rising from the mire of my worry.

"Please keep her safe, Lord," I whisper again and again.

"Kasey," DJ interrupts my troubled thoughts, "I'm bored. Can we go outside to make a snowman?"

I turn away from the window to see him at my side, his hazel eyes peering up at me from underneath outgrown, ruffled hair. The yellow flecks in his eyes catch the light from the lantern. I run my fingers through his messy hair, smoothing it away from his eyes.

"And get all soaked and cold from the snow, buddy? Wouldn't you rather play blocks with Janie? Or I can make you a cup of hot cocoa. Or I can read to you."

I'm bribing him, but I don't trust myself to have the presence of mind right now to play in the snow like a carefree auntie.

DJ considers my offers carefully. "Can I read to you?" he replies with enthusiasm.

"Sure."

He leads me away from the window. Sinking onto the floor, my upper back leans against the bed frame as DJ chooses a book from the small shelf in the corner. To my surprise, he brings back an illustrated children's Bible that Emma gifted to him the last time we stayed at the ranch. When he opens it, the pages automatically part as if they've been opened a thousand times. Colorful illustrations splash across the spread.

Over the long months since we've been stuck up here, I've been working faithfully with DJ on his reading skills. While he's learning rapidly, when he begins to read with an unusual fluidity and confidence, I realize he's reciting the passage from memory.

"The Lord is my Shepherd," DJ says slowly, the illustrations clearly prompting some of his words.

Janie, not to be left out, rises from her blocks and totters over to me, falling on my lap. Finn follows closely at his tiny queen's heels and settles next to my leg.

The children's Bible features the original passage alongside a simplified, easy-to-read, story-like version and illustrations to visually demonstrate the concept. I've never seen anything like it before, and I follow my nephew's small finger in fascination as it trails across the page.

Unfolding in the artwork before me is the story of a Shepherd who loves His flock and is willing to sacrifice His own comfort and safety to ensure they are protected and provided for. Because of this Shepherd's faithfulness, the flock doesn't have any need to fear; whether by waters still and sweet or in the valleys dark and dreary, He guides them with the comfort of his Shepherd's hook.

And when their steps falter, He picks them up and carries them far away from danger in His strong, protective arms. He does all this because the sheep belong to Him, and leading them home means more than His own life.

As DJ recites the words that I assume Emma taught him, and Janie rests her sleepy head on my chest, what Dean has been trying to show me becomes suddenly crystal clear. With a sharp inhale, I see the truth unfold before me like a road map. My mind spins, but my heart goes incredibly still.

I think I see it now. We're the flock, and He's the Shepherd. And when the sheep follow His voice like they are designed to, He leads them through the dangerous places without harm. I want that assurance of safety. I want You to be my Shepherd, Lord.

A heavy pressure that's been pushing down on my heart for nearly six months seems to lift with the unspoken prayer, and I wrap my arms around Janie and press a kiss to the top of her head as DJ's boyish voice continues to recite the soothing words of the psalm.

. . .

I've forced myself to begin organizing and packing our things to occupy my mind. The snowstorm finally ceased last night, though the gray and gloomy sky is a promise that it will soon return. I'm trying to pack discreetly so as not to alert the children, and I'm so focused that I almost ignore the faint cry of a voice outside. When I register it for the second time, my ears sharpen, and my head snaps up.

The soft, urgent cry sounds again.

My boots pound the floor as I run to the door and fling it open.

I spot the brightness of her strawberry blonde hair first.

Amy grasps a low-hanging pine bough and pulls herself up the slight incline to step off the trail into the cabin's clearing. Our eyes meet at the same time, and instantly, her face crumples. She stumbles forward, gasping for air and grabbing her chest as sobs rack her small frame.

Without hesitation, I run to her down the snow-covered path.

"Kasey! Ka-a-sey!" she wheezes. "I thought I'd taken the wrong trail and would be lost all night out here."

Her hands reach for me, and I throw my arms around her, pulling her close. She's still tiny, but the frail, breakable frame of months ago has filled out with healthy weight. I stare into her eyes, and the whites are clear, her pupils alert. She looks like the Amy of ten years ago, like the little sister I wish I'd never left behind. Her clothes are caked with snow, and even the ends of her hair look frosty.

"I can't . . . Are you . . . How did the treatment go?" I ask, my throat choked by emotion. Night after night, I've prayed that the burden of the addiction that took her away from us would roll off her back like a boulder tumbling down a hill into a canyon so deep it could never resurface.

Her tears flow freely, but the joy on her face is palpable. "I know I still have work to do, but He saved me," she murmurs. "God found me in the deepest darkness, and He walked with me into the light, never letting go, even when it felt like the devil sent the wolves to the door of my breakthrough again and again." Her hands grip mine with surprising strength. "I never thought I'd say this, but I'm not afraid anymore of the battles to come to maintain my victory."

My heart feels as if it is going to overflow. Words fail me. Amy squeezes my hands.

"My . . . my . . . babies?" she says.

"In the cabin," I reassure her, turning to lead her down the narrow trail. I fling open the wooden door.

Finn rises as she stumbles in.

"Mama?"

DJ and Janie see her at the same time. With screams of joy, they leap up and fling themselves forward into her arms. Instantly, the cabin is a chaotic tumble of tears, hugs, questions, and happy shouts of laughter. I stand back and take it all in.

Hours later, Amy rises from the floor. Late morning has turned into afternoon, and the shadows across the clearing are already deepening. Janie is propped on my sister's hip; DJ clings to her side as if he is afraid to let her go lest she disappear into thin air. She turns to me with a beaming smile.

"She's gotten so big I can hardly pick her up," she remarks in disbelief.

"I think they've both grown an inch since you left." I return the smile.

"Kasey," Amy begins, and I stop her before she can go on. I know what she is about to say. I want to know where she's been and everything she's been through in the long months since her departure, but if we start talking about it now, I know we'll be here for hours.

"You can tell me everything later," I place a gentle hand on her arm, "but for now, what do you want our next steps to be? We can stay here for a few days to let you rest. I have plenty of food and firewood, but if you want to leave, we have to pack up and go now before it gets too dark."

My sister presses her cheek to Janie's chubby one and pulls DJ closer. She looks at me with a soft expression before her gaze breaks to roam over the small cabin. "I don't want to leave," she murmurs. "I just want to stay and soak up every second with the three of you. Can we stay for a few days at least before we have to make any decisions, Kasey?"

The tightness that has begun to grow in my chest again loosens. I pull the three of them in for a hug, relief in my voice. "Of course, we can stay. I'll put more wood on the fire and make us something hot to eat."

She sinks onto the cot gratefully, cuddling Janie as if she'll never put her down again. The wood box is nearly empty. I grab the canvas bag and draw my coat over my shoulders as I pull open the door and step outside. I can't help but smile as I walk around the cabin toward the woodshed. There are a thousand things to discuss and plan, but for now, my sister is home.

The cell phone is still stuffed into my pocket. Dean's handsome face surfaces in my mind, and I wonder when enough reception will return for me to call him with an update. A newfound freedom seems to settle over me.

I'm gathering logs to add to the fire when I hear an unusual scuffling sound in the forest behind the cabin. Instantly, I'm on alert. I set the canvas bag onto the snow and reach for the pistol on my hip, wishing I had my rifle, but I left it in the cabin on its hooks above the door.

Are the wolves finally here?

Before I can move, bright, feminine laughter reaches my ears, punctuated by a lower-pitched, masculine echo. Locked in place, I wait. Running back to the cabin to hide is useless. If someone is in the woods, they'll see the smoke from our fire as soon as they step into the clearing. Likely, they can smell it from a mile away. I think of the snowshoers hiking down from the lodge that Dean mentioned and remind myself that they are probably just passing through when I catch sight of them.

A woman tumbles out of the forest a short distance away from the woodshed. Her long, dark hair obscures her face from me at first. She's bundled up in a tan coat, a cream pom-pom-topped beanie perched on her head. She's laughing, and suddenly, I recognize the sound as her face turns toward me.

A man steps out of the trees close on her heels, his snowshoes flicking up sprays of white into the air.

Jenna stares at me in disbelief. "Kasey, what in the world are you doing up here?" Her lips widen in a surprised, but friendly, smile.

Hunter's mouth also turns up at the corners as he lifts his hand to wave.

My brain feels like scrambled eggs. Their walking poles dig into the piles of snow as they fully exit the forest and approach me.

Jenna continues chattering with good-natured cheer. Her

cheeks are bright red, and the tips of her hair are frosty. "Is this your cabin? I knew you lived in the mountains, but I didn't even realize you were out this way."

Finally, I pull myself together enough to form a coherent sentence. "What are you two doing out here?" Even though the reason for their presence is obvious from the snowshoes attached to their boots.

Jenna pauses in front of me, her olive skin rosy, her dark eyes bright. "Since the snow finally took a break last night, Hunter and I came up to get a little activity in. People can only stay cooped up for so long before they go stir-crazy. We won't say any names. We parked one car down by the main road and took a second car up to the lodge, just like Dean said you could do. But it turns out that even with snowshoes, that was quite the strenuous hike when the trail's not clear. I'm not even sure we are on the trail anymore because someone insisted on navigating." She looks over her shoulder and grins back at her fiancé.

"You're not on the trail," I mutter, but she doesn't hear.

Jenna turns back to me. "I want to see your place. It looks so . . . rustic and cute."

She clearly has no idea this cabin doesn't even belong to me. I've been squatting here for months, and this is the first time I've seen a soul up here besides Dean. I don't know what to do other than to turn around and trace my steps back down the path. Their snowshoes shuffle along behind me.

My brain races, searching for any excuse to prevent them from invading our space, but I can't think. It doesn't feel right to let them into the makeshift home where I've hidden and protected my niece and nephew all this time. No matter what the future holds, this time and place belong to us. The sudden appearance of humans after months of near-solitude has thrown me for a loop.

We reach the porch, and I wait for them to unbuckle their snow gear. The couple stomps their boots on the old porch planks. An excuse pops into my head.

"You know, Janie hasn't been feeling well, so I don't know if you should come inside. Wouldn't want you two to catch anything," I blurt out.

"Nonsense." Hunter pushes forward, his eyes glowing gold in the shadows creeping across the porch. "We'll be perfectly fine. I could use a warm-up by your stove."

I'm about to push back and insist they leave when I feel a gust of air behind me as DJ flings open the door. I swing toward him.

"Is Dean here?" he shouts. His gaze travels up to Hunter and Jenna, and his eyebrows draw together as he studies them. He doesn't look away, the confused expression only growing as he speaks over his shoulder, his eyes fixed on Hunter. "Mama, you have to meet Dean. He's a cowboy, and he has horses and huge cows and . . ."

I catch the look on Amy's face just beyond the doorway. She rises from the cot, staring toward us as she clutches Janie to her chest, her eyes wide and full of fear. Her voice shakes. "Kasey, don't let that man . . ."

Jenna screams just as I feel the cold press of a steel muzzle jammed through my coat. I reach for my gun, but the pistol is already being ripped from its holster on my hip. I freeze.

Hunter's voice is a growl in my ear as he speaks over my shoulder. "Hello, cousin. Glad to see you back and looking so well."

Chapter Thirty-Six

Dean

"It's a good thing you seem to be a man of leisure these days," Samantha hops from Vincent's truck, her snow boots landing on the frozen earth in front of Caleb's farmhouse with a thud, "and didn't need your truck after all."

She glances at me with a smirk, but her gaze is quickly pulled away when Caleb—who was waiting when we turned into the driveway—draws her into his arms.

"How's my future wife today?" he asks quietly, leaning over to press a gentle kiss to her forehead.

"Missing you, future husband," she murmurs in reply.

She whispers something else to him, and wanting to give them a moment of privacy, I turn away to assess the snow clouds gathering again over the valley.

My sister insisted on driving me back to the Kane ranch this afternoon to collect my truck, which she left stranded at the property before the storm began the day after Christmas. I'm certain that she offered to tag along as an excuse to spend more time with her fiancé, but she's right that I haven't had a need to use my own truck the last couple of days.

Given the intensity of our first big snowstorm of the season, I stayed close to home and kept a watchful eye on the cattle and ranch animals. Winter means new demands on a rancher's attention, including distributing extra forage and supplemental feed among the herd, plus ensuring they have access to water and bedding to keep them warm in their shelters. Winter calving season is almost upon us, and since extreme changes in weather can trigger a cow to go into labor, Vincent, Knox, and I have spent extra time checking the pregnant cows and watching for any signs of distress.

The additional chores are a relief, an efficient way to keep my mind off Kasey, whom I can only assume is snowed in on the shadowy mountain that rises formidably in the distance, heavy clouds hiding its peak.

At least for now, the storm has abated, and before it begins again, I'm determined to check on the trio even if I have to snowshoe in. Pacing around to the driver's side, I ready my snow gear. Mountain travel can be extra unpredictable in the winter, but I plan to only go as far as I can with my truck and hike the rest of the way.

Samantha turns to me again. "Caleb and I want to go up with you if that's okay? I'm going to grab some snowshoes for the hike." She starts to walk away but pauses to look at me as if confirming I'm okay with this abrupt change in plan.

I'm caught off guard, but in the softness of her tone, I hear the sisterly concern. While I'm confident in my ability to get the small family safely off the mountain, it seems she and Caleb feel better if they can help. Distressing her is the last thing I want to do.

"Sure." I smile. "I'd like you to get to know Kasey a little more before you go back to Spain anyway."

Her eyes shine. "She's important to you, isn't she?"

I nod. "Very."

"Then I can't wait to spend more time with her." She grins and runs toward the porch where Caleb disappeared a minute ago. He's just stepped out with two pairs of snowshoes in his hands. He looks toward me, and I give him a nod.

Ten minutes later, we're in the truck, and the mountain looms ahead.

. . .

"Tell me it's been a while since you went snowshoeing without telling me it's been a while since you went snowshoeing." I glance back at my sister with lifted eyebrows.

She glares at me, her chest heaving and her cheeks almost as red as her hair. "I remembered this activity differently when I was younger," she huffs out.

While the main road leading up the mountain had already been mostly cleared, the logging road that turns off toward Kasey's cabin was still a sketchy pass of ice and snow, so rather than risk taking the truck up too far and getting stuck, we parked a couple of miles downhill and hiked up the rest of the way. Kasey's cabin—Danny's cabin—is well off the beaten path, tucked into the forest below the Bear Creek Lodge summit, though far away from the ski lanes. I've been to the cabin so many times that it isn't hard to find the hiking trail that leads up to it. When we begin our ascent, the scuffled and broken snow indicates that someone has already come this way.

But I'd forgotten how strenuous snowshoeing even on a slight uphill climb in several feet of soft, fluffy snow could be. Teasing Samantha about huffing and puffing as she works her way up the trail is only to cover my own heavy breathing. I'm hot and sweaty under the layers of snow gear. Only Caleb appears to be unbothered by the cardio, patiently bringing up the rear and helping my sister through the heavier patches of snow.

As we climb, the faint scent of smoke gets stronger and stronger. I press forward and step first into the clearing, Kasey's cabin straight ahead. The only sign of life is the steady puff of smoke coming from the stovepipe on the roof.

"Is this where she's been living?" Samantha steps off the trail behind me, her quick eyes scanning the scene. Caleb looms just behind her. "When you said cabin, I thought . . ."

I know she's thinking of the children's well-being out here in the middle of nowhere, and I jump to reassure her. "She's made it homey and functional, sis. Don't worry."

Relief crosses her face, and she pushes past me, pausing to unbuckle the clumsy snowshoes. The path to the cabin has been cleared away, and the snow is firmly packed. I have my own snowshoes unbuckled in ten seconds, watching the front of the small building all the while.

It's unusually quiet, the cabin face dark and unfriendly, as if the little family inside has disappeared into the ether. Stepping around my sister, I stride down the path toward the door, my muscles tensing with sudden anxiety. Did they leave before the storm began? Stubbornly, my brain reminds me that the fire is still burning inside.

I cross the small porch in a single stride, lifting my fist and knocking on the weathered door.

"Kasey, it's Dean," I call.

There is no answer, and I'm about to knock again when I hear a shuffle and what sounds like a hoarse whisper behind the door. Samantha and Caleb linger just off the side of the porch.

"Are you in there?" I call again. "We just came to see how you weathered the storm and give you some company."

The latch pulls back. When the door swings inward, I try to hide my surprise.

"Oh . . ." I stare down at the petite woman just inside the cabin. "Jenna, what are . . .?"

Peering over her head into the dark interior, I spot Kasey immediately. She is sitting with her hands folded at the small wooden table in the center of the cabin. At her side sits a pale, strawberry-blonde woman, and I know from the features they share that she is Kasey's sister. DJ and Janie cling to their mother. An uncomfortable silence radiates from them with palpable tension.

But it's the figure who steps forward from behind the door that surprises me the most.

Jenna backs away as Hunter pulls the door fully open, a broad and welcoming smile spreading across his face. "Did you think you could take a nice hike and end up getting lost like we did, McCade?" He glances around the doorframe at Samantha and Caleb and beckons us into the cabin.

"Is that what you two are doing up here?" I drawl, my senses fully alert, eyes darting around the cabin. "It's easy to get lost in these mountains."

I step inside, the warmth of the stove immediately dispelling the chill of the outdoors.

"Jenna and I thought we could park up by the lodge and snowshoe back down the mountain to the spot where we parked

Jenna's truck," Hunter answers as Caleb walks in just behind me.

"That's literally miles, Jenna," Caleb says gravely, eyeing the young woman rather than her fiancé.

I notice he's placed my sister in a protective position by having her enter behind him. The two of them pause just inside the door as Hunter replies.

"It wasn't so bad. We were going downhill most of the way."

I can't stop looking at Kasey. Finn is posted by her side like a statue. She doesn't rise when I enter, so I walk over to her. Slowly, her chin lifts, and she stares up at me. The bright hue of her eyes has darkened to a stormy ocean gray.

Lightly, I set my hand on her shoulder. The muscle is tight under my touch. I sink into a squat, peering up into her face.

"Hey," I say softly, "how are you?"

"Fine." She inclines her head toward the woman sitting next to her. "Dean, this is my sister, Amy. She just arrived today."

Briefly, I acknowledge the woman, but I can't tear my attention away from Kasey. She seems to have retreated into a shell, so I'm surprised when she lifts her hand to slip it into mine. My thumb rubs across the back of her palm tenderly, as the pressure of several pairs of eyes on us bores into the back of my head. I try to communicate with her in an undertone that can't be heard by the rest of the room as Hunter shifts into my peripheral vision, Jenna close to his side.

"You seem tense." I glance at her sister, whose face is buried in Janie's hair. "Is everything—"

At the familiar scrape of a safety sliding back and a startled cry from Jenna, I rise, spinning to face the threat.

Hunter presses the handgun against Jenna's temple, his arm wrapped tightly around her neck. Her olive skin has gone pale, her eyes wide with terror.

"Whoa, whoa, whoa," Caleb and I say at the same time.

Samantha gasps in horror. "What are you doing?"

My friend and I tighten up our stances simultaneously. His hand goes to his hip where his own weapon sits; his other hand presses Samantha behind him.

"Don't even think about it," Hunter snarls in his direction.

Caleb drops the hand on his weapon and backs away as chaos erupts in the cabin. A guttural growl emits from Finn's throat. Teeth bared, he rises and stares at the man, the fur around his neck raised. He takes a single step forward.

"Get your dog under control, or I'll shoot him," Hunter says calmly. "And hand over your guns, all of you."

The big dog takes another step.

"Finn!" DJ cries out as his sister begins to wail. She shrinks into her mother's chest.

"Finn! Down," Kasey yells over the din, and the big dog obeys her immediately, though the harsh growl continues to emit from his throat. His dark eyes stay locked on Hunter, and I have no doubt he would rip the man to shreds if he could.

My palms lift outward in a nonthreatening gesture. "What's going on here, Hunter?" I ask, keeping my voice even and neutral. I grasp at the only scenario that makes sense. "Are you and Jenna fighting? I'm sure we can work it out if we just sit down and talk about it."

Caustically, his laugh scrapes the air. "You've got it all wrong." He presses a rough kiss to the top of Jenna's head. She cringes and shrinks away. "I'm sorry to say that my dear fiancée here is merely a casualty of the situation. This was supposed to be a private family matter, but now you three have made yourselves an unfortunate part of it as well."

"And what is the situation?" I ask, my veins running cold.

His chin tips upward toward Kasey and her family. "I'll let my cousin-in-law and her meddling sister tell you all about it."

Startled, I look toward the two women at the table. Kasey is staring at the floor, but Amy lifts her head and speaks for the first time. Her eyes are rimmed with red, her already-pale features ghostly.

"He's my husband's cousin." Her weak voice falters and breaks. "He sent him here to bring us . . ."

"Tell him the rest of it," Hunter growls again when she can't continue. "Tell him how you ran off and hid his children from him while he suffered in prison. Tell him how I had to scour the country looking for DJ and Janie—to make sure you hadn't hurt them—and when I finally tracked down where your sister had taken them, I had to wait months for you to return because you were nowhere to be found, Amy. You left your own kids with a stranger. What kind of mother are you?"

Her eyes, though full of tears, flash at him with sudden fury. "You think I wanted to leave them? I needed help, Hunter! Your cousin watched me spiral, and he just left me like that."

"You are his wife," Hunter spits. "He trusted you to take care of his children while he was away, not leave them with *her.*" His finger points accusingly at Kasey.

"He's a convicted criminal! And she's a better person than you or me or my husband combined," she cries. "I knew if I didn't get help while he was gone, I'd never have the chance to make things right." Amy's voice cracks. "And the crazy thing about this is that you didn't have to hunt me down and ambush me as soon as I resurfaced anyway." She shakes her head in disbelief. "I was coming back to try to work things out with him. I thought he deserved the chance to try again."

Hunter tightens his hold around Jenna's neck. "Oh, you're

going back all right." Briefly, he pulls the muzzle away from his fiancée's temple. He motions toward Caleb and me but directs his words toward Samantha. "Miss McCade, I take it? Please take the zip ties in my backpack over there and tie these gentlemen to those chairs."

"No," Caleb says firmly.

"Yes," Hunter replies with surly determination. "Do it now, or . . ." The muzzle of the gun is pressed to Jenna's head again as he stares at us with a grim expression.

"What does Jenna have to do with any of this?" Samantha speaks up, her sharp tone demanding answers. "How could you treat her this way?" She glowers at him. "Can't you see you're terrifying her?"

Back in the summer, Samantha distrusted Jenna's intentions, but her protective instincts seem to be surfacing as she boldly defends the woman now. In contrast to my sister's assertive stance, Jenna's petite frame seems to shrink away as Hunter jeers over her. She trembles, and I hear a soft cry of fear as he shakes her good-naturedly.

"You can't expect a man to come all the way out here on a stakeout with no end in sight and not seek a little female companionship while he is at it, can you?" The snide grin he flashes toward my sister sends a wave of revulsion through my limbs. "And when she gave me an ultimatum, I knew I had to act fast. After all, a single man hanging around a small town like Cascade Valley looks suspicious, but a man in love . . . well, he just becomes part of the scenery. Besides, it's what everyone expected us to do, and I've certainly enjoyed myself as long as Amy was gone."

He glances at me. "Thanks for dropping that little hint about the location of Kasey's cabin, McCade. I was getting worried that

I wouldn't find it in time. I've been looking for months. And when I followed her Jeep down from the party the other night, it wasn't hard to scout out the location of the cabin, given your convenient hints. Timing our recreation to coincide perfectly with Amy's arrival was just pure good fortune and math, though."

The realization that Hunter used Jenna to ingratiate himself into our community disgusts me. I've known Jenna for years, and my anger rises for her, used and manipulated for a cruel man's gain. Her pale olive skin and despondent expression tell me she feels the same.

Caleb glances at me, and I know what he is thinking. He and I are of similar height and build, and his muscular frame looks as tightly wound as mine feels as he readies himself to strike. If we both rush Hunter at the same time, we'll have a good chance to overpower him before he can react. But making a move on the man is a risk I'm not willing to take with Jenna's life on the line.

Before we can act, Hunter grunts. "Now, get to it," he orders. "I don't have all day. We have a family reunion to get to."

Almost imperceptibly, I shake my head at Caleb, warning him not to move. When my sister draws a handful of plastic ties out of the backpack on the bed, I don't put up any resistance. Hunter directs her to hand over our weapons and secure our legs and hands to the two extra chairs on the other side of the table. He collects everyone's cell phones and shoves them into his jacket pocket. He keeps a close eye on Kasey as Samantha works the ties around our wrists and ankles. Once, she glances up at me, a combination of fear and worry in her expression, and I give her a reassuring nod. Caleb glares at Hunter with a deadly fire in his eyes as I test the restraints. They are tight, but I feel as if I could snap them loose if I had some time.

"I still don't understand how you happened to arrive here just a few hours after my sister," Kasey suddenly demands.

"I should have warned you, Kasey," Amy's head drops, and she speaks in an undertone, "but I never thought to show you a picture of Dmitry's bodyguards."

Hunter drags a yelping Jenna around to stand in front of her. His eyes reflect his resentment. "Well, I've been around a couple of times this week, little lady. Once I located where you were hiding, I couldn't risk you disappearing on me again." His fake Montana drawl is nauseating. "It took some doing to track the flight your sister took to Florida, but after that, her trail ran cold. You should have paid cash for a new car to avoid the paper trail, cousin." He glances at Amy, whose face looks sick, the thought no doubt hitting her of what a colossal blunder she'd made. "Once you registered for that rental car, we figured you'd head straight out here. Calculating her arrival time was just a matter of mathematics and simple guesswork."

"But how did you find *me* in the first place? Way out here, with no ties to any of this." Kasey shakes her head. Her hands grip the fabric of her snow pants, tightening it in her fists.

Hunter shrugs. "Dmitry had all of us digging up everything we could about you once we figured out it was you who had taken them, not Amy." He glances at the frail woman next to Kasey. "That was a clever move on your part, pulling your absent sister into your scheme. I'll admit the connection to your army teammates was hard to find. We ran down every lead. It was a stroke of good fortune that we stumbled across Danny Gardener's hometown and his social media account—which is still active, by the way—in which he shared all about his remote cabin in the woods. The mountains of Montana seemed like the perfect place to hide, and we'd already clocked your Jeep's license plates entering the state. I volunteered to come out and look around.

"Though, it was by complete chance that I stumbled across you in that shooting range that day. But I've been trekking all over this mountain searching for this place. Thanks to Dean here," he casts cruel, taunting eyes at me, "I finally got a lead."

"Where is Dmitry?" Amy interrupts, her voice desperate and shrill. "Let me talk to him. This is between him and me. Leave these people out of this."

His free hand threads itself through Jenna's hair, and she yelps as he yanks her head back. He motions to Samantha to secure Kasey to her chair as well, checking the watch on his wrist.

"Oh, you'll be reunited tonight," Hunter says. "Your husband just drove into Bozeman. He's on parole, you know, so we couldn't exactly put him on a flight. It's unfortunate you three got mixed up in this," he says, looking between Caleb, Samantha, and me. "But now, I have a couple of extra insurance policies to make sure all goes as planned while we head out." He glares down at Kasey, whose arms and legs are now strapped to the chair. "I wasn't looking forward to wrangling the veteran out of here, but you ladies shouldn't give me too much trouble."

Roughly, he shoves Jenna toward the door and uses the gun to motion for Amy and Samantha to follow.

"You're not taking them anywhere," I demand.

"That's where you're wrong, McCade," Hunter replies calmly. "We're hiking out of here, and you're going to stay put. This is a family matter, and that's all it is. Once my cousin's family has been returned to him, I'll let your sister and my fiancée go. I'm sure they'll be back up to set you free as quickly as they can." He holds two fingers up to his forehead. "And if they behave, I won't hurt them. Scout's honor."

Amy stumbles toward the door, struggling to hold Janie in one arm while pressing DJ to her side with the other. The little boy clings to her silently, his eyes wide with fear.

Ignoring Hunter's shouted commands, Samantha hurries around the table toward Caleb. Leaning over him, she places both hands on either side of his face and presses a kiss on his lips with tender force.

"I love you," she tells him fiercely, "so much, and I'll be back for you as soon as I can."

"I love you," he replies. Then in a softer tone, "Don't be afraid."

Tearing his eyes away from my sister, Caleb looks at Hunter. His dark eyes glower in the shadowy cabin. "You lay one finger on my girl's head . . ."

"Let's go," Hunter snarls from the doorway, and reluctantly, Samantha moves toward him, her head high.

Jenna and Amy are already on the porch, and as I watch them through the open doorway, I notice that the shadows across the clearing are deepening as the afternoon wanes toward evening. Dusk will fall soon. If they haven't reached the second car that Hunter said he left behind before nightfall, the steep terrain out of here is going to become treacherous. And with two small children in tow . . .

"If you try to break loose and come after us . . . If you alert the sheriff after you're freed . . . If you do anything to impede what I'm here to do . . . You'll regret it." With a lingering glare in our direction, Hunter grabs the rifle from where it hangs over the door, steps outside, and pulls the cabin door shut behind him.

Chapter Thirty-Seven

Kasey

A heavy silence falls over the cabin when Hunter shuts us in. I listen, barely breathing as the crunch of his boots gradually fades down the path toward the trail. The sound of Janie's wail is the last to fade away. There isn't a clock in the cabin, and the minutes seem to drag into hours as the light in the clearing darkens. Dean struggles against the restraints as my heart sinks.

Finn whines softly at my side, and I know how he feels. The big dog rises and nudges my leg, but I can't reach down to pet him.

Somehow, in the space of an afternoon, everything has gone from right to wrong. Months of carefully protecting my niece and nephew, waiting for my sister's return, and praying that I get another chance to be the sister and aunt they deserve slip through my fingers.

And I allowed it to happen. My brain roils with self-blame.

Stupidly, I let my guard down and allowed a lying, sneaking, plotting intruder to walk right into our safe haven. I should have seen this coming, stayed out of sight, moved locations, something. But Hunter wasn't connected to Dmitry's court case. He wasn't in any tabloid photographs. He came like a wolf in the night, waiting until the moment was right.

I let myself get too comfortable. After Dean inserted himself into our little world time and time again, I let my feelings for him draw me in, giving me blinders to the danger that being in public would guarantee.

I don't blame Dean. I could never blame Dean. Even as I strain against the zip ties, trying to find some weak point to break free, I glance over at him and find him staring at me with a gentle expression that breaks my heart in two.

"Stop blaming yourself." His tone is kind.

The plastic wrapped around my right wrist feels looser than the others. I wiggle my hand, trying to get leverage. Maybe Dean's sister left it slack on purpose.

"Why not? This whole thing is my fault," I reply bitterly.

"Kasey."

"There's so much you don't know, Dean," I insist, my voice shrill and panicked. A sob from deep within my chest cuts off the rest of my sentence. I hang my head.

Dean leans forward as far as he can to peer into my face. "We're going to get them help, but in the meantime, I promise you that God cares more about all of them than you do. Do you trust Him, Kasey?"

I nod, the words coming out in a whisper, but I mean them with everything within me. "Yes, I do. I trust Him."

"Well, then let's get out of here," Caleb drawls, speaking for the first time.

In shock, I stare as the dark-haired man rises calmly from the chair and quickly cuts Dean's ties before striding around the table to me. I see the small pocketknife in his hand.

"How did you . . .?" I ask as he releases the plastic binds.

"I always carry a pocketknife on my belt. Hunter didn't see it under my jacket, and Samantha made sure she didn't 'discover' it when he made her check for weapons. Took me all this time to work it free, though." He looks annoyed with himself for taking so long.

When I rise on shaky legs, Dean is at my side in an instant, his strong arms pulling me into his chest. The fierceness of his feelings is evident as he places a gentle hand under my chin and tilts my face upward.

"We're going to get them back safe and sound." He leans over me and brushes his lips across mine. "I promise."

It isn't the time or the place to be kissing Dean, but the reassurance of his touch seems to infuse me with strength. A soft voice in my head whispers that, despite the dire situation, he is telling the truth. As I stare up at him, I almost forget that we're not alone.

"And we're going to throw Hunter into the slammer for unlawful imprisonment and kidnapping," Caleb fumes, going to the cabin door and yanking it open. Immediately, Finn shoots through the doorway like a bolt of lightning.

"Finn!" I call after him, but the German Shepherd has already disappeared, obscured by the piles of snowdrifts as he runs away.

"We'll get him back," Dean physically restrains me from racing after my dog, "but right now, we have to focus."

I stare up at him, my vision blurring as panic starts to set in again. We've already lost so much time, and if we can't follow their trail . . .

"Not to mention threatening with a deadly weapon," Caleb continues to growl.

"He took my guns," I blurt out. "I had a pistol in my holster, and he disarmed me when Amy saw him." I feel like a fool for letting the man gain the advantage over me, but tussling over a loaded firearm with my niece and nephew a few feet away hadn't been an option.

Caleb swings to face me. "Do you have any other firearms in here, or did he take them all with him?"

Something shifts in my head, years of military duty reminding me that I've been equipped for this scenario. I lost this battle, but I'll win the war. I snap to attention and pull myself out of Dean's arms.

"The woodshed," I reply. "I have another pistol in a locked box hidden under some logs. I hung another rifle out there too. And I've got more ammo," I stride over to our bags, which are packed and waiting in the corner of the cabin, "in here."

Caleb darts outside and around the corner toward the woodshed. I pull out a couple of small but heavy ammunition boxes from the depths of my bag, handing them off to Dean. By the time I rise, Caleb is back. He hands me the small lockbox, and I enter the code to retrieve the Glock I'd stowed safely away when we first arrived, not wanting to risk the prying of tiny, curious hands if they found it while I was otherwise occupied. The other firearms were out of their reach or on my person at all times.

"You only brought four firearms?" Caleb asks.

"I certainly didn't think I'd end up needing more than that," I reply dryly.

"Fair point," he concedes.

One by one, we file out the door. I keep the handgun, while Dean takes charge of the rifle. My fingers itch for it, but the smaller gun will be better at close range. The snowy path to the trail that leads down the mountain is roughly scuffed, disappearing under the heavy boughs as it leads away.

I pause before entering the trail, hesitating, fear of the unknown getting the best of me. "Hunter said they would all be unharmed if we didn't follow. Are we making a mistake going after them?"

Suddenly, my chest grips painfully. The memory of that fateful day when Danny died—a day never far from my mind—comes screaming back to me. With a tight cry, I lean over and plant my hands on my knees, my breath coming in desperate, wheezing gasps. Sharp pains shoot through my stomach, and my vision spins, the edges going black.

An ugly thread of words coils around and around my mind.

You couldn't save them then, and you can't save your family now.

"I can't do this. I can't do this." I come to and realize I'm saying the words over and over. My limbs lock as I freeze with fear, becoming one with the snowy forest floor.

All at once, a sudden warmth begins to permeate the chill. Dean's hand rests on my shoulder comfortingly, and when I look up, the terror partially recedes as his blue gaze captures mine.

"We're not taking orders from a guy like that," he says firmly. "That's our family he's kidnapped and threatened. There's no question that we're going to find them and bring them safely home."

Hearing his calm but firm declaration acts like a balm to my mind. The hot terror running up and down my veins turns into icy resolve. My vision sharpens, my hearing reaching out to catch the slightest sound. I may have walked through the fire to get here, but perhaps the God who saw it all before I was even created brought me through everything I've faced for such a moment as this. There's no question in my mind that rescuing my family is a mission I'll sacrifice everything to complete.

The men follow me into the forest, allowing me to lead the way without question. I proceed with caution, one hand on my holster, eyes scanning, and ears alert. The wind rustles through the trees with a scream, and a pine bough rubs against another, its creaking ghostly underneath the wind. And once, far in the distance, my ears think they catch the echo of a wolf's howl.

I shudder and press on, my boots fighting to find footing in the snow.

Digging my Jeep out of its hiding spot at the base of the trail isn't an option because the logging road is too impassable. Hunter said the spare car was parked below, on the main road leading up the mountain.

He must be pushing the little group hard because they are nowhere to be seen when we hit the road below the trail. The snow at the base is rough, like many feet have passed over it. He is hiking them out as fast as he can. If one of the women breaks an ankle or takes a fall . . .

The mountains lose their light fast in the dead of winter, especially under the heavy cover of the pines. As we hurry along the logging road, the shadows deepen into an inky black, and the snow flurries begin to drift through the trees again. With each minute that passes, they seem to increase in intensity.

Dean stops me with a hand on my arm. He draws me close, my rifle slung over his shoulder. "We should have caught up with them by now," he says.

"They can't have gotten that far," I reply, "and we have their trail to follow."

Caleb shifts in my peripheral vision, his expression grim as his eyes continuously scan the trees.

Dean shakes his head. "Samantha, Caleb, and I came up this trail earlier, too, remember. I'm starting to wonder if they left this way at all. But the bigger problem is that we don't know where Hunter and Jenna parked their second car. It could be hidden on any one of a dozen off-roads going up the mountain. If they get to it before we find them . . ."

He doesn't have to finish the sentence. Hunter's plan sinks with clarity in my mind. "He planned all of this out," I say, an edge of defeat creeping into my voice.

Caleb's deep voice breaks the heavy silence. "Dean, do you remember that summer we went camping with Danny and Knox up here, and the two of them took off in the truck? We used an old deer trail to go straight down the mountain to head them off, and we ended up beating them there because they had to take the switchback."

Dean's free hand swipes at the stubble on his jaw. "Yeah, I do remember that."

"There's got to be a deer trail going down this mountain," Caleb continues.

"There's a creek that often has deer droppings around it where I get water. Could there be a trail leading off there?" I interject.

Dean pauses and looks down at me, his face hazy in the dark. "Possibly. But the trail is going to be rough, Kasey. We won't be able to find it from here. We'll have to hike back up to the top."

"I don't care." Vehemently, I shake my head. "We have to try."

Without a word, he turns and motions to Caleb to lead the way. Dean places me in front of him, and we rapidly retrace our steps. I'm out of breath by the time we resurface in the clearing, my body hot despite the frigid chill of night.

Caleb brushes his hand around the snow at the head of the trail. "Two pairs of our snowshoes are gone," he states. "Hunter and Jenna had their own."

Meaning Amy and Samantha are wearing the others. I imagine the women must be carrying the children out. I hope DJ isn't having to stumble through the snow on his own. My brain snaps to attention.

"There are snowshoes in the cabin!" I exclaim, feeling like an idiot for not thinking of them earlier. Rushing up the path, I burst through the wooden door. The fire is dying in the stove, and already, the room doesn't feel like the warm and cozy home we've made it over the past few months. It feels empty and cold, like the residents ran away unexpectedly and left all their belongings behind.

The snowshoes hang in a dark corner, and I snatch them off the wall, hoping that they are a size we can actually use. I grab a lantern and a pair of flashlights to light our way as well.

Caleb has already brought the third pair in from the path, and we distribute them among ourselves. It feels like a small blessing to realize that we are all outfitted with snowshoes, and hope inches its way back into my heart.

"The creek just over there runs straight down the mountain." I rise and double-check my holster.

When we reach it, I wait impatiently while the men debate, finally agreeing that it is the most straightforward path. The snowflakes have increased in speed and size.

The temperatures have been low enough the last couple of weeks that the edges of the creek are almost frozen over and covered by a thick dusting of snow. For the past few days, I've been gathering our water from the piles of snow around the cabin and melting it.

I pick my steps carefully, the clumsy snowshoes attached to my boots making it difficult to walk at first. My leg throbs, the cold quickly seeping in and causing it to drag behind with a momentary delay. I force myself to keep pace, gritting my teeth against the throbbing pain. Caleb falls in step behind me, and Dean naturally moves into the leader's position, hiking ahead of me to assume the hard task of breaking a path through the snow. I watch his strong back as he pushes ahead, his hands gripping the rifle, head on a constant swivel.

It takes my distracted brain a few minutes to realize he's not watching for the people we're chasing.

The howling is louder this time, a call and response that seems to have moved closer under the high-pitched whine of the wind. The sound is clearer than any of the nights I kept watch in the cabin. As the mournful calls ring around us, I feel as if I'm going to crawl out of my skin.

"They are out there with these animals," I gasp, pitching forward and grabbing the sleeve of Dean's coat.

"Wolf calls can be heard up to several miles away, Kasey. They probably aren't anywhere near here," he reassures me, but I catch the moment he makes eye contact with Caleb behind me as the howls echo around us again.

Collectively, we move even faster, picking our way downhill, only speaking when we have to, our ears straining for every sound.

We reach a road, but if there were tire tracks once, the fresh snowfall has erased them.

"Let's keep going," Caleb urges. "Let's go straight across and get to the road below this one. They are going to be walking the switchback at some point. If Hunter and Jenna parked another car on their way to the lodge, it's going to be much lower and close to the main road for a faster getaway."

We move quickly, fighting through the heavy underbrush. Every now and then, the chilling calls of the wolf ring across the mountain. It sounds like they are getting closer, but I push the thought away. The cold is beginning to penetrate my layers of clothing, ice clinging to my legs. The men are much taller, their long legs an advantage as we break through the snow. I struggle to keep my weak leg from dragging, my knee throbbing as I fight through the pull of the drifts. Gritting my teeth, I refuse to let it slow me down, pulling on those crushing weeks of basic training I endured to join the army years ago. Everything that I've lost seems to stand in the back of my mind like a chorus of witnesses, driving me not to fail.

Help me, please. My Heavenward call is desperate.

Just when my leg feels as if it's finally going to buckle under the pressure, Dean holds up his fist.

"I see something through the trees ahead," he calls over his shoulder in a whisper.

We creep forward, and I nearly fall when I catch sight of a dark-colored truck parked just off the roadway. Dean glances back at Caleb, and I hear his gruff tones confirm that the truck looks like Jenna's. We all hasten to unlatch the cumbersome snowshoes, leaving them discarded among the trees.

"Have we beaten them here?" I whisper. "Where are they?"

The scene feels like a trap, the lonely vehicle a lure to draw us in.

"I'll check it out," Dean replies, stepping fully out of the timberline onto the road. My hand goes to my hip, my fingers closing around the familiar, rounded grip of the Glock. Cautiously, Dean progresses forward, the rifle in his hands at the ready. When he reaches the truck, he makes a sweep, checking through each window.

Nothing.

He looks back at us and shakes his head.

He's walking back when a tree limb cracks loudly in the distance, and I hear the cry of a child somewhere in the forest. There's a crashing sound and a shout.

In one big stride, Dean steps back into the trees, still a distance away, and Caleb and I follow suit. We watch as Samantha stumbles onto the roadway first. I recognize DJ clinging to her neck, his pant legs and boots etched in snow. Jenna is right on her heels, and then I see Hunter and Amy bringing up the rear, Janie clutched in her arms. Roughly, the man shoves my sister forward.

Caleb's hand on my arm holds me back from leaping onto the road.

"Hurry up! Get to the truck," Hunter shouts.

The group rushes forward. They discarded their snowshoes at some point, and I see Dean's sister and Jenna break into a run toward the vehicle, but Amy struggles in the back. She looks ready to collapse.

Hunter's pistol is still in his hand, and he keeps looking back over his shoulder, his free hand clamped firmly on Amy's arm. He seems to be the only reason she hasn't fallen to the ground. My heart races, and I begin to panic.

"Is he just going to let them get away?" I fume under my breath.

Dean steps out of the trees and raises the rifle to his shoulder just as the eerie call of a wolf rings out from the forest directly behind the small group.

In a horrifying instant, I realize what they are running from, but I can't get the warning out in time.

"Drop it!" Dean shouts.

Chaos descends on the snowy mountain road. Samantha and

Jenna start yelling, and immediately, Hunter yanks Amy toward him, the muzzle of the gun rising to her temple. She screams in fear as I rush down the incline. Caleb leaps out in front of me, racing forward. He and Dean order Hunter to drop the weapon. Their voices rise louder and louder, echoing off the mountain.

I'm the only one who sees the first wolf emerge, and my breath catches in a painful gasp. My heart pounds furiously. The animal's fur is smoky gray. It's massive with alert ears and glittering, yellow-tinged eyes focused in our direction. The wolf is followed by six or seven other wolves, their shoulders hunched, the black tips of their fur standing up as they regard us aggressively.

The ragged sound of their snarls rattles over the shouting. The Glock is in my hand, and I'm sighting the pack before I even register that I've moved.

"Are you going to let that pack of rabid dogs eat us? Let us get in the truck and go!" Hunter shouts, but he doesn't remove the gun from my sister's head.

Janie is wailing, her cries heartbreaking and shrill in the night. Samantha runs to Caleb with Jenna on her heels, and he shields them protectively, his attention distracted by his fiancée. With Caleb focused elsewhere, it's down to Dean and me to face off against a sudden multitude of threats.

Dean doesn't lower the rifle. "Drop the gun now, and step away from her," he orders.

The wolf pack paces behind the group, and I step in tandem with them. I don't know what propels me across the snow, the fear running its icy course down my limbs nearly freezing me to the road. But somehow, I drop to one knee, the gun lifted level with my shoulders. And underneath the panic, I feel my instincts kick in, my breath shifting from heavy and labored to deep and even. I don't dare look at Amy lest my resolve crack, never taking my eyes off the wolves currently surrounding us.

Despite the chaos of the frosty road, the wolves don't seem deterred, closing the distance a foot at a time. I could send them running with a single round, but I don't dare for fear the shot would tip Hunter's already shaky hand as he and Dean continue to exchange warnings.

My indecision waffles as I watch for an opening to rescue my sister. The mayhem escalates.

Without warning, a flash of brown and black leaps out of the forest in the corner of my peripheral vision. Finn rushes the pack without hesitation, his hair standing on end, his fangs bared as a snarl of rage rattles in his throat. Stance wide and shoulders low, he faces them down. The canines whip around, their bulky bodies nearly double his size as their attention diverts to him.

"Finn, no!" I scream, and then, the panic does set in. Leaping to my feet, I break into a run.

When the German Shepherd charges, the tumultuous sound of barking dogs and angry growls erupts. The snarls catch Hunter off guard. Nearly yanking my sister off her feet, he turns toward the fray, his eyes wide and frightened as he sees the fight behind him.

Dean doesn't hesitate. Rushing forward, he slams Hunter against the truck, wrestling with him for control of the pistol. Suddenly released, my sister cries out and stumbles to her knees.

Caleb jumps into the fight as I send a few rounds into the air, hoping it will scare the wolf pack away. But the dogfight continues, and I run straight for it.

I skid across the snowy road, closing the distance between me and the pack. One hundred yards. Fifty yards. Finn's fierce snarls have turned to pained yelps as the wolves snap at him, but he doesn't back down.

I grind to a stop and raise the gun, sighting down the short barrel. The pack is now one roiling mass of fur. I can't identify my dog in the snapping tangle, meaning I might only have one shot to save his life. Finn yelps again, and I tense, panic paralyzing me, the fear of losing him taking hold. With a violent punch to the gut, the guilt I carry from the last time I tried to save my teammates and failed slams into me, causing my hands to shake. I may have been powerless against the forces that came against us that day, but I won't let it happen again. I fight the feeling, shoving the past down and away.

"God, please help me!" I cry aloud.

Taking aim for the largest wolf in the bunch, I wait for a split-second opening, and when it appears, I pull the trigger and send a bullet flying toward the predator. It lands directly at his feet, and the ground splinters, snow and mud flying up. I aim and shoot again, and the reverberation of the shot splits the pack apart. Yelps pierce the forest.

"Go! Go on!" I scream, and as if an unseen force sweeps across the road, the wolves fall back, tails and ears tucked, and retreat into the forest, disappearing as quickly as they appeared.

Whipping around, I lift the gun again but instantly lower it. My chest sobs in relief, the tears that I've withheld for so long finally breaking free.

Caleb has Hunter pinned to the ground, and Samantha and Jenna have already run forward to support my fragile sister. DJ is kneeling at Amy's side, and a terrified Janie still wails in her arms, but immediately, I know that my family is safe.

Only Dean has broken away and is running toward me. When I see his eyes fill with alarm and shift over my shoulder, I swing back to look behind me again.

Finn is standing in the middle of the road, his head hanging low. A dark pool of blood is gathering at his feet. Heaving, he looks up at me once, and then his furry body collapses on the snow.

Chapter Thirty-Eight

Dean

The next few hours are pure chaos. The snowstorm knocked out most of the reception on the mountain, but we're down low enough to reach the Cascade Valley sheriff's office on my cell phone, which I retrieved from Hunter's pocket. They dispatch five officers and two ambulances to retrieve us. We can hear their patrol cars speeding up the mountain from miles away.

Caleb keeps Hunter pinned to the snowy ground, his knee planted firmly on the man's back. Once we disarm him, the man's bluster disappears. I get Jenna's truck unlocked and the heater turned on full blast. Amy is struggling to stand upright, so I gently lift her and Janie into the seat, tucking a blanket I grab from the back around them. Her neck is bent, her head hanging low.

"Help will be here soon," I promise her.

She looks up then. Her hand slips out from under the blanket and reaches out to me, her fingers locking onto my wrist with a grip that is shockingly strong. Her light eyes peer up, gleaming in the dark.

"Thank you . . . Dean, is it? I'm so sorry about all of this."

I nod.

"Please take care of her," she continues fiercely. "She'll try to take care of everyone else and forget that she needs help too." Her gaze extends past the truck and locks on her sister.

Extricating myself from her grasp, I step away. Samantha moves toward Amy to take my place, fussing over her and Janie.

Kasey is fifty yards up the road, kneeling next to Finn, her hands cradling the wounded dog's head. Once she drove the wolves away and Hunter was secured, she went straight to her sister's side. Her family clung to her, but once she assured herself that they were alive, unharmed, and help was on the way, she raced back to her dog.

Miraculously, he's alive but bleeding out fast on the snow. She ripped off her coat and is now using it as a bandage to suppress the blood flow.

I'm still in shock at the scene that unfolded tonight. Kasey would have been well within her right to shoot to kill, but she'd refrained, driving the aggressive wild animals away with expertly placed warning shots. Her marksmanship skills came screaming to the forefront today.

Briefly, I wonder what would have happened if Finn hadn't shown up when he did. The wolf pack was only following its nature, but if my sister or future brother-in-law had been attacked . . . or Kasey . . . or the kids. I shudder thinking about what could have happened tonight. We were faced with danger from every side, but God prevailed.

Thank You for Your protection tonight, Father, I lift up the prayer with gratitude.

I kneel on the snow next to Kasey as the sound of sirens grows closer. "He's going to be okay." I slip my hand over hers. "We may be a little town way out in the boonies, but we've got the best vets in the world here in Cascade Valley. We need 'em for the cows and horses, you know."

The road lights up with flashes of blue and red, pushing the darkness away enough for me to see a look of appreciation cross Kasey's face. "I'm going to hold you to that promise," she bends lower and strokes the dog's soft head, "because he deserves nothing less than the best."

. . .

After a couple of days of investigation, our local law enforcement officials decided that the issue needs to be settled in family court.

It turns out that since Dmitry was incarcerated and Amy had sole custody of the children while he was in prison, she will face little, if any, legal consequences for sending DJ and Janie away with their aunt. At least, according to the family lawyer Amy already has on retainer. They were placed in the care of a responsible family member, and Amy did the right thing by seeking help with her addiction. When they go before the judge, he will most likely see her actions as an unconventional plan, but after he learns of Dmitry's prison record and character, in combination with Hunter's actions—whose name isn't Hunter anyway—it's unlikely he'll blame her for it. Best case scenario, Amy will be required to continue counseling and check in weekly with an approved mentor until she gets back on her feet.

The rest of their family's future is, as of yet, unknown.

Hunter, on the other hand, will end up receiving the maximum punishment his offenses allow, including potential prison time. Our county doesn't have the resources to process him, so he is sent upstate to await sentencing. When Dmitry showed up in Cascade Valley the following day after his cousin never appeared, our local sheriffs were more than happy to place him under arrest as well. He posted bail soon after and hightailed it out of town, never even setting eyes on his family. He will most likely be investigated for stalking and harassment, not to mention violating his parole by leaving the state.

When Mom found out what had happened to us on the mountainside, she descended into full mother hen mode. All of us will probably come out of this ten pounds heavier after eating the smorgasbord of casseroles, cookies, and sweet drinks she keeps pressing into our hands. I think her heart aches to be a mother to Kasey, DJ, and Janie, but she's having to settle for me, Samantha, and Caleb instead. Vincent and Knox are fortunate side beneficiaries of her love.

Amy, DJ, and Janie were medevacked to Bozeman for treatment after the ordeal. They've spent three nights in the hospital there. Kasey refused medical aid and has divided her time between watching over them and making the trek back to Cascade Valley on icy highways to make sure Finn is recovering well at the small animal hospital run by our local farm veterinarian.

To all our shock, the big dog is going to make a full recovery, though the vet warns Kasey that he most likely won't be as spry or nimble in the future, and she'll need to ensure he doesn't get into any more fights with wolf packs.

She's agreed.

Kasey and I have spoken only briefly since those fateful last moments on the mountain together. And I get it; she's preoccupied with making sure her human and furry family members are on the road to recovery. Her attention is needed elsewhere.

I just wonder if things will ever be like they were between us again.

When her Jeep showed up in town today, Esther sent me a text. I probably break a few speed limit laws getting there. My truck tires skid just a little as I park behind her vehicle and wait for her to exit the vet's office after her daily visit.

She finds me leaning against the front bumper of my truck thirty minutes later.

"Hey," she says when she spots me, her manner startled, her eyes wide and wary.

"Hey," I reply.

Stepping off the sidewalk, she nearly slips on one of the many patches of snow now turning into ice everywhere in town, her boots sliding and making her throw out her arms for balance.

It's natural to reach out and grasp her arms, pulling her light frame close to prevent her from falling on the ice. It isn't until her arms go around my waist and she hugs me back that I realize how long I've been waiting for this moment.

The moment when there aren't any secrets between us.

The moment when the truth—even though it's ugly and full of trauma—is spread out on the table in front of us.

The moment when I can ask—with nothing holding me back—if there's any chance of a future for us.

And yet, now that the moment has come, I don't know how I would recover from the gut punch it would be if she says no.

I've waited years to meet the woman God has for me. I've prayed for her, believed for her, hoped for her. For months, something about Kasey has whispered to my heart that she is the one whom my soul loves. But is she meant to be the wife God designed for me?

I know she believes in God; Mom led her through a rededication and the sinner's prayer weeks ago. I've seen the fruit of His hand in her life. I've watched how her faith has grown as she's walked through the fire to be reunited with her family.

I'm just not sure if she's ready for what comes next. The way I feel about her can only soothe her broken heart so much. At some point, she'll have to fully surrender her future and all that she's loved and lost to God.

But if the happily-ever-after I long for isn't from the One who shepherds my heart with the utmost care, I don't think I want it.

I am the first to release our hug. She steps back, steady now, and presses her back against the Jeep. Her arms are folded across her chest, but she doesn't look defensive. There are people around, but I focus only on memorizing the exquisite details of her face. If this is the last time I see her, I want to remember.

"It's been rather quiet around here the last couple of days without you," I venture first with a regretful tone, hoping I can inject more lightheartedness into this conversation than I feel.

It draws a short laugh from her. "Hey now, you'll make me think my flying-under-the-radar skills are no good if you keep talking like that."

"Oh, but you definitely have the cranky-hermit-on-top-of-a-mountain vibe down," I reassure her with a smirk.

She grins. "Thanks. That's what I was going for."

My mood shifts to serious. "So what's next for you?"

Please say you're going to stay.

Her head tilts toward the vet's office. "They are discharging Finn later today. He'll need a lot of care, but he should be on his feet in a few weeks. Once I pick him up, I'm going back to Bozeman to get Amy and the kids. I'm driving them home to Connecticut. And then I'm . . ." She falls silent.

The words she doesn't say shout across the chasm between us.

"Don't go." My voice is hoarse.

Her eyes sweep toward the floor. "I have to," she whispers. "I haven't been home in months, and there are things I need to . . ."

"And where's home for you?" I interject, swallowing hard and realizing there's so much I don't know about her life, about who she is when she's not in crisis mode. All I can think about is how much I want to know every detail.

"Tranquility Bay Beach, Oregon, believe it or not." She smiles at me. "It's ironic, given the trajectory of my life and the way I've been living the past six months."

I reach for her, and she doesn't hesitate but puts her hand in mine. My thumb brushes the back of her palm. "I don't know. I'd say Danny's cabin was one of the most tranquil places I've ever been to while you were there."

Her blue eyes shine up at me with a stormy ocean of emotion in their depths. I feel the weight of every word she wants to say, though something seems to hold her back.

"Are you going to be okay?" I ask the question that keeps pressing into my brain.

Her sigh is deep, but there's peace in the sound, nonetheless. "Yeah . . . probably . . . hopefully?" She turns her face up to me, a grimace across her mouth. "I just want to be there for my family, make up for time lost . . . If that makes any sense?"

It does. And it's painful because what she's about to gain contrasts sharply with what I'm about to lose.

"I've got to get going now," she murmurs. "I'm hiking up to the cabin one more time to retrieve all of our things before I pick up Finn and head out."

"Do you want me to come with you?" I ask.

She shakes her head. "Thanks, but I think this is something I want to do on my own. Don't worry," she hastens to assure me. "I'll make sure I put everything back just as I found it. It'll be like we were never there."

A stab of pain twists in my gut, but I nod and drop her hand. "I understand. Be safe up there."

"I will," she whispers.

With a mighty effort, I force myself to move toward my truck. If I don't walk away now . . .

"Dean!"

Her voice calls me back, and I turn. Kasey is staring at me.

"Take care of yourself and your wonderful family, okay?" she says, and her smile lights up the whole world.

My smile aches at the corners of my mouth. "Take care of yourself too. And Kasey . . ."

She freezes and looks at me with a frightened expression, as if what I'm about to say is going to be too much for her to hear, so I wink in her direction.

"If you find yourself hankering for a scenic mountain getaway again, I know of a great local ski lodge that's going to reopen soon. It's got electricity, running water, and plumbing. If you like skiing, that is."

Her reply is soft, her eyes filled with a gentle light. "I like skiing," she says. "Although, I'm not very good at it."

"I know a great instructor," I reply. "I'll set you up with a recreational package you can't beat."

Her laughter rings in my ears long after I've stepped into my truck and driven away.

Chapter Thirty-Nine

Kasey

My lungs burn as I ascend the snowy trail that leads to Danny's cabin for the last time. The air is crisp and fragrant with the scent of snow and pine and winter. The storms have passed for now, and the birds have reemerged, their songs accompanying me cheerfully up the path. I'm not too worried about the wolf pack reemerging. Dean sent me a report the other day that the pack had been spotted miles away. I don't have a weapon since I haven't gotten my pistols or rifles back from the sheriff yet.

But the ache in my limbs as I choose my steps carefully doesn't begin to match the ache in my heart.

I'm prepared to walk away from Dean McCade and everything I've ever wanted because, after making so many wrong decisions based on my disappointment . . . fear . . . and wounded heart in my lifetime, I'm ready to make the right one.

And the right choice is to stay by my sister's side until I know she is truly safe.

Even if leaving this valley and the man I love breaks me.

Because I love Dean. There's no denying what is simply true.

To my surprise, the sight of Danny's cabin sitting in the clearing feels like being welcomed home. The diminutive wooden structure is untouched when I walk up and push the door open. The interior is cold and dim, the fire in the stove going dark days ago, but our bags still sit in the corner where I left them, my own unzipped and my belongings scattered about from my search for ammo. Kneeling, I replace everything neatly and then sit back on my heels to look around for the last time.

"Thank you for being my friend, Danny Gardener," I murmur aloud. My heart prompts me, and I continue, "And thank you, Lord, for protecting us and bringing us safely home."

Over the past few days, I've finally realized the truth I overlooked my entire life. All through the dark days and nights when I thought I was walking through my troubles and sorrows alone, the Good Shepherd was there, carrying me through to safety on the other side. I may have still walked through the valley, but Someone was there to guide me to the other side.

When I rise, DJ's illustrated children's Bible catches my eye from its spot on the cot. Tenderly, I lift it, tucking it into my bag for safekeeping. I replace Danny's Bible in the center of the table.

It takes me two trips to load all our things into my car. The sheriff had the snowplow clear the logging road, so I was able to retrieve my Jeep the other day. On my final trip to the cabin, I do one last sweep. The majority of the jars of preserved food and supplies Emma prepared for us, I'll leave here for anyone else who happens upon this spot.

My cell phone rings when I'm at the bottom of the trail, hoisting the final bag into the car. After so many months without a phone, the sound startles me at first, but I quickly recover and dig it out of my pocket.

Amy's voice is still weak, her recovery steady but slow. "Are you headed back yet?"

"Soon," I reply. "I'm just loading the last of the bags now. Are the kids okay?"

"They miss their Aunt Kasey." The smile is clear in her voice. "I think they are ready to get out of here. They keep asking when they can show me 'the cows and the horses at the ranch.' "

My heart constricts. "They'll forget all about Cascade Valley when they are playing with their toys back in your big house in Connecticut again."

Amy sighs heavily on the other end of the line. "Kasey, I . . ." she hesitates, her breathing shallow, "I called because I'm not sure if I want . . . What if . . . Do you think it's possible that . . .?"

I wait, my breath quickening.

"I don't want to go back," my sister finally blurts out, her voice panicked. "There's nothing back there in that superficial, pretentious world for us. I hated living there, but when you grow up in it . . ."

My exhale is loud on the quiet road. "Amy, that's your home, all your things, your life. When everything settles, you'll want a comfortable life."

"I just want a *life*," she protests. "A life of peace and joy in a little house with my children and my sister. DJ and Janie keep talking about a woman named Emma and her farm animals and her garden. That's the life I want."

It hurts to breathe. Amy rushes on.

"I know you have your house in Oregon, and we'll have to go back to Connecticut to deal with all the legal stuff at some point. Obviously, that cabin you were in is a little primitive for permanent living," she laughs, "but couldn't we find a house somewhere in the valley? I've got Dad's money, and you're welcome to it too. It's ours. And I can cook and plant a garden in the spring . . ." She trails off.

I find myself laughing, the sound ringing through the forest and bouncing back at me.

"Is that a yes?"

I can hear her smile on the other end of the line. "But are you sure about this, Amy?" I press her. "Life here is simple. Even from what little I saw during my few visits to town, there isn't a lot to do. It isn't exciting. Church, the local diner, and outdoorsy sports are about it."

"I've had enough excitement to last me awhile," she replies dryly. "I found a lot of peace in the quiet life at the recovery center. And I'd love to find a church to call home. I'm ready to grow my faith."

The crunch of tires across snow startles me, and I spin around. A familiar truck scrapes to a stop just down the road. I inhale sharply.

"So can we stay, Kasey?" Amy asks again.

"Sis, can I call you back?" I blurt out. "Or better yet, I'll call you when I'm on my way to pick you up tonight."

She acquiesces, and I disconnect the call.

Dean steps from the truck onto the road. He pulls off his sunglasses and stares at me, lifting a hand to run it through his wavy hair. The intensity of his expression takes my breath away.

Stepping forward at the same moment, we walk toward each other. When I've closed some of the distance between us, I halt and look at him.

"You're a little late to help. I already loaded everything in." I motion over my shoulder toward the Jeep.

Deliberately, Dean stalks toward me, his strides slow and measured, his gaze dark and stormy. "I didn't come to help you," he says, and I shiver at the rough huskiness of his voice.

"Oh," I falter. "Then why did you come all the way up here?"

"I came to tell you that losing you isn't an option for me." He keeps walking. "If you have to leave for a while to take care of your family business, that's fine. But if you're not back here in time to ride up the mountain to take the cows to graze with me in the spring, I'm going to have to show up wherever you are and beg you to return. Because I love you, and I want you to stay."

My heart constricts. It beats in time with each step as we move toward each other.

The space between us fully closes; we're mere inches apart. He towers over me, his hands hovering just behind my elbows, ready to pull me close, but I know he's giving me the space to choose. Tilting my head back, I stare at him, my hands rising to rest against his chest.

And my heart whispers that it's finally found its way home.

"What if I don't want to live on a ranch in the middle of nowhere?" I venture, but I'm unable to hold back the grin his presence draws from me.

His hands slip around my back, and I sway as I allow myself to lean into him.

"Well, then, I'll remind you that we can choose from plenty of mountains in the middle of nowhere to live on as well," he replies dryly.

The smirk creeping across his face sends a shiver down my limbs. As if drawn by invisible strings, my hands slip up and around the back of his neck. His forehead lowers until it presses against mine. Our breath mingles as my eyes close.

"I love you," I whisper, and his arms tighten around my waist.

"I don't want to leave," I whisper.

"And I don't want to let you go," he murmurs.

"If I stay, I'll have a lot of baggage coming with me."

"Our farmhouse has lots of storage closets. Plenty of room," Dean replies. His voice lowers. "And it would be an honor to help you store it for as long as you need."

I cling to him and feel his silent plea. Pulling back, I wait until our eyes are locked. The joy that bubbles up inside my chest can't be contained. I can feel it beaming out across my face.

"Well, it's a good thing for you that I'm a very good auntie, and DJ and Janie have decided that they want to live close enough for Miss Emma to help them plant a garden this spring. I'll need a job, though, so if you know of any good positions available . . ."

"Why don't we discuss you getting a job after we plan our wedding?" His eyes smolder.

My breath hitches in my throat. "You're not saying you want to marry me?" I gasp, shaking my head in disbelief. I expected him to welcome me to the valley. This is beyond my wildest expectations.

"I'm not saying anything but that," he whispers in reply, and hot tears spark in my eyes. "What do you say? Will you marry me, Kasey?

I can only whisper "yes" over and over and over.

Dean draws me close, his stormy eyes consuming me until the whole world is nothing but him and us and this moment. And when he sweeps me up and lifts me off my feet, I'm ready to meet his lips with my own as he spins me with a kiss so delirious that the snowy forest becomes a blur, and all I can see is the man I know will walk through the valleys with me until we emerge together into the light.

Epilogue

Kasey

"Are you ready for this?"

When he leans over me, the cap of his trucker hat shields me from view. His breath turns to fog in the chilly snap of the midwinter air, but the gentle press of his palm warms my forearm, and a familiar tingle races along my skin, traveling a sure path straight to my heart.

My experience in Cascade Valley has already canceled out all the long, lonely years that came before.

Dean waits for me to reply, and before I do, I peek around his broad frame at my sister, who walks a few paces ahead, her two small children bouncing around her slender frame as they progress down the snow-cleared walkway. I glance back up at him, a grimace contorting my face.

Just moments ago, my fiancé (I'm still in shock that I'm marrying a rancher) drew me aside as the five of us climbed out of his big truck in front of the small, country church that I now attend every Sunday. Pastor Miller waits for us inside, preparing to begin our family counseling sessions.

The counseling sessions were suggested by Emma McCade a few weeks ago, as the chaos of the past few months settled, and Amy and I moved into the same house for the first time in our lives. It's been a lot to navigate and a struggle at times. I recognize the need for healing in both of our lives. When we scheduled these meetings with Pastor Miller, I asked Dean to accompany us.

With a wink, he said he might as well join us since he and I will be back in Pastor's office for our own premarital counseling sessions shortly.

Drawing in a long, heavy breath, I shrug. "Yes, no, maybe? I'm not really sure what to expect." I slip my hand in his, and it's an instant comfort.

Slowly, we follow the path my sister took to the side door of the church. DJ and Janie have taken off around the corner, and she's been forced to chase them, breaking through the untouched snow spread across the open land.

"I'm just grateful that she's so invested in her own recovery," I continue before he can reply. "This would all be really tough if she weren't."

Dean's voice is a low rumble in my ear. "God can change any heart, but we have to want what He offers us first. Otherwise, we're just chasing our flesh around and around the foot of the mountain. Amy's heart was transformed by His redemption, but that doesn't mean there isn't still work to do."

I find myself nodding thoughtfully as he speaks. I'm still getting used to the McCade family's special language of "scripture-ese," as I've taken to calling the way their faith flows out during even the most normal conversations. It speaks to a comfort with the Word of God that I find myself longing to emulate.

Before I can reply, the side door bursts open, slamming backward and almost striking Amy in the face as she retraces her snowy footsteps back to the building with Janie on her hip.

A waterfall of straight, dark hair is the first thing I see, but it takes me a moment to recognize Jenna as she nearly flings herself outside.

"I'm sorry," she gasps. "I didn't mean to . . ." Her apology is choked off as she recognizes Amy and the kids. Her expression goes from chagrined to horrified, and she quickly backs away and hurries down the walkway.

Amy's eyes follow her, eventually meeting up with mine as Jenna approaches. My sister stares at me, looking pointedly between me and the younger woman.

When she spots us ahead of her, Jenna freezes briefly, her dark eyes staring at us like a frightened deer in headlights. Her olive skin is pale and drawn tightly over her face, her lustrous hair dulled and greasy. My heart constricts, and as she pivots on her heel and begins to break a fresh path through the snow across the church lawn, I know what I need to do.

"Stall them for a few minutes, will you?" I squeeze Dean's hand, and following my gaze, the firm press of his fingers tells me he approves.

Taking off after Jenna, I shuffle through her trail and catch up to her just as she reaches her truck in the parking lot.

"Jenna, wait up," I call.

Spinning, she slams her back against the side of her truck and stares at me as I close the last few feet separating us. I recognize the look of anguished torture immediately.

"How are you?" I keep my voice soft and low.

Her throat works, her mouth opening and closing as if her

tongue is suddenly too big for her mouth. I'm expecting tears, but when she finally gets the words out, her voice is harsh and guttural.

"Will you just leave me alone?"

I'm taken aback. "I just wanted to check on you, make sure you're okay. We haven't seen you since . . . Amy and I wanted to . . ."

She doesn't let me finish. "I don't want to see anyone, especially the two of you. Don't you think I've suffered enough?" Her hands fly out to her sides, and I see a spark of anger replacing the dullness in her eyes. The words pour out. "I'm sorry for everything that happened. I'm sorry for bringing your enemy straight to your doorstep. I'm sorry for getting caught up in what I thought was turning out to be my future. But I'm the laughingstock now. Everyone knows what a fool I was to let that man . . . And to think I let him . . ."

I stretch out a hand in the space between us. "Jenna, stop. What happened wasn't your fault. You couldn't have known—"

She snaps angrily. "I should have known. He wasn't an honorable man, and the red flags were right in front of me."

Pausing abruptly, she squeezes the center of her brow bone with two fingers, her eyes closing as her chest heaves. Her voice has dimmed to a hoarse whisper.

"And I can't take the way everyone is looking at me anymore, like I'm broken."

Without another word, she turns, yanks open the truck door, climbs inside, and with a skid of tires kicking up muddy snow, disappears down the street. I watch her truck until it's out of sight, wishing there was something I could say or do to comfort her.

I turn around with a heavy heart and see Dean waiting for me across the snow. When I close the final distance between us, he draws me into his arms, his strength a balm to my troubled mind.

"What was that about?" he says.

"She's hurting. I'm worried for her," I reply.

"We'll do what we can to help Jenna. But are you ready for this now?" he asks again.

And as I take a deep breath and breathe in his pine-infused scene, I know that no matter what the future holds, I don't have to run from discomfort anymore. I am finally home at last.

Acknowledgments

There are some stories that simply live in your head for years, waiting for the right time to be written. This is one of those. For almost a decade, I've wondered what would happen if an isolated and world-weary woman were asked to do the impossible to make things right for those she loves, and what would happen if her secret were to be discovered.

Born out of the ramblings of my imagination came a story that spoke not only of romance but of the lengths we will go to in order to protect the ones we love—and of the ultimate sacrifice of the Good Shepherd, who laid down His life that we might be saved.

The Twenty-Third Psalm has been my watchword for a very long time. It's of great comfort and a source of deep study in my personal faith journey. The psalm speaks of a Shepherd who walks with His flock even in the darkest and deadliest of valleys. We are promised that we are not alone, even when all hope seems lost.

His love is so deep and far and wide for us that just when we think we can't take another step, He will lift us in His own strong arms to carry us to safety, sending just the right people along our path to help us. If you aren't familiar with the poem *Footprints in the Sand*, I think you'll find it a beautiful representation of what I tried to capture with this book. *The Shepherd Trilogy* by Phillip Keller has also been a valuable Bible study aid for me. (Many thanks to my dear friend, Sara North, for the beautiful copy she sent me!)

In Kasey and Dean's journey, I hope you've found a renewal of your own hope, faith, and strength and the conviction that even in the darkest valleys of life, you are not alone.

To our brave veterans and those currently serving in the military: Thank you for your service. Your sacrifice, devotion, and dedication to duty are not forgotten.

To the ranchers and farmers who feed the world: Thank you!

To my stunning community of book lovers, hype team, and ARC readers who make me feel as if they love my characters as much as I do and remind me daily of why I write: Thank you for being in my corner! Your support and encouragement mean the world!

To Erica: It felt so odd not to be cowriting this book with you, but I hope it made you proud! I couldn't ask for a better critique partner, fellow-author-in-the-trenches, and dearest friend to do life with. Thank you for all your help and support, and let's write another book together soon!

To Finnegan: You are missed every day. The fearlessness and loyalty of Kasey's faithful canine companion were inspired by our many (but far too few) years together. Thank you for showing me that there's nothing like the purehearted love of a dog.

To Joe: My real-life Dean, as strong and steady as the mountains we both love. Thank you for your endless support, enthusiasm for my work, and for telling everyone that I'm an author even when I'm too shy to talk about it. You are my safe haven, and I love you.

And to Jesus: There isn't a season of life when I haven't felt Your presence. May I lean ever harder on your never-ending mercy and grace. Thank you for being my Good Shepherd. I love you.

Britt Howard is a contemporary romance author who strives to create thrilling stories that ultimately encourage readers to pursue a deeper relationship with God. She lives in Idaho with her husband. When she is not editing books for other authors, dreaming up a new love story, or trying to tackle her never-ending TBR, she can be found in the mountains where she feels most at home.

www.britthoward.com
www.instagram.com/britthowardauthor